A MIRACLE FOR HIS SECRET SON

BY
BARBARA HANNAY

AND

PROUD RANCHER, PRECIOUS BUNDLE

BY
DONNA ALWARD

MILLS & BOON

He had a son. A boy.

His mind flashed back to their past, to the last magical summer he'd spent at the bay—three halcyon months between the end of high school and the start of university. Twelve years had passed since then, and in many ways it had felt like a lifetime. Now, for Gus, it felt like a lifetime in exile.

Shoulders back, chin lifted, Freya met his angry gaze. "Yes, Gus, you're Nick's father."

A terrible ache bloomed in his throat, swiftly followed by a tumult of emotions—alienation and loneliness, frustration and anger. He fought for composure. The sea breeze buffeted his face and he gulped in deep, needy breaths.

"Let's hope I can help him, then."

Freya's mouth trembled. She wanted to shower Gus with gratitude—but her instincts told her that he wouldn't welcome such effusiveness from her. He was still shocked and angry. Just the same, she had to say something.

"I—I'm so sorry to land this on you. I know it's a terrible shock and a huge imposition, and I—"

He held up a hand, silencing her. "I'm the boy's father. I'll do everything in my power to help him."

A MIRACLE FOR HIS SECRET SON

BY
BARBARA HANNAY

All the characters in this book have no existence outside the imagination of
the author, and have no relation whatsoever to anyone bearing the same name
or names. They are not even distantly inspired by any individual known or
unknown to the author, and all the incidents are pure invention.

First published in Great Britain 2010
Harlequin Mills & Boon Limited,
Eton House, 18-24 Paradise Road, Richmond, Surrey TW9 1SR

© Barbara Hannay 2010

ISBN: 978 0 263 88834 8

23-1010

Harlequin Mills & Boon policy is to use papers that are natural, renewable
and recyclable products and made from wood grown in sustainable forests.
The logging and manufacturing processes conform to the legal environmental
regulations of the country of origin.

Printed and bound in Spain
by Litografia Rosés S.A., Barcelona

Barbara Hannay was born in Sydney, educated in Brisbane, and has spent most of her adult life living in tropical North Queensland, where she and her husband have raised four children. While she has enjoyed many happy times camping and canoeing in the bush, she also delights in an urban lifestyle—chamber music, contemporary dance, movies and dining out. An English teacher, she has always loved writing, and now, by having her stories published, she is living her most cherished fantasy.

Visit www.barbarahannay.com

For my daughters Emma and Victoria,
always ready with bright ideas.

PROLOGUE

TELLING Gus about the baby was never going to be easy. Freya knew that.

Gus was ambitious and, in the long hours they'd spent talking about the future, he'd actually told her that he didn't want children till he was at least thirty. Just the same, all the way from Sugar Bay to Brisbane she tried to reassure herself that once she'd shared her news with Gus, he'd change his mind. How could he not want their baby? Surely everything would be fine.

Sitting on the train for five hours, nibbling dry crackers to ward off morning sickness, Freya had plenty of time to picture their reunion.

Details of the setting were hazy, but she knew exactly how Gus would look. His summer tan would have started to fade, but that was to be expected now that he was a city-based university student, attending lectures all day and poring over books at night. On the weekends too, apparently, as he'd been too busy to travel to the bay to see her.

At least his dark hair would be as soft and silky as ever, and it would still have that adorable habit of flopping forward onto his forehead. Best of all, Freya could picture the special way his dark eyes would light up when he saw her.

He would probably call her Floss, the funny nickname he'd given her within days of his arrival at Sugar Bay High. He'd look at her with one of his heartbreakingly beautiful smiles and he'd gather her in so close she could feel his heart pumping. She'd breathe in the scent of his skin, and her off-kilter world would settle back into place.

Later, when they were quite alone, she would find the courage to tell him.

Then, it would be OK.

She was silly to worry. Once Gus got used to the idea of the baby, they would work out *something* together and her future would no longer be a scary black hole. She would have Gus and their baby. Everything would be fine.

Deep in her heart, Freya knew that she might be nervous now, but by the end of the day, she and Gus would have a plan. Really, there was no need to worry.

CHAPTER ONE

LATE on a Friday afternoon, Gus Wilder was only half paying attention when he lifted the receiver.

'A long-distance call for you, boss,' Charlie from the front office told him. 'A Freya Jones from Sugar Bay in Queensland.'

Freya Jones.

Just like that, Gus was zapped from his demountable office in the remotest corner of the Northern Territory to a little beach town on the coast of Queensland. He was eighteen again and standing at the edge of rolling surf, gazing into a lovely girl's laughing sea-green eyes.

It was twelve years since he'd left the Bay and he hadn't seen Freya in all that time, but of course he remembered her. Perfectly.

Didn't every man remember the sweet, fragile magic of his first love?

So much water had flowed under the bridge since then. He'd finished his studies and worked in foreign continents, and he'd traversed joyous and difficult journeys of the heart. Freya would have changed a lot too. No doubt she was married. Some lucky guy was sure to have snapped her up by now.

He couldn't think why she would be ringing him after all

this time. Was there a high school reunion? Bad news about an old schoolmate?

Charlie spoke again. 'Boss, you going to take the call?'

'Yes, sure.' Gus swallowed to ease the unexpected tension in his throat. 'Put Freya on.'

He heard her voice. 'Gus?'

Amazing. She could still infuse a single syllable with music. Her voice had always been like that—light, lyrical and sensuous.

'Hello, Freya.'

'You must be surprised to hear from me. Quite a blast from the past.'

Now she sounded nervous, totally unlike the laughing, confident girl Gus remembered. A thousand questions clamoured to be asked, but instinctively, he skipped the usual *how are you?* preliminaries… 'How can I help you, Freya?'

There was an almost inaudible sigh. 'I'm afraid it's really hard to explain over the phone. But it's important, Gus. Really important. I…I was hoping I could meet with you.'

Stunned, he took too long to respond. 'Sure,' he said at last. 'But I'm tied up right now. When do you want to meet?'

'As soon as possible?'

This obviously wasn't about a high school reunion. Gus shot a quick glance through the window of his makeshift office to the untamed bushland that stretched endlessly to ancient red cliffs on the distant horizon. 'You know I'm way up in Arnhem Land, don't you?'

'Yes, they told me you're managing a remote housing project for an Aboriginal community.'

'That's right.' The project was important and challenging, requiring a great deal of diplomacy from Gus as its manager. 'It's almost impossible for me to get away from here just now. What's this all about?'

'I could come to you.'

Gus swallowed his shock. Why would Freya come to him here? After all this time? What on earth could be so suddenly important?

His mind raced, trying to dredge up possibilities, but each time he drew a blank.

He pictured Freya as he remembered her, with long sun-streaked hair and golden tanned limbs, more often than not in a bikini with a faded sarong loosely tied around her graceful hips. Even if she'd cast aside her sea nymph persona, she was bound to cause an impossible stir if she arrived on the all-male construction site.

'It would be too difficult here,' he said. 'This place is too… remote.'

'Don't planes fly into your site?'

'We don't have regular commercial flights.'

'Oh.'

Another eloquent syllable—and there was no mistaking her disappointment.

Grimacing, Gus scratched at his jaw. 'You said this was very important.'

'Yes, it is.' After a beat, Freya said in a small frightened voice, 'It's a matter of life and death.'

They agreed to meet in Darwin, the Northern Territory's capital, which was, in many ways, an idyllic spot for a reunion, especially at sunset on a Saturday evening at the end of a balmy tropical winter. The sky above the harbour glowed bright blushing pink shot with gold. The palm trees were graceful dancing silhouettes on the shorefront and the colours of the sky were reflected in the still tropical waters.

Not that Freya could appreciate the view.

She arrived too early on the hotel balcony. It wasn't very crowded and she saw immediately that Gus wasn't there, so she sat at the nearest free table, with her legs crossed and one foot swinging impatiently, while her fingers anxiously twisted the straps of her shoulder bag.

These nervous habits were new to her and she hated them. Having grown up in a free and easy beachside community, she'd prided herself on her relaxed personality and as an adult she'd added meditation and yoga to her daily practice.

Her serenity had deserted her, however, on the day she'd needed it most—when the doctor delivered his prognosis. Since then she'd been living with sickening fear, barely holding herself together with a string and a paper clip.

Freya closed her eyes and took a deep breath, then concentrated on imagining her son at home with Poppy, her mother. If Nick wasn't taking his dog, Urchin, for a twilight run on the beach, he'd be sprawled on the living room carpet, playing with his solar-powered robot grasshopper. Poppy would be preparing dinner in the nearby kitchen, slipping in as many healthy vegetables as she dared.

Already Freya missed her boy. She'd never been so far away from him before and, thinking of him now, and the task that lay ahead of her, she felt distinctly weepy. She dashed tears away with the heel of her hand. Heavens, she couldn't weaken now. She had to stay super-strong.

You can do this. You must do this. For Nick.

She'd do anything for Nick, even tell Gus Wilder the truth after all this time.

That thought caused another explosion of fear. The process of tracking Gus down and making the first telephone contact had been the easy part. The worst was yet to come. Gus still didn't know why she needed him.

A tall, flashily handsome waiter passed Freya, carrying a tray laden with drinks. The smile he gave her was flirtatious to the point of predation. 'Would you like something from the bar, madam?'

'Not just now, thanks. I'm waiting for…' The rest of Freya's sentence died as her throat closed over.

Beyond the waiter, she saw a man coming through the wide open doorway onto the balcony.

Gus.

Tall. Dark-haired. White shirt gleaming against tanned skin. Perhaps a little leaner than she remembered, but handsome and athletic enough to make heads turn.

Angus Wilder had aged very nicely, thank you.

But what kind of man was he now? How many gulfs had widened between them, and how would he react to her news?

As he made his way towards her, weaving between tables, memories, like scenes in a movie, played in Freya's head. Gus at sixteen on his first day at Sugar Bay High, desperate to throw off the taint of his posh city high school. Gus, triumphant on the footie field after he'd scored a match-winning try. Herself, floating with happiness as she danced in his arms at the senior formal.

The two of them walking together, holding hands beside a moonlit sea. The sheer romance of their first kiss…

Suddenly Gus was beside her, leaning down to drop a polite kiss on her cheek. 'Freya, it's good to see you.'

He smelled clean, as if he'd just showered and splashed on aftershave. His lips were warm on her skin.

Without warning, Freya's eyes and throat stung. 'It's great to see *you*, Gus.' She blinked hard. This was no time for nostalgia. She had to stay cool and focused. 'Thanks for coming.'

He pulled out a chair and sat, then slowly crossed his long legs and leaned back, as if he were deliberately trying to appear relaxed. His smile was cautious, the expression in his dark eyes warm, but puzzled. 'How are you?' Quickly, he countered his question. 'You look fabulous.'

Deep down she couldn't help being pleased by the compliment, but she said simply, 'I'm well, thanks. How about you? How's business?'

'Both first-rate.' Gus sent her a slightly less careful smile, but his throat worked, betraying his tension. 'So, I take it you still live at the Bay?'

'I do.' She smiled shyly and gave a careless flick of her long pale hair. 'Still a beach girl.'

'It suits you.'

Freya dampened her lips and prepared to launch into what had to be said.

'How's your mother?' Gus asked, jumping in to fill the brief lull.

'Oh, she's fine, thanks. Still living in the same crooked little house right on the beachfront. As much of a hippie as ever.'

He let his gaze travel over her and, despite the nervous knots tightening in her stomach, Freya indulged in a little staring too. His eyes were as rich and dark as ever and his hair still had the habit of flopping forward onto his forehead.

She felt an ache in her chest—she couldn't help it. She'd missed Gus Wilder so much. For a dozen years she'd been out of his life. She knew he'd worked in Africa, and there was so much more she wanted to know. Where exactly had he been? What had he done and seen? Whom had he loved?

'I know you have something very important to discuss,' Gus said, 'but would you like a drink first?' Without waiting for her answer, he raised a hand to catch the waiter's attention.

'What can I get for you?' The waiter's manner was noticeably less cordial now that Gus had joined Freya.

'A lemon, lime and bitters, please,' she said.

'And I'll have a mid-strength beer.'

'Very well, sir.'

After he'd gone, another awkward silence fell and Freya

knew it was up to her to speak. If she didn't get to the point of this meeting quickly it would become impossibly difficult. Taking a deep breath, she folded her hands carefully in her lap.

'I really am very grateful that you've come here, Gus. I know you must be puzzled, but I'm hoping that you might be able to help me.'

'You said it was a matter of life and death.'

She nodded.

'I hoped you were being melodramatic.'

'Unfortunately, no.'

The last remnants of Gus's smile vanished. Leaning forward, he reached for her hand. 'Freya, what is it? What's happened?'

His touch was so gentle and he looked so worried she had to close her eyes. She hadn't been able to broach this subject twelve years ago, and it was a thousand times harder now. Just thinking about what she had to tell him made her heart race and her stomach rebel.

'Gus, before I tell you, I have to ask—are you married?'

It was the worst possible moment for the waiter to return. Wincing, Freya dropped her gaze while the drinks were set on cardboard coasters in front of them.

She reached for her purse, but Gus beat her to the draw.

'My shout,' he said.

'But I owe you. You've come all this way.'

He was already handing money to the waiter and she didn't feel strong enough to argue. Instead, she thanked him and stirred her drink with a slim black straw, making the ice cubes clink and the slices of lemon and lime swirl.

Frowning, Gus touched the tips of two fingers to the frosty outside of his beer glass. 'I can't help being curious. What does my marital status have to do with your problem?'

She felt her cheeks grow hot. 'It…could…complicate

everything. If you were married, your wife might not want you to help me.'

Heavens, she was making a mess of this and Gus looked understandably puzzled. She wished she could find a way to simply download everything she needed to tell him without stumbling through explanations, or grasping for the right words, or the right order to put them in. Surely, negotiating world peace would be easier than this.

Clearly bewildered, Gus shot a glance to her left hand. 'What about you? Are you married?'

'Still single.'

His eyes widened. 'That's a surprise. I thought you'd be snapped up by now.'

I never gave them a chance, Freya thought.

Gus set his glass down and eyed her levelly. 'I *was* married three years ago,' he said.

She had steeled herself, determined not to mind, but this wasn't just a matter of hurt pride. She did mind. Very much. Now Gus would have to discuss her problem with his wife and how could she be sure another woman would be sympathetic?

Gus swallowed, making the muscles in his throat ripple. 'My wife died.'

'Oh.' A whisper was all Freya could manage. She was swamped by a deluge of emotions—sympathy and sadness for Gus mixed, heaven help her, with jealousy for the woman who'd won his heart. 'Gus, I'm so sorry. Were you married long?'

'A little over a year. We met when we were both working in Africa. My wife, Monique, was French—a doctor with Médecins Sans Frontières.'

So his wife had been clever, adventurous and courageous, and filled with high ideals. In other words, she was exactly like Gus. She'd been perfect for him.

'That's so sad.' To her shame, Freya was torn between compassion for Gus's pain and her relief that one hurdle had been removed.

Gus said grimly, 'I guess you'd better tell me what this is all about. What's your problem?'

Her heart took off like a steeplechaser. 'Actually, it's my son who's in trouble.'

'Your *son*?' Gus repeated, clearly shocked.

All the worry and tension of the past weeks rose inside Freya and she felt like a pressure cooker about to blow its lid. Her lips trembled, but she willed herself to hold everything together. She mustn't break down now.

'So you're a single mum?'

She nodded, too choked up to speak.

'Like your mother.'

She managed another nod, grateful for the lack of condemnation in his voice. Of course, Gus had never been a snob like his father. He'd never looked down his nose at Sugar Bay's hippies.

Just the same, his observation was accurate. Freya had followed in her mother's footsteps. In fact, Poppy had actively encouraged her daughter into single motherhood.

We can raise your baby together, darling. Of course we can. Look at the way I raised you. We'll be fine. We're alike, you and me. We're destined to be independent. You don't need a man, love.

Unfortunately, Poppy had been wrong. The terrible day had arrived when neither of them was able to help Nick— and Freya had no choice but to seek help from this man, his father.

Gus was watching her closely, his expression a mixture of frowning puzzlement and tender concern. 'Are you still in contact with the boy's father?'

It was too much. Her eyes filled with tears. She'd waited

too long to tell him this—twelve years too long—and now she had to deliver a terrible blow. It was so, *so* difficult. She didn't want to hurt him.

She had no choice.

Clinging to the last shreds of composure, she looked away from him to the flat sea stained with the spectacular colours of the sunset. She blinked hard and her throat felt as if she'd swallowed broken glass.

Beside them, a party of young people arrived on the balcony, laughing and carefree, carrying their drinks and calling to each other as they dragged tables together and sat in a large happy circle. It was a scenario Freya had seen many, many times at the pub on the Sugar Bay waterfront. Once, she and Gus had been part of a crowd just like that.

Terrified that she might cry in public and cause Gus all kinds of embarrassment, she said, 'I'm sorry. Would you mind if we went somewhere else to talk about this? We could go for a walk, perhaps?'

'Of course.'

Gallantly, he rose immediately and they took the short flight of steps down to The Esplanade that skirted Darwin Harbour.

Offshore, yachts were racing, bright spinnakers billowing, leaning into a light breeze. The same breeze brought the salty-sharp smell of coral mingled with the scent of frangipani blossoms. The breeze played with Freya's hair and she didn't try to hold it in place. Instead, she wrapped her arms protectively over her front as Gus walked beside her, his hands sunk in the pockets of his light-coloured chinos.

'Are you OK, Freya?'

'Sort of.' She took a deep breath, knowing that she couldn't put this revelation off a second longer. 'You asked if I've been in touch with my son's father.'

'Yes.'

'I haven't, Gus.'

She slid a wary sideways glance his way and she saw the exact moment when he realised. Saw his eyes widen with dawning knowledge, and then a flash of horror.

He stopped walking.

The colour drained from his face as he stared at her. 'How old is this boy?'

His voice was cold and quiet, and Freya's heart pounded so loudly it drummed in her ears.

'He's eleven—almost eleven and a half.'

Gus shook his head. 'No way.'

He glared at her, his eyes angry—disbelieving—already rejecting what she had to tell him next.

CHAPTER TWO

GUS struggled to breathe, struggled to think, to believe, to understand…but, all the while, gut-level awareness was shouting the truth that Freya still hadn't told him.

He had a son. A boy. Now eleven years old.

'Gus, I'm so sorry.' Freya stood on the path in front of him, wringing her hands, her face a blurred wash of tears.

His mind flashed back to their past, to the last magical summer he'd spent at the Bay—three halcyon months between the end of high school and the start of university—when he and Freya had been almost inseparable.

Twelve years had passed since then and in many ways it had felt like a lifetime. Now, for Gus, it felt like a lifetime in exile.

He rounded on her. 'Say it, Freya. Spit it out. This boy is my son, isn't he?'

Shoulders back, chin lifted, she met his angry gaze. 'Yes, Gus, you're Nick's father.'

'Nick?'

'He's Nicholas Angus.'

A terrible ache bloomed in his throat, swiftly followed by a tumult of emotions—alienation and loneliness, frustration and anger. He spun away from her, fighting for composure. The sea breeze buffeted his face and he gulped in deep needy breaths.

He tried to picture his son, this boy he'd never seen. His flesh and blood. Damn it, he had no idea what the kid might look like.

How crazy was that?

His thoughts flew haphazardly. He had a son. Every boy needed a dad. What right had Freya to keep such a secret?

Had it worked both ways? Did the boy know anything about him?

Unlikely.

Gus whirled back to challenge Freya. 'Why? Why the hell didn't you tell me?' He knew he sounded bitter but he didn't care. He *was* bitter. 'Did you keep this to yourself because you didn't know who *your* father was? Is it some kind of warped tradition in your family?'

'No, of course not.'

Her protest wasn't convincing but he didn't stop to investigate. 'Why then? Why didn't you tell me that I had a son?'

'I thought—' Freya's hands flailed with a wild kind of helplessness, then fell to her sides and she gave a groan of frustration. 'I tried, Gus. I did try to tell you.'

'When?' he shouted, not trying to hide his disbelief.

'The day I came to the university to see you.'

His mouth sagged open as memories of that day arrived in a sickening rush. His skin flashed hot and cold and a feeling suspiciously like guilt curdled unpleasantly in his stomach.

Over the years, he'd blotted out Freya's sudden appearance on the St Lucia campus, but he couldn't deny that he'd never felt comfortable about the last time they'd met.

Now, she was walking away from him, leaving the walking track and hurrying across the velvety lawn to the rocks that bordered the foreshore. By the time Gus reached her, she'd pulled tissues from a woven shoulder bag and was blowing her nose.

'We have to talk about this,' he said.

'Of course. That's why we're here.' She spoke with quiet resignation.

They found a flat rock to sit on—side by side, looking out to sea—and it was uncannily like old times, except that, unlike the pounding surf in Sugar Bay, this sea was flat and calm. And they were facing west now, rather than east, so the setting sun was suspended inches above the horizon like a giant glowing balloon.

Freya shoved the tissues back into her bag, then drew an elaborately deep breath and let it out very slowly.

Despite his rage and frustration, Gus couldn't help thinking how lovely she looked, sitting on the rock beside the sea.

She directed her steady gaze his way, giving him the full effect of her darkly lashed aquamarine eyes. 'Do you remember that day I came to see you at university?'

'Of course.'

'I was, honestly, planning to tell you that I was pregnant.'

'But you didn't say a thing about it. Not a word.' He fought to speak calmly. 'Why?'

She dropped her gaze. 'It's hard to explain now, after such a long time. I know I was very young and immature back then. I was totally freaked by the whole university scene.'

The wind plucked at her hair and she caught a strand and tucked it behind her ear. To his dismay, Gus found himself noticing the delicate shape of her ear and the small hole pierced in the middle of her neat pale lobe.

'The whole journey to Brisbane was such a big deal for me,' she said. 'I had to travel such a long way from the Bay on the train, and I had to get up at something like four o'clock in the morning. And I had morning sickness, so I was pretty fragile. Then, when I got to Brisbane, I had to catch the bus out to St Lucia. When I arrived there, and the university was so—'

She waved her hands, searching for the word.

'Intimidating?'

'Yes. So huge and important-looking. All those sandstone buildings and columns and courtyards.'

Gus nodded. It was incredibly easy, now, to imagine how a girl from a sleepy beach village had felt, but he'd been young, too. Looking back, he suspected that he had, quite possibly, been insensitive.

Freya pouted. 'I'd told you I was coming, so I thought you'd skip a lecture to see me. But I had to wait around for ages for you to come out of the lecture hall and then, when you did, you were surrounded by a tribe of adoring women.'

Gus felt his neck redden as he remembered. 'Hardly a tribe. And there were other guys in the group.'

She dismissed this with a sharp laugh. 'I was naïve, I guess, but I got such a shock to see how you'd changed so quickly. After all, it was only about six weeks since I'd seen you.'

'I couldn't have been too different, surely?'

She lifted her hands, palms up. 'Believe me, Gus, you were different in every way. You had this scholarly air. And you were so full of how awesome university was. You couldn't stop talking about your college and your lecturers, your career plans. After six weeks at uni, you were going to single-handedly save the Third World.'

Gus swallowed uncomfortably, knowing she was right.

'And those girls were such snobs,' Freya said. 'Designer jeans, masses of jewellery, perfect hair and make-up. I hated the way they looked down their noses at me.'

'I'm sure they didn't.'

Freya rolled her eyes as if he hadn't a clue. 'They made it clear that I had no right to be there, chasing after you.'

Gus remembered how Freya had looked that day, dressed in her hippie, beach girl get-up like something out of the seventies, in a batik wrap-around skirt, a silver anklet complete with bells and brown leather sandals.

He'd thought she'd looked fine. She was Freya, after all. But he could guess how those city girls might have made her feel. No doubt they'd used that particularly sinister feminine radar that sent out signals undetected by males.

Why hadn't he been more perceptive? More protective of his girlfriend?

Even to him, it no longer made sense.

But *hang on*. He might not have shown exemplary sensitivity, but Freya still should have told him she was pregnant.

Gus turned to her. 'How could you have been pregnant? We took precautions.'

She lifted an eyebrow and the look she sent him was decidedly arch. 'If you remember, you weren't exactly an expert at using a condom.'

He groaned, muttered "Idiot" under his breath.

Face aflame, he looked out to sea where the last of the sun's crimson light was melting into the darkening water. 'If you'd told me, Freya, if you'd given me a chance, I would have faced up to my responsibilities.'

'I suppose you would have.' Her fingers began to twist the woven straps of her shoulder bag. 'But you'd told me you didn't want children for ages.'

'That didn't mean—' Gus grimaced and shook his head.

'I didn't want you to see me as a responsibility. I wanted to be so much more to you, Gus, but when I saw you that day I lost all my confidence. I knew what becoming a father would have cost you. Your father had such high hopes for you. And you had big dreams too. A baby would have wrecked everything you had planned.'

'I'd have found a way.'

Her steady gaze challenged him. 'Be honest. Your father organised a transfer back to Brisbane, just so he and your mother could support you through uni. You were their eldest son, the jewel in their crowns. They'd never have forgiven you. And how would you have felt if you'd had to leave your studies to earn enough money to maintain a family?'

'I don't know,' Gus said glumly. 'I wasn't given the opportunity to find out.'

It was ages before Freya said softly, 'Well, OK, I think we've established that I made a bad call.' She dropped her gaze, but not before he saw the glitter of tears in her eyes. 'I've said I'm sorry. But sometimes mistakes are made with the best of intentions.'

Gus let out a heavy sigh and wondered to what degree his overbearing parents had swayed Freya's decision. The irony was that as soon as he'd graduated he hadn't gone into the kind of high profile executive position his father had planned for him. He'd quietly rebelled and gone off to Africa instead. Bursting with high ideals, he'd dived into aid work.

For the next nine years he'd been committed to doing good work for strangers and, sure, they'd really needed help. But, all that time, there'd been a son who'd needed him back in Australia.

The thought of that boy made him want to cry out with rage. Despair. Self-pity. Where was the morality in trying to save the world when he'd contributed absolutely zilch to his own son's welfare?

The worst of it was that Freya *had* tried to tell him.

She'd turned to him in trouble and, instead of becoming the prince who rescued her, he'd let her down. Very badly, it seemed.

Oh, he'd gone through the motions that day. Resisting the crass option to sneak her back to his college room for a quick tumble between the sheets, he'd taken Freya back into the city on the bus and splashed out on an expensive supper at a posh café overlooking the Brisbane River. But throughout the meal she'd been strained.

Looking back, he could see that he'd been far too impressed

with himself as a student. Too caught up in his new and exciting world. He probably hadn't given Freya a chance to get a word in edgeways.

Guiltily, he remembered that he'd been rather relieved to put her back on the train to Sugar Bay. It was only when he'd walked along the railway platform, keeping up with her carriage as the train lumbered off, that he'd seen the tears streaming down her face.

Too late, he'd understood that he'd disappointed her. And now, *way* too late, he realised that he'd been so self-absorbed he'd left no room for her to offload her dilemma. He'd been a complete ass.

The big question was—if he *had* known about the baby, would he have made room in his life for Freya? Happily? Without resentment?

He'd loved her, sure. That summer with her was his sweetest, most poignant memory. But, in that first term at university, he'd loved the idea of Freya waiting back in Sugar Bay far more than the reality of her intruding into his busy new life.

Gus sat in silence, mustering his thoughts while he listened to the soft lapping of the sea. After a bit, he said, 'You stopped answering my letters.'

'We decided it was better to make a clean break.'

'We?' For a moment he imagined she was talking about another boyfriend. Then he remembered Poppy. Freya's mother had always been more like her sister or her best friend than her mother. 'I suppose Poppy was in on this too. She very effectively blocked my phone calls.'

'She was a tower of strength.'

Oh, yeah, she would have been, Gus thought grimly. Poppy would have been in her element. She'd never been able to hang on to a man for long, but she would have clung for dear life to Freya and the promise of a grandchild. She would have aided and abetted Freya's decision to end it with him and raise the baby alone.

So it boiled down to the fact that his relationship with Freya had just faded away. She hadn't answered him and he, distracted by his bright new world, had simply let her go.

In other words, he, Freya and Poppy had made separate choices twelve years ago, and now they were paying the price.

Rather, the boy, Nick, was paying the price.

Gus looked up at the darkening sky—navy-blue, almost black—and he saw the evening star, already shining and sitting alone in the heavens like a bright solitaire diamond.

Staring at it, he felt shock like a fist slamming into his solar plexus. *Hell.* He still didn't know why Freya had contacted him so urgently. He'd been hung up about what happened in the past, but hadn't she said that her son had a problem right here and now?

A matter of life and death?

He bit back a horrified groan. 'There's more, isn't there? You still haven't told me why you need my help.'

To Gus's dismay, Freya seemed to slump beside him as if her strength had suddenly deserted her. He reached out, wanting to draw her against him, to rest her head against his shoulder, but his hand hovered inches from her. 'What is it? What's happened?'

A sob tore from her throat and she covered her face with her hands.

A hot knife of fear sliced through Gus. For an instant he felt an urge to flee, to refuse to listen to her bad news. He couldn't bear the tension.

He forced himself to speak. 'Is…is the boy sick?'

Freya nodded and the knife in his guts twisted sharper, deeper. *Life and death.* Terror chilled his blood. Was his son dying?

His throat tightened painfully. He hadn't known it was possible to care so instantly and painfully for a boy he'd never met.

Freya, sensing Gus's distress, lifted her head. Hands clenched in her lap, she sat very still, willing herself to be strong. This was the point of no return, the worst part of her mission. She couldn't fail her boy now.

So many times she'd thought about what she would say to Gus at this moment, and she'd searched for the wisest and kindest starting point. Each time she'd come up with one answer. She had to tell him the hard news straight up.

This wasn't a time for breaking things gently. To pussyfoot around would be both cruel and unhelpful.

But…oh, God. She felt as if she were plunging from the highest possible diving board into the tiniest thimble of safety.

She thought of Nick again—her gorgeous, talented rascal of a boy—and she knew she had no choice. Taking a deep breath, she said, quietly but clearly, so there could be no mistake. 'Nick's kidneys are failing and he needs a transplant.'

It was almost dark but Freya didn't miss Gus's reaction. It was like watching a man in agony turn to stone.

Horrified, she began to shake and she closed her eyes, unable to bear the sight of his distress. *I'm sorry, Gus. I wouldn't have done this to you if I'd had a choice. But I had no choice. I'm so, so sorry.*

The awful silence seemed to stretch for ever. Somewhere overhead fruit bats screeched and chased each other, tattered black wings flapping noisily as they raced on their nightly raid of local gardens.

It was a full minute before Gus spoke and, when he did, his voice was dull and lifeless, dropping into the tropical night like a handful of pebbles thudding onto sand.

'I guess you're on the hunt for a donor. That's why you need me.'

Freya tried to answer but when she opened her mouth a noisy sob broke from her. Blindly, she groped in her bag for her tissues.

'I'm so sorry,' she spluttered. 'I know this is the worst possible way to find out.'

'You're not wrong.' His tone was disturbingly unreadable.

She bit down on her bottom lip to stifle another sob. She couldn't imagine how Gus felt, but she knew it would be beyond heartbreaking to be told one minute that he had an eleven-year-old son and then... *Oh, by the way, we're hoping you can give the boy your kidney.*

Gus couldn't help but be shocked and angry but, when he spoke, his tone was almost expressionless. 'I assume you're not a suitable donor.'

Freya shook her head. 'Poppy and I both wanted to help, but we're the wrong blood type.' The breeze blowing across the water turned chilly and she shivered.

'We're both type B and Nick is O, so we knew that you must be O as well. Apparently, type B people can receive type O kidneys, but people who have O blood can only receive a kidney from another type O donor.'

Beside her, Gus was moving, lurching to his feet. In a heartbeat he'd shifted from the rock onto the grass. When Freya tried to follow, he held up his hands, warning her to stay put.

'Give me a moment,' he said stiffly. 'I just need to...to get my head around this.'

'Of course.'

He began to pace back and forth, jaw tight, hands thrust deep in his pockets, his dark hair lifted by the wind. Abruptly, he stopped pacing and stood glaring out to sea.

Freya opened her mouth to say something—anything that might serve as a peace offering—but she had no idea what to say. She knew Gus was battling a storm of emotions and he needed space. Head space. Emotional space.

She could only pray that, somewhere within that turmoil, he could find it in his heart to help Nick.

Suddenly, he whirled on her, his face pale, eyes wild, arms stiff by his sides, fists clenched.

'Gus,' she said hesitantly, 'are you OK?'

Oh, God, what a stupid, *stupid* question.

His cold laugh mocked her. 'You've got to be joking.' He prowled closer, his body taut as a hunter's, his expression dark and menacing. 'Of course I'm not OK. I'm mad, Freya. I'm mad with you. With Poppy. With a crazy universe that lets this happen to *my* kid. To anybody's kid.'

She hadn't moved from the rock but she realised now that she'd drawn her knees up and wrapped her arms around them, turning her body into a defensive ball.

She'd never seen Gus like this. 'I don't blame you for being mad with me.'

'Hell. If this hadn't happened, you'd never have told me about the boy, would you? You only made contact with me now as a last resort.'

What could Freya say? It was the awful truth. Things might have been different if Gus hadn't been away in the depths of Africa for nine years…or if her own father hadn't turned up, out of the blue, proving that family reunions could be disastrous…

'Damn it, Freya, if you or Poppy had been able to help Nick, you'd have let me go my entire lifetime without ever knowing my son existed.'

She shook her head, but Gus had already spun away again. He'd had too many shocks at once and he was hurt, deeply hurt.

She wished she hadn't had to do this to him. Wished she'd made wiser choices earlier. But, even if she had been braver, even if everything had turned out miraculously and she and Gus had been married and raised Nick in a perfect fairy tale family, she couldn't have stopped Nick getting sick.

Gus still would have faced this challenge.

But of course he had every right to be angry. She half-expected him to grab a rock and hurl it into the sea.

Instead, he slammed a balled fist into his palm, then stood, hands on hips, breathing deeply, dragging in lungfuls of fresh sea air.

Watching him, Freya felt a band of pain encircle her heart, squeezing painfully. Her vision blurred.

She reached for the tissues again. She'd been tense for weeks and now she felt stretched to breaking point. She still didn't know if Gus would help her.

Was she asking too much of him?

Poor man. He'd had such a lot to deal with—the death of his wife and the demands of Africa and, more recently, managing big remote area projects. And they were just the few things she knew about—heaven knew what else he had on his plate. And now, her news about Nick must have hit him like a bombshell exploding in his face.

She remembered how she'd felt a couple of months ago on the day the doctor had given her the bad news. Heartsick and desperate, she'd paced along the beach and she'd soon found that she couldn't stop. She'd forgotten to take a hat but she didn't care. She'd walked the entire length of Sugar Bay and then she'd climbed over the headland and onto the next bay and the bay after that.

She'd come home sunburnt and exhausted but she still hadn't been able to sleep that night. Actually, she hadn't slept properly since that day, and even when she had slept she'd either had nightmares about losing Nick or dreams in which

Nick was cured and well, only to wake to cruel reality. She'd lived with gnawing fear as her constant companion.

Now, Gus was turning back to her once more, his expression grave yet purposeful. Freya wondered if this meant he'd reached a decision and nervous chills chased each other down her arms.

Her stomach bunched into terrified knots but she forced her facial muscles to relax. She didn't want to let Gus see how frightened she was.

As he approached her, she scrambled stiffly to her feet and, to her surprise, he held out his hand to help her down from the rock.

Freya held her breath.

'Relax, Freya. I'm more than willing to help Nick, if I can.'

A massive wave of relief washed over her.

She knew that at some point in the very near future she'd be ecstatic and dancing with gratitude, but right now she couldn't manage words of more than one syllable. 'Thanks.'

'Hey, you're shaking,' Gus said.

He was still holding her hand and, for a moment, she thought he was going to put his arms around her. Her mind took a ridiculous leap, instantly imagining his embrace and her head cradled against his broad shoulder.

Oh, heavens, how she longed to be there, in the protective shelter of Gus Wilder's arms, whispering her thanks while she drew strength and comfort from him. She could almost imagine the remembered scent of his skin mingled with the fragrance of the tropical night.

But of course Gus had no intention of hugging her. How silly to have even thought of it. She'd surrendered that privilege a very long time ago.

'You're cold,' he said. 'Your fingers are practically frozen.' In a purely practical gesture, he rubbed her fingers between

his warm palms and she loved it, even though she shouldn't.
'You should go inside, Freya. You're dressed for summer.'

'I didn't think it ever got cold in Darwin.'

'Sure it does. Every year there are at least three days when
Darwinians have to put their jackets on.'

He'd almost cracked a joke. Surely that was a good sign.

Gus let her hand go and they walked side by side across the
grass to the well-lit concrete path that led back to the hotel.

'So,' he said briskly, 'I guess you'd better tell me what
you know about Nick's condition. I'd like to be fully in the
picture.'

He deserved no less, and she'd almost learned to talk about
Nick's illness dispassionately, the way the doctors did, hiding
the personal terror that lurked behind every word.

'It started with a bad case of stomach flu. Vomiting and a
high fever. I realised Nick was getting dehydrated, so I took
him to the doctor, to our local GP. He took one look at him
and rushed him to hospital, to emergency.'

She couldn't help shuddering, reliving the horror. 'Nick
seemed to make a good recovery from that, but there were
follow-up blood tests, and that's when possible problems
showed up.' A sigh escaped her. 'So we were sent to Brisbane
then, to see a specialist, and they discovered that Nick had a
disease called global glomerulosclerosis.'

'That's a mouthful.'

'Yes. I'm afraid I've had plenty of practice at saying it. Nick
calls it his global warning.'

'What a champ.' Gus's smile was tinged with sadness. 'It
takes courage to make a joke about something so personally
threatening.'

'He's been incredibly brave.' Freya blinked back tears. 'I've
been a mess. So scared. I used to burst into tears without
warning. Day and night. But then I saw how strong Nick was
and I realised I had to toughen up for his sake.'

Gus remembered young mothers in Africa, broken-hearted, watching their children grow weaker while they covered their fear behind a mask of stoicism. He hated to think of Freya bearing the same kind of pain for her son—*their* son.

'Basically,' Freya continued, 'this disease means that Nick's kidneys are filling up with scar tissue. Eventually it leads to complete kidney failure.'

She stopped walking. They were almost back at the hotel and the carefree sounds of laughter and music from a jukebox spilled into the night.

'He's been on medication for the past couple of months,' she said. 'And it's working really well. He feels fine but, unfortunately, the medication will only work for a limited time.' She looked up and met Gus's stern gaze. 'That's why he needs a transplant.'

'Poor kid.' Gus's throat worked furiously. 'Does he understand?'

Freya nodded and, despite her tension, she smiled. 'On the surface, he doesn't seem too worried. He feels fine and he doesn't need dialysis. That's a huge plus. The drugs have allowed him to carry on as usual. He can still swim and play sport, take his dog for a run.'

'He has a dog?'

'Yes. An ugly little mix of terrier and heaven knows what from the Animal Shelter. Nick adores him. Calls him Urchin. They share every spare minute Nick isn't at school. They're the best of mates.'

Gus's eyes took on a misty faraway look and Freya was almost certain that he was picturing the boy and the dog, running on the beach at Sugar Bay. The fond warmth in his eyes made her throat ache.

Next moment, Gus blinked and the soft light was gone. His expression was sober again. 'So he understands about needing a transplant?'

'Yes.' She gave an imitation of Nick's typical shrug. 'But he doesn't dwell on it.'

'The benefits of being young, I guess.' Gus dropped his gaze and sighed.

'We don't talk about the alternative,' she said softly. 'I've promised him I'll find a donor.'

'Have you tried elsewhere?'

Freya looked away. 'We're on a waiting list, but the doctor said that you were our best chance, Gus.'

He nodded grimly. 'And the time frame?'

'The sooner he has the transplant, the better.'

'Let's hope I can help then.'

'It would be—' Freya's mouth trembled. She wanted to shower Gus with gratitude. This was such a huge thing he was offering—to submit to an operation, to hand over a vital organ.

But her instincts told her that he wouldn't welcome such effusiveness from her. He was still shocked and angry. Just the same, she had to say something. 'I...I'm so sorry to land this on you. I know it's a terrible shock and a huge imposition, and I—'

He held up a hand, silencing her. 'It's not an imposition.' Harsh anger simmered beneath the quiet surface of his voice. 'I'm the boy's father.'

Chastened, Freya nodded. Gus's reaction was just as she'd expected. He was prepared to help his son, and that was the best she could hope for. It would be too much to expect him to forgive her secrecy.

'You never know,' Gus said less harshly. 'This might be Nick's lucky day.'

To her surprise, he smiled. Admittedly, it was a crooked, rather sad smile, but it encouraged an answering smile from her. 'I certainly hope so.'

'But it's not just a matter of matching blood types, is it?'

'Blood type is the major hurdle, but there are other tests they need to do. I know there's a chest X-ray, but I'm not totally sure about everything else. I was ruled unsuitable before I got past first base.'

It was then Freya realised that she'd been so stressed and worried about Nick that she hadn't actually planned anything for this meeting beyond asking Gus for his help. Now, she wondered if she should ask him to join her for dinner. 'Are you staying in this hotel?'

'Yes.'

Unexpected heat flamed in her cheeks. 'Do you have plans for this evening?'

'Nothing special beyond meeting you.'

'I wasn't sure…if you'd…like to have dinner.'

Looking mildly surprised, he said dryly, 'I certainly need to eat.'

Had he deliberately missed her point? Freya felt confused but she also felt compelled to hold out an olive branch. She was so enormously indebted to him, and so very much in the wrong.

Running her tongue over parched lips, she tried again. 'Please, let me take you to dinner. After all, it's the least I can do.'

His wary eyes narrowed ever so slightly and she held her breath, knowing she would enjoy dining with him very much. There was so much to talk about, and they could possibly begin to build bridges.

'Thank you, but not tonight,' Gus said quietly and he reached into his shirt pocket and pulled out his door key, checking its number. 'I'm in Room 607,' he said. 'Perhaps you could ring me in the morning to give me the doctors' contact details.'

'Yes, sure.'

'For now I'll say goodnight, then.'

Freya swallowed her disappointment. 'Goodnight, Gus.'

Just like that, their meeting was over. No peck on the cheek. Not even a handshake. Clearly, no bridges would be built tonight.

Maybe never.

With a polite nod, Gus turned and, without hurrying, he moved decisively and with a distinct sense of purpose, away from her, up the stairs and into the hotel.

CHAPTER THREE

Gus downed a Scotch from the minibar, then ordered a room service meal. Promptly, a box of Singapore noodles arrived and he ate lounging on the bed, watching National Rugby League live on TV. The Roosters were playing the Dragons and normally he'd be riveted, not wanting to miss one tackle or pass.

Tonight he was too restless to pay attention. The best he could hope was that the charging footballers and the voices of the commentators would provide a familiar and reassuring background to his rioting thoughts.

He was out of luck.

Before the game reached half-time, he set his meal aside, grabbed the remote and switched the TV off. Pushing the sliding glass doors open, he went out onto the balcony and looked out at the shimmering stretch of dark water.

Breathing deeply, he told himself that he *had* to let go of his anger. Anger wasn't going to help Nick. The only way he could help the boy was to give him his kidney, although at this stage even that wasn't guaranteed.

The boy might die.

Despair threatened to overwhelm him. He fought it off by concentrating on the positives of this situation. He was in a position to volunteer his help. He was fit and healthy and in the right blood group and he would donate the organ gladly.

From what he'd heard about these transplants, there was every chance they'd have a good result.

He just wished he could let go of the hurt he felt whenever he thought about the eleven and a half years that Nick had been on this earth.

In many ways he felt as if he'd been living a lie. Not only had he married another woman, but he'd spent those years working hard to help people in Africa, to give them better lives. He'd even managed to feel noble at times, but all the while, here in Australia, he'd had a son he'd done nothing for.

There could be no doubt that the boy was his. Freya wouldn't have come looking for him otherwise.

But it was so hard to accept that he'd made his girlfriend pregnant and then she'd chosen not to tell him.

It was even harder to accept the reasons Freya had given him for keeping her pregnancy secret—that she'd felt unworthy, or a nuisance, or just plain unsuitable for him.

Looking at it another way, he'd been deemed unworthy for a role most men expected as their right.

Thoughts churning, Gus stared at the harbour. In total contrast to his turmoil, the water was still and calm, reflecting the smooth silvery path of the moon. His thoughts zapped back to Africa, to the many nights he'd sat on the veranda of his Eritrean hut with Monique, his wife, eating traditional flatbread and spicy beef or chicken, while looking out at this very same moon.

He wondered what Monique would have thought about his situation.

Actually, he knew exactly how she'd have reacted. As a doctor with a fierce social conscience, she would have expected him to donate a kidney without question. She would have supported the transplant, if she'd still been alive and married to him. Monique was a pragmatist and his illegitimate son from a previous girlfriend wouldn't have fazed her. She'd had a realistic, unromantic attitude to relationships.

Once, he would have said that Monique and Freya were polar opposites. His wife had been a practical scientist and aid worker, while his first girlfriend was a romantic and dreamy artist. After tonight, he wasn't so sure. Freya, the romantic artist, had made a very hard-headed decision twelve years ago.

A heavy sigh escaped Gus as he looked at the rocks where he'd sat earlier tonight with her.

Freya, the siren.

There'd always been an element of enchantment in his attraction to her, and it seemed she still had the power to cast a spell over him. This evening, sitting on those rocks, listening to her explanations in her soft, musical voice, he'd almost fallen under her spell again.

He'd become enchanted by visual details he'd almost forgotten—the way she held her head, the neat curl of her ear, the way she smiled without showing her slightly crooked front tooth. Hers was a natural beauty that no amount of fashion sense or make-up could achieve, and she'd always had a kind of fantasy mermaid aura.

There were no salon-induced streaks or highlights in her long silky hair and her clothing was utterly simple—a slim-fitting plain sleeveless shift in a hue that matched her eyes— somewhere between misty-green and blue.

Her only jewellery had been an elegant string of cut glass beads, again in blues and greens, which she wore around one slim tanned ankle.

Gus remembered that she'd always worn anklets when she was young and this evening, despite his anger and shock, he'd found this one disturbingly attractive. He'd felt the same helpless stirrings of attraction he'd felt at eighteen, and he'd seen a look in her eyes that had sent his blood pounding.

He'd almost been willing to forgive her for not telling him about Nick.

Then she'd dropped her bombshell about the boy's illness and he'd understood that this meeting was not a voluntary move to reunite father and son. It was simply a search for an organ donor and, without that desperate need, Freya might never have told him.

Suddenly, there'd been so much anger raging inside him he doubted he could ever forgive her.

Should he try?

Wasn't it too much to ask?

A cloud arrived quickly, covering the moon, and the silver path on the water vanished. Wrapped in darkness, Gus felt unbearably lonely. Alienated. Angry. So angry it blazed like a bushfire in his gut.

But tangled up with the anger was niggling guilt.

If only he'd been more perceptive on that day Freya had come to him. Why hadn't he realised how insecure she'd felt? And, when she'd stopped answering his mail, why hadn't he gone back to Sugar Bay to demand a response?

Instead, he'd listened to his mates, who'd embraced the plenty more fish in the ocean philosophy, and he'd let his relationship with his schoolboy crush fizzle out.

The weight of those choices wrenched a groan from Gus. But it was too late for regrets and, no matter where the blame lay, the one person who mattered now was his son.

He had to make sure that Nick didn't suffer because of his anger. Hell, he could remember what it was like to be eleven going on twelve, all the frustrations, the hopes, the energy and the awkwardness. And he hadn't been facing the prospect of kidney failure.

That thought sent a cold chill snaking over his skin. Sickening desperation gripped him and he prayed that he was a suitable donor. But then he reasoned that, if all went well and he was a match for Nick, he and Freya and their son would find themselves caught up in an even deeper whirlpool of emotions.

So it made sense from the outset to have a very clear plan of how he would negotiate the pitfalls.

Watching the moon shimmer faintly from behind the cloud, he made a decision. He would do whatever was in his power to help his son, but he would maintain a clear emotional distance from the boy's mother. He had to accept that he would always find Freya attractive. Spending time with her, being close to her would be sweet torture, but he mustn't contemplate revisiting temptation.

The last thing their boy needed now was the distraction of estranged parents trying to recapture their youth.

Gus had made all kinds of wrong assumptions about Freya when they were young, and this time he wanted no confusion. He was always prepared to admit his mistakes, but he prided himself on never making the same mistake twice.

Normally, Freya didn't mind dining alone.

Although she'd had several almost-serious boyfriends, she was well and truly used to being seen in public without an escort. This evening, however, when the waitress in the hotel's bistro showed her to a table for two, then removed the extra place setting, Freya felt unusually conspicuous.

It was ridiculous, but she felt as if everyone in the room could guess that she'd invited a man to dine with her and he'd turned her down.

But, in all honesty, she wasn't sure if she was relieved or disappointed that Gus had declined her invitation.

She knew she should be relieved. She'd won Gus's cooperation but he was going to keep his distance, which meant she would be spared any unnecessary complications. It was, really, the best possible outcome.

Too bad for her that seeing Gus again had stirred up all sorts of longings and heartaches. Too bad that she kept remembering the warmth of his hands, and the deep rumble of his voice, and the exact shape of his curvy, kissable mouth. It was especially too bad that she could still remember from all those years ago the bone-melting fabulousness of his lips on hers.

She was a fool to think about that now. It would be the worst kind of madness to start falling for Gus again. Surely she'd learned, once and for all, that she wasn't his type.

Her unsuitability had been a painful discovery when she'd visited Gus at university. This evening he'd confirmed it when he told her that the woman he'd loved and chosen as his wife had been a doctor, not just any doctor, but a brave, unselfish, generous woman who worked with the Médecins Sans Frontières. Freya knew she could never live up to such high standards. Not even close.

She had no choice but to squash her romantic memories and to bury them deep, just as she had years and years ago, before Nick was born.

The waitress came back to take Freya's order, but she'd been so lost in the past she hadn't even looked at the menu. Now she gave it a hasty skim-read and ordered grilled coral trout and a garden salad and, because she needed to relax, she also asked for a glass of wine, a Clare Valley Riesling.

Alone again, she sent a text message to Nick reassuring him that she would be home by tomorrow night. She sent her love but she didn't mention the F word.

Father.

When she'd flown to Darwin, she'd merely told Nick she was meeting a 'potential donor.' At this point, she wasn't sure how she was going to handle the next huge step of telling Nick about Gus Wilder.

If only there was a way to tell him gently without the

inevitable excitement and unrealistic hope. She knew from bitter experience that meetings with fathers could be hazardous.

Freya was brisk and businesslike next morning when she phoned Gus. 'I have the doctors' phone numbers and addresses ready for you.'

'Thank you.' He sounded equally businesslike. 'Why don't we meet in the hotel's coffee bar?'

'I'll see you there in five.'

She'd tidied her room in case Gus planned to drop by, but the coffee bar was a sensible alternative—neutral ground, in line with his aim to retain a discreet distance.

She knew she shouldn't have checked her appearance in the mirror—it didn't matter what she looked like—but she did check. Twice. Once to apply concealer to the purple shadows beneath her eyes. The second time to give her hair a final run through with a comb and to add a touch of bronze lip gloss.

When she saw Gus, she noted guiltily that he also had telltale dark smudges under his eyes. *And* there were creases bracketing his mouth that she hadn't noticed yesterday. Even the bones in his face were more sharply defined. Clearly, his night had been as restless and sleep-deprived as hers.

Gus didn't waste time with pleasantries. As soon as they'd ordered their coffees, he got straight down to business. 'Do you have those contact details?'

Last night, she'd listed everything he needed. Now she retrieved the sheet of paper from her purse and handed it over.

He read the page without comment, then folded it and slipped it inside his wallet. When he looked up again, she was surprised to see the faintest hint of warmth in his dark brown eyes. 'Your handwriting hasn't changed. It's still the curliest, loopiest script I've ever seen.'

Freya risked a brief smile. 'I'm an artist. What do you expect?'

'So you've kept the art up? I've often wondered if you continued with your plans to study painting.'

The word *often* made Freya's heart flutter. Had Gus really thought about her often?

She tried not to let it matter. 'I've studied in dribs and drabs. A part-time course here, an evening class there.'

'It must have been difficult with a baby.'

'I managed. I still paint.'

Their coffees arrived—a soy cappuccino for Freya and a long black for Gus.

As Gus picked up his cup, he asked, super-casually, 'Does Nick have any artistic flair?'

'Oh, no.' With a nervous smile, she selected a slim packet of raw sugar from a bowl of assorted sweeteners, tore off the end and tipped half of the crystals into her coffee. 'Nick's sporty and brainy.'

Avoiding the intense flash in Gus's eyes, she began to stir the sugar. 'He's good at maths and science and football.' Her face grew hot. 'Like you.'

She looked up then and wished she hadn't. The stark pain in Gus's face made her heart thud painfully.

Don't look like that, Gus.

Last night, as she'd tossed and turned, she'd assured herself that it was possible to get through this without becoming too emotionally entangled with him. But was she fooling herself? He'd merely asked one simple question and now she was struggling, on the brink of tears. And she suspected that Gus was too.

Their situation was so delicate and complicated. They shared a son whose life was in danger, and they shared a past that still harboured a host of buried emotions.

Freya's wounds were twelve years old and she'd thought

they were well and truly protected by thick layers of scar tissue, but the smallest prod proved they were still tender. Gus's wounds, on the other hand, were new and raw and clearly painful.

'About the medical tests,' she said quickly, sensing an urgent need to steer their conversation into safer, more practical waters. 'I'm pretty sure you can have them done in Darwin. The hospital can send the results on so, with luck, you shouldn't have too much disruption to your building project.'

Gus dismissed this with a wave of his hand. He frowned. 'What have you told Nick about…about his father?'

'I…I said you were someone I knew when I was young.'

'Does he know my name?'

Freya shook her head and a pulse in her throat began to beat frantically. 'I said you were a…a good man…that you'd spent a lot of time overseas.' Her fingers twisted the half-empty sugar sachet. 'He did ask once, ages ago before he got sick, if he was ever going to meet you. I said it would be better to wait till he's grown up.'

'For God's sake, Freya. Why?'

Unable to meet the blazing challenge in his eyes, she looked away. 'I knew you were in Africa, and I couldn't go chasing after you there. I did look up what was involved and it was terribly complicated.'

Gus looked shocked.

Freya shrugged. 'I…I guess I was waiting for the right time. But then we went through the experience of meeting *my* father, and it was a disaster.'

'What happened?'

'Let's just say it was a bitter disappointment. Very upsetting for all of us.'

Gus let out his breath on a slow huff. 'OK…so…I take it Nick doesn't know you're meeting me now?'

She shook her head.

His jaw tightened. 'Do you have a photo of him?'

'A photo? Oh…um…I…' Freya gulped, swamped by a tidal wave of embarrassment.

'I'd like to see what my son looks like.'

Good grief. Why hadn't she thought to bring a photo? She didn't even carry one in her purse.

She was rarely separated from Nick. His school was just around the corner from her gallery and she hardly ever left the Bay, so she'd never felt the need to carry her son's photo. And, coming here, she'd been so stressed, so focused—her mind was a one-way track.

Saving Nick's life filled her every waking thought.

From over the rim of his coffee cup, Gus was watching her discomfort with a stern lack of sympathy. 'No photo?'

'No…I'm sorry.' How could she have been so thoughtless? 'I'll get photos for you, Gus. Of course, you must have photos. Absolutely. I'll scan the whole album and send them by email just as soon as I get back.'

'When are you flying back to the Bay?'

'This afternoon.'

Gus placed his coffee cup carefully on its saucer and, with his mouth set in a grim line, he leaned forward, arms folded, elbows on the table.

To Freya, the pose made his shoulders look incredibly wide and somehow threatening.

'I'd like to come too,' he said.

Thud. This was *so* not something she'd bargained for. Not today. Not so soon.

'I'm sure you understand that I want to meet my son.' Gus spoke with the quiet but no-nonsense determination he probably used to push aid projects past obstructionist Third World governments.

'You mean you'd like to fly back to the Bay today?'

'Yes… Why not?'

We're not ready. I'm not ready. 'I…I thought you were in the middle of a very important building project.'

'I am, but there's a window of opportunity. The designs are finished, the materials have been ordered and there's another engineer supervising the foundations. So I phoned the site and the elders are happy to shoulder more responsibility for a limited time.'

'Oh, I…see.'

Freya had known from the start that eventually Gus would want to meet Nick, and their meeting would be emotional and wonderful—but terribly complicated. She hadn't dreamed, though, that Gus would want to come back to the Bay with her straight away. She needed time to prepare Nick, to warn him.

She couldn't help remembering her own brief encounter four years ago with her male parent—she shied away from thinking of Sean Hickey as her *father*… Meeting him hadn't been worth it. Nick had learned then, at the age of seven, that happy reunions were also potential disasters.

Gus would be different, almost certainly. But so soon?

Freya found herself grasping at straws. 'There probably won't be any plane seats available at such late notice.'

'There are seats.' A faint smile played on Gus's face, making attractive creases around his eyes.

'You've already checked?'

He pulled a very smart state-of-the-art phone from his pocket.

'I suppose that has Internet connection,' she said faintly.

'Yes. It's so easy.'

In other words, Gus was five steps ahead of her.

'Well…that's…wonderful.' Freya forced enthusiasm into her voice. Which, in all honesty, wasn't so terribly difficult. There had been a time when this possibility had been her

secret dream, and she'd longed for Gus Wilder to come back
to the Bay. The only problem was that in her fantasy he'd
claimed her as well as Nick. He'd been incredibly understanding and considerate, and her secret hadn't been an issue
between them.

In her fantasy, Gus had fallen in love with her again and
he'd adored Nick and in no time they'd been married and
formed a perfect little family.

How pathetic that dream seemed now. Thank heavens she'd
come to her senses.

Gus was frowning. 'You don't object to my seeing the boy,
do you?'

'No-o-o, of course not.' *Not in theory.*

His eyes narrowed as he studied her. 'But you look worried.
Is there a problem?'

Freya shook her head. 'No. No problem. Not if we're
careful.'

'I want to help Nick any way I can, Freya.' He watched her
for another beat or two, then said quietly, 'I promise I won't
rush in and do anything rash.'

Yes. She would make sure of that.

CHAPTER FOUR

IT WAS mid-afternoon when they landed at Dirranvale, a short distance inland from Sugar Bay. After collecting Freya's car from the airport's overnight car park, they drove to the coast along a road that wound through tall fields of sugar cane.

Everything was exactly as Gus remembered—the gentle undulating countryside, the rich red soil, the endless sea of feathery mauve plumes on top of the waving stalks of cane. He was caught by an unexpected slug of nostalgia.

He remembered the first time he'd made this journey at the age of sixteen, slouched beside his sister in the back of his parents' station wagon. Back then, they were both furious about their father's transfer to the Bay, hating that he'd dragged them away from their city school and their friends.

They'd sulked and squabbled throughout the entire journey from Brisbane…until they'd crested the last rise…and the Bay had lain before them in all its singular, perfect beauty.

Remembering his first sight of the beach town that had been his home for two magical years, Gus felt a ripple of excitement. His nostrils twitched, already anticipating the briny scent of the sea and the tang of sunscreen. He could almost feel the sand, soft and warm under his feet, and the sun's burning heat on his bare shoulders.

He could practically hear the rolling thump and rush of the surf and, for the first time in a very long time, he found himself remembering the out-of-this-world thrill of riding a board down the glassy face of a breaking wave.

He'd loved this place. Why on earth had he taken so long to come back?

He turned to Freya. 'I bet Nick loves living here.'

'Oh, he does. No doubt about that.'

Most of her face was hidden by sunglasses, but Gus saw the awkward pucker of her mouth and he knew she was nervous, possibly even more nervous than he was.

They hadn't talked much on the plane, mainly because a nosy middle-aged woman who'd sat next to them had tried to join in every conversation.

He'd learned, however, that Nick was staying at Poppy's place while Freya was away, but that Freya and the boy normally lived in a flat attached to an art gallery. They'd agreed that Gus would stay at the Sugar Bay Hotel.

'I suppose you've warned Poppy to expect me?' he asked.

'Actually, no,' Freya said, surprising him. 'I haven't told her yet.' She chewed at her lip.

'Is there a reason you haven't told her? Does she still have a problem with me?'

Not quite smiling, Freya shook her head. 'I knew she wouldn't be able to help herself. She wouldn't have been able to keep the news to herself. She might have told Nick about you, and got him all worked up.'

It was understandable, Gus supposed, given how restless and on edge he'd felt ever since he'd learned about his son. 'So how do you want to handle this? Will I go straight to the hotel and wait to be summoned?'

They'd come to a junction in the road and Freya concentrated on giving right of way to oncoming traffic before she turned.

When this was accomplished, she answered Gus's question.

'Nick's playing football this afternoon and I thought it might be a good idea if you went to the game.' Quickly she added, 'It would be a more relaxed atmosphere.'

At first Gus was too surprised to speak. All day he'd been trying to imagine meeting his son, and he'd always pictured an awkward introduction indoors with Poppy and Freya hovering anxiously over the whole proceedings. A football match was the last thing he'd expected, but the idea of meeting Nick at a relaxed social event appealed.

'That's smart thinking,' he told her. 'What kind of football does Nick play?'

'Rugby league.'

Gus swallowed against the rapid constriction in his throat. There'd been a time when he'd lived to play rugby league. He'd loved it almost as much as surfing. 'How can Nick play league in his condition? It's such a tough game.'

'I know.' Freya shrugged. 'I thought the doctors would put a stop to it, but they said he's fine to play while his medication's still working.'

'That's amazing.'

'Except…as I told you, the medication has a time limit.'

Gus scowled. 'So when will you tell him who I am, and why I'm here?'

'I don't think we can talk about that sort of thing at the game. We should go back to my place.'

Her place.

Unreasonably, that cold feeling of exclusion encircled Gus again. Freya and Nick had a home where they'd lived as a special unit for all these years. Without him.

It was only then that he realised they were cresting the last rise—and suddenly there was the Bay lying below them, even more beautiful than he remembered.

Considerately, Freya stopped the car so he could take in the view. The small town hugged the pristine curve of pale yellow sand strung between two green headlands that reached out like arms to embrace the sparkling, rolling sea.

'Wow.' He hadn't dared to hope that it might still be the sleepy seaside village he remembered. 'It hasn't changed.'

'Not too much.'

'I was worried the beach would be crawling with tourists by now, or spoiled by developers.'

'There are a lot more houses.' Freya waved to the cross-hatching of streets and rooftops that stretched back from the beachfront. 'And there are new blocks of units on The Esplanade.'

She pointed out a handful of tall buildings that stood, boldly out of place, near the shops overlooking the sea. 'The local councillors have been very strict, though. They won't allow any building taller than six floors.'

'Good thinking.'

Disconnected memories came rushing back. Eating fish and chips on the beach straight from the paper they were wrapped in. Watching the flashes of summer lightning out to sea. Surfing the waves and feeling at one with the forces of nature, with the whole universe.

That last summer, which he'd forever thought of as Freya's summer.

Gus felt as if a thorn had pierced his heart.

Freya started up the car again and, as they headed down the hill, he saw the house his parents had owned, perched on a clifftop overlooking the bay. Lower down, they reached the suburban streets where many of their friends had lived, and then the high school, with the new addition of an impressive brick gymnasium.

Neither Gus nor Freya spoke as they continued on two blocks beyond the school to the football field ringed by massive banyan trees.

Gus stared through the windscreen and his throat was

tighter than ever as he glimpsed the grassy sports oval between the trees. He saw the white timber goalposts, the young boys in colourful jerseys, the rows of parked cars and the players' friends and families gathered along the sidelines, or sitting on folding chairs in the shade.

For two happy years, this had been his world.

Now it was his son's world.

The picture swam before him and he was forced to blink.

Freya turned off the engine.

'How are you feeling?' he asked her.

'I'm a bit shaky.'

Gus nodded. Shaky was exactly how he felt. This was such a big moment. Huge. Almost as momentous and huge as getting married, or witnessing a birth. Twelve years too late, he was about to become a father.

A roar erupted from the crowd as they got out of the car and Freya sent a quick glance over her shoulder to the field.

'Looks like the other team has scored a try.' She pouted her lower lip in mock despair.

'Who's the opposition?'

'Dirranvale. They usually beat us.'

'Nothing's changed, then.' Gus sent her a quick grin, and he was rewarded by an answering grin.

Wow.

Wow. Wow. Wow. Even when Freya's face was half hidden by sunglasses, the grin transformed her. She was the laughing beach girl of his past, and his heart leapt and rolled like a breaking wave.

Impulsively, he reached an arm around her shoulders, moved by an overpowering urge to plant a deep, appreciative kiss on her smiling mouth.

Just in time, he remembered that she'd chosen to keep him out of her life, out of his son's life, and he stamped down on the impulse.

Just as well. Freya wouldn't have welcomed it. Even his casual hug troubled her. Her lips trembled, her smile disintegrated and she moved away, leaving his arm dangling in mid-air.

Fool. Gus shoved his hands in his pockets. He was here to meet Nick, to *save* Nick. Flirting with the boy's mother was not an option. Neither of them wanted to rake up out-of-date emotions and he'd promised himself he wouldn't put a foot wrong during this visit.

Hurrying ahead of him, Freya had already reached the sideline and some of the bystanders turned, smiled and waved to her or called hello. As Gus joined her, they eyed him with marked curiosity, but he paid them scant attention. His interest was immediately fixed on the team of boys in the blue and gold Sugar Bay jerseys.

His son was one of those boys.

Right now, they were standing in a disconsolate row, watching as the opposition's goal kicker booted the ball over the bar and between the posts. The whistle blew, the Dirranvale team's score jumped another two points, then both teams regrouped, ready to resume the game.

Fine hairs lifted on the back of Gus's neck. 'Where's Nick?' he murmured to Freya. 'Is he on the field?'

She nodded. 'I bet you'll recognise him.'

Gus felt a spurt of panic. Was he supposed to instantly know which boy was his? Was this some kind of test?

Freya's sunglasses hid the direction of her gaze and his heart thumped as he scanned the field. There were thirteen boys out there in the Sugar Bay jerseys. He had no idea if Nick was dark or fair, tall or thickset, if he took after the Wilder family or the Joneses.

Should he be looking for a kid who was frailer than the rest? Or was his son the chubby kid, red-faced and panting and avoiding the ball?.

The Sugar Bay team had possession of the ball and parents yelled instructions from the sidelines. The boys were running down the field, throwing passes, trying to make ground and dodge being tackled. As far as Gus could see, they were all happy and healthy and bursting with energy. It was hard to believe that any one of them could be seriously ill.

The boy in the number seven jersey suddenly broke ahead of the pack. He had a shock of black hair and dark grey eyes, and there was something about his face. Gus felt a jolt, a lightning bolt of connection. *Recognition?*

'I don't suppose that could be him, could it?' His voice was choked. 'Number seven?'

'Yes, that's Nick!' Freya's cry was close to a sob and she stood beside him with her arms tightly crossed, hugging her middle.

Nick. His kid. Nicholas Angus. Gus felt a rush of adrenaline as he watched the boy and he tried to pinpoint why he was so familiar. Apart from colouring, they weren't really alike.

But there was *something*.

Gus's eyes were riveted on Nick's dashing dark-haired figure as he cleverly sidestepped an attempted tackle, then passed the ball.

He was good. Hey, Nick was really good. He moved forward again, ready for another chance to take possession, and Gus couldn't suppress a fierce glow of pride.

The kid was fast. He was a halfback, a key position in any team, requiring speed and ball-playing skills and a quick mind rather than brute strength.

Chest bursting, Gus watched as Nick took the ball once more and passed it on neatly and deftly, a split second before he was tackled to the ground.

Gus elbowed Freya's arm. 'You didn't tell me he was terrific.'

Her mouth pulled out of shape, halfway between a happy grin and heartbreak.

And suddenly Gus felt as if he'd swallowed the damn football. He looked away, staring into the canopy of one of the ancient trees as he willed his emotions into some kind of order. Once the game was over, he would meet Nick and he'd have to play it cool.

But it was such a massive thing to know that this wonderful kid was his child. He was flooded by a rush of emotion—of responsibility, of happiness and pride—and all of it tangled with fear and the weight of loss for all the years he'd been deprived of this pleasure.

If I'd seen him in the street I would have walked straight past and totally ignored him.

Knowing made such a difference.

But there was so much more he wanted to know. How could he and Nick possibly bridge all their missing years?

Freya thought she might burst with the tension.

She'd hoped that viewing the game from the sidelines would be an easier induction for Gus, giving him the chance to take a good long look at Nick before he had to cope with introductions. But *she* wasn't finding it easy at all. With each minute that passed, she was more on edge.

She'd watched Nick play football many times, but she usually chatted with other mums and paid only fleeting attention to what was happening on the field. Today, she couldn't drag her eyes from her boy, kept trying to see him though Gus's eyes.

She knew she was hopelessly biased, but Nick was gorgeous, with his lovely dark hair and beautiful, soulful, intelligent grey eyes. She couldn't imagine what it must be like for Gus to be seeing his son for the first time.

She remembered her own introduction to Nick. All those years ago.

With Poppy at her side as her birthing coach, there'd been gentle music playing in the background and the scents of lavender aromatherapy candles. Poppy had helped Freya to breathe through her contractions and, although the whole process was hard work, Nick's arrival had been a calm and beautiful experience.

And he was perfect. Eight and a half pounds, with lovely dark hair, sturdy limbs and great energetic lungs.

It was only later, after Poppy and the midwife left Freya alone to rest, that she'd allowed herself to cry.

She'd cried for Gus.

And she'd cried oceans. She'd missed him so terribly, and she'd longed for him to see their baby. She'd cried and cried so hard and for so long that the nurse had called the doctor, who'd come hurrying back, and he'd been worried and wanted to prescribe a sedative.

Freya had been breastfeeding and she was sure a sedative couldn't be good for her baby, so she'd rallied. From her first days as a mother, she'd always put Nick's needs first.

But, because she'd managed just fine without ever meeting her dad, she'd convinced herself that her son could manage without a father. She'd told herself that she would unite the boy and his dad once Nick was old enough to understand… but by then Gus had been in the depths of Africa.

Freya was so wrapped in her worries she hadn't even realised that the game was over until she saw the boys on the field shaking hands and reaching for water bottles. It was obvious from their body language that the Sugar Bay team had lost.

She glanced quickly at Gus. His body language spoke volumes too. He was so tense he was practically standing to attention.

Out on the field, Nick's coach, Mel Crane, was giving the

boy a pat on the back. Nick turned and saw Freya and he grinned and waved, called to his team-mates, then began to jog across the field towards her.

Nick was halfway to them before he saw Gus and his pace slowed. By contrast, Freya's heart began to canter. She took deep breaths, trying to calm down, and she stifled a longing to reach for Gus's hand. How crazy would that be? Gus was here to help Nick, and for no other reason.

She mustn't give the impression that she needed him too. And she certainly mustn't send Nick mixed messages about her relationship with his father. There must be no confusion.

Beside her, Gus dipped his head and spoke close to her ear. 'I'll take my cues from you.'

She nodded and pinned on a smile. *Always assuming I know how to handle this.* Problem was, etiquette advice didn't cover this kind of introduction.

Nick didn't run into Freya's arms as he might have done a few years ago, but he let her kiss him. He smelled hot and dusty and sweaty and she relished the smell—the scent of a normal, healthy eleven-year-old footballer.

'You were fantastic,' she told him, as she told him after every game. 'And you'll beat them next time, for sure.'

Nick accepted this with a smiling shrug. Then he shot a curious glance at Gus.

Freya jumped in quickly. 'Nick, this is Gus Wilder. He's come back from Darwin with me.'

Nick's dark eyes widened and a mixture of tension and curiosity crept into his face. 'Hi,' he said.

'How do you do, Nick?' Gus's deep voice held exactly the right note of friendly warmth. He held out his hand and Freya's heart tumbled as her son and his father exchanged a manly handshake.

'You made some great plays out there,' Gus said.

'Thanks.' Nick grinned, clearly warmed by the praise. He

looked at Freya, his eyes flashing questions. Dropping his voice, he asked, 'Is Mr Wilder—'

'You can call him Gus, Nick. He's a friend.' Conscious of the people milling around them, Freya chose her words carefully. 'He's hoping to be a good match for you.'

'Really?' Nick's grin widened and this time when he looked at Gus, his eyes absolutely glowed. 'Wow!'

Gus's eyes glowed too as he cracked a shaky smile.

'So how did you find—'

'Hey, Gus, is that you?' a voice called from behind them. 'Gus Wilder?'

Mel Crane, the football coach, was an old classmate from Sugar Bay High and he grinned madly and slapped a beefy hand on Gus's shoulder. 'Thought it was you. Good to see you, mate.'

'Mel, how are you?'

'Not bad. Not bad. What brings you back to the Bay? Are you here for long?'

Gus's smile was guarded. 'Just a short trip.'

Mel Crane's pale blue eyes flickered with keen interest, and Freya's anxiety levels began to climb. As Nick's coach, Mel was one of the few people in the Bay who knew about the boy's condition. He also knew that Freya and Gus had once been an item.

It wouldn't be long before he put two and two together.

'Young Nick played a terrific game today.' Mel ruffled the boy's hair. 'But you know, Nick, Gus here was a *great* footballer.' He gave Gus another hearty thump on the shoulder. 'Lucky for me, he was also good at maths. He used to let me copy his homework.'

Nick laughed and Freya could see that his admiration for Gus was rapidly escalating to hero worship.

'How do you know my mum and my coach?' Nick asked Gus. 'Did you used to live here?'

'Ages ago,' Gus said, carefully avoiding Freya's eyes. 'But I only lived here for a couple of years. Last two years of high school.'

Stepping in quickly before too many memories were laid bare, Freya said, 'I'm afraid we're going to have to whisk Gus away now, Mel. We want to catch a few of the sights before it gets dark.'

'Yeah, sure,' Mel said. 'If you've got a spare moment while you're here, Gus, drop in to the garage.'

'Still the same place down on The Esplanade?'

'Yep. My brother Jim and I have taken over from the old man.'

Gus shook Mel's hand. 'I'm staying at the hotel. I'll call in.'

'Lovely,' said Freya quickly. 'I think we'd better get going now.' Keen to avoid being held up by anyone else, she shepherded Nick and Gus ahead of her to the car.

The worst wasn't over yet.

For Gus, it felt surreal to be sitting in the car beside Freya, with their son in the rear, unaware that his life was about to change for ever.

'So what sights do you want to see, Gus?' Nick asked, leaning forward eagerly.

Gus shot Freya a questioning glance.

'I think we should go straight home,' she said.

'But you told Mr Crane—'

'I know what I told Mr Crane, Nick, but I needed an excuse to get away. I want to take Gus back to our place. There's a lot to talk about.'

'About the kidney?'

'Yes.'

Nick flopped back in his seat and stopped asking questions. In the stretch of silence, Gus stole a glance back over his shoulder and found the boy watching him, his eyes huge and wondering. Gus sent him a smiling wink. Nick smiled shyly, and Gus felt his heart turn over.

Freya turned the car onto The Esplanade, where late afternoon shadows stretched across the beach. Sunbathers were packing up but a handful of hardy board riders were still catching waves. He watched them. He'd been like them once, not wanting to leave the water till it was almost dark, much to his mother's consternation.

To his surprise, he saw that Freya was turning into a driveway. 'Do you live here? Right on the beachfront?'

'Where else?' A quick smile flitted across her features, but it disappeared in a hurry and Gus knew she was nervous again.

The driveway ran next to a modern building of timber and glass. He caught sight of a sign in the front garden, with *The Driftwood Gallery* painted in pale tan on a cream background.

'Hey, Urchin!' A doggy blur and a wagging tail greeted Nick as they got out of the car. After giving the dog a rough and enthusiastic hug, the boy called to his mother, 'I'm starving.'

'Nothing new there,' Freya responded with an elaborate roll of her eyes.

Gus retrieved their overnight bags from the boot while Freya opened bi-fold doors, and he followed her into an open-plan living area.

'Hey, this is beautiful,' he said, looking around him.

'Not bad, is it?' She dumped her purse and keys on a granite topped counter. 'I manage the gallery, and this flat is part of the deal. Please, take a seat and I'll make some coffee. Is plunger coffee OK?'

'Yes, perfect, thanks.'

Gus remained standing, taking in details of the off-white

walls, gleaming pale timber floors and large picture windows looking out to the sea.

The place felt perfect for Freya. It was so much like her—close to the beach and decorated simply but beautifully in neutral tones with soft touches of peach or sea-green. The colours were repeated in the watercolours that hung on the walls and there was a wistful elegance about the paintings that made him wonder if they were hers.

Nick was at the fridge and helping himself to a brightly coloured sports drink. 'What can I have to eat?'

'The usual,' Freya told him. Already, she'd filled a kettle and switched it on and was retrieving the makings of a sandwich. She shot Gus a quick apologetic smile. 'Excuse us for a moment, please.'

'Of course. You have to feed the hungry beast.'

Nick grinned at him and came to the counter beside his mother, took slices of cheese from a packet and added them to the bread she'd buttered.

'I hope you've washed your hands.'

'Washed them at the sink just now.'

'Would you like tomato with this?'

Nick shook his head. 'Cheese is fine.' He added an extra slice, then fetched a plate for his sandwich.

They looked so at home, Gus thought. This routine was so familiar to them, and his outsider status washed over him like a physical pain.

As if sensing how he felt, Freya said, 'What about you, Gus? Are you hungry? Would you like a sandwich?'

He smiled. 'No, thanks. Coffee's fine.'

Leaning against the counter, plate in hand, Nick munched on his snack. He was still wearing his football gear and Gus saw green smears where he'd landed heavily on the grass, and there was a graze on his knee.

How the hell can this kid be sick? Gus thought. *He looks so normal.*

It seemed so wrong. So cruel.

'So has Mum told you all about my global warning?' the boy asked suddenly, smiling between mouthfuls.

Gus's stomach took a dive. 'Yes, it's rotten luck, but I'm hoping we can turn that around.'

Freya, in the middle of retrieving coffee mugs from an overhead cupboard, appeared to freeze.

'Awesome,' said Nick. 'So do you have O blood, the same as me?'

'I do.'

'But Gus still has to have more tests before we can be absolutely sure he's a perfect match,' Freya countered.

Nick nodded and looked thoughtful as he chewed again on his sandwich, while the kitchen filled with the smell of coffee.

Across the silence, Gus met Freya's gaze. She sent him a wobbly smile.

'If you could help to carry these things, we can make ourselves comfortable,' she said.

'Sure.' Immediately he snapped into action, and they carried the pot and mugs, a milk jug and a plate of pecan cookies to a low coffee table set amidst comfortably grouped squishy armchairs upholstered in cream linen.

'You want me to hang around?' Nick asked.

Freya's throat rippled as she swallowed. 'Yes, honey, of course. We need to talk to you.'

He came and perched on the arm of one of the chairs, sports drink in one hand, plate with the remains of his sandwich in the other, and he frowned as he watched his mother pour coffee. 'So did you guys know each other before? When Gus used to live here?'

'Yes.' Freya's voice was a shade too tight.

Nick stared at her and his face sobered. He slid a quick look to Gus, then another glance back to his mother. 'You're not going to tell me anything really crazy, are you? Like Gus is my father or something?'

CHAPTER FIVE

FREYA almost dropped the coffee pot. It clattered onto the table and Gus was instantly attentive.

'Did you burn yourself?'

She shook her head. She was too mortified by Nick's question to worry about the stinging patch of skin on the inside of her wrist. She wished she could think more clearly, wished she could find the right words so that everything made instant sense to Nick. And she wanted to defend Gus.

When she opened her mouth, nothing emerged.

She looked helplessly at Nick, who was watching her and Gus with his lips tightly compressed and a look of anguish in his eyes, as if he wished he could bite back his words.

I have to answer him.

But, as she struggled to find the words, she heard Gus's voice above the fierce hammering of her heartbeats.

'That's exactly right, Nick.' Gus spoke quietly, calmly. 'I've come here because I'm your father and I'm the best person to help you. I want to help you.'

There…

It was out.

Thank you, Gus. Freya felt relief, but a sense of failure too. She should have been ready for this. She knew exactly what her son was like, knew he was smart and perceptive.

When at last she found her voice, she hurried to make

amends for her silence. 'Gus really wants to help you, darling. We know there could be other donors, but Gus is your best chance for a really good match.'

A bright red tide was creeping up Nick's neck and into his cheeks. His eyes shimmered with tears.

The sight of his tears tore at Freya's heart. She felt lost. Totally thrown.

Slowly, her son slid from the arm of the chair and he set his plate and drink down on the coffee table.

'Thanks,' he said shakily, not quite meeting anyone's gaze. 'That's great.' Then he shot a nervous glance to Freya. 'If it's OK, I'm going to get changed and take a shower.'

This was so not what she'd expected, so out of character. Nick hardly ever volunteered to have a shower. Freya usually had to shove him into the bathroom. Now, she felt compelled to let him go.

The adults watched in uncomfortable silence as the boy walked from the room, sports shoes squeaking on the polished floors. Neither of them spoke nor moved until they heard Nick's bedroom door close down the hallway.

Freya let out a soft groan. 'That went well.' She felt terrible for Gus. What must he be thinking? Of her? Of their son? 'I'm sorry, Gus. That wasn't quite the reception I imagined.'

'Do you want to go and speak to him?'

'I don't know,' she said, feeling dazed. 'I'm not sure it would help. I…I'll try.' Her legs felt as weak as limp rope when she stood. 'Won't be a moment.'

She went down the hall and knocked on Nick's door. 'Nick?'

'I'm getting undressed.'

'Do you want to talk?'

She heard the thump of his shoes hitting the floor. 'Later.'

'Don't be long,' she called.

When she went back into the living room, Gus gave an easy non-judgemental shrug.

'The boy's had a shock.'

'But you've come all this way to meet him.'

To her surprise, Gus didn't seem angry.

'All in good time,' he said smoothly. 'Nick needs a chance to get his head around everything.'

Gus would know what Nick was going through, of course. He'd had a similar shock less than twenty-four hours ago.

As Freya picked up the coffee pot again, she gave him a grateful smile. 'So…would you still like a cuppa?'

He was staring at her arm, frowning. 'You *did* burn yourself.'

She'd been trying to ignore the stinging, but now she looked down and saw the angry red welt on the pale skin of her inner wrist.

'You need to get something on that,' he said. 'Do you have burn cream?'

'Oh—I have some of Poppy's aloe vera growing in a pot. That'll fix it.'

Frowning, Gus rose and followed her into the kitchen, watching as she snapped off a piece of succulent herb growing on the windowsill.

'Here, let me,' he said, taking the aloe vera from her. 'That will be hard to manage one handed.'

Before Freya could protest, he was holding her arm, gently, ever so kindly. He squeezed the plant to break up the juicy fibres and began very gently to rub it over her reddened skin.

His touch sent an electric shiver trembling through Freya. She was remembering a time when they were young, when she'd had a coral cut on her ankle, and Gus had been so caring—just like this—washing the cut clean and making sure she got antiseptic straight onto it.

OK, so he's a caring guy. I know that. It's why he's here. It's why he's been working in Africa for all these years. That's no excuse for swooning.

'Thanks,' she said extra brightly when he was done. 'That's feeling better already. Now, about that coffee—'

Gus was still holding her arm. She was still flashing hot and cold. And when she looked into his eyes, she saw a look she remembered from all those years ago.

An ache blossomed inside her, treacherous and sweet, and she almost fell into his arms.

He let her wrist go and said, 'I'd love a coffee.'

Just like that, the moment was gone and, as Freya crashed back to earth, she wondered if she'd imagined that look.

She went back to the coffee table, filled their mugs and handed one to Gus.

He sat down and took a sip and made an appreciative noise. 'I remember now. You make very good coffee.'

She smiled faintly and sat very still, holding her coffee mug without tasting it, thinking about Nick, and Gus and… the repercussions of the decision she'd made all those years ago.

From down the hallway came the sound of a shower turning on. Freya and Gus exchanged cautious glances.

'I'd always planned to warn him, to get him ready before he met you,' she said defensively. 'But you insisted on meeting him today.'

Gus sent her a strange look and took another sip of coffee. 'You said Nick had a bad experience when he met your father.'

'Yes. I think it's safe to say he was quite disillusioned.'

'Do you mind telling me what happened?'

She let out a slow huff. 'Well…my father turned up here a few weeks before Christmas. He sailed into the Bay in a pretty little yacht called *Poppy*.' She rolled her eyes. 'You can picture it, can't you? All smart white paint and lovely tanned sails.'

'Like a romantic fantasy,' Gus suggested.

'Exactly.'

'What's his name?'

'Sean Hickey.' Freya drank some of her coffee, then settled back in her chair, as if getting ready to tell a long story. 'He certainly looked the part, all lean and sunburned, with a weather-beaten sailor's tan. Quite handsome, actually, in a wicked, boyish way. White curly hair and bright blue eyes—*and* a charming Irish lilt to his voice.'

'How did Poppy react to seeing him?'

'Oh, she welcomed him with open arms, and she seemed to grow ten years younger overnight. Nick adored him, of course. I mean, he had another male in his family for starters.'

As she said this, she felt a stab from her guilty conscience. She'd always felt bad about denying her son a male role model. 'Nick was seven at the time, and he was over the moon. Sean was the ideal grandfather—lively and friendly and full of fun, and very interested in his grandson.'

Gus regarded her steadily. 'And you?'

'Oh, I was beyond excited too. I had a father, at last.' She avoided Gus's eyes as she said this and her cheeks grew uncomfortably hot. She stumbled on, hoping to make amends. 'Admittedly, Sean wasn't quite the way I'd pictured my father.'

'I seem to remember,' said Gus dryly, 'that you had a list of famous Australians who might have been your father.'

The heat in Freya's face deepened. Gus hadn't forgotten. She, however, had conveniently pushed that memory underground, hadn't let herself think that Nick might feel equally deprived. Or worse.

'Well, Sean wasn't a film star,' she said tightly. 'He was more like a charming pixie, but he lavished praise on my paintings and I lapped it up. He even told me about an artistic grandmother who still lives in County Cork in Ireland.'

Gus smiled. 'So that's where your talent comes from.'

'I'm not sure any more.' Freya shrugged. 'Anyway, he taught Nick how to sail, and he took the three of us out in *Poppy*, and we sailed to the islands and had lovely picnics. He even painted Poppy's house for her.' This was said with an accompanying eye roll. 'Do you remember how Mum's cottage used to look?'

'Of course. It was fabulous. The only house right on the edge of the sand. And painted every colour of the rainbow. It was a talking point in Sugar Bay.'

'Yes, well...wait till you see it now.'

'Why? What did Sean do to it?'

'Painted it white.'

'The whole house?'

She nodded. 'Spanking white with neat aqua blue trims. Spotless and tidy, just like his boat.'

'My God. *Spotless* and *tidy* are two words I'd never associate with Poppy. Did she hate it?'

Freya gave another shrug. 'She pretended to love it. She was smitten at the time, though, so her judgement was clouded.'

'But I take it your dad eventually blotted his copybook?'

'Oh, yes. Big time. A week before Christmas he totally blackened his name. He and his little yacht just disappeared into the wide blue yonder.' Freya paused significantly. 'Along with Poppy's savings.'

It was gratifying to watch Gus's jaw drop.

'How did he manage that?'

'Oh, you know Poppy. Didn't trust banks, and didn't worry much about money. What little she did accumulate she kept at home in a ginger jar.' Freya sighed. 'It was the gloomiest, most depressing Christmas ever. We tried to be cheerful for poor Nick's sake, but we weren't very good at it, I'm afraid.'

Leaning forward, she put her coffee mug back on the table. 'I found out later from one of the local fishermen that Sean had moved on, up to Gladstone. He'd changed the name of his yacht to *Caroline*, and he was living with a new woman, a widow named Mrs Keane. *Caroline* Keane, of course. *And* he showed no sign of an Irish accent.'

'So he was a con artist.'

'Through and through. And Poppy admitted later that he'd always had a gambling addiction. She'd known that, and she still wasn't careful.'

Gus let out his breath in a whoosh, then rose and paced to the big picture window and stood with his hands resting lightly on his hips as he looked out to sea. 'I see why fathers have a bad name around here.'

Freya stood too and followed him across the room. 'I know you're nothing like Sean, Gus. In fact, you're the opposite. You've come here to give, not to take.'

'That's certainly the plan.' He didn't turn from the window. Outside, it was almost dusk and the sea and the sky had turned a deep pearlescent grey.

'I know Nick liked you, straight off,' Freya said. 'Actually, I'm sure he wants to get to know you. He's just—'

'Scared.'

'Yes.' *We're both scared.*

Trouble was, though Gus might not be a con man, he still had his own special brand of dangerous charm. If he entered their lives, even for a short time, and then left again, as he must, he would almost certainly leave a huge raw-edged hole.

Gus turned from the window. 'I guess I should head off now. You need to talk to Nick, and I need to book into the hotel.'

'You're welcome to stay here.' Freya had no idea she was going to say that. She was pretty sure Gus wanted to stay in the hotel, to keep an emotional distance, but the invitation had tumbled out spontaneously and she couldn't take it back without looking foolish. She held her breath, waiting for his answer.

To her surprise, his lip curled in a faintly amused smile. 'Don't you think you should consult Nick before making such rash offers? He hasn't exactly welcomed me with open arms, has he?'

'But you're doing a wonderful thing for us, Gus, and we're in your debt. What if I go and talk to him? He's sure to have calmed down by now.'

'Not now, Freya.' Gus wasn't smiling any more. He was deadly serious. 'It will be better for all of us if I stay at the hotel.'

It was ridiculous to feel disappointed. Freya was dredging up a smile when Gus surprised her by reaching for her arm.

'Before I go, let me see that burn. I'm not sure you should trust Poppy's home-grown remedies.'

'Oh, it's fine.' It was true. The burn no longer stung and, when she looked at her arm, the aloe vera was already working. The angry redness was fading.

Gus's fingers, however, encircled her wrist and, in spite of her beach girl's tan, they looked very dark and strong against her skin. His other hand touched her wrist gently, unbelievably gently. So gently he was killing her.

A tiny gasp escaped her and he went still. She looked up and something in his burning gaze sent a high voltage current through every vein in her body.

She couldn't bear it, had to look away.

He said, 'I'll make contact with Nick's doctor in the morning.'

She was almost too breathless to respond. 'If you need me, I'll be here in the gallery all day.'

'OK. I'll call you.'

Without another word, Gus went to the kitchen door where he'd left his overnight bag. Snagging it with two fingers, he let himself out and he didn't look back.

Freya was chopping mushrooms and onion for a homemade pizza when Nick came into the kitchen. His hair was still wet from his shower, and she always thought he looked younger somehow when his hair was wet. More vulnerable. Tonight, he looked shamefaced too.

He sent a quick glance around their open-plan living area. 'Where's Gus?'

'He's gone to the hotel.' She continued methodically to slice mushrooms.

'Is he buying wine or something for dinner?'

'No, Nick. He's staying at the hotel.'

'Why? Didn't you ask him to stay here?'

Setting down her knife, Freya folded her arms and she sent her son a rueful smile. 'Gus thought it would be better. He wanted to give you time to get over your shock.'

'Oh.'

'He's a good man, Nick. He's not like Sean. He really wants to help you.'

The boy stared at the partly assembled pizza. 'Are you going to put bacon on that?'

'Of course.'

'Plenty?'

'Just the right amount. You know what Dr Kingston said. You're supposed to have lots of vegetables and not too much salt.'

Nick sighed theatrically and, for a moment, Freya thought the subject of Gus had been dropped.

Not so.

Leaning with his elbows on the counter, her son scowled. 'I don't get it. I really don't get it. If Gus is such a great guy, why isn't he a proper father? Why doesn't he live here with us?'

Freya's heart thudded and her brain raced as she searched for the exact words to explain. This moment was so critically important. The explanation was complicated, but she had to get it right.

Clearly, Nick thought she was taking too long and he rushed in with more questions. 'If Gus is so helpful, why'd he go away in the first place? What's wrong with us?' Sudden tears spilled and Nick swiped at them angrily with the backs of his hands. 'What's wrong with our whole freaking family?'

'Oh, darling.' Freya gave up searching for perfect words to answer *these* questions. Instead, she rushed around the kitchen counter to hug him.

On Monday morning Gus looked out of his hotel window at blue skies and perfect rolling surf and wished his heart felt lighter. He'd spent another restless, unhappy night thinking about Freya and Nick and he'd resolved nothing.

Still yawning, he showered and shaved and went down to the hotel dining room for breakfast. Coffee, fresh fruit and scrambled eggs helped.

Then, as he left the dining room, he came to a sudden, heart-thumping halt. Nick was in the foyer, speaking to a woman at the front desk.

The boy was dressed for school in a blue and white polo shirt with grey shorts and sneakers. He had a school bag slung over his shoulder and he fiddled nervously with its zip while he spoke to the woman behind the counter.

What was he doing here? Gus's heart picked up pace as he hurried forward. 'Nick?'

The boy whirled around. His eyes widened and he smiled nervously. 'Hi, Gus.' He turned back to the desk and said to the woman, 'No need to call the room. It's OK. I've found him.'

I've found him.

The words were like music to Gus, or the world's finest poetry. His son was looking for him. His heart swelled with elation. 'It's good to see you,' he told Nick thickly.

The boy nodded. 'I was hoping I'd find you.'

'Have you had breakfast?' Gus smiled, trying to put the boy at his ease.

'Yes, thanks.' Nick swallowed nervously. 'Mum didn't send me here or anything. I just wanted to see you—to…to talk.'

'Sure. We could go up to my room or—' A glance through the hotel's large plate glass windows showed the beach sparkling in the morning sunshine. 'We could go outside.' Gus smiled again. 'I think I'd rather be out in the fresh air. How about you?'

'Yeah. Outside would be better.'

They went out through automatic sliding glass doors into the pleasant subtropical sunshine. Children zipped past on bikes or dawdled to school. Ubiquitous surfers carrying surfboards mingled with early shoppers strolling on The Esplanade. Gus and Nick walked over soft grass strewn with pine needles to an empty bench seat beneath Norfolk Island pines.

'Look at that.' Gus gestured to the curling waves and the pristine curve of the beach. 'You know you're lucky to be living here, don't you?'

'Yeah.' Nick smiled shyly. 'But it's not so great when you have to go to school all day.'

'Although…as I remember, the surf's still here when school's out.'

'Yeah, I know.' Nick grinned. 'It's a cool place to live, except lots of people only stay for a while, then move away.' He shot a sideways glance to Gus. 'Like you.'

Making a deliberate effort to appear casual and relaxed, Gus leaned back against the seat's wooden slats and propped an ankle on a knee. 'There aren't a lot of jobs in these parts. That's why people move on. I had to go away to university and then, later, I worked overseas.'

'Yeah, Mum told me.' Nick looked down at his school bag, dumped at his feet, and he reached for the strap, twisting it with tense fingers. 'Like I said, Mum didn't send me here. I told her I had to get to school early. She doesn't even know I'm talking to you.'

Pleased by the boy's honesty, by his obvious concern for Freya, Gus felt a strangely warm glow. 'Maybe we can tell your mum…later.'

'I guess.' Nick kicked at a fallen pine cone. 'We talked last night. About you. Mum told me what happened.'

'Happened—as in—?'

'Why you two split up. She said you didn't deliberately leave us. You didn't even know about me.'

'Well…yes…that's right.'

'And she said it was her decision not to tell you about me.'

Gus couldn't resist asking, 'Did she explain why?'

Nick shrugged. 'Kind of. It didn't really make sense.'

You and me both, kiddo, Gus thought. Even though he understood Freya's motives, her secrecy still hurt, still didn't make proper sense to him. Just the same, he tried to explain it to the boy. 'Sometimes we do things that feel right at the time that don't always make sense when we look back on them later.'

'Especially in my weird family.'

'Trust me, Nick, every family has its own kind of weirdness.'

Wind ruffled the boy's dark hair and he seemed to consider

this for a moment, then shrugged it aside. 'The way Mum tells it—sounds like she wasn't good enough for you.'

Gus lost his casual pose. 'Freya told you that?'

'She didn't say those exact words.'

'But she told you that she couldn't fit into my life?'

'Yeah. Something like that. Sounded pretty lame to me.'

A heavy sigh escaped Gus. How could he ask Nick to understand that he and Freya had been young, that most young people made bad judgements one way or another, although they never felt like mistakes at the time?

The boy was eleven and he couldn't be expected to look on eighteen-year-olds as young, especially when he faced a shockingly uncertain future.

'The good thing is, your mum found me now,' Gus said.

'Yeah. Thanks for coming down here, and offering the kidney and everything.' Nick sent him another shy smile. 'That's actually what I wanted to say.'

Gus smiled back at him. He loved this kid. Heck, he wanted to wrap his arms around Nick's skinny shoulders and hug him hard. But maybe it was too soon, so he resisted the urge. 'I've got a kidney to spare, and you're welcome to it. But I have to have the tests first.'

'I emailed Dr Kingston last night.'

'You what?'

'Sent him an email,' Nick said nonchalantly.

'I didn't know you could do that.'

'My doctor's pretty cool. And he wrote back to say he's really pleased we found you, and you can get most of your tests done at the Dirranvale hospital, if you want.'

'That sounds good.'

Nick's grey eyes, which were the same shape as Freya's eyes and had the same thick, dark lashes, took on an unexpected twinkle. 'If you're going to Dirranvale, there's something I should warn you about.'

'What's that?'

'One of the nurses up there is a vampire.'

For a split second, Gus wasn't sure how to respond to this. He was about to laugh it off, then he caught the spark of mischief in Nick's grin and changed tack. 'No kidding? A vampire?'

'I reckon when she takes your blood, she keeps some of it for herself.'

'No!' Gus gave an elaborate shudder. 'You'd better describe her to me, so I'll know to avoid her.'

'She's easy to pick. She has long black hair and really, really pale skin.'

'And fangs?'

Nick giggled. 'No. She's actually kind of pretty.'

'Oh, yeah. That would be right. Vampires are often exceptionally beautiful. That's why they're so dangerous. Do you think I should tell her that we know what she's up to?'

Nick's smile lost a little of its certainty. 'I'm not asking you to drive a stake through her heart or anything.'

'Well, that's a relief.' Gus chuckled. 'So you're determined to save her bacon. Does that mean you're keen on her?'

'No way.' The boy went bright pink.

'All right, then. I won't say a word.'

From somewhere in the distance came the ringing of a bell.

'Oh-oh.' Nick scrambled to his feet and scooped up his bag.

'You're going to be late for school.'

'Yeah. I'd better go.'

'You'd better run,' Gus said. 'But be careful crossing the road, won't you?'

'Course.'

'Thanks for the advice about the vampire.'

'Good luck!' Nick flashed a final quick grin, and Gus

watched the boy dashing across the grass beneath the pines, dark hair lifting in the breeze, school bag bumping against his hip, and he felt, for a fleeting moment, as if he'd known his son all his life.

Then reality returned like a fist in his guts. He'd been deprived of this fabulous feeling, deprived for the past eleven and a half years.

Freya's concentration was shot to pieces. Gus had phoned to say that he'd hired a car and was driving to Dirranvale for blood tests, X-rays and scans and, although she went through the motions of her normal everyday activities—opening the gallery, smiling at visitors who wandered in, checking mail, answering phone calls—her mind was at the hospital.

She'd been there so many times with Nick and she could picture exactly what Gus was going through—sitting patiently, or perhaps impatiently, on those hard metal seats outside X-ray, then having to change into one of the awful gaping hospital gowns. Afterwards, going on to Pathology to be stuck with needles.

The thought kept her dancing on a knife-edge between hope and fear. This morning, Nick had been so excited, so certain that his dad would save him. He had all his faith pinned on this. And of course she was hoping too...

Even though Nick wasn't in immediate danger, he was on a national waiting list and they'd been assured there would be a donor match out there, but she knew they all, including Gus, wanted him to be the one who gave.

The tissue match had to be perfect, however, so wasn't it foolish to build up too much hope?

She must have whispered *good luck* to Gus at least a thousand times this morning.

When she wasn't doing that, she was thinking about last

night and the way Gus had held her wrist and looked at her…
She kept seeing the dark shimmer of emotion in his eyes…

The memory filled her head and how crazy was that, to be
obsessed by such a teensy, short-lived moment?

It was nothing.

No.

It was something. There'd definitely been *something* happening when Gus had touched her skin…intensity in his face
that couldn't be ignored. He'd looked that way all those years
ago…on so many occasions during their perfect summer.

Thinking about that summer, Freya found herself drawn
into a web of memories…beginning with the first time Gus
had asked her out, when he invited her to be his partner at
their senior formal.

She could recall every detail of that afternoon in their last
year of high school…

Wednesdays always finished with double history, one of
the few classes Freya shared with Gus. And on that particular
mid-week afternoon he spoke to her just outside the school
gate.

Her heart started a drum roll the minute she saw him standing there and realised he was waiting for her.

She'd been hopelessly smitten from the day Gus arrived at
their school two years earlier, but she'd been quite stupidly
shy around him and, as Gus had been rather shy too, they'd
hardly spoken.

Oh, there'd been a little flirting…and a lot of smiling…
but he'd been caught up with his surfing, his football and his
studies, and he'd never asked her out on a date. As far as Freya
knew, Gus hadn't taken any girl out and there were plenty of
girls who'd been hoping.

But, on that special afternoon, he approached her with
endearing nervousness.

'Hey, Freya?'

'Hey.' She'd tried to sound casual, as if this wasn't a big deal, like maybe the biggest deal of her life to date...

'I was wondering...if you have a partner for the formal.'

'Um...no, I haven't.' *Oh, God.* Her knees were shaking. 'Not yet.'

Mel Crane shuffled past and sent them a goofy grin.

Gus scowled at him, then offered Freya a shy tilted smile. 'I was wondering if you'd like to come with me.'

'Um.' Her tongue was suddenly paralysed. *Speak, simpleton!* 'Yes,' she managed at last.

'Yes?' Seemed he was about as inarticulate as she was. Why did he look so disbelieving? As if she wouldn't jump at the chance? His shock gave her courage.

'Yes, Gus, I'd really like to go to the formal with you.'

'Sweet.' He was smiling properly now, smiling fully at her in a way that was a little short of dazzling. 'Terrific. I don't know any details yet, about what time I'll pick you up or anything.'

'That's OK. There's no rush.' She smiled at him bravely. 'Thanks, Gus.'

He walked with her then for three blocks, and she wasn't sure that her feet were touching the ground. They talked about their history teacher, about their friends, about surfing...

When they reached The Esplanade they said goodbye. Their houses were at opposite ends of the Bay.

Oh, man. Freya rushed home to Poppy, bursting with excitement.

And, immediately, she met her first hurdle.

Poppy didn't like the idea of her only daughter going out with a football jock. Weren't they all smart-mouthed thugs? Wasn't there a nice boy Freya could go with? Someone more artistic and sensitive?

Naturally, Freya insisted that Gus was nice. He wasn't just

good at football; he was practically top of their class. He was lovely, and she was going with him or with no one.

When Poppy finally, but unhappily, acquiesced, they moved on to the Battle of The Dress.

'I can do wonderful things with a sewing machine and a bucket of dye,' Poppy suggested.

Freya was beyond horrified. She loved her mum, but she flatly refused to go to the formal dressed like a tie-dyed hippie.

'All the other girls are getting their dresses from Mimi's in Dirranvale. Phoebe's mother's even taking her to Brisbane to buy her dress.'

'That girl's mother never had any sense,' Poppy muttered darkly. 'And you know we can't afford so much as a handkerchief from one of those fancy salons.'

'That's OK. I'll earn all the money I need.'

'How?'

'I'll sell aromatherapy candles at the markets.'

Poppy rolled her eyes. She'd gone through her 'market phase', as she called it. She'd sold handmade soaps and candles and jewellery and she'd made quite good money, but she hated the long hours of constant toil that were required to replenish her stocks week after week, and she'd opted for a part-time job caring for seedlings at a local plant nursery instead.

Freya, however, was determined. She went with her best friend Jane and Jane's mother to Mimi's in Dirranvale and she fell in love with a most divine off-the-shoulder dress and put it on lay-by. Then she gathered used jars from all her neighbours' households and spent hours in the evenings melting wax and adding essential oils and wicks, then decorating the candle jars with silver and gold calligraphy pens.

For a month she spent every weekend doing the rounds of the craft markets in the local seaside towns. She was exhausted, especially as she had to catch the bus back and forth, *and* she had to burn the metaphorical candle at both ends, sitting up till midnight to finish her homework.

But it was worth it. She'd earned enough to buy her dream dress from Mimi's, as well as divine shoes that were dainty enough to make Cinderella jealous, *and* there was money left over for a trip to the hairdresser and a French manicure.

On the night of the formal, Freya slipped into the soft misty-blue chiffon dress that everyone said matched her eyes perfectly. And she felt—amazing!

Gus arrived at her door with a corsage and he looked all kinds of perfect—so tall and dark and handsome in his black tuxedo that Freya thought she might die and go straight to heaven.

And that was *before* they danced, touching each other for the very first time.

CHAPTER SIX

WALKING home with Gus that night was even more sensational than dancing with him. They had to go all the way along the beachfront because Poppy's house was at the far end of the Bay, and it was Freya who suggested they should take off their shoes and walk on the sand.

Gus agreed with gratifying enthusiasm, and they left their shoes beside a pile of rocks. Gus shoved Freya's evening bag into his trouser pocket and rolled up the bottoms of his trousers, while Freya scooped up the hem of her dress in one hand, leaving her other hand free to hold his. *Bliss City!*

If there were other couples on the beach that night, they stayed well in the shadows and Freya and Gus felt quite alone as they strolled hand in hand on the edge of the sand beneath a high, clear sky blazing with stars.

Freya could have stayed out all night. She'd never felt so happy, so unbelievably alive. She kept wanting to turn to look at Gus. To stare at his gorgeousness. There were so many things she loved about the way he looked—his dark hair with the bit that flopped forward, his deep-set dark eyes, his strong, intelligent profile, his broad shoulders, his long legs, his sturdy hands.

Then there came *that* moment, the moment when Gus let go of her hand and touched the back of her neck.

Freya usually wore her hair down, but that night it was swept up by the hairdresser into a romantic knot.

'Did you know you have the most gorgeous skin right here?'

The feel of Gus's fingers on her nape made her want to curl into his arms.

'I sit behind you in History,' he said. 'And your hair falls forward, and I spend hours admiring the back of your neck.'

'So that's why I get better marks than you in History.'

'Could be.' His fingers stroked just below her hairline. 'I love this bit just here.'

And while she was melting from the touch of his fingers, he touched his lips to her neck.

Freya was shaking. His gentleness was excruciating. She bowed her head, exposing her skin in a silent appeal, begging for more. The touch of his lips on the curve of her neck made her ache deep inside, made her want to cry and to laugh, to dance, to lie down in the shallows.

Then Gus kissed her lips.

Of course it was late when they finally reached her house, especially as they forgot their shoes and had to go back to search for them, and it took ages to remember which pile of rocks they'd left them beside. They were laughing, giggling like children, drunk with happiness.

Gus kissed her again on the front steps. He was still kissing her when Poppy flung the front door open, letting bright light spill over them, and making them blink.

Arms akimbo, her mother glared at Gus.

'Freya should have been home hours ago. Who do you think you are, coming down here and making all sorts of assumptions about my daughter?'

To his credit, Gus was very restrained and polite, but he

left in a hurry. It was Freya who lost her cool, later, after he'd gone.

'How could you be so mean, Mum? We were only kissing. Why did you have to be so awful to Gus?'

'I don't trust him, or any of that snobby lot up on the hill.' Poppy picked up the damp hem of Freya's dress and frowned elaborately at the clinging grains of sand.

'Well, *I* trust him, and surely that's what counts?'

It was an argument that came back to bite Freya four months later, at the end of the summer, after Gus had already left for university in Brisbane and she missed her period.

Now, Freya was so lost in the mists of the past that when the bell at the front door rang, letting her know that yet another visitor had come into the gallery, she didn't look up. Most people liked to be left to wander about looking at paintings without being observed, and she wasn't in the mood for an exchange of happy banter with a tourist.

When a shadow fell over her desk, she realised she was out of luck. She looked up and heat rushed into her face. 'Gus!'

Gus's heart was pounding, actually pounding. As he'd walked into The Driftwood Gallery, he'd seen Freya sitting at the pale timber desk in the corner. She had her back to him and she was wearing jeans and a grey knitted top that shouldn't have looked sexy, but it was soft and it clung lovingly to her shoulders before falling loosely to her hips, and somehow it managed to look incredibly feminine.

She was leaning forward so that her hair, light brown and streaked with gold, parted like a curtain to show a V of smooth, pale skin on her neck. And suddenly he was remembering every detail of falling in love with Freya Jones and the heady, blinding happiness of that magical summer.

Their summer.

To his dismay, he felt the sting of tears and he found himself recalling all the silly nicknames Freya had given him—Huggy Bear, Hot Stuff, Angel Eyes.

Her favourite had been Sugar Lips, while he'd simply called her Floss.

Memories pulled at him as he approached her desk but, when she looked up, he saw shock in her eyes and then unmistakable fear, and their happy past disintegrated like a jigsaw puzzle breaking up into a thousand separate scattered pieces.

Gus was wrenched back into the present in all its unhappy complexity.

'Hi,' he said, forcing the breezy greeting past the constriction in his throat. Freya's smoky blue eyes were so clouded with worry that he tried to cheer her with a joke. 'I've finally escaped from the evil clutches of the vampire.'

'The vampire?' She looked more worried than ever.

'Hasn't Nick mentioned her?'

'No.'

Damn. Gus grimaced.

'I thought you were at the hospital. What are you talking about?'

'I *have* been at the hospital,' he assured her. 'Every one of my vital organs has been X-rayed and scanned from every conceivable angle, and I've given vast quantities of blood.'

'Oh. Is that the vampire connection?'

'Yeah. Bad joke. But you can blame Nick. He told me about the vampire nurse when he called in this morning on his way to school.'

'Really?' Freya was on her feet, twisting a locket at her throat with anxious fingers.

'I'm so glad Nick called in to see me, Freya. He came to thank me, and it meant a lot. He's a great kid. You must be proud of him.'

She showed no sign that his words reassured her. She

looked distressed and rubbed at her temple, as if her head ached. 'Nick didn't tell me he was going to see you.'

'Well, I think he felt bad about yesterday's reception. And he's entitled to see me. I'm his father, after all.'

'Yes, of course.' She was still frowning and not looking at him.

Gus's jaw tightened. If Freya was going to be a dog in the manger about their son, she'd have a fight on her hands.

'So what will you do now the tests are out of the way?' she asked. 'Will you fly straight back to the Northern Territory?'

'Why?' he asked coldly. 'Are you keen to be rid of me?'

'No. But you said you had commitments.'

'I don't want to rush away till I've had a chance to get to know Nick.'

Freya regarded him thoughtfully. 'But you do know it will be a week or more before we get the results?'

'A week, Freya? What's a week when you've had Nick for more than eleven years? Don't you understand that I need a chance to get to know my son?'

'Yes, of course I understand that. I'm sorry.' She looked as if she might weep.

'They're giving Nick's case priority,' he said in a more conciliatory tone. 'So we might hear quite soon.'

'That's good news, at least.'

Gus glanced at his wristwatch. 'It won't be too long before school's out and I thought Nick might like to come swimming with me this afternoon.'

'Oh?'

'I won't keep him too long. I know he has homework.' He frowned at Freya. 'Nick does swim, doesn't he?'

'Of course. He's like me. He loves the water.'

Out of nowhere, something about the soft, vulnerable droop of her lower lip triggered a memory for Gus. Damn it. He was recalling a folk song he'd heard years ago, a song about a forsaken mermaid.

He'd only heard it a couple of times—once at an outdoor folk festival and once on the radio—but each time the lament about a lost and heartsick mermaid had drenched him with memories of Freya.

For days afterwards, the memories had haunted him. He'd only shaken them off, eventually, by convincing himself that Freya Jones had moved on with her life just as he had. But how could he have guessed that she hadn't settled down with some lucky man? How could he have dreamed there was a child, a living connection that would link him to her for ever?

Perhaps it was because of the memory that he said, 'Freya, you're welcome to come swimming with us, if you like.'

'I…I can't go. I've got a gallery to look after.'

Gus looked about him at the empty rooms and the walls filled with artwork. He lifted an eyebrow in a silent question.

'I know it doesn't look very busy at the moment,' she said, reading his thoughts. 'But you never know who might drop in. I can't close on a whim.'

'Pity.' He let his gaze travel over the colourful walls. 'You have some great paintings here.'

'Yes, I've been lucky.' Freya moved into the centre of the room, looking about her with evident satisfaction. 'I've managed to capture quite a bit of interest in this little gallery. It's developed a reputation and people are starting to come here from all over Australia. Now I have top artists asking me if they can hang their work here. It used to be the other way round.'

'That's quite an achievement,' Gus said, genuinely impressed.

She nodded, smiling, unable to hide her satisfaction.

'So are any of these paintings yours?'

'Yes.' Freya lifted a hand, about to point out her work.

'Hang on,' Gus said. 'Let's see if I can find yours.' After finding Nick in a tribe of similarly dressed footballers, he was feeling a tad smug.

Now, with vague memories of the sketches that Freya had drawn twelve years ago, Gus began to wander the rooms checking out the landscapes, seascapes, vibrant arrangements of tropical flowers and fruit, portraits, abstracts...

Freya stood watching him with her lips curled in a small smile and her eyes sparkling with an *I dare you* gleam.

It wasn't long before Gus was forced to admit defeat. He sent her an apologetic grin. 'I give up. These all look really good to me, but none of them screams *you*.' He made a circling gesture to the paintings all around him. 'I have to say, if you've painted any of these, you've improved a hell of a lot since high school.'

'I should jolly well hope so.' Smiling archly, she came and stood beside him, arms folded over her front. 'Just out of interest, which paintings do you like? Which ones appeal to you most?'

He must have looked anxious because Freya laughed. 'This isn't a trick question, Gus. I'm not going to slash my wrists if you don't pick mine. I'm just curious.'

'I'm no expert.'

'I know that.'

His gaze flickered over the fruit and flowers, paused briefly on a bright, daring landscape with sand and palm trees, then on to a realistic seascape with waves crashing onto rocks. He stopped at a piece that seemed to be a collage of watercolours and paper of varying textures. It was beautiful and incredibly clever—the sort of thing he would buy for a woman, the sort of thing he *should* have bought for Monique, perhaps.

He moved onto an abstract with stripes in browns and ochres overlaid with splashes of charcoal and crimson. 'If I was buying something for myself, I would probably choose this one,' he said, pointing.

Freya nodded. 'That's a Carl Barrow.' She smiled. 'You have good taste. It's probably the most expensive painting here.'

'Really?' He pointed to the collage. 'What about that one? It's beautiful.'

'That's one of mine,' she said, turning pink.

'Wow.' Genuinely excited, he moved closer. 'I really like the way you've grouped everything and the combination of colours. It's incredibly pleasing to the eye. Intricate without being cluttered.' He turned to her, beaming. 'Floss, you're brilliant.'

'Well, thank you, sir.'

She was blushing prettily and her eyes were glowing with pleasure and he wanted to kiss her so badly he couldn't breathe.

Instead, he found himself saying, 'Why *don't* you come with us to the beach? Couldn't you put one of those signs on the door? *Closing early today. Sorry for the inconvenience*.'

Pink-cheeked, she pursed her lips as she considered this. Gus watched the slow blaze of concentration in her eyes as she weighed up the pros and cons. He had a fair idea that her curiosity about his fledgling bond with Nick would win out.

'I guess I could close up for an hour,' she said.

Gus grinned.

Freya smiled back at him. Their gazes held and, without warning, the flame of their old attraction burned brightly.

'Hey, Mum.'

Nick's voice startled them. He was standing at the door, hair awry, school bag dangling from one shoulder.

'Oh, Nick, that's good timing.' Freya's voice was strangely high-pitched and the colour in her cheeks deepened. 'Gus was just asking if you'd like to go for a swim.'

'Would I ever?' Nick's face was instantly alight. 'Thanks, Gus. Hey, what about you, Mum? Are you coming too?'

'Yes. I thought I might as well.'

'Awesome.'

This is so not wise, Freya told herself as she thrust her feet through appropriate holes and wriggled into her swimming costume. Closing the gallery for a swim with Gus on a Monday afternoon was quite possibly the dumbest thing she'd ever done.

She knew jolly well that she should have left Gus and Nick to go swimming alone, but she'd let two things sway her and neither of them were admirable. First—she was jealous of the newly developing relationship between her son and his father. She didn't want to feel left out.

Second—those few minutes alone with Gus in the gallery had been over-the-moon wonderful and, even though she knew such moments were as fragile as soap bubbles and could only lead to heartbreak, she wanted more.

She was a fool.

She sank onto the edge of her bed. She had to think this through before she made a serious mistake.

Surely she wasn't really so selfish that she was jealous of any time Gus spent with Nick? Not after she'd had the boy to herself for eleven and a half years? No, she might feel a tad worried that Gus could somehow steal Nick from her, but if that had been her only concern, she wouldn't have closed the gallery to play hooky at the beach.

The true cause of her foolishness was the other reason—the intoxicating glow she'd felt when Gus praised her painting. It was the *zing* in her veins when he looked into her eyes and the scary knowledge that she'd never stopped loving him, that she would steal any time to be with him, no matter how brief or unwise.

But, the trouble was, trying to recapture those moments was *very* unwise. A few moments could never add up to a lifetime, and it was a lifetime with Gus that Freya wanted. Why couldn't she remember that her lifestyle and Gus's were worlds apart?

When he'd chosen a wife, he'd chosen a woman who was as different from her as it was possible to be.

Why couldn't she remember that Gus was here to help Nick and for no other reason?

'Mum!' Nick stuck his head around Freya's bedroom door. His face was smeared with white sunscreen and he was dressed in bathers. A beach towel was draped around his neck. 'Are you ready? Gus is back and he's waiting.'

'Almost ready. Give me a minute.'

Freya jumped up and butterflies danced in her stomach as she checked her swimsuit in the mirror. The last time Gus had seen her in bathers she'd been a girl in a bikini. What would he think of her now?

She'd chosen her favourite bathers in a pale yellow Hawaiian print because they gave her skin a rather nice glow. But were they too revealing? Did her backside look too big?

'Mum?' Nick called again from the hallway.

She would have to do. She grabbed a long beach shirt and slipped it on, pushed her feet into flip-flops. Out into the hall, she collected her hat and beach bag.

Nick was skipping ahead of her with excited glee.

Through the front window, Freya could see Gus waiting on the footpath and her heart skipped too, although she was more nervous than gleeful.

'This is so cool,' Nick sang. 'I'm going to the beach with my mother *and* my father.'

Oh, help.

'Nick,' Freya called.

The boy turned, read the caution in her face and looked instantly worried. 'What's the matter?'

'You mustn't get your hopes up. You…you can't expect…'

'What?' the boy demanded, frowning.

Freya looked at Nick's shining eyes. She saw her beautiful, clever, courageous half-man, and her heart shuddered as she thought of the terrible shadow that hung over him. Given everything he faced, it was cruel to let him hope for the impossible.

'I'm talking about Gus and…and me. We're not…um…we won't…' She groaned, angry at her clumsiness. 'Your father is here to help you, darling, to make sure you get well. But you mustn't hope that he and I will get back together.'

Right now, Nick was too excited to let anything bother him. He simply grinned and said, 'Whatever. Hurry up.'

Should she have spelled it out even more clearly? 'Nick!'

He turned back, eyes shining and Freya hadn't the heart to spoil his fun.

'Just remember, don't swim out too far,' she said.

'Aw, M-u-u-m.'

As they left their towels and jogged across the warm sand to the sea, Gus felt a need to suck in his abs. He was a long way from tubby, but he wasn't quite as streamlined as he'd been at eighteen, and for the first time in a long time it mattered.

The surf was magic. He'd forgotten the sheer exhilaration of catching a wave, of feeling it pick him up and rush headlong with him, carrying him forward with magnificent force, then dumping him in the foaming shallows, chest scraping on sand.

And he hadn't dreamed that this primitive pleasure would be so greatly enhanced by the company of a child. Nick was at his side the whole time, sometimes acting like a little kid, laughing and squealing, reaching for Gus's hand, even jumping onto his back as they dived through a wave.

At other times he was fiercely independent, catching waves fearlessly. Showing off.

The surf was a little rough and Gus felt a need to keep an eye on the boy the whole time and, truth be told, he was grateful for the distraction. If he hadn't been watching Nick, he would have been constantly staring at Freya in her stunning lemon and white swimsuit. He would have been mesmerised by her glistening and smooth wet skin and her long mermaid's hair, sleek against the curve of her neck and shoulders.

Actually, he wouldn't have simply been staring; he probably would have found a need to be close to her, finding excuses to touch.

But Freya was wiser than he was. She kept her distance. When the strap of her bathers slipped, she pulled it up a lot faster than she would have when she was younger, and there were no flirtatious smiles.

So it was a good thing that Nick was there, always jumping between them, shrieking with glee and distracting Gus's attention, and preventing him from doing anything foolish. And, when the boy finally admitted he'd had enough of surfing, they went back to their beach towels, dripping and exhausted, and Poppy Jones provided a new distraction.

She was waiting for them, sitting on the sand beside their towels, looking as unconventionally glamorous as she always had in a colourful kaftan and with her long silver hair in a loopy chignon.

It was Nick who made the introductions.

'Hey, Poppy, guess what? My dad's here.'

'So I see.' Poppy smiled warmly at Freya and her grandson and a tad uncertainly at Gus.

Hello, here we go… Gus thought, drawing a sharp breath. Poppy had been no fan of his when he was young and he had no idea how she would receive him now. He wasn't even sure how big a role she'd played in Freya's decision to keep her pregnancy a secret.

One thing was certain; Gus would have preferred to be wearing more clothing when he met Freya's mother after such a long time. It was hard to feel dignified when he was half naked and dripping wet, especially when he was uncomfortably aware that this woman viewed him as the son of snobs and totally unsuitable for her daughter.

He manufactured a smile. 'How do you do, Poppy?'

'I'm very well, thanks, Gus.' Hopping nimbly to her feet, Poppy scooped up Nick's beach towel and wrapped him in it, giving him a fond hug as she did so.

To Gus's surprise, the boy didn't seem to mind his grandmother's public display of affection.

'Gus has spent the whole day at the hospital,' Freya told her mother.

Without releasing her embrace, Poppy turned to Gus. 'Freya tells me you've come back to help our boy.'

'Fingers crossed,' Gus said, nodding.

This time Poppy's smile was definitely warm. 'That's wonderful news. We're very grateful.' As she began to towel Nick's hair dry she said, 'Freya and Nick always come to my place for dinner on Monday nights. Would you like to join us tonight, Gus?'

'Yes!' Nick punched the air with a triumphant fist.

Gus sensed rather than saw the way Freya stiffened.

'Easy there, Nick,' she said in a gently warning tone. 'Remember what I said. Gus might have other plans.'

Freya flashed a significant glance Gus's way and he knew she was giving him the perfect opening to bow out. He wondered if she was worried that this could be an awkward evening and he thought fast, trying to decide what was best.

'I have a curry simmering away,' Poppy told him. 'There's plenty for everyone.'

Never once in the time he'd gone out with Freya had Poppy offered him a meal, but now, with her grandson's life hanging in the balance, that barrier appeared to be finally down.

Gus couldn't help feeling pleased, but hadn't he planned to keep an emotional distance? Dining with this trio would be rather like playing Happy Families, and it might confuse Nick. Even so, Gus wanted to accept. He'd been an outsider for too long.

Three pairs of eyes were watching him, waiting for his answer. Poppy was looking mildly amused, Freya was as tense as an athlete waiting for the starter's gun, and Nick looked full of hope.

It was the hope in Nick's eyes that decided Gus. After all, the boy was the reason he was here. 'Thanks, Poppy,' he said. 'I'd love to join you, but I need to duck back to the hotel to change.'

Nick began to dance a little jig of excitement.

'We have to change, too,' Freya said and she seemed surprisingly relieved. 'And Nick has to do his homework.'

Poppy gave them all a pleased smile. 'Dinner will be ready at seven.'

Dining in Poppy's warm, cosy kitchen *did* feel like Happy Families. Dangerously so. Despite the super-neat sparkling white exterior, the inside of her cottage was as exotic and colourful as her clothing, and when Gus was welcomed at the front door by Nick, he was also met by the smells of jasmine-scented candles mingled with the fragrant aroma of curry.

Nick's eyes popped wide when he saw the wine and flowers Gus carried. 'Are they for my mum?'

Gus winced inwardly when he saw the boy's delight. 'Actually, they're for your grandmother. Poppy's the hostess,'

Gus explained. 'She's gone to all the trouble of cooking a meal for us.'

The boy shrugged and pulled a face as if he'd never understand grown-ups, then led Gus down a pea-green hallway to the kitchen.

Gus's eyes were drawn immediately to Freya, who was setting the table. She'd fixed her hair into a high twist and had threaded gold hoops in her ears, and she was wearing jeans with a top made from something soft and floaty in muted browns, beiges and pinks. When she saw Gus she smiled and he came to a heart-thudding standstill.

Her smile seemed to glow, as if she was lit from within, and heaven knew how long he might have stood there, drinking in the sight of her, if Nick hadn't piped up.

'Poppy, Gus has brought you presents.'

Coming to his senses, Gus handed the gifts to Poppy, who blushed like a girl and gave him an unexpected hug. 'I can't remember the last time a man brought me flowers.'

'What a lovely thought, Gus,' Freya said and she smiled so warmly, he kissed her on the cheek.

The kiss felt more significant than it should have.

Poppy was animated as she deftly arranged the flowers in a vase and set them on a brilliant pink dresser. 'Freya, find us some glasses, dear. Do we need a corkscrew? It's in the drawer next to the sink. Can you deal with that, Gus? Oh, and there's lemonade in the fridge for you, Nick. Help yourself, darling.'

For a few moments there was general fuss as drinks were organised and steaming pots of rice and curry were set on mats in the centre of the table. The hubbub died as everyone sat down. A gentle breeze drifted in through the kitchen window along with the sounds of waves breaking. *Thump, crump, swish.* Poppy's house was right on the edge of the sand, as close to the sea as it was possible to be.

'I'd forgotten what it's like to live so near to the sea that you can hear it all the time,' Gus said.

'I don't know if I could live without it now,' said Poppy. 'It's almost like having another heartbeat.'

'And when I sleep over at Poppy's the waves sing me to sleep,' Nick chimed in happily.

Yes... Gus could remember all too clearly a night when he'd slept here with Freya, close to the singing of the waves. Had there ever been a more perfect night?

He wondered about the times Nick stayed at his grandmother's. Where was Freya on those occasions? Out on dates? He discovered this wasn't a question he wanted to dwell on.

'This smell of curry reminds me of Africa,' he said.

Of course they plied him with questions then and, as Poppy dished up spoonfuls of rice and fragrant meat, he told them about Eritrea in the horn of Africa.

'Where's the horn of Africa?' demanded Nick.

'Go and get the globe from the lounge room and Gus can show you,' Poppy told him.

Nick was back in a moment, bearing a large old-fashioned globe, which he handed to Gus. Then he stood leaning against the back of Gus's chair with a hand resting casually on his shoulder, his breath soft and warm on the back of Gus's neck.

'The names of the countries have changed since this globe was made,' Gus told him. 'But here's Eritrea, next to Ethiopia.' He traced Eritrea's borders. 'And here's the Red Sea, which forms another part of its border.'

'Isn't Asmara the capital?' asked Freya.

'That's right.'

As Nick went back to his place and they started to eat, Gus told them about Asmara's beautiful Italian colonial architecture, and about the islands and reefs in the Red Sea and the desolate magnetism of the wastelands of Dankalia in the south.

'Did you see lots of elephants?' Nick asked.

Gus shook his head. 'I'm afraid I didn't see many at all. There are only about a hundred elephants left in Eritrea.'

'What's happened to them?'

'Most of them were killed in the war.'

Nick looked horrified. 'Which war?'

'A long, long war with Ethiopia. The people in Eritrea were struggling for independence and it went on for years and years. It was a very hard time for the people and the animals. There were droughts as well as war, and lots of sickness.'

Gus looked from Freya to Poppy. 'Sorry, this isn't exactly a pleasant subject to discuss over dinner.'

Freya smiled. 'We're used to it. These aren't the worst questions Nick's asked at dinner time.' To Nick she said, 'It's because of the wars and the drought that Gus went to work in Africa, to help the Eritreans.'

Nick was wide-eyed, clearly impressed. 'How did you help them?'

'Mainly by working alongside them. My job was to help them to fight the drought, so I was involved in sinking wells and building dams and finding drought-resistant crops for them to grow.'

'What about your wife? Was she helping them, too?'

Across the table, Freya's eyes met Gus's in a direct, cool challenge, and it took him a second or two to respond.

'Monique taught in one of the hospital medical schools,' he said. 'And she worked to educate people generally about health care.'

Nick's eyes were huge. 'How did she die?'

'*Nick!*' There was both a warning and an edge of panic in Freya's voice.

CHAPTER SEVEN

Gus managed a shaky smile. He knew Freya was upset, but he didn't want to reprimand Nick. The boy was bright and almost certainly understood that his hold on life was at risk. Chances were the whole question of death plagued him much more than he let on.

It was even possible that an honest answer would help Nick.

Even so, talking about the way Monique died always brought a sickening chill that soaked Gus to the bone. At least he was used to the feeling now. After two years, he knew it would come whenever he spoke about this.

'My wife was killed in an explosion,' he told them. 'She took a wrong turn and she drove her truck over a landmine left behind from the war.'

'Oh, God,' Poppy whispered.

'I'm so sorry,' said Freya, white-lipped.

An uncomfortable silence fell over the table and, rather than allow it to go on for too long, Gus felt a need to resurrect the mood. 'Wars are terrible things, but the Eritreans are getting on with their lives now. Freya, have you seen any of the contemporary art coming out of Africa? I think you'd love it.'

Freya brightened visibly. 'Actually, I've been lucky enough to see an exhibition in Canberra. I thought it was amazing. So much energy and excitement in the work. I especially loved the sculptures.'

She went on to tell Gus about the artists she particularly admired and, to the adults' relief, Nick found this topic boring and he stopped asking questions.

He saved them for much later...when they were home again and Freya had tucked him in and kissed him goodnight and was turning out his bedroom light.

'Mum?' the boy called through the darkness. 'Do you like Gus?'

The question zapped through poor Freya as if she'd been spiked by an electric probe. Her legs threatened to give way and she clutched at the door frame for balance. 'Of course I like him.'

'I mean *really* like him.'

Oh, help. She thought she'd nipped this in the bud. Tonight, however, after they'd washed up Poppy's dishes together, Gus had walked home with them and Nick had walked between them, talking animatedly the whole way, skipping at times, even linking arms with them in moments of pure elation. When they'd said goodnight to Gus at the front gate, the boy had given him a bear hug and clung to him for dear life.

Remembering the poignancy of that moment now, Freya felt tears prick the backs of her eyelids. Her knees were distinctly wobbly as she walked back to Nick's bed and sat on the edge of the mattress.

'Nick, you haven't forgotten what I told you, have you? You know Gus and I won't be getting back together.'

'But that's crazy. Why won't you?'

Freya sighed. 'You know Gus hasn't come here to see me. He's only here because of you.'

'But he wants to see you, too. He's always looking at you. I reckon he likes you.'

He's always looking at you. Freya pushed aside the silly

little thrill these words caused. 'Well, yes…Gus likes me as an old friend, but that's all. Darling, you have to understand it doesn't mean we're going to…er…start living together or anything like that.'

Moonlight shining through the blinds above Nick's bed illuminated the pout of Nick's lower lip, and then the glitter of tears in his eyes.

Freya hugged him. 'Nicky boy.' It was an endearment from his baby days. 'Don't be sad, darling. Now that Gus knows about you, he's going to want to stay in touch with you always. I'm sure you'll see lots of him. He's so proud of you.'

'But what if he just disappears again?'

'He won't, Nick.'

'Grandpa did.'

'Oh, darling.' Freya gave him a hug. 'I told you Gus is a very different man from Grandpa. Everything about this situation is different. Gus is thrilled that you're his son. I know how much you mean to him already.'

She stroked Nick's hair away from his forehead. It had the habit of falling forward the same way Gus's did. 'Now he's met you and knows how fantastic you are, there's no way he'd want to lose contact.'

Using a corner of his sheet, Nick swiped at his eyes. 'I suppose if Gus gives me his kidney, he'll have to come back to make sure I'm looking after it properly.'

'You bet he will.' Somehow, Freya held back the emotion that threatened to choke her. She was so aware of how the boy picked up on the smallest unconscious messages, positive or negative.

Now she forced herself to picture Nick healthy and strong, spending precious times with his dad long into the future. 'And that will be perfect, won't it?' she said.

Everything would be perfect, she told herself as she left the room, once Nick was well and happy.

But how would she cope with Gus dropping in and out of their lives? It would be so much easier if she wasn't still hopelessly in love with him.

Waiting to hear back about the tests was a new form of torture for Gus. He tried to keep busy, staying in touch with the project in the Northern Territory via phone calls and email, and he used his hire car to tour the district, rediscovering forgotten haunts. He saw Nick when he could in the afternoons after school and they went swimming or for runs on the beach with Urchin.

Freya emailed an entire photo album devoted to Nick and he pored over these snaps, fascinated by the gradual transformation of his son from tiny baby to chubby toddler to small child, then schoolboy. Sometimes he caught glimpses of Freya's smile, or he saw an expression in Nick's eyes that reminded him of himself as a child. But mostly Nick was his own unique self, his features becoming more clearly defined as he grew.

To Gus's surprise, he discovered that he no longer felt the same raging disappointment for the lost years when he hadn't known his son. He knew Nick now and that seemed to matter more.

The past was gone and, for all he knew, he might have stuffed up being a father. But he and Nick still had the present. And, heaven help him, if he was a perfect match and if the surgeons did their job well, Nick could look forward to a long and healthy life, and Gus planned to be involved.

Right now, with his heart melting over these glimpses into his son's life, Gus knew without question that, even if he lived on the other side of the globe, even if his relationship with the boy's mother remained fragile, he would make sure he was a part of Nick's future.

More than once Gus considered inviting Freya to join him

for lunch at the hotel. Despite his lingering sense of injustice, he wanted to get to know her better, for all kinds of reasons, and her intimate knowledge of Nick was only one of them. There was a quiet self-assurance about Freya now that intrigued him, and a mysterious allure—sadness and shyness mixed with beauty and courage.

She'd changed in many ways and Gus wanted to understand how and why.

But he didn't invite her. She'd made it clear that she didn't want to get too pally with him, and she was sensible to be wary. Nick was her focus and the boy needed every ounce of her attention and love. The very last thing she needed right now was the distraction of an old boyfriend.

Just the same, Gus couldn't believe how hard it was to keep his distance from Freya. To start with, he saw her every day and each day she seemed to grow more beautiful. She was still like a Siren and being back in the Bay, surrounded by the sights and sounds and smells that accompanied their long-ago romance, was almost more trying than waiting for the test results.

Gus found himself recalling every detail of falling in love with her.

It had been so amazing to discover at the end of high school that the shy, elusive girl he'd been lusting after for two years was as interested in him as he was in her. At first it had felt like a miracle but, as the weeks of that summer rolled on, and in spite of their parents' misgivings, he and Freya had grown closer and closer.

They would walk for miles along the coast just to be completely alone. The first time they made love, they were in a tiny secluded cove that was a two-hour hike from Sugar Bay.

Thinking about it now, Gus could still remember the heady scent of the sun on Freya's skin and the silky smoothness of her tanned limbs, could remember her eagerness, her sweetness, her boldness.

And she hadn't minded his fumbling nervousness.

He'd made love with more assurance and finesse the next time…on a stolen weekend in Poppy's house…

Poppy hardly ever left the Bay, but she'd been invited to a birthday party for a friend who lived in Gympie and she was away for the entire weekend.

Freya had rung Gus at home. 'Guess what? We have the house to ourselves for a whole weekend.'

'Damn.'

'Damn?'

'I'm supposed to be giving Mel a hand on the petrol pump this afternoon.'

'Can't you get out of it? Swap with someone?'

He'd tried to con several mates into taking his place at the garage and he'd eventually bribed Fred Bartlet, promising to let Fred use his surfboard every day for a fortnight.

When he arrived at Freya's, she greeted him at the front door wearing nothing but a smile and a pink sarong, and she'd lit scented candles and decorated her bed with a lavender tie-dyed sheet and frangipani petals.

They made love. They went for swims, came home and showered and made love again. They were sweet and tender. They were wicked and wild. They kissed and touched in ways they'd only read about or heard about, and they almost cried with the beauty and out-and-out fabulousness of it all.

They talked long into the night and cooked up a midnight feast, and Gus discovered that a girl like Freya could be so much more than a lover—she could also be his best friend.

Hell.

How had he ever forgotten that? How had he let her slip away? Had he been under a spell that had broken the minute he left the Bay?

One thing was certain. It was too late to go back to the golden age of eighteen and he would drive himself mad if he kept asking these questions now.

After three restless days, Gus poked his head in at the Crane Brothers' garage, where he found Mel in the middle of rebuilding an engine.

Mel lifted his cheery grease-smeared face from beneath the bonnet of a cream Citroën. 'Sorry, mate, can't stop. Old Bill Nixon wants this running smoothly for his granddaughter's wedding on Saturday. Won't get away till this evening. But how about we sink a cold one at the pub, say around half past six?'

Early evening found the two old friends perched on high stools at a bar overlooking the bay, reminiscing about their youth as they munched on salted peanuts and drank beer from tall frosty glasses. Mel had always been a great story-teller and Gus enjoyed hearing what their old friends were up to these days, as well as receiving proud updates about Mel's wife Shelley and their two children, a boy and a girl.

But eventually, inevitably perhaps, the conversation swung around to Freya and Nick.

Gus came back from the bar with their second round of drinks and set them down, and Mel said without preamble, 'That boy of Freya's is a fabulous kid, Gus.'

Despite the skip in Gus's heartbeats, he nodded carefully and sampled his beer.

'And I'm not just talking about his football skills,' said Mel. 'Nick's been amazing, the way he's handled this whole business with his kidneys. He never whinges or talks about it. Just gets on with his life.'

Emotion tied painful knots in Gus's throat and he was suddenly unable to speak.

Mel eyed him shrewdly. 'Shut me up if I'm speaking out

of turn, mate, but I reckon maybe Nick's a chip off the old block.'

Something inside Gus struck hard, as if his heart had sounded a gong. 'Which old block would that be, Mel?'

Momentarily, Mel was taken aback, but he recovered quickly and shrugged. 'The one sitting right in front of me, perhaps?'

There was no point in trying to deny the truth. Gus let out his breath slowly. 'I suppose the whole Bay knows by now?'

'Well, maybe not the *whole* Bay.' Mel sent him a cautiously crooked smile. 'Three-quarters maybe, but not *everyone*.'

'Which means that almost the entire population of Sugar Bay found out I'm Nick's father just a day or two after I did.' Gus scowled as the anger and hurt he'd almost laid to rest blasted back with a vengeance.

'You were in the dark? You're joking.' Mel grimaced uncomfortably. He took a swig of beer. 'That's rough.' Then another swig. When he set the glass down, he regarded Gus thoughtfully. 'You mean to say Freya never told you she was pregnant?'

'I had no idea,' Gus said coldly. Damn it, he thought he'd come to grips with the years of secrecy, but talking about it to Mel ripped the wound wide open.

Mel shook his head. 'That's a shocker. At the end of high school we all thought you and Freya were the couple most likely to—'

'Likely to what?'

Mel grimaced. 'I don't know—get together and stay together, I guess.'

Gus gritted his teeth so fiercely he was surprised they didn't crack. He knew it was true. Back in that summer between the end of high school and leaving Sugar Bay, he and Freya had been infatuated with each other, inseparable.

Looking back, he found it almost impossible to pinpoint how and when he'd changed, but it must have started almost as soon as he left for Brisbane. How else, after six short weeks, had he been able to let her go so easily?

Eighteen was such an impressionable, fickle age.

But was that an excuse?

The worst of it was that he'd changed so fast and so radically he'd frightened Freya off. But he wasn't about to confess to Mel Crane that she'd actually tried to tell him about their baby.

'I know it's not really any of my business,' Mel said, watching Gus carefully. 'But, for what it's worth, no one around here knew who Nick's father was. One or two thought it might have been you, but Freya and Poppy went away up north for a few months. Freya was pregnant when she came back, and she was very close-lipped about the circumstances.'

'I guess Poppy took her away to muddy the waters,' Gus said moodily.

'I guess.' Mel thought about this for a bit, then brightened. 'I can tell you one thing, Gus—Freya's done a great job with that boy. A fantastic job.' Mel shrugged. 'As a footie coach, I've seen every kind of family. In my teams there are kids with no mum, no dad, parents who never turn up to watch their kids play, other parents who scream at their kids and yell abuse at the ref.'

Mel eyed Gus steadily over the rim of his glass. 'There's no argument. You would have been a huge bonus in Nick's life. But, putting that aside, the simple fact is Freya's done a great job. Heck, she let the boy play a game she doesn't even like, and I really respect that. I'm sure she'd rather he played tennis.'

Gus smiled in wry acknowledgement of this.

'Shelley really likes Freya,' Mel went on. 'So do her married friends, and that's saying something. I've seen other good-looking single women who bring out the claws of the married ones, but everyone here likes Freya.'

Still staring moodily into his drink, Gus said, 'What surprises me is that she hasn't married.'

'Too right. And it's not for lack of opportunity. Nearly every bachelor in the district has set his cap at her.'

Mel started to chuckle, then seemed to think better of it. His face sobered. 'So, mate, what's the story with Nick? Is he going to be OK?'

'That's the plan. I'm certainly hoping he'll be absolutely fine.'

'With the help of a kidney from you?'

'Yeah. We're still waiting to hear if I'm a suitable match.' As Gus said that, his mobile phone began to buzz in his pocket. 'Excuse me.' His chest tightened as he retrieved it and saw the number. 'Bit of a coincidence. This is from the renal physician's office. I'll take it outside.'

Gus's heartbeats were thundering as he hurried quickly from the bar. 'Hello?'

'Mr Wilder? I have a message from Dr Kingston.'

Thud. 'Yes?'

'He has the results back from the blood and tissue cross-matching, and he'd like you to make an appointment to see him.'

'Yes, sure. When?'

'As soon as possible. Is there any chance you could be in Brisbane by tomorrow morning?'

'Absolutely.'

'Great. We can fit you in at eleven.'

A week later, Gus made the journey to Brisbane again, this time with Freya and Nick. During the entire trip down the highway Freya's stomach churned as she swung through a spectrum of emotions from hope and excitement to fear and abject terror.

The past week had been such a whirlwind of preparations ever since they heard that Gus was a perfect match for Nick. His blood type, his tissue samples, the state of his kidneys, his heart, his lungs and his mind made him a perfect live donor. If everything went well, Nick could live to a healthy old age.

But if it didn't…

Freya couldn't bear to think of failure, couldn't let her imagination go there. And yet, no amount of level-headedness could hold off the knife-edge of panic.

Now she wasn't only worried about Nick. She was worried about Gus, too. The procedure should be straightforward but in any operation there was always a risk.

Two people she loved were facing possible danger…

'Don't look so glum,' Gus told her when they stopped for a cuppa at a roadside café.

'Sorry.' For Nick's sake, she knew she had to be totally optimistic and excited.

As they stood at the counter placing their orders—tea, a long black and a strawberry milkshake—Gus leaned close and whispered in Freya's ear, 'It's going to be OK.'

She looked up, saw the warmth and confidence in his eyes and her heart took wings. When Gus pressed a warm kiss on her cheek, she longed to let her eyes drift closed and to lean into his strength.

Perhaps if Nick hadn't been watching them so closely she might have done exactly that.

In Brisbane they stayed in adjacent suites in a hotel close to the hospital. Gus insisted on paying for their accommodation and he wouldn't listen to Freya's protests. 'So far, I haven't contributed a cent to Nick's upkeep,' he said.

Their appointment with Dr Lee, the transplant coordinator,

was for three o'clock. As they sat in the waiting room, Nick read a comic that Freya had bought him—one of his favourite space adventures—while she flicked through a celebrity gossip magazine without seeing anything on the pages.

Gus reached for her hand and gave it an encouraging squeeze and she answered with a brave smile. His touch had the power to make her feel hopeful and she would have liked to keep holding his hand.

At last they went inside. Dr Lee greeted them warmly, then took them through what would happen over the next few days. Tomorrow, they were to arrive at the hospital early for a final day-long evaluation of Nick that would include more blood tests and an ECG. The medical team would do a final cross-match to make sure Nick could still receive Gus's kidney. And Nick would begin taking drugs to prevent his body from rejecting the new kidney.

The doctor took them calmly through every step of the procedures, making the transplant sound very routine and unthreatening. Freya stole glances at Gus and Nick, caught them exchanging fond, almost excited smiles, and her heart filled to overflowing with love for both of them, and with pride and admiration, too. They were both so strong. They were her heroes. For their sakes, she resolved to remain calm and optimistic.

It was, after all, the only way to get through the next few days.

After the journey and the appointments and a meal at Nick's favourite pasta and pizza place, the boy was ready for bed quite early. Neither Freya nor Gus was sleepy though, so they sat on the balcony outside Freya's hotel suite, looking at the city lights and talking.

Mostly they talked about Nick.

Freya filled in details, giving Gus a potted history of their son's milestones—when he'd crawled and learned to walk, and how he'd skinned his knee trying to fly off Poppy's top step. She told him about the time, when Nick was three, that he'd wandered away from home, and how terrified she'd been until she'd found him at the shop around the corner.

'He'd found ten cents and he was trying to buy fish food,' she said, smiling at the memory. 'He wanted to feed the little fish he'd seen swimming in the shallows.'

They both chuckled over that, and it was all kinds of wonderful for Freya to sit with Gus while their son slept in a room nearby. She could almost pretend they'd been doing this for years. And what a seductive picture that was—to imagine that she and Gus were conventional parents, happily living under one roof, an intact family.

For a reckless moment she let her mind elaborate on the fantasy. She saw herself sharing meals with Gus, saw them curled on a sofa enjoying glasses of wine, sharing the same bed.

Oh, God. She was sure her face was glowing bright red. What a fool she was.

But she was so happy for Nick that his father had come into his life. The man was handsome and friendly and thoughtful and generally wonderful. Over and above that, he was making a huge sacrifice. It was no wonder the boy adored and worshipped him.

If only…

No…it was pointless to wish she'd made different decisions in the past. They had felt right at the time and it was a useless exercise to keep going back over them and wondering…

'Nick talked to me about your father,' Gus said, suddenly breaking into Freya's thoughts. 'You're right. That old con man has shaken the boy's faith.'

'That was such a terrible Christmas.' She shook her head, remembering. 'Poor Nick. He was singing in the Nippers' choir at Carols by Candlelight and he thought his grandfather was out in the crowd, watching and listening. But that was actually when Sean took off. During the carols. It was such a dirty trick.'

'He's still worried I'm going to disappear, too.'

'I've tried to reassure him.'

'So have I. I told him I have to go back to the Northern Territory once this is over, but I plan to keep seeing him on a regular basis. I mean it, Freya. I'll stay in touch. And I'll come back as often as I can.'

Her soft whoosh of relief was barely audible, thank heavens. She knew there was no point in feeling too happy just because Gus promised to stay in touch. It was Nick he wanted to visit. He might even want to take Nick away with him from time to time and she would have to get used to waving them goodbye.

Those thoughts made her unnecessarily gloomy, so she forced herself to smile. 'Nick told me you'll have to keep coming back to make sure he's looking after your kidney properly.'

'Yeah.' Gus tried to laugh, but the sound was strangled. He cleared his throat. 'He's such a brave little guy.' His face softened and he looked away into the distance, then let out a heavy sigh.

'Actually,' he said quietly, 'I took the opportunity to tell Nick that he has more than one grandfather.'

'Oh...well...yes.' Freya winced as her guilty conscience gave a nasty jab in her solar plexus. 'I'm sorry, Gus. I should have asked before. How *are* your parents?'

'They're both very well, thank you. They live in Perth these days. My sister moved over there when she married, and she has a baby now. Mum couldn't bear to be living on the opposite coast from her grandchild.'

For the first time in too long, Freya recalled Gus's

conservative middle-class parents. When they'd lived in Sugar Bay, Gus's father had been the town's most influential and hard-nosed bank manager. He and his wife had never mixed with the hippie commune at the far end of the Bay.

Bill and Deirdre Wilder had always found it very hard to hide their disapproval of Freya but, to give them their due, they'd behaved no more coldly towards her than Poppy had towards Gus.

'Have you told your parents about Nick?'

Gus nodded. 'I rang them two days ago.'

'That must have been hard.'

'It wasn't the easiest phone call I've made.'

Freya looked down at her hands, tightly clenched in her lap. There was no condemnation in Gus's voice, but she couldn't help thinking that here were more people hurt by her secrecy. 'Were they shocked?'

'Of course. Shocked and concerned.' Shooting her a bright sideways glance, he said, 'They'd like to fly over here to see Nick.'

'That would be lovely.' She forced her hands to relax. 'So I take it they've recovered from their shock?'

'Yes, and with surprising speed. Mum rang straight back to assure me.'

Freya wasn't proud of the way her heart sank, but the thought of dealing with Gus's parents on top of everything else was rather daunting. She hunted for a nice safe direction to steer their conversation but, to her surprise, Gus frowned suddenly and his jaw jutted as if he was preparing to confront her.

A shiver skittered over her. Instinctively, she straightened her shoulders and lifted her chin. She almost demanded *What?* the way Nick did when he knew he was about to get into trouble.

Gus's eyes were a dark challenge. 'I have to say I'm very surprised that you haven't married.'

If he'd zapped her with a stun gun he couldn't have startled her more.

'M-married?' she repeated stupidly, while her heartbeats took off at a gallop.

'You're a lovely woman, Freya, and I know you've had plenty of admirers.'

'Who've you been talking to?'

'Mel.'

'Oh.' She tried to shrug this off. 'Mel could gossip for Australia.'

Gus didn't respond. He watched her with a moody frown as he leaned back in his chair, legs stretched casually in front of him, waiting for her to talk about the men in her life.

If any other man had asked Freya this, she would have told him what he could do with his nosy questions, but this was Gus, the father of her son. He wasn't asking about her boyfriends out of jealousy, or because he wanted to make a move on her. He probably wondered why she hadn't found a man to stand in as a male role model for Nick.

'Mel's right,' she said. 'There have been boyfriends. Mostly local fellows, who were good company.' She shrugged. 'A few years ago, I met a really nice guy from Melbourne through my work.' She stopped, unwilling to add that this man was interesting and intelligent, and he'd liked Nick, and he'd been keen to commit to something more permanent.

Gus frowned at her savagely. 'Go on. Why didn't it work out?'

Didn't he know? Couldn't he guess?

Freya's mouth curled in a sad smile as she shrugged elaborately. 'No sparks.'

'None?' Gus challenged, glaring fiercely.

'Not enough.' Not enough to commit to a long-term

relationship. Freya had been scared that Jason's niceness would bore her eventually, but she wasn't going to tell Gus that.

Her face was burning, so she turned away and missed his reaction. He didn't speak and for long, uncomfortable moments they both sat very still, staring down at the ceaseless lines of traffic while she wondered about the women in *his* life—especially his wife.

Eventually, she couldn't help herself. If Gus could interrogate her, surely she could ask at least some of the questions that were keeping her awake at night.

'What about you, Gus? Can you tell me about Monique?' She saw the tightening in his facial muscles. 'Unless it's too painful to talk about.'

'It's OK,' he said gruffly. 'What would you like to know?'

Nothing. Everything…

'Oh, I don't know—how you met, perhaps?'

Gus shifted uncomfortably. 'It was all very straightforward. We met through our work. We were both in a remote village, the only non-Africans around, so we kind of drifted together, I guess.'

The way he told it, their relationship sounded more like a convenient friendship than a romance. But it must have been romantic. Freya had seen Gus in love and she knew how very passionate and tender he could be.

'Did you ever bring her back to Australia? Were you married here?'

'No, we were married in Africa. Our parents came over for the wedding.'

We were married. The words pierced Freya as if Gus had fired them from a blowgun.

The pain was so much worse than the familiar ache she usually felt when she thought about Gus Wilder and it proved to her, once and for all, that she was, unfortunately, still seriously hung up on him. Then she tortured herself further by picturing Gus as a bridegroom with his beautiful, happy bride on his arm.

She could imagine his delighted parents meeting Monique's delighted parents. *Don't they make a beautiful couple? And so worthy of each other.*

To ask more questions would be like pushing something sharp beneath her fingernails, but Freya couldn't leave the subject alone.

Was Monique beautiful? She mentally cancelled that and asked him instead, 'What did Monique look like?'

Gus frowned. The smallest smile flickered. 'Very French. Dark eyes. Straight black hair. French nose.'

'What does a French nose look like?'

He grinned. 'Oh, you know. Rather pointy.'

Freya could hear the fondness in his voice and she wished she didn't mind so very much. Of course Gus had loved his wife.

But a loud sigh escaped him and suddenly he slumped forward, elbows sunk on his knees.

'Gus, I'm sorry. I'm as bad as Nick, asking far too many awkward questions.'

'It's OK. It's not the questions…'

'But the memories must hurt…'

Gus lifted his head. 'Yes, they do, but perhaps not quite in the way you imagine.'

As Freya puzzled over this, he stood abruptly and went to the balcony's railing. For a moment or two he looked down into the lines of traffic below, and when he turned back to Freya his face was bleak. 'Actually, it's the guilt that bothers me more than anything.'

'Guilt?' Freya's heart lurched sickeningly. What on earth could he mean?

'Monique was ready to leave Eritrea,' Gus said. 'But I persuaded her to stay on for an extra six months, till I'd finished the dam project.'

And some time during those six months Monique had driven over the landmine, Freya guessed. Her heart went out to him. 'Gus, you mustn't blame yourself.'

When he didn't respond, she said, 'But I think I understand. When something bad happens to someone you love, it's easy to convince yourself that you're somehow to blame.'

Frowning, Gus lifted his gaze to meet hers. 'You don't blame yourself for Nick's condition, do you?'

'It's easy to do. There are times when I beat myself up, thinking that maybe I did something wrong. Or there was something I didn't do that I should have. So many times I've wished I'd taken him to the doctor sooner...'

The bleakness left Gus's face and his eyes were suddenly unexpectedly tender. 'Freya, from what I've heard, you've been a fabulous mother. Perfect, in fact.'

She'd been far from perfect but, under the circumstances, it was generous of Gus to say so. 'I suppose I'm like most mothers. I do my best. You can only ever do your best.'

But she was sure Gus must have been wondering, as she often did, whether things might have been different if the two of them had raised Nick together.

The blast of a car horn reached them from the traffic below. Freya looked at her watch. 'I shouldn't be keeping you up too late,' she said. 'You need to be in tip-top condition for the final round of tests tomorrow.'

Apparently Gus agreed, for he left quite promptly. After he'd gone, Freya made herself a cup of hot chocolate using one of the sachets provided by the hotel and she drank it in bed, but she took ages to get to sleep.

It was so silly. After so many sleepless nights worrying about finding a match for Nick, that weight had been taken off her shoulders. She should have been relaxed, not tossing and turning, not questioning the decision she'd made all those years ago.

Thing was, until Gus had turned up, she was sure she'd made the right decision for both of them, but now...

The more she saw of Gus being wonderful and charming and sexy, the more she remembered how much she'd loved him. When she'd made that fateful journey to the university to see him she'd thought he was changing, but he hadn't changed at all. Not only was he as attractive and sexy as ever, he was warm and kind and thoughtful...

Freya groaned and buried her face in her pillow but she couldn't block out her memories. *Oh, help.* She could remember the comfort of Gus's embrace, and she could still taste his kisses. Could still feel the warm eagerness of his lips on hers, and the sensual heaven of his lips on her throat and her breasts.

She could remember kissing him all over, discovering the scents of the sea on his skin.

Oh, God. It was no good. She couldn't go on tormenting herself like this. She got up to make another cup of hot chocolate and to find something safely unromantic to read.

CHAPTER EIGHT

DR LEE strode into the waiting room, grinning and giving the thumbs-up signal. 'Good news. It's all systems go.'

The tests were completed and he'd come to report that the transplant would take place the very next day, beginning at nine o'clock in the morning and finishing some time around one in the afternoon.

Freya's stomach began to churn with a mixture of hope and fear.

With Dr Lee's blessing, she and Gus took Nick to a late afternoon matinee to watch a space adventure with a guaranteed feel good, happy ending. But then they had to go back to the hospital where he would stay overnight to start the anti-rejection medication.

Sitting in his hospital bed in brand-new pyjamas covered in rocket ships, Nick grinned at Gus. 'By this time tomorrow I'll have your kidney inside me.'

'You're very welcome to it, mate.' Gus's voice was rough with emotion.

'No more global warning.' Nick grinned again, but Freya could see the fear lurking behind the bright smile and she felt impossibly weepy. Of course, she'd known for ages now that her boy was a super brave little guy, but his courage still got to her every time.

'I'll be here first thing, early in the morning,' she told him when he began to look sleepy.

'And you'll bring Gus, won't you?'

'Yes, darling, of course.'

As she hugged Nick, she willed herself to be braver. If he could get through this without a whimper, then she must, too.

Gus gave Nick a hug. 'I've checked out the nurses and I haven't seen any vampires, have you?'

Nick shook his head and giggled.

'But, just in case, I brought you a weapon.' Gus reached into his deep trouser pocket and produced a little string of garlic cloves.

Where on earth had he found them?

'These will keep the hungriest vampire at bay,' he announced. 'They're in all the hospitals, you know. They try to look normal.'

Nick laughed. 'Thanks for the warning.' Eyes sparkling, he surveyed the sparsely furnished room. 'Where will I keep this? Under my pillow?'

'Garlic might be a bit smelly,' Freya suggested tentatively, worried that Nick might get into trouble, but not wanting to spoil their game.

'I'd say we should put in here,' Gus said, pulling out the drawer in the bedside table. 'Can you reach it?'

'Easy.' Nick demonstrated a quick snatch. 'Cool. I was wondering what I'd do if a vampire snuck in here in the middle of the night.'

'There will be nurses in and out all night,' Freya felt compelled to explain.

'Yeah, Mum, I know.'

Nick winked at Gus, and just for a moment, Freya felt on the outside, then she squashed the feeling. She really was delighted that her son and his dad were getting on so well.

For all sorts of reasons, Freya was glad of Gus's company as they tiptoed out of Nick's room and down the long hospital corridor. They'd waited till he dropped off to sleep, but she'd hated leaving him, even though he'd insisted he didn't need his mum and he wasn't a baby.

'You've got a big day tomorrow, too,' she told Gus as they reached the ground floor.

He turned to her with an easy smile. 'But we have to eat, and I'd like to take you out to dinner.'

'Oh…'

Amusement danced in Gus's eyes. 'Oh? Is that a yes or a no?'

Freya gave a flustered little laugh and gestured to her T-shirt and jeans. 'I was only thinking that I don't have a thing to wear.'

'We can find somewhere casual,' he suggested.

She thought she caught an edge of disappointment in his voice and she could well understand why he might want to spend this last evening enjoying himself. Then she remembered that she *had* brought black trousers and a couple of blouses that were almost evening wear.

'I could probably manage something better than casual.'

'Fantastic. Let's splash out on somewhere grown-up.'

Freya teamed a cream silk blouse with her black trousers and she wound her hair into a knot, which she hoped looked sophisticated, and added black hoop earrings and black toe-peepers, a black pashmina for warmth.

'Wow!' Gus grinned when he saw her. 'If that's casual, remind me to ask you to dress up some time.'

She realised that Gus had never seen her really dressed up—unless she counted the senior formal, which was so long ago he couldn't be expected to remember. She wished she was wearing high heels and stockings and something slinky and backless to make him really take notice.

Of course he looked wonderful in a dark sports jacket, white shirt and beige trousers.

'Maybe I should put a tie on,' he said, fingering the open neck of his shirt.

'No, don't. You look—' Freya could hardly say *wonderful*. 'You look fine.'

'I've wangled a late booking at a seafood restaurant near the river, and there's a taxi waiting. I didn't want to have to worry about trying to find a park.' He touched the small of Freya's back ever so lightly and she almost went into orbit as the warmth of his hand branded her skin through the thin silk fabric. 'Let's go.'

It was well after eight when they arrived, and the restaurant was very well patronised. Freya was sure every seat had been taken, but they were shown to a table for two at a window with beautiful sweeping views of the city skyline and the full beauty of the lights shining on the water.

'How on earth did you wangle such a good table at short notice?' she asked when they were alone.

Gus grinned. 'I can be quite persuasive when I put my mind to it.'

She felt a blush coming on and quickly picked up the menu. Fortunately it was large and she could almost hide behind it, studying the selection with earnest attention. The last thing she wanted now was to let her thoughts stray. There was no point in remembering how devastatingly persuasive Gus Wilder could be.

The meal was superb. Freya chose a starter of salt and pepper calamari, while Gus chose seafood chowder. Their mains were a delicate baked fish with mango and avocado salsa, and steamed crab with chilli jam.

Gus was perfect company and Freya relished this chance

to sit opposite him; it gave her the perfect excuse to look into his gorgeous dark eyes whenever she wanted to. For brief moments she could almost—not quite, but *almost*—stop worrying about Nick. She could almost pretend she and Gus were dating again, and that he was in love with her.

Perhaps he knew that she'd be weepy if they talked about Nick, because he entertained her with light-hearted anecdotes about the wonderful people he'd met in Africa. He also told her about the Aboriginal elders who were working alongside him on his current building project and, because she was genuinely interested, he explained how the project worked.

'It's all about empowering the Aboriginal communities,' he said. 'In the past, they've had big, all purpose housing designs imposed on them. With this project, they're involved in every step. They decide what kind of housing they want and where it will be built. Hopefully, we avoid the culturally insensitive mistakes that have been made in the past.'

'It sounds like you're following a similar model to the one you used in Eritrea?'

'That's right. It works well. The community pitch in with the construction and there's built-in training, so the younger people are skilled in various trades. The people end up with a real sense of community ownership.'

Watching him carefully, Freya could see how very important the project was to Gus. 'I guess you'll be eager to get back to see how things are progressing.'

'I can't leave them in the lurch,' he said, answering her question obliquely.

'So you'll be heading back as soon as you're well enough?'

'That's the plan.'

Gus's eyes narrowed as if he was trying to gauge Freya's mood. She pinned on a smile and hoped it didn't look too forced.

After dinner, they walked along the path beside the river. It was such a perfectly romantic setting that they should have been holding hands but, even though they weren't, Gus walked close to Freya and the sleeve of his jacket kept brushing against the thin silk of her blouse. Each time she felt the contact she held her breath and her nerve endings went into a frenzy.

The tiniest stumble would have had her falling against the solid bulk of his chest but, as luck would have it, she walked as smoothly as a supermodel.

A light breeze blew, rippling the satin-smooth surface of the water and shattering the perfection of the reflected lights. Freya knew she should be soaking up the big-city atmosphere but, now they were away from the busy restaurant, her thoughts kept bouncing between her awareness of Gus and her worries about Nick.

'I wonder how he is,' she said.

Gus didn't have to ask what she meant. 'He's sure to be sleeping soundly,' he assured her.

'Maybe I should ring the ward to check if he's missing me?'

'But they have your mobile number. The sister promised to ring if Nick's upset.'

Freya knew Gus was right and, although she'd turned off her phone in the restaurant, she'd checked it as soon as she got outside and there were no messages, no missed calls.

She watched the stream of cars travelling over Victoria Bridge. The headlights and tail lights looked like rubies and pearls strung on necklaces.

'Nick loved the garlic necklace,' she said. 'It really helped to distract him tonight.' She came to a halt, drew a deep breath.

Gus stopped too, and he smiled at her. 'Do you remember the last time we walked beside this river?'

'Twelve years ago. You took me out to dinner, then you walked me to the station.'

And by then she'd already decided not to tell him about the baby.

Why?

Tonight, after their lovely evening together, and after the past week when Gus had slipped so easily into his role as Nick's father, it was hard to remember how she'd actually felt when she'd made such a rash, life-altering decision.

She drew a deep breath. 'Gus, before we get to the taxi rank, I want to thank you. For everything. I know you're terribly hurt that I never told you about Nick, and I'm sorry. Truly sorry. I—' Her throat was tight and she swallowed, took another breath and tried again. 'I want to thank you for being so good about it—about everything.'

To her dismay, he didn't respond and his face was in shadow now, so she couldn't even guess his reaction.

What had she expected? Sudden and total forgiveness?

Gus was helping Nick. Wasn't that enough?

Her voice was so shaky she almost sobbed. 'I also want to thank you for being such a willing donor. I wasn't sure how you'd respond after all this time.'

'It's what any father would do. I love the boy, Freya.'

'Yes, I know.'

'Besides, I have two healthy kidneys and I can manage with one. I get to give. Nick gets to live.'

'Yes.'

He made helping Nick sound like another of his well meaning and well thought out projects. Freya knew it was unreasonable to feel depressed.

Stop it, she told herself. *Be grateful for what he's doing. You can't hope for more.*

But, having him back in her life, she was so terribly aware of everything she'd given up. She hadn't only rejected Gus's lifestyle; she'd rejected *Gus*—the only man she'd ever met who could fill her with happiness and longing in equal measure.

I'm greedy. His help for Nick has to be enough. I mustn't wish for more.

How many times did she have to tell herself this? When would it finally sink in?

In the back of the taxi, Gus sat beside Freya, watching the play of streetlights and shadows on her lovely face and he knew that the defences he'd been struggling to hold in place were toppling, finally and completely.

Once again, he was under Freya Jones's spell and he no longer wanted to fight it. Just the same, his timing was off. This was hardly the night to be thinking of seduction.

As if to prove it, when the taxi stopped at the hotel, Freya slipped out quickly while he paid the fare and she opened her mobile phone again.

'I've got to ring the hospital, Gus. I just have this awful feeling. I'm so frightened that something will go wrong.'

Her earnestness confirmed what he'd already known. Romance was out of the question. Hell. How could he be thinking about anything remotely romantic when he knew Freya was desperately worried about Nick?

She'd bravely avoided talking about the boy at the restaurant, but that didn't mean she hadn't been thinking about him the whole time.

Gus knew he could say nothing to allay her fears and he watched with concern while she rang the hospital. He saw the frown creasing her smooth forehead and the dark shadow of worry in her sea-green eyes. Watched her teeth gnaw at her soft lower lip.

'Hello? It's Freya Jones. Nick's mother. I was just wondering…is everything OK?'

She was a touching picture of worried concentration as she

listened to the person speaking on the other end. She looked vulnerable and yet unbearably lovely and Gus wished with everything in him that he could take away her pain and banish it for ever.

'Yes…' Freya was saying and she nodded. 'Yes…all right.' Then he saw the sudden brilliance of her smile. 'That is good news. Thank you.'

As she flipped her phone shut, she turned to him with a beautiful happy grin. 'You were right. Nick's sound asleep and absolutely fine.'

Almost giddy with relief, she stumbled towards Gus and, without hesitation, he opened his arms to catch her.

Her silky hair brushed his cheek; her warm breasts crushed against him. He could even feel her heartbeats. Freya, after all this time…

It was beyond blissful to be hugged by Gus.

Freya felt so reassured by him and so filled with hope. She wanted to stay in his arms, absorbing his strength and protectiveness and general gorgeousness, and she never wanted to let go. Her arms seemed to be stuck to him with Velcro. Stepping away from him took a huge force of willpower, but she managed it somehow.

'Thank you,' she said, trying hard to sound normal and nonchalant. 'I needed that hug.' *Understatement of the century.*

Gus's eyes were twinkling. 'You're welcome. Any time.'

'I needed to go out tonight, too,' she told him as he opened the heavy glass doors of the hotel. 'Our dinner was perfect. I've been tense for so long, and tomorrow is going to be so… so…' She shivered. 'I would have been in such a mess if I'd had to spend tonight on my own.'

Gus placed a protective arm around her shoulders as they crossed the hotel's lobby. The concierge smiled at them—he probably thought they were lovers. Freya tried, unsuccessfully, not to mind that they weren't.

There was no one else using the lift. Gus let her enter ahead of him, which was gentlemanly, but she would have been happier if he'd kept his arm about her.

'How are you feeling?' she asked him.

To her surprise, he gave her a puzzled smile as if her question was extraordinarily difficult to answer.

'Are you nervous about tomorrow?'

'Oh.' He gave a soft self-deprecating laugh. 'Yes. Terrified.' Smiling again, he reached for her hand.

She knew he was only being playful and it was silly to get all hot and breathless about a little hand-holding.

Or was it?

Freya stole another look at Gus and his eyes flashed a message that made her bones melt. When the lift stopped at their floor and the doors slid open, she wasn't sure that her legs would support her.

Fortunately, she made it down the hallway to her room.

'Thanks for a lovely evening, Gus.' The words felt trite, inadequate. She wanted to invite him in for coffee, or a drink, but this wasn't a date and Gus wasn't just a comfortable old friend she could relax with, so she wasn't quite sure if an invitation would be appropriate. They were in a relationship no-man's-land.

While she was dithering, Gus smiled, then reached out and gently touched the side of her face. 'You're not going to lie awake all night worrying about tomorrow, are you?'

'I…I hope not.' The touch of his fingers was electrifying.

'Maybe you shouldn't spend the night alone, Freya.'

Zap! The very thought of spending the night with him sent wave upon wave of excitement rolling through her, but he was joking, wasn't he?

Freya saw the look in his eyes—a kind of smiling, yet serious intent. *Oh, heavens.* Maybe he wasn't joking.

Then his fingers trailed ever so gently down the side of her cheek and she knew for sure that this was something else entirely. Now she tried to remember why it wasn't a good idea to spend an entire night with Gus Wilder.

Her brain absolutely refused to cooperate.

All she could think was that this night was their only chance to be alone together, and she couldn't come up with a single reason why she should turn Gus away. He was, after all, the man who'd resided in her heart for twelve long years.

Her knees were trembling so badly she leaned against the door. 'I…I don't think I want to be alone, Gus.'

She lifted her eyes to meet his and a silent message flashed between them. Heat flared as if a thousand matches had been struck inside her. She wanted this so badly, couldn't believe it might actually be happening. When she took the key from her clutch purse, her hand was shaking and she couldn't fit it into the lock.

'Here,' Gus said gently and, taking the key, he slotted it smoothly home.

The door clicked open.

Freya stepped forward into darkness and silence, her heels sinking in luxurious thick carpeting. Gus followed and used the hotel door key to turn on the power. Immediately, the room came to life, lit by the discreet golden glow of table lamps. The air conditioner began to hum.

Freya prised her tongue from the roof of her mouth and she turned to him with a shy smile. 'Would you like coffee or a nightcap?'

'No, thanks.' He shrugged out of his jacket and tossed it onto a chair, then stepped closer and took her evening purse from her tightly clenched hands, dropped it lightly onto a glass-topped table.

Freya's heartbeats thundered. Her lips tingled with expectation as Gus's head dipped to hers. She closed her eyes and their lips touched.

Gus. At last.

The taste of him and the scent of his skin were exactly as Freya remembered. She sank into his embrace, letting his kiss flow through her like a wave breaking on the shore and washing over the sand.

It was almost too good to be true. After so many years, Gus was kissing her, holding her close to his long, hard body, holding her as if he never meant to release her.

She'd thought she might be shy or embarrassed after such a long time, but there wasn't a chance. Being with Gus felt perfectly, wonderfully *right*.

In a kind of blissful daze, they drifted towards the king-size bed and tumbled together onto the antique gold quilt. For a moment or two they just lay there, gazing into each other's eyes and smiling, as if they were eighteen again and couldn't quite believe their luck.

Gus lifted Freya's hair away from her face. 'Your eyes are still all the colours of the sea. They keep changing with your moods.'

'Your eyes don't change,' she said, looking dreamily into their chocolate depths. 'But I like them like that. Having them stay the same makes you very—'

'Predictable?'

'I was going to say grounded.' She smiled again and he smiled back and she suspected that right now, at this moment, she was as happy as she'd ever been. 'What colour are my eyes now?' she asked him.

'Sultry green.'

'Sultry?' She pouted, pretending to be disappointed.

'Stormy, then.'

'Yes, that would be right.' She wriggled closer into the arc of his body heat and a fresh tide of longing washed over her. 'I'm feeling quite stormy.'

'Me, too.'

They kissed again in the most deliciously leisurely manner, nipping, tasting, then slowly delving deeper, letting their desire rebuild in wave upon glorious wave. Then, in a burst of impatience, Freya sat up and began to undo the pearl buttons on her blouse as fast as her trembling fingers would allow.

Gus was beside her, making short work of his shirt, his shoes, his trousers. Their clothes flew about the room and the last of Freya's inhibitions went with them.

Her skin was burning as she lay down again. Gus was so beautiful and she was aching for his touch. A gasp broke from her as he knelt over her, as he lowered his head and scattered warm kisses over her jaw, over her throat and breasts.

She felt the hot sting of tears in her eyes. She didn't want to cry, but this was Gus and her happiness was tinged with sadness too, for everything she'd lost.

'Freya.' It was only a whisper, but she caught the black note of despair in his voice. 'How did I ever let you go?'

It was too much. Her emotions spilled and she clung to him, pressing her face into his shoulder, trying to smother her tears. But Gus gently eased away from her and he kissed her damp face and her wet eyelids and then he kissed her trembling, sobbing mouth. She tasted the salt of her tears on his lips and their kiss turned wild.

Much later, Gus turned out the lamps and gathered Freya close. Holding her in the darkness, he pressed his face into the curve of her neck and breathed in the scent of her skin. Was it his imagination, or could he smell a hint of frangipani?

'Gus?' she murmured sleepily.

'Mmm?

'What are you thinking about?'

'Sparks,' he said.

'Our sparks?'

He smiled as he kissed her neck. 'Seems to me, we don't have a problem with any lack of them.'

'Seems to me, you could be right.' Rolling onto her back, she picked up his hand and began to kiss each of his fingers. The simple intimacy wrapped around his heart and he found himself needing to confess one truth that had been nagging at him all evening.

'In case you're wondering, it wasn't like that with Monique.'

Freya stopped her kisses. 'Actually, I did wonder. I couldn't help it.'

Gus lay very still, momentarily caught between an urge to tell her everything and a desire to save himself the pain. His conscience, as always, won.

'The thing is, our marriage wasn't working too well.' He hated admitting this, but tonight—before tomorrow—he wanted Freya to know. 'In some ways, I suppose you'd say we had a marriage of convenience.'

'Really?' She was shifting in the darkness, turning and propping herself up on one elbow. 'Why?'

'Oh…it seemed like a good idea at the time. Two young, like-minded adults living remotely in a foreign country…with healthy…needs.'

'But you weren't in love?'

After a beat, he said, 'No. I think we were fond enough, but not really in love.'

'Wouldn't it have been easier if you'd just had an affair?'

Gus smiled. Freya really was her mother's daughter. 'Is that what you'd have done?'

'I have occasionally. Very occasionally.'

'Yes, well…it sounds pretentious now, but Monique and I were trying to set a good example. Social responsibility—respectable

NGOs and all that. We had an image to protect, so we thought it would be better to marry.' Even though the room was pitch-black, he closed his eyes, as if somehow that made the confession easier. 'It was a mistake.'

Gus grimaced into the darkness, not wanting to tell Freya the next bit but, now that he'd started, he needed to get the whole truth out. Not being able to see her face helped. 'That's why Monique wanted to leave Eritrea.'

'You mean she wanted to leave you?'

'Yes, she asked for a trial separation.' A sigh escaped him. 'But my damn pride got in the way. I've never liked admitting to failure.'

'Your parents would have been upset.'

'That's putting it mildly.' His voice was rough and choked. Black clouds of despair threatened to smother him, but he forced himself to go on. 'I was totally committed to building the dam and I persuaded her to stay on for another six months, till the end of my term.'

'Oh, Gus, then the landmine happened.'

'Yes.' The word fell from his lips with a shudder.

'How awful for you.'

Gus heard the sob in Freya's voice and realised he was a fool. Why on earth had he started this conversation? Why was he trying to offload his regrets when he was supposed to be offering Freya comfort? Now he'd upset her and they were both wound up and disturbed when they were supposed to be sleeping, resting up for tomorrow.

Beside him, Freya was sitting up. 'Roll over, Gus.'

'Over?'

'Yes. You're upset and your shoulders are all tense. I'm going to give you a massage.'

'But I'm supposed to be helping you to relax.'

'You have helped, believe me.' She gave his shoulder a gentle shake. 'Now do as you're told.'

Smiling, he rolled obediently onto his stomach. 'I can't remember the last time I had a massage.'

'That's exactly why you need one now.'

Her hands began to work on his shoulders, kneading the muscles firmly and expertly in a way that was soothing rather than sexy.

Then again, Gus amended as warmth and contentment spread through him, those skilled hands were Freya's…and she *was* naked…

Morning arrived all too quickly.

Freya heard the beep of the alarm on her mobile phone and she gave a sleepy groan as she reached to turn it off. Reluctantly, she opened one eye and saw the pale light of early morning. She'd slept better than she had in months.

Then she remembered. *Oh, God.* Nick. The transplant. Gus. They had to be at the hospital early.

Chilling fear froze her.

'Morning, sleepyhead.'

Through the open doorway that led to the bathroom, she saw Gus at the basin, wearing black and white striped boxers while he shaved. One half of his jaw was clean and smooth, the other covered in white lather.

He looked amazingly relaxed and calm and, when he sent her a cheerful grin, her anxiety receded slightly. She remembered her vow to be brave and confident.

Admittedly, even with the ordeal that faced them today, she couldn't help thinking that Gus was a perfectly lovely sight to wake up to. Couldn't help admiring the very masculine way his broad shoulders and nicely defined muscles tapered down to his waist.

His skin glowed with a hint of bronze and there was a shadowing of dark hair on his chest, and every cell in her body tingled as she remembered what had happened last night.

Making love with Gus had been beautiful and emotional and cathartic—every kind of wonderful.

Mmm… No wonder she'd slept so well.

But today his beautiful, strong and perfect body was going to be marred. For their son's sake.

A rush of gratitude filled her, tangling with her happiness and her fear. She swung out of bed and grabbed a towelling robe.

Hurrying over to Gus, she dodged his shaving cream and hugged him.

He chuckled softly; his arms came around her and, for just a moment, her world was perfect.

Then her fingers traced the line of ribs on his left side and she stopped at the place where the surgeon's knife would make its incision. Her stomach clenched.

She loved Gus. There was no escaping this truth. In the past she'd loved a sweet, sexy boy, but now she loved a soulful, generous and beautiful man. Whenever she was with him she felt strong and assured. Right at this moment, she was ready to fight dragons, to trek through dark jungles or endure four hours alone while today's surgery took place.

Forcing her fear aside, Freya smiled up at him bravely and she kissed him, shaving cream and all.

CHAPTER NINE

FREYA'S assurance faltered at the hospital's admissions desk. Gus expected her to abandon him here, but how could she?

'I don't need your help to fill in a form,' he told her gently. 'You hurry on to see Nick. He needs you now.'

'But I'll try to get back to you before you go to Theatre.'

'Stay with Nick, Freya. I'll be fine.'

She'd never felt so torn. She was desperate to see Nick, but it was so hard to leave Gus. Above his lopsided smile, his dark eyes seemed to smoulder and glow, as if his emotions were as riotous as hers.

'If I don't make it back before you go down to the theatre...' Freya hesitated, fighting tears while her heart played leapfrog with her stomach. She wanted to tell Gus she loved him but the admissions nurse was watching them and, besides, Gus might not want to hear her confession. Mightn't he be shocked that she'd jumped to conclusions about their relationship after just one night together?

'All the best,' she offered instead. 'Good luck, Gus. Break a leg.'

With a soft sound that might have been a groan, he pulled her into his arms and hugged her.

'Thanks,' she whispered into his shirt. 'Another hug just might get me through this.'

'Me, too.'

Releasing her, he gave her a wink and dropped a warm, comforting kiss on her cheek. 'Off you go. Give my love to Nick. And don't forget to grab a coffee. You're not expected to fast just because we have to.'

No way could Freya drink coffee—her stomach was churning. As she hurried away, the happiness and confidence that had buoyed her since she'd woken crumbled hopelessly and her fear returned.

Doubts rushed back. Today was going to be such a huge emotional strain. How could she stay strong for hours and hours? What if anything went wrong? Could she bear it?

She wanted to be brave—she *had* to be brave—but what could be scarier than having the two people she loved most in the entire world undergoing major surgery?

Outside Nick's room, she stopped and took a deep breath. Nick was so quick to pick up on her mood. Her reaction became his reaction, so she couldn't let him see any sign of her fear. Squeezing her face muscles, she fixed her smile into place.

To her relief, the smile held as she breezed through the doorway.

'Hey, Mum.' Nick was beaming. 'Look who's here.'

Freya's smile slipped when she saw the dignified silver-haired couple standing by her son's bed. The man was in a grey suit, the woman a picture of elegant conservatism in navy linen and pearls. It had been years—but she recognised them instantly.

Gus's parents.

Freya's hand leapt to press against her rioting heartbeats. Of course, she'd known that at some stage she would have to face up to Bill and Deirdre Wilder, but she hadn't expected to see them this morning.

'My grandmother and my grandfather have come to see

me,' Nick announced proudly. 'They're Gus's parents and they've flown all the way from Western Australia.'

Freya managed a shaky smile and extended her hand. 'Mr and Mrs Wilder, how lovely to see you again.'

Gus's parents nodded. His mother's eyes, which were the same dark brown as Gus's, regarded Freya sternly.

At least they returned her handshakes.

Gus's father nodded solemnly. 'How do you do, Freya?'

'Hello, Freya.' His mother spoke cautiously and without smiling.

'It's wonderful that you could get here so quickly.' Freya spoke in her warmest tones. 'You must have flown all night.'

Deirdre Wilder's mouth tilted awkwardly as she smoothed a non-existent crease in her navy linen jacket. 'Actually, we arrived last night. We tried to ring Angus at his hotel, but we couldn't seem to raise him.'

Freya couldn't miss the mild accusation in her tone.

'Is Gus all right?' This question was fired by Gus's father.

'Oh, yes.' Freya gulped. 'He's being admitted right now, as we speak.'

Freya hoped she didn't look guilty. No doubt the Wilders already viewed her as the scarlet woman who'd seduced their son and stolen their grandchild. She knew it was silly, but she couldn't shake off the feeling that they'd also guessed that their son had spent last night in her bed.

In the awkward pause that followed, Freya said, 'You have no idea how grateful I am—how grateful both Nick and I are. If it wasn't for Gus…' She had to stop as tears threatened. She was very aware that this situation was as hugely emotional for Gus's parents as it was for her.

Taking a deep breath, she slipped an arm around Nick's shoulders. 'Now Nick gets to meet his grandparents.'

As much to reassure herself as anyone, she bent to kiss Nick's cheek and she couldn't resist stroking his hair. 'So how are you feeling, champ?'

'Hungry. The nurses won't let me have any breakfast.'

Freya smiled. 'Gus can't eat anything either.'

Deirdre Wilder said in a choked voice, 'Nick looks so much like Angus.'

'Poppy always says my eyes are like Mum's.' Nick was lapping up being the focus of everyone's attention, and Freya found that she was grateful for any distraction from the impending operation.

'Well, yes…your eyes are quite light.' Deirdre Wilder smiled at Nick with surprising gentleness, although a chill crept into her features as she turned to Freya. 'Is your mother here, Freya?'

Deirdre managed to look down her nose as she said this, as if she'd clearly expected Poppy Jones to renege on her grandmotherly duties.

'Poppy's on her way,' Freya said. 'She's coming down on the train this morning.' She gave Nick another reassuring smile. 'Poppy will be waiting to see you when you wake up.'

Truth be told, Freya had been surprised when Poppy hadn't insisted on coming to Brisbane at the same time that she and Gus had driven down with Nick. But her mother had been adamant that Nick, Freya and Gus needed time alone together.

'To bond,' Poppy had said with mysterious significance. 'I'll mind Urchin till then. Then Nick's friend Jamie will have him, and I'll jump on the train first thing on the day of the operation. I'll be ready for Nick when he needs me most.'

Freya wondered how much 'bonding' her mother had anticipated. She suspected that Poppy was feeling a tad guilty about her insistence all those years ago that her daughter didn't need a man in her life, that they could raise Nick just fine on their own.

Whatever her mother's reasons had been, Freya was beyond grateful for that time with Gus. Heavens, how could she have dreamed they would become so close, so quickly? But it would be impossible to explain any of this to Deirdre Wilder.

Sudden footsteps outside announced the arrival of a nurse.

'Good morning, Nick.' She breezed into the room with a bright nursey smile. 'I've come to wash you with special soap and to dress you in this gown.' Grinning, she held up a green cotton hospital gown. 'What do you think of the latest fashion?'

Nick eyed it dubiously. 'Will my dad have to wear one of those, too?'

'He's probably getting into his right about now,' the nurse said. 'And without any argument.'

Deirdre Wilder stiffened and turned to her husband. 'We'd better hurry if we want to see Angus.'

There was a flurry of kisses and calls from the door of 'good luck, darling', and then Gus's parents were gone.

As the nurse began to unbutton Nick's pyjamas, he sent Freya a satisfied grin. 'Now I've got a father and four grandparents. How cool is that? I'm like Jamie Galloway now.'

Seeing the shining excitement in her son's eyes, Freya felt her throat tighten painfully. She wanted to tell Nick that he mustn't expect that his family would suddenly be like Jamie Galloway's.

Jamie, Nick's best friend, had both sets of his grandparents living right in the Sugar Bay hinterland. Both families had cane farms and they hosted huge get-togethers at Christmas and on birthdays. Their homesteads regularly overflowed with aunts and uncles and cousins, and Nick viewed these family gatherings as his version of heaven.

It was impossible to imagine that the Joneses and the Wilders would ever get together for something like that. But, as the nurse began to wash Nick, the boy grinned at Freya.

'Actually, I'm even luckier than Jamie. His dad hasn't given him a kidney.'

Oh, help. Freya almost sobbed aloud. Instead, she focused on giving him another brave smile.

Almost as soon as Nick was bathed and dressed, a friendly young anaesthetist arrived to insert an IV line into his arm.

'This is where the medicine goes while you're having the operation,' the doctor told him.

Nick paled as he eyed the tubes and syringe. 'Is my dad having these in him, too?'

'I've just finished fitting his.'

That was enough to satisfy Nick and he submitted without a grimace. Freya wished she could rush back to Gus to tell him how wonderfully reassured Nick was, just knowing that his dad was sharing his ordeal.

But she wouldn't leave Nick now. Besides, the thought of Gus's parents watching her interaction with their son made her distinctly nervous.

To Gus's shame, his spirits took a dive when the footsteps in the corridor materialised into his parents. He hadn't expected to see Freya again, but a guy could always hope. How had his folks got here so soon?

'Angus,' his mother sobbed, rushing to hug him. 'You poor darling.'

'Whoops. Watch the IV tube, Mum.'

Gus submitted to her hugs and to his father's handshakes and backslaps.

'Are you OK, son?'

'Yes, I'm fine, thanks. I've had so many health checks

lately.' He managed to crack a grin. 'Seems I'm close to perfect.'

His mother chatted nervously while she stroked his hair as if he were ten years old—although Gus couldn't actually remember her being so demonstrative when he was a kid and had longed for signs of affection.

'We had to see you before you went down to Theatre,' she said. 'But we've met Nick, and he's a lovely boy, isn't he? He's so much like you.'

'How's he doing?' Gus asked, hoping his mother hadn't upset the boy. 'Is he OK?'

'Oh, yes. He's being very brave. And we saw Freya, of course. She looks—'

'Is she OK, too?' Gus interjected. Despite his concern for Nick, it was Freya who filled his head. Poor girl, she must be so stressed right now.

His mother's mouth pursed, sour lemon tight. 'Freya looks well.' She managed to make Freya's glowing health sound like a character fault.

Gus's father cleared his throat. 'You're doing the right thing, son. Your mother and I want you to know we're proud of you.'

'Thanks, Dad.' Gus's gratitude was genuine. 'Thanks for coming.'

He'd half-expected to be hammered by questions—about why Freya hadn't told him about their grandson, and would they have ever known about Nick if he hadn't needed a transplant?

He could just hear his mother's questions. *What's happening about access? Freya can't keep you out of Nick's life any more, Gus.*

No doubt the questions would come later.

Something to look forward to, Gus thought, mentally wincing.

'Now, don't worry about a thing,' Deirdre said. 'We'll be here to look after you once you're through with this.'

'There's no need. I'll be—'

'Of course there's every need, darling. We've come all this way, just to care for you. You've been looking after other people for far too long. It's time you had some pampering.'

That might be so, but the only pampering that interested Gus was the kind that involved Freya. He wasn't going to argue about it now though, and he was rather relieved when two male nurses arrived.

'Time to take you down to Theatre,' they announced cheerily.

At last. Gus was keen to get on with it. In vain, he tried to reassure his mother, who'd begun to cry. 'Don't worry. I'll be fine.'

Tears streamed down her face as she waved him goodbye.

'Keep an eye on Freya,' he called.

His mother cried harder than ever.

It was the longest day of Freya's life.

While Gus's surgery commenced, she waited with Nick in his room. He played with his Game Boy and she tried to read a magazine, but she couldn't concentrate on photos of celebrities pushing babies in prams or holidaying in the South of France. And, although Nick madly pressed the buttons on his tiny screen, his face expressed none of his usual enjoyment in high-speed battles with aliens.

One good thing—the doctors in the operating theatre sent word back that Gus's procedure was going according to plan, and that was a wonderful relief. Then it was Nick's turn to go down to Theatre.

Freya's stomach flip-flopped. This was the moment she'd dreaded but, for Nick's sake, she had to hold up a brave front.

She thought of Gus, already down at Theatre, giving up his kidney, and she clung to the doctors' assurance that everything was going well. Nick was simply going down there to receive Gus's gift. That was all.

When this was over, Nick would be healthy again and, with luck, he would go on living healthily for a very, very long time.

But, as he was lifted onto a trolley, he looked impossibly young and small and vulnerable. She remembered the day he was born and how she'd fallen instantly in love with his tiny pink perfection.

Tears prickled her eyelids. She ignored them. 'Off you go, then,' she said, lightly kissing him goodbye as if he was heading off to school or to a football game. 'Poppy will be here when you wake up.'

Nick tried to smile but his face was pale and worried as he disappeared around a corner.

Freya was left alone.

Too anxious to sit still, she paced the corridors. She passed a water fountain and realised she hadn't had anything to drink all morning. Sipping iced water from a paper cup, she told herself again that everything would be fine. Nick and Gus were in good hands. Even so, her insides were hollow with dread.

She should probably eat something, or at least get a coffee from a vending machine, but the very thought of ingesting anything stronger than water made her ill. She tried to ring Poppy, who would be midway through her train journey to Brisbane by now. The sound of her mother's warm, smoky voice would be such a comfort, but she couldn't get through. Poppy hated modern technology and hardly ever turned on her mobile phone.

Leaving a message, Freya continued her pacing. She was desperate to stay positive so she pictured Nick in the future, living with Gus's kidney, happy and well. *No rejections, please, please...*

She imagined Nick graduating from university, getting a plum job and getting married, becoming a father. She so wanted her boy's life to be perfect in every way. She would have to be careful not to interfere. She would let Nick make his own decisions, his own choices. She only hoped he'd make wiser choices than she had.

When it came to thinking about Gus, however, Freya couldn't picture his future, or perhaps she was afraid to. Her mind seemed to freeze whenever she tried. Could she dare to hope or was that totally foolish?

She wished she'd talked to Gus about the future last night when she'd had the chance. But he'd offered her nothing more than one night, and that night had been so fabulous, she hadn't wanted to spoil the magic.

Of course, she couldn't help reliving all the lovely memories. Gus's special mix of tenderness and passion couldn't be faked, surely? Her heart did a tumble turn every time she thought about it, especially when she thought about his surprising confession about his marriage. Poor man. Guilt, even when it wasn't really warranted, was a heavy burden to carry.

She tried to hold the memories close, like a protective fire blanket around her vulnerable heart, but already the night was beginning to feel like a dream. Had it been too good to be true?

All she actually knew about Gus's plans was that he was going back to the Northern Territory as soon as he was well enough, and his project would take months to complete. There was nothing in that scenario that encouraged rosy dreams.

Reluctantly, she turned her thoughts to Deirdre and Bill Wilder, who were no doubt sitting quietly and sensibly in the waiting room, as they'd been told to, as any news from the theatre would be relayed there.

So what am I doing, trying to avoid them and blundering around in corridors?

Dismayed by her foolishness, Freya hurried back down the maze of corridors. Twice she got lost, but eventually she arrived at the waiting room, shaking and rather breathless.

There was no sign of Gus's parents.

CHAPTER TEN

THE family group sitting in the corner of the waiting room turned in unison when Freya came in.

'I'm sorry to trouble you,' she said. 'I…I don't suppose you saw an older couple waiting in here?'

'Their son was having surgery, but he's out now,' a woman told her. 'They've gone back with him to his room.'

'Oh.' Adrenaline made Freya's heart pound. 'Thank you.'

She felt sick as she hurried back down the highly waxed corridors, pausing at the nurse's desk to ask where Gus's room was, then speeding on as quickly as her shaky legs allowed.

When she reached Gus's room, she caught a glimpse of him lying in the bed, apparently asleep and with a distressing number of tubes attached to him. He was flanked by his mother and his father, and Deirdre Wilder rose quickly and hurried to the door on tiptoe, a finger raised to her lips, her eyes fierce, demanding silence.

'Angus shouldn't be disturbed,' she hissed.

'Is he OK?'

Frowning elaborately, Deirdre stepped out into the corridor. 'He came through the operation splendidly, but he's sleeping off the anaesthetic. The nurses warned us he'll need strong painkillers and they might make him sleepy.'

'Poor Gus.'

'Indeed,' Deirdre said tightly.

Peering over Deirdre's shoulder, Freya saw Gus's eyes flicker open. 'Can I go in, just for a moment?'

'Under the circumstances, I think Angus's father and I are the best people to help him now.'

'I'd just like to—'

'He may be well enough to receive visitors later.' Gus's mother's eyes were hard and decidedly unfriendly. 'For short periods.'

Her meaning was clear. *We're Gus's family and you, Freya Jones, are a rank outsider and more trouble than you're worth.*

'Please give him my best,' Freya said, but she very much doubted that her request would be granted.

Unsure how much longer she could hold it together, Freya went back to the waiting room. She still had ages to wait and she feared she might cave in before the time was up.

But Poppy was there.

And what a sudden, uncomplicated joy it was to see her mother, swathed in her customary colourful layers. How lovely to be welcomed into her familiar embrace.

At last the waiting became almost bearable. Poppy had brought a basket with a Thermos of tea, still surprisingly hot, and a tin of shortbread made by the mother of one of Nick's school friends. She talked about Sugar Bay—about the glorious weather they'd had this past few days, how Urchin had been happy to stay at Jamie Galloway's while she was away, and how she'd been inundated with calls from well-wishers.

The snippets of gossipy news from home were a welcome diversion and Poppy didn't ask prying questions about the past few days, for which Freya was especially grateful.

Somehow they got through the remaining hours and, eventually, Dr Lee appeared at the doorway. Freya's heart jolted as she leapt to her feet.

'Things couldn't be better,' he said. 'The kidney's in place and everything's working. Nick's already making urine on the table.' He grinned at them. 'He's peeing like a racehorse.'

'How wonderful!' Freya hugged him and thanked him, and she hugged her mother and thanked her. 'What about Gus?' she asked. 'Does he know the good news?'

Dr Lee shook his head. 'Not yet.'

'Then you must excuse me.' She was already at the door. 'I'll have to go and tell him.'

Freya began to run.

The pain was bad.

Gus had been prepared for it but the severity was still a shock. He woke, fighting it, and opened his eyes to find his mother sitting beside his bed. 'How's Nick?' was the first thing he wanted to know.

'We haven't heard yet, darling.'

Gus closed his eyes, needing all his strength just to deal with the pain. He felt drugged and he drifted in and out of sleep. At one time when he woke he was aware of whispers and he thought he heard Freya's voice. His eyes snapped open.

His mother was at the door, but now she came silently back to the side of his bed.

'Was that Freya?'

'Yes, dear. She came to tell us that everything went very well with Nick. He's out of the theatre and on his way to the children's intensive care, but he's fine.'

'Ohhhh... that's great.' Gus managed to crack a grin. 'That's fabulous. I'm so glad.' Then he remembered. 'Why didn't she come in to see me?'

'You need to rest, darling.'

'You mean you sent her away?' He tried to sit up and gasped as fiery pain ripped through his left side.

'You're not ready for visitors,' his mother said.

Gus wanted to disagree, but a wave of exhaustion hit him and he hadn't the strength to argue.

'That Wilder woman's always been a dragon,' Poppy told Freya. 'And she hasn't mellowed with age.'

'I was thinking she was more like a Rottweiler.'

Mother and daughter shared rueful smiles over the dinner table. There was nothing more they could do at the hospital overnight while Nick and Gus rested in expert care, so they'd come away for an evening meal.

'Pasta is wonderful comfort food,' Poppy had declared as they passed tempting smells from an Italian restaurant. Thus, here they were at a corner table with a crisp white cloth and gleaming silver, each with a glass of Sauvignon Blanc and deep bowls of divine melt-in-the-mouth gnocchi Gorgonzola.

It was the first proper meal Freya had eaten all day and she felt herself finally beginning to unwind. Perhaps that was why she was so willing to express her disappointment about Gus's mother.

'She won't let me near Gus. She blocked me like a footballer.'

Poppy dismissed this with a hand-waving gesture that made her silver bracelets tinkle. 'She won't be able to stop him from getting near you once he has his strength back.'

'I wouldn't be too sure about that.'

'Oh, Freya, stop being so negative.'

Freya sighed. She was feeling strangely 'out of it' and exhausted now that most of the tension had left her. Of course, a degree of tension would continue for some time while they waited to see if Nick's body would accept the new kidney, but so far the indications were excellent.

Why couldn't she feel happier? She'd expected to be elated

tonight. She should be elated. She'd been waiting for this day
for such a long time and now the weeks of longing and dread
were behind her. In a couple of weeks, Nick and Gus could
resume their normal lives.

That was the problem, wasn't it? Gus's normal life was far
off in the Northern Territory, and she was going to miss him
horribly. And the gnawing dissatisfaction that she felt at the
end of this day of triumph was caused solely by the fact that
she hadn't been able to see him.

She hadn't been able to look into his eyes the way she had
with Nick, to see for herself that he really was OK. Hadn't
been able to reassure herself that his feelings for her were still
as strong as they'd been this morning.

*Shame on you, Freya. The poor man's in pain and you're
being disgustingly selfish.*

'Stop worrying, Freya.' Poppy was frowning at her and her
voice expressed an edge of impatience.

'Sorry. I think I must be down because I'm so tired.' Freya
reached over and squeezed her mum's hand. 'You know what
you've always said. Everything always seems better after a
good night's sleep. I'll be right as rain tomorrow.'

Gus couldn't believe his mother was back on guard duty early
next morning. Not that she saw her ministrations in that light,
of course. She arrived with flowers and fruit and three paper-
back novels, and set up camp in the corner of Gus's room as
if she planned to read her women's magazine from cover to
cover and had no intention of shifting.

Gus loved his mother, of course he did, but she had an
unfortunate habit of trying to smother. This trait had been
behind his escape to Africa, while his sister had taken off
to Perth on the other side of the continent, only to have their
parents follow.

Now he suppressed a groan of irritation. He wasn't an

invalid. The IV tubes had been removed and he'd been up and had a shower and he was eager to get on with his recovery.

'Mum, you're not expected to stay here all day,' he said in his most diplomatic tones.

'Oh, darling, I don't mind. It's such a long time since I've been able to do anything for you. I want to be on hand in case you need anything.' She gave his hand a possessive pat. 'Anything at all.'

'Well, to be honest, what I need most is to see Nick.'

Her eyes widened. 'Well, of course, that would be lovely. I believe he's out of Intensive Care and back in his room.'

'Great.' Gus threw off the bed sheet.

'But you can't be thinking of walking to him, Angus. You're not strong enough.'

'Of course I am.'

Alarmed, his mother dropped the magazine. 'No! Wait! I'll see if I can find a wheelchair.'

'I don't need a wheelchair.'

'But you do.' Her voice was becoming querulous. 'Don't be foolish about this. I'll go and make enquiries.'

Gus wasn't prepared to wait. He wanted to see Nick and, for crying out loud, he wanted to get there under his own steam, not to be pushed along by his mother. As soon as she'd left, he eased himself cautiously out of bed. The soreness under his left ribs was still pretty grim, but he would just have to put up with it.

He could walk quite well if he held himself very straight.

It was Poppy who greeted Gus in Nick's room. 'Gus, how wonderful to see you up and about. Nick, look who's here.' Her face broke into a beaming smile and she hurried to the door and took his elbow.

'Easy does it, hero,' she murmured in an undertone as she guided him to a chair, which he sank into gratefully. 'I'll leave you two to have a nice chat,' she said, then discreetly retreated outside.

Gus took in the boy's bright eyes and healthy colour. 'Nick, you look fantastic.'

'I feel great. Dr Lee said my new kidney is in better shape than his.'

'How about that?'

'Thanks, Dad,' Nick said softly.

To Gus's dismay, he felt the sting of tears. *Damn it*, he loved this kid so much and he'd been so scared this transplant wouldn't work. He forced a shaky smile. 'Knowing you're going to be well is the best news I've ever had.'

The boy's eyes shone. 'Sister says I can get up later today.'

'Amazing.'

Without warning, Nick's smile vanished. 'But there's one bad thing.'

'What's that?' Gus asked, heart sinking.

'I can't play tackle football any more.'

The relief that the problem was so small made Gus want to smile. But he hadn't forgotten how he'd felt at Nick's age, when rugby league had dominated his life and he'd dreamed of playing for the Australian Kangaroos. 'That's a low blow.' He gave Nick's shoulder a gentle punch. 'But you know what it means, don't you?'

Nick pouted. 'What?'

'You'll have more time for surfing, and for being a life-saver, and for climbing mountains and sailing oceans, chasing girls…'

At the mention of girls, the boy giggled.

'Speaking of girls,' Gus said, hoping his voice sounded casual, 'where's your mum?' He *had* to ask. In spite of everything else, he couldn't stop thinking about Freya and the question burned in him.

'She had to go and make phone calls. Something to do with the gallery. She should be back soon.' The boy was watching Gus with a carefully knowing gaze.

'What's that look for?' Gus asked.

'I was thinking maybe you do still like Mum.'

'Well, of course I like her.' The back of Gus's neck grew hot.

'But does that mean—?' Nick flushed and looked awkwardly down at his hands as he twisted a corner of the bed sheet between his fingers. 'I don't suppose…I mean…are you thinking about marrying her?'

Slam! It was like running into an invisible brick wall. The last thing Gus had expected was that his son, barely out of Intensive Care, would morph into a matchmaker.

Somehow, he manufactured a chuckle to cover his consternation. 'You're jumping the gun, aren't you, mate?'

'What do you mean?'

'You're rushing things.' Gus scratched his jaw as he tried to figure how to handle this question. Of course, it would be helpful if he knew the answer.

Despite the pain and his parents' visits and the intrusions of the hospital staff, he hadn't stopped thinking about Freya. The night he'd spent with her had been incredible, even better than when they were young. One night with Freya could never be enough.

But they needed time to discover where this fabulous chemistry might take them.

They didn't have time. Not for romance.

And he didn't want to give Nick false hope or confuse him. The kid needed a chance to heal, to stabilize at home with his mother and grandmother…to ease back into school life…and into a new sport…

Gus suppressed a grimace. Nick was watching his every

reaction with the intensity of Sigmund Freud combined with Sherlock Holmes.

'Since your mother and I met up again in Darwin, our focus has been on you,' Gus said. 'All my time's been taken up with getting you better. I haven't had much chance to think about other things, like romance…or…or marriage.'

'But you have time now, don't you?'

'Not really, Nick. As soon as I can, I have to get back to my work in the Northern Territory. A whole community is depending on me.'

The boy's face fell and Gus hastened to mollify him. 'But I'll be staying in touch with you…and…with your mum.'

Nick nodded very slowly, as if he needed to think this through. 'Are you still angry with Mum for not telling you about me?'

Gus let out his breath on a whoosh. 'No,' he said after a bit. 'Not any more. I think I stopped being upset about that as soon as I got to know you.'

The boy smiled shyly.

'But you shouldn't be bothering your head about these things.' Gus ruffled Nick's hair.

'I'm not really worried.'

'Good.'

'Thing is, I reckon I've worked out what probably happened between you and Mum, and why she never told you about me.'

'No kidding?' Was there no end to the surprises with this kid? Gus couldn't help asking. 'So? Maybe you'd better fill me in?'

'Well…something happened at school.' Nick dropped his gaze. 'Everyone knew why I had to go to hospital and on the last day…this girl in my class…' He shot Gus a quick glance. 'She's usually quiet and sort of sensible.'

'They're often the best sort,' Gus said, biting back an urge to smile.

'Anyway, when I was leaving,' Nick went on, 'she ran after me and called out, to wish me good luck.'

'She sounds nice.'

'Yeah, I know.' The boy's mouth developed an embarrassed lopsided twist. 'The thing is, I didn't do anything. I went all weird. I pretended I didn't hear her. I wanted to say something back, but I just kept walking with my head down, like a…like a…'

'Numbskull?'

'Yeah.'

'And now you wish you'd handled it better?'

The boy nodded.

Gus swallowed to ease the log jam in his throat. 'Don't worry. You'll be able to say something nice to her when you get back.'

'If I'm brave enough.'

'You're a brave kid. Never doubt that.' Gus smiled. 'So you think that I probably stuffed up when I was young, and never said the right thing to your mum?'

'Well…maybe.'

Out of the mouths of babes. Gus sighed, remembering the day he'd put Freya on the train, remembering his dismay when he realised, as it drew out of the station, that she was crying.

If only he'd found out why…

His life might have been so different.

He might not have graduated. He certainly wouldn't have gone to Africa…or been involved in fascinating projects in distant parts.

Freya's life would have been so very different too. She'd spent so many years battling on her own.

Hell… The truth of this was like a sounding bell deep

inside Gus. He saw Freya's decision to keep the pregnancy a secret in a whole new light.

Truth was…when he'd made her pregnant, he'd stolen the future she'd planned. But, by remaining silent, she'd handed him his future as a gift.

He sent Nick a rueful smile. 'You could be right,' he said softly. 'Maybe being a numbskull runs in the family?'

Nick grinned at him, but then his attention was caught by someone at the door. 'Oh, hi, Mum.'

Gus whirled around, wincing as pain scorched through his left side. He could tell by the look on Freya's face that she'd heard at least some of their conversation.

Her smile was awkward as she came into the room. 'It's just wonderful to see you two on the mend so soon.'

Pink tinged her cheeks as she perched on the edge of Nick's bed. She was wearing an outfit Gus particularly liked—jeans and a soft grey cardigan that should have looked school-marmish, but on Freya looked incredibly attractive. Make that sexy.

'I came across Poppy and your mum down the hall,' she told him. 'They seemed to be involved in a cold war over a wheelchair.'

Gus groaned. 'That's mothers for you. Mine's determined to strap me into that thing and wheel me around like a baby.' He pulled a face that made Nick laugh, then sent the boy a surreptitious wink. 'I'm setting you a bad example here, so don't take any notice.'

To Freya, he said, 'Do you think you could escort me back to my room? I'd be safe with you. I can't imagine that my mother would arm wrestle with you just to get me into that blasted chair.'

Freya gulped as if she'd swallowed a beetle, but eventually she recovered enough to say, 'Of course. I'm happy to help.'

Her skin tightened all over and her cheeks burned as she helped Gus out of the chair.

He was wearing a dressing gown over striped pyjamas, and he looked a little pale and he certainly moved cautiously, but none of these things could diminish his masculinity, or the effect of his proximity on her heartbeats.

After flashing a farewell grin at Nick, they set off with Gus folding Freya's arm through his and holding it close against his good side. She savoured the warmth of him and the now familiar smell of his aftershave but, coming on top of overhearing his conversation with Nick, it was all rather overwhelming.

This morning she'd woken to a huge sense of anticlimax. Now she was back to feeling tense, hot and bothered.

In the corridor, they found Poppy alone.

'You're off the hook, Gus. A nurse finally convinced your mother that it's desirable for fit patients like you to be up and walking as soon as possible after surgery, so she's taken the wheelchair back.'

'Bless the nurse,' Gus said.

Poppy laughed. 'Your mum took some convincing.'

She sent Freya a bright, pleased smile, which Freya did her best to ignore. Her mother was almost as bad as Nick when it came to wanting to see her and Gus reunited. No way did she want Poppy to read too much into this simple act of walking Gus back to his room.

Freya half-expected Gus to release her now the wheelchair threat was gone, but he tucked her arm more tightly beneath his and when he smiled at her his eyes smouldered sexily.

Deep down, she was totally, over-the-top thrilled by this simple contact, but she was also scared and on edge. Now that the transplant was behind them, she had no idea where their relationship stood. She wasn't even sure they had a relationship and she didn't want to start hoping, only to be disappointed.

But poor Gus could hardly be expected to think about

romance after everything he'd been through. He looked pale and exhausted by the time they reached his room.

'You need to rest now,' Freya said after she'd helped him back onto the bed and given him a drink from the water jug.

'I'm fine.' He reached for her hand. 'Please, don't rush away. I've hardly seen you and we need to talk.' He patted a space on the bed beside him. 'Sit here.'

Time alone with Gus was like discovering gold, so of course Freya sat, even though she was sure he really needed to rest. Her heartbeats went haywire as she wondered what he wanted to talk about. The other night, after they'd made love, they'd talked about his marriage but they hadn't talked about their own relationship, past, present or future.

Of course, they talked about Nick—quietly relieved that the worst was behind them.

Gus's fingers touched the back of her hand. 'You know I'm going to miss you.'

Freya wasn't sure if she was pleased that he would miss her, or sorry that he was already thinking ahead to when he would leave for the Northern Territory.

'You won't be heading off for a while yet, will you?'

'I'm hoping to get away next week.'

'So soon?'

'The doctors aren't thrilled about it, and if my parents had their way I'd spend another week at the Gold Coast with them. But I'm confident I'll be fine, and I need to get back.'

Freya nodded, tried to smile.

'The people up there are trusting me,' he said. 'Politicians have let them down in the past, but I'm determined to keep my word. We can't afford any more delays, and we have to get the work completed before the start of the wet season.'

It made perfect sense, of course. From the start, Freya had known she was dragging Gus away from important work, and he'd already given her so-o-o-o much. She had no right to be disappointed.

'Nick and I will have to stay here in Brisbane for a few more weeks,' she said. 'Even after Nick gets out of hospital, he has to have daily blood tests to check for rejection.'

'He wouldn't dare to reject my kidney.'

'Oh, God, I hope not.'

Gently, Gus smiled and he touched her cheek. 'Don't worry, Floss.'

Floss. Her old nickname. Freya loved that he remembered. His hand cupped her face and she felt a warm rush of happiness. All it took was Gus's smile and his touch and her heart was flying. She closed her eyes and pressed her cheek into his palm.

'To be honest, I've had enough of worrying,' she said. 'From now on I'm going to have perfect faith that your wonderful gift will keep Nick well for ever.'

'Absolutely.' His thumb roamed lazily over her skin. 'I've promised Nick I'll stay in touch.'

'That will mean a lot to him.'

'And, with luck, this job should be finished by Christmas.'

Six weeks away. Even though Freya knew the time would fly, it still felt such a long time to wait. And there was no guarantee that Gus would come rushing straight to the Bay as soon as he was free. 'I guess your family will expect you to spend Christmas with them.' She tried not to sound downhearted.

'They might.' Gus's fingers traced the shape of her ear lobe now. 'But I might have to disappoint them. A very important member of my family lives in Sugar Bay.'

He was talking about Nick, of course.

'Perhaps you shouldn't get Nick's hopes up about Christmas,' Freya said quietly. 'Just in case you can't make it.'

'You're worried I'll disappoint him, the way your father did.'

'We certainly wouldn't want another Christmas disaster.'

'I promise I won't let the boy down, Freya.' Gus slipped his hand behind her neck and his fingers rubbed her nape. 'And I won't let you down.'

What did that mean, exactly?

Before Freya could work out the best way to ask Gus, he drew her face closer to his. She saw the mix of passion and tenderness in his eyes and her heart began to dance.

Gus gave her a rueful smile. 'Come closer,' he murmured. 'I want to kiss you and I can't unless you lean in.'

'Are your ribs hurting?'

'A bit.'

'Maybe you shouldn't excite yourself,' she said, even though she leaned closer and her blood began to fizz.

'Maybe a little excitement is just what the doctor ordered.'

Their noses were almost touching. Their lips brushed. Freya's body shot sparks. 'And why should I let you kiss me?' she whispered, partly to tease him and partly because she really needed to know.

'Good heavens!' a woman's voice shrilled from behind them. 'Gus will open up his stitches. What on earth do you think you're doing?'

Freya flinched and she heard Gus's groan. His mother stormed into the room like a battleship with cannons blazing.

Freya wanted to echo Gus's groan. Now she'd confirmed Deirdre Wilder's worst fear that she was a brazen hussy, intent on seducing Gus over to the Dark Side.

'I can't believe—' Deirdre began.

'Mum, please, you've said quite enough. We're not children.'

Gus's air of cool command clearly surprised his mother. Her self-righteous lips flapped for a beat or two, then snapped unhappily closed.

Taking her cue from Gus, Freya threw off the feeling that she'd been caught in flagrante delicto, and she rose from the bed with perfect dignity. She caught Gus's eye, read his flash of apology.

'As I was saying,' she told Gus, 'you really do need to rest.'

'Don't worry, I plan to.'

Freya smiled. 'I'll leave you to it, then.' She smiled at his mother and said, ever so politely, 'Good morning, Mrs Wilder.'

When there was no response, she slipped quietly from the room.

Once outside, she allowed herself to recall every detail of her precious moments with Gus, right to the breathtaking second before he almost kissed her.

Her face broke into a smile and she gave a little skip, happier than she'd been in months.

Gus eyed his mother squarely. 'I'm sorry, but you can't go on like this, Mum. Do you realise how over the top you were then?'

'I was only worrying about you. Freya's worried about Nick. I'm worried about you.'

He nodded. 'I appreciate that, but there was more to it than that. You've still got a problem with Freya and Poppy, haven't you?'

'A problem with their lifestyle.' Deirdre's shoulders lifted in a half-hearted shrug. 'It's always been so different. So casual.'

'But you have to admit Nick's a wonderful boy,' Gus said. 'I'm proud to be his father.'

'Oh, yes, dear. You're quite right. He's adorable.'

'Well behaved,' Gus added. 'Thoughtful and coura-geous.'

'Of course.'

'And you have to remember that he didn't get to be like that on his own, and yet we had nothing to do with his upbringing.'

Deirdre opened her mouth as if she wanted to say some-thing, then shut it as she changed her mind.

'If Nick's turned out well, it's thanks to Freya and Poppy,' Gus said. 'I think Freya's done a remarkable job, and I'd really like you to ease off on her.'

Looking distinctly abashed, Deirdre nodded her silent agreement.

Satisfied, Gus closed his eyes as a wave of exhaustion washed over him. He began to drift towards sleep, thinking about Freya and Nick and Poppy, about what an effective unit they were. He wondered how exactly he could fit into that picture.

But the big question was—should he revisit that territory? What if he tried to get back with Freya and it didn't work? Wouldn't that make things worse for Nick? It was a big risk. Dared he take it?

Weariness overcame him before he found any answers.

CHAPTER ELEVEN

SIX weeks was a very long time.

After twelve years of separation from Freya, six weeks should have felt like a blink of an eye, but Gus had never been more impatient for the hours, days and weeks to fly.

Instead, time crawled with tedious, excruciating slowness.

Sure, the Arnhem Land project was still very interesting and important to him, but now there were two people who were so dear to his heart he hated the separation. Just the same, he'd already stolen weeks from the project and he needed to complete it before the wet season began, so he couldn't take more time off. As it was, he was working round the clock to have everything finished in time.

Nick was constantly on his mind. In a strange twist of fate, Gus now felt as if he was linked to his son more closely than most fathers could ever be. He delighted in every phone call and email as the boy continued on his road to full recovery.

As for Freya…

Gus spent far too much time thinking about Freya.

Number one in his thoughts was the amazing night they'd spent together. Over and over he replayed every precious moment. He would start with the dinner, recalling each shared glance across the table, each smile.

He'd remember how he and Freya had walked close beside

the river, remember the longing, the electricity, the overpowering desire that consumed him. Then, later, the unreasoning joy of discovery—her longing matching his. Then the kisses, the caresses, the soft, sweet sighs of pleasure. The marvellous, passionate intimacy.

Their night had been so perfect, as sweet as when they were young, yet so much more powerful and poignant after the long, lonely journeys they'd both travelled.

There were other memories, too. So many wonderful memories of Freya, from the time he'd first seen her in Darwin till their damp-eyed farewell at Brisbane airport.

'I'll be back before Christmas,' he'd told her as he stole yet another last-minute kiss goodbye. 'And I'll make sure I'm back in plenty of time, so Nick won't have to worry.'

Despite the pressure of work, Gus was more determined than ever to keep his promise. He loved Nick. Loved Freya. Loved her with the deep, unavoidable, heart-grabbing certainty that had evaded him in his marriage.

He wasn't going to let her go a second time.

For most of November Freya was upbeat and optimistic. Nick was growing stronger every day and whenever Gus phoned or sent her an email, he was warm and affectionate and flirtatious and she was quite sure her most dearly cherished dreams were about to come true.

She just wished the time could pass more quickly. She wouldn't be completely at peace and happy until she saw Gus again and could look into his eyes and know she wasn't building up false hopes.

There were still black moments of doubt, especially when she lay in bed in the wee small hours and remembered that other time she'd been separated from Gus for six weeks and how much he'd changed in that time.

Could it happen again?

She told herself no. But she wished she could be absolutely sure. In reality, she was basing all her romantic hopes on the flimsiest of foundations—a few days in Brisbane when their emotions were running high and when nothing beyond the hospital had seemed real.

Had she been foolish to imagine that Gus cared for her deeply in the same way that she cared for him? If she really examined their recent relationship, there had only been a single evening of romance. One night of lovemaking between two consenting adults, who'd had a previous relationship, then turned to each other in a moment of huge emotional need.

Her past history with Gus hardly counted so, except for that one night, their shared love of Nick was their only point of connection. On that basis, could they really hope for a future together?

Their lifestyles were poles apart. Gus couldn't be expected to settle back into the quiet life of sleepy Sugar Bay, and he wouldn't want a woman and a boy trailing after him as he continued his important work in the world's remote outposts.

Although she knew all of this, Freya clung blindly to a vain hope. Those stolen moments with Gus had been so special. Memories of his electrifying touch, of his kisses, his voice, his smile…haunted her day and night.

She hadn't imagined the deeper meaning of those moments, had she?

If only she could be sure. If only it was Christmas already.

Gus scowled at the radar map on his computer screen. A huge low pressure system was moving across from the Indian Ocean and was about to dump its load on Australia's Top End.

Already, the sky was thick with cloud and the air was heavy and dense, making everyone's clothing stick to their skin.

The smell of rain was in the air. It wouldn't be long before it arrived.

Damn.

The small plane destined to take him out of here wasn't due for another day, but once the rain arrived, the dirt airstrip here could be transformed in a matter of hours into a dangerously slippery mudslide. It would be impossible to land.

Gus had put through call after call, trying to locate a spare plane that could come sooner, but so far he'd had no luck.

He wondered if he should call Freya to warn her that he mightn't get away for Christmas after all.

Hell, no. He couldn't do that to her. Couldn't do it to Nick. He would find a way to get out of here, and there was no point in putting them through unnecessary worry.

Standing at the window, he watched the dark clouds roll in. If he started off now in the truck, he might reach the nearest all-weather airport in a day. He'd probably be racing against rising creek waters, but he'd get there.

He had to.

'I'm not wearing these stupid antlers. They're dumb as!' Nick sent the red velvet and pasteboard headpiece flying across the room.

'For heaven's sake,' Freya cried as she watched the antlers smash into the opposite wall. 'What's got into you, Nick? Pick them up right now.'

'Why should I?' Arms folded, Nick glowered at his mother. 'I don't need them. I'm not going to dumb old Carols by Candlelight. The songs are stupid and I hate Christmas.'

'I know you don't mean that.'

'I do.'

The boy was on the edge of tears, but he was fighting them valiantly and Freya's heart ached for him. It was such a disappointment to see him unhappy when he'd been doing so well. All the post-surgery worry and danger was behind Nick now and, apart from not being allowed to play football and the need for regular checks with their local GP, his life was miraculously back to normal. He'd been so looking forward to Christmas.

Damn Gus Wilder and his broken promises!

Freya wanted to throw something too—something that made a loud and satisfying smash. How could Gus do this to them after all his assurances?

Not that she could let Nick get away with such bad behaviour. Suppressing a sigh, she eyed her son. 'You asked me to buy those antlers and I paid good money for them, so the least you can do is pick them up.'

Her quiet, firm manner did the trick. Reluctantly, Nick collected the headpiece from the corner, but he showed no remorse as he fingered a broken antler prong.

'Bring it into the kitchen,' she said. 'I'll have to try to fix it with sticky tape.'

'What's the point of fixing it?'

She didn't bother to answer. She knew how fragile Nick's emotions were right now.

The timing for Gus's failure to show couldn't have been worse. The last few years, Nick always got tense the week before Christmas and, for him, Carols by Candlelight brought back the bitterest of memories. He'd been singing carols down on the beach with the Sugar Bay junior lifesavers on the night his grandfather had stolen away.

This year was going to be so much worse. Nick had been worked up for weeks and over the moon with excitement and anticipation because Gus was coming to the Bay. Gus had even named an arrival date a full week before Christmas.

Now they were four days past that date and there'd been no apology or explanation for Gus's no-show. Nick was devastated. Freya was furious.

And hurt.

And confused and disappointed.

With a heavy sigh, she looked across the room to their Christmas tree. She and Nick had scoured the seashore, searching for perfect branches of driftwood. They'd had so much fun and they'd come home, happy and excited, to arrange the silvery branches in a bucket of sand.

Then they'd hung tinsel and lights and Freya's delicate handmade ornaments alongside a variety of crude but cute Santas and angels that Nick had constructed over the years—a virtual record of every Christmas since he'd started kindergarten.

Beneath their tree, there now sat a red and green striped package with *'Dad'* written on the tag in Nick's clear handwriting. It was a book on the history of vampire legends for Gus. Nick was so proud of himself for tracking it down on the Internet.

And while Freya had tried to hide her excitement about Gus's return, she'd been as pumped as Nick, maybe more so. She'd been to the hairdresser's for glamorous streaks, and she'd had her legs waxed and her eyelashes tinted. She'd invested in new clothes in the hottest styles, including a slinky, summery dress and divinely sexy heels.

All to impress Gus Wilder.

But now she had to admit she'd been foolish.

She hadn't the heart to force Nick to go to the carols. The choir would manage without her boy. He could barely hold a tune anyway, not that it mattered. He sang with gusto and the night was all about community spirit rather than choral excellence.

'Well, this looks almost as good as new,' she said, holding up the mended antlers. 'But I suppose I'd better ring Maria and tell her you can't sing tonight. If we don't go to the carols, what would you like to do instead? We could go and see if the turtles have started making their nests.'

To her surprise, Nick didn't leap to accept her offer. Frowning glumly, he fiddled with the sticky tape dispenser. 'I s'pose I'd be letting the choir down if I stayed away.'

'Well…yes…I guess,' Freya echoed, surprised.

She waited, one curious eyebrow raised, but, as the seconds ticked on, her son didn't seem ready to explain his change of heart. 'We'd better get going then,' she said eventually. 'If you want to sing, you can't be late.'

Had she imagined it or had Nick's eyes betrayed a flash of excitement, even though he let out a theatrical sigh as he picked up the antlers and headed for the door?

Outside, a beautiful summer's twilight lingered and the beach was bathed in a soft mauve half-light. The sting had gone out of the day and a sweet breeze blew in from the ocean. Sugar Bay's families were making themselves comfortable on the grassy parkland at the edge of the sand, spreading picnic rugs and cushions.

Poppy was there, helping to hand out candles in cardboard holders. A stage was set at one end of the long lawn and children, wearing antlers and Santa caps, were lining up beside it.

'Off you go,' Freya told Nick and he dashed to join them, one hand holding the antlers in place as he ran.

Freya tossed a cushion onto the grass and flopped down onto it. She knew lots of people here, of course, and normally she'd be kept busy chatting and catching up on news, but tonight she wasn't in the mood to be social. She sat hugging her legs, with her chin propped on her knees, watching Nick in the distance as he joined the choir and exchanged shy greetings with a slim, very pretty girl with long dark hair.

Well, well, she thought. *Is Milla Matheson the reason Nick decided to come here after all?*

Her little boy was growing up.

She'd never felt more alone.

Damn you, Gus.

The light was fading swiftly. Glowing dots of candlelight appeared, dancing in the warm purple night like fireflies. Children ran on the grass waving coloured fluoro glow-sticks and their parents called to them to come and sit quietly, while the junior lifesavers' choir filed up makeshift steps and onto the stage.

Close by, the sea kept up its regular constant rhythm. Thump, dump, swish…

Everyone looked so happy, but behind Freya's eyelids hot tears gathered and her throat felt raw and painful. She was shaking, in danger of falling apart, and she knew she'd be a mess the minute the children started to sing. She always felt emotional when she saw them trying so hard to please their watching families. Tonight she was a dam about to burst.

She hugged her knees tighter and kept her eyes fixed on Nick in the back row of the choir, noticed that the mended antler prong was beginning to droop.

He looks so much like Gus, she thought with a pang, and then she swiftly cancelled that thought. *I'm so lucky he's well. I have no reason to be unhappy.*

But she had every reason to be angry.

Maria Carter, the choir's conductor, came onto the stage wearing a red and white polka dot sundress that showed off her tan. She tapped the microphone and smiled out at the crowd. Any minute now the singing would start. Freya hugged her knees more tightly than ever and kept her eyes on Nick.

Traditionally, he sent Freya a smile just before the singing started, but tonight his eyes were straying to the dark-haired girl in the row in front of him, and then out over the crowd.

Don't, Nick. Don't keep looking for Gus. You'll only break your heart. And mine.

Maria, the conductor, lifted her baton and Nick's face broke into a huge grin.

Concentrate, Nick.

The choir burst into an Aussie version of *Jingle Bells*, but Nick wasn't singing about dashing through the bush. He wasn't singing at all. He was grinning and waving to someone at the back of the crowd.

Freya stopped feeling weepy and began to feel embarrassed instead. Since when had her son developed behaviour problems? She turned around to see what had distracted him but it was so dark now, it was hard to see what had caught his attention.

And then her breathing snagged…

Poppy, clearly visible beneath a lamp post, was at the back of the crowd. There was no mistaking her silver hair and green kaftan. Beside her stood a tall, dark, manly figure…

Gus.

Freya's heart slammed against the wall of her chest.

Poppy was pointing in Freya's direction and Gus was listening carefully. He lifted a hand to shade his eyes from the lamp post's glare as he peered at the crowd, then he nodded. Next minute, he was moving, weaving his way through the crowd.

Freya tried to stand but her legs were like water. Her heart thudded madly as she watched the gleam of Gus's white shirt as he moved through the darkness and dancing candlelight.

No wonder Nick was smiling and forgetting to sing. Freya looked down at her old jeans and T-shirt and thought wistfully of her hot new outfits languishing at home.

This time when she tried to stand she was successful. She waved and Gus waved back, and she caught the white flash of his teeth as he smiled.

Stumbling over legs and apologising, she hurried to the edge of the crowd.

At last.

Gus hauled her into his arms and hugged her close and she

felt the warmth and strength of him. She smelled his spicy cologne and his clean shirt, felt the thudding of his heartbeats, and she knew this was as good as it got.

Complete, perfect happiness.

Jingle Bells finished and the choir was given a round of hearty applause, and it was only then in the lull between carols, that Freya remembered she was supposed to be angry with Gus.

'Where have you been? You said you'd be here four days ago.'

'I know. I'm sorry.'

It was hard to be angry when Gus was fingering her hair and kissing her forehead.

'The wet season arrived early,' he said. 'The first of the big monsoons caught us all by surprise. The airstrip was too boggy for the plane to land so I had to drive to an all-weather strip, but the rivers and creeks were already flooding so there were more delays.' He looked down at her with a crooked smile. 'I fought flood waters and crocodiles to get here.'

Freya had to admit that, as excuses went, this was convincing. 'Couldn't you have let us know?'

Gus shook his head. 'All the lines were down and we had to rely on mobile phones, but a huge section of that Top End is out of the network. It was damn frustrating. I knew Nick would be disappointed.'

'Well, yes, he was. Very.'

'By the time I got to Darwin, my battery was dead and I had to rush to make the plane, so I simply jumped on and hoped I'd surprise him.'

'He'll be thrilled,' Freya said, and she couldn't help smiling. Here they were, talking about Nick, who couldn't possibly be as thrilled as she was.

Gus held her closer. 'Nick looks well.'

'He is. He's never been better. All thanks to you.'

The choir began a new carol—*Deck the sheds with bits of wattle…*

Gus's arms encircled Freya, drawing her back against the solid wall of his chest. They stood like that, bodies aflame, at the edge of the crowd, watching and listening. Above them, stars appeared in the inky heavens and the warm December night seemed to close in around them—a benevolent and comforting darkness.

Freya might have felt completely at peace if she hadn't had so many questions and hopes and fears clashing in her head. Could she dare to assume that she was as important to Gus as Nick was?

As the second carol finished, Gus dipped his lips close to her ear. 'How long does this singing go on for?'

'Oh, about half an hour. Then Mel Crane dresses up in a Father Christmas suit and drives in on a tractor, handing out ice creams to all the kids.' She turned in Gus's arms and searched his face. 'Why? Are you bored already?'

'Not bored.' His eyes sparkled and his lips brushed her ear. 'But I'm desperate to be alone with you.'

Freya's body zapped and flashed like a Christmas tree out of control. Perhaps it was just as well that another carol started—a song about six white kangaroos that pulled Santa's sleigh through the Outback.

She told herself not to get too excited. After all, it wasn't surprising that a bachelor, newly arrived from a remote outpost, might want to be alone with a woman. Just the same, her body continued to zap and flash, but somehow she remembered to keep breathing as one carol flowed into the next.

Then the children finished their last song and took their bows amidst a blaze of applause. Gus kept a tight hold on Freya's hand as they made their way to the front to greet Nick.

'Dad!' the boy yelled, practically leaping into Gus's arms.

A warm glow burned inside Freya as joyous grins spread over both Nick's and Gus's faces.

Gus told Nick how great the singing was and then he started to explain why he'd been delayed, but Nick didn't seem to care now that his dad was here. Gus's presence was all that mattered.

Pretty, dark-haired Milla Matheson walked past again and sent Nick an extra-bright smile. He waved to her, then stood on tiptoe and whispered something in Gus's ear.

Gus turned and took a surreptitious glance at the girl as she walked away, then he gave Nick a nod and a winking smile of approval.

'What are you two whispering about?' Freya *had* to ask.

Nick looked abashed and Gus laughed. 'Secret men's business.' Then he looped one arm around the boy's shoulders while he drew Freya to him. 'Nick was just pointing out a nice sensible girl from his class at school.'

'Oh.' It was the only response Freya could manage. When she was this close to Gus, her brain went into meltdown and she could think of nothing but him, of how she felt about him, how she wished...

Oh, dear God, was she wishing for too much?

She was feeling shaky again as Poppy made her way towards them.

'You sang like angels!' she exclaimed, giving her grandson a bear hug that knocked his antlers sideways. Poppy beamed at Freya and Gus. 'Weren't the children wonderful?'

'Wonderful,' they agreed.

'And now the ice creams are on their way.' Poppy sent Gus a pointed glance.

'Yes.' Gus took Freya's hand. 'And it seems to me that if Nick's going to be guzzling ice cream, this is the perfect time for me to take his mother for a walk.'

'Can't I come, too?' asked Nick.

'I thought you were lining up for ice cream?'

The boy shrugged.

'Thing is, I have something very important to say to your mum,' Gus said, making Freya's heart leap. 'But I promise we won't be too long.'

'Take as long as you like,' Poppy told them. 'Nick and I won't mind waiting. Will we, Nick?'

The boy looked as if he might disagree, but something in Poppy's expression must have changed his mind.

'Sure.' Nick's face was split by a sudden grin. 'We don't mind how long you take.'

'You know, those two are jumping to all sorts of conclusions,' Freya told Gus as he led her away from the crowds and onto the dark, deserted beach.

His response was a long look deep into her eyes and a smile that made her face flame.

Hastily, she tried to think of something else to say. 'Um... if we're going to walk on the sand, we should probably take off our shoes.'

'Good idea.'

They left their shoes beside a pile of rocks, then walked towards the water. The sea was relatively flat with only small waves lapping the shore, and the tide was out, leaving an expanse of firm sand that was cool and damp beneath their bare feet. On the horizon, a beautiful almost full moon was rising.

Freya took deep breaths of clean sea air, hoping it might help her to calm down.

Gus's arm was around her shoulders again. 'It's so good to be back,' he said. 'It's so beautiful here, so quiet. I always feel at peace.'

'That's why the Bay's such a popular holiday destination.'

Gus stopped in his tracks.

Freya's heart took a dive. 'What's the matter?'

'I was talking rubbish. It's not this *place* that gives me peace. I've been to oodles of quiet and beautiful places but I've never felt how I feel when I'm with you, Freya.' He took both her hands in his. 'In Brisbane, with all the medical drama on the go, whenever I was with you, I felt—'

'Peaceful?'

In the moonlight she saw Gus's smile.

'Not peaceful exactly. Most of the time I was filled with blinding lust—but I was happy. Bone-deep happy. Like I'd been sailing for a long time, lost at sea, and I'd found a perfect mooring.'

He trapped her hands against his chest and held them there, enclosed in his hands.

She could feel his heartbeats.

His throat rippled. 'I was hoping…that maybe…you might feel—'

'I do,' Freya whispered. 'I'm exceptionally happy whenever I'm with you.'

'Floss.' Her old nickname floated on the night air as he pulled her in and kissed her.

It was a long time before they walked on, arms about each other, skirting the edge of the water, and Freya was no longer worried. She was drenched in happiness.

'We were always meant for each other,' Gus said. 'You know that, don't you?'

'But I made the worst mistake when I didn't tell you about the baby.'

'I was as much to blame. I was a conceited uni brat and I never gave you a proper chance to explain. But that's behind us. Now we have the future.'

'Are you saying—?'

'Yes.' Gus's finger traced the shape of Freya's ear. 'I'm saying that I love you, Floss. I've been thinking about little else for the past six weeks. I was so anxious to get here to ask you to marry me.'

Marry.

Freya stumbled. She couldn't help it. Her knees gave way completely and she sank towards the sand.

Taken by surprise, Gus tried to catch her, but when she grabbed at his shirt she tipped him off balance.

Next moment they landed in a tangled heap.

Splash.

A wave washed over them.

'Are you all right?' Gus sounded worried.

'I'm fine.' Freya was laughing, helpless with surprise.

Sandy and damp, they clung together, breaking into giggles like teenagers.

'Sorry about that,' Freya gasped between giggles.

Another wave washed in, soaking them again and they didn't care. They rolled closer and lay in their wet clothes, grinning goofily and gazing at the glistening stars in each other's eyes.

'I didn't mean to shock you.' Gus lifted a damp strand of hair from her face.

'It's OK. Being proposed to is the best kind of shock.'

'But you didn't give me an answer.'

'Didn't I?' Freya kissed him, adoring the cool saltiness on his lips. 'I meant to say yes. I'd love to marry you, Gus Wilder.'

Another long and lovely kiss and another soaking wave later, Freya said, 'But how's it going to work? Do you have any plans for us?'

Gus's happy gaze searched her face. 'Does it matter? At the moment, all I want is for you and me and Nick to be together. I don't really mind where we are or what happens, as long as we're a family.'

'Sounds good to me. I'd be happy to go anywhere if you

were there, and as long as Nick had access to decent health care.'

'We'd make sure of that.' He drew her into him. 'Mmm,' he whispered, trailing kisses over her throat. 'I've always thought of you as my sexy mermaid.'

Suddenly, the kisses stopped as Gus sat up. 'Hell.' Swearing softly, he patted at his damp pockets.

'What's the matter?' Freya sat up too. 'Have you lost something?'

'I hope not.'

Gus's face was grim and distinctly worried as he dealt with a button on his shirt pocket. Of course, the task would have been so much easier if his clothes weren't wringing wet.

At last, he had the pocket open and he reached inside. 'Thank God. I thought it might have washed out.'

'What is it? Your wallet? Your phone?'

'This,' Gus said, reaching for her hand, and he slipped a ring onto her finger.

'Ohhhh.' Freya saw the flash of silver and diamonds and the gleam of a dark faceted stone and she gasped at the enormity of what might have happened if the ring had been lost. 'An engagement ring,' she whispered.

'You can't see it properly in this light, but the main stone's a sapphire. A mixture of blue and green to match your eyes.'

'Gus, I love it. I'd love it if it was made of barbed wire, but this is gorgeous.'

'What happened to you two?' Poppy tut-tutted as Gus and Freya finally arrived back from the beach with sodden clothes and dripping hair. 'You look like a pair of good-for-nothing teenagers.'

'I almost drowned trying to ask Freya to marry me,' Gus said, grinning happily.

This was met by squeals from Poppy and Nick.

'And then we got engaged but we were more or less un-
derwater,' Freya added, laughing as she held out her hand to
show them her beautiful ring.

This news was greeted by even more satisfying reactions.
Nick gave another squealing whoop and broke into a war
dance. Poppy smiled enormously and hugged them both, wet
clothes and all.

It was a week later, with the happiest Christmas ever behind
them, that Gus told Freya about his parents' surprise.

They were walking along the beach as they did most afternoons, floating on happiness, still marvelling that being
together could be so good, that life could feel so wonderful. Nick was there too, running ahead of them with Urchin,
throwing a ball for the dog to catch.

'See this land,' Gus said, pointing to a vacant double al-
lotment that fronted both the beach and the mouth of a small
creek.

'It's fabulous, isn't it?' Freya said. 'The best piece of un-
touched real estate in the Bay.'

'My father bought it when he was living here. I guess, being
a bank manager, he had an eye for a good investment.'

Freya's lovely eyes widened. 'I hope he hung on to it. It
must be worth a fortune now.'

'He hung on to it,' Gus said quietly, then he smiled. 'He
and Mum want to give the land to us as a wedding present.'

Her shock must have rendered her speechless. It was ages
before she spoke. 'That's so generous,' she said at last. 'But—'
She frowned and looked out to sea, to the dancing waves and
dazzling sun pennies. 'But would you want to build a home
here? Wouldn't it be too much of a tie?'

Gus chuckled, felt the excitement inside him begin to
bubble over. 'Ever since Dad's phone call on Christmas Day,
I've been hatching a plan. I'd like to build a cluster of cottages

here for the families of seriously ill children. It would be somewhere peaceful, with a holiday atmosphere for them to come to—after a big operation perhaps, or chemotherapy. A place for the whole family to relax and recover.'

Freya was shaking her head.

'You don't like the idea?'

'I do like it,' she said. 'I'm just taking it in.'

'It's what I do best, Freya. I've got the experience and the contacts.'

'And we both know what it's like to have a seriously ill child.'

'So I'd have your support?'

Her eyes were shining. 'Absolutely.'

'We could stay on here then,' Gus said. 'At least until Nick finishes school. You could run your gallery. I'd set up a foundation to fund the cottages, and manage the construction. I'd create a website to handle publicity and bookings.'

'It sounds perfect.' Freya was laughing and hugging him. 'Gus, I can't imagine anything better.'

'I can,' he said, gathering her into him.

'What's that?' she asked on a breathless whisper as he began to kiss her bare shoulder.

'A lifetime with you.'

As he kissed her again, he heard a boy's happy shout and a dog's bark and the slap and roll of the sea.

Dear Reader,

As a writer, I'm often asked, "Why romance?" It's an easy question for me to answer. Romance is about hope. Not just a happily-ever-after, but the hope that there is someone out there to love us, and accept us, and face the ups and downs with us. It's the hope that even after we've faced challenges life can be good again. Not just good—even better than ever before.

Hope. It is, I think, the most optimistic word in the English language.

If anyone is in need of hope, I think it is Elli. Life has dealt her a rough hand, and she's taken some time away to regroup. Wyatt, too, hasn't had it easy. And when they first meet they don't exactly hit it off. But then something happens. Maybe it's a miracle. Because somehow a tiny baby enters the picture and she changes everything. Baby Darcy might bring a whole lot of trouble, but she also brings something to Wyatt and Elli that is desperately needed: hope.

Why romance? Because in my heart I believe in love, and healing, and happiness. I wish that for you, too.

Happy reading!

Donna

PROUD RANCHER, PRECIOUS BUNDLE

BY

DONNA ALWARD

First published in Great Britain 2010
Harlequin Mills & Boon Limited,
Eton House, 18-24 Paradise Road, Richmond, Surrey TW9 1SR

© Donna Alward 2010

ISBN: 978 0 263 88834 8

23-1010

Harlequin Mills & Boon policy is to use papers that are natural, renewable
and recyclable products and made from wood grown in sustainable forests.
The logging and manufacturing processes conform to the legal environmental
regulations of the country of origin.

Printed and bound in Spain
by Litografia Rosés S.A., Barcelona

A busy wife and mother of three (two daughters and the family dog), **Donna Alward** believes hers is the best job in the world: a combination of stay-at-home mum and romance novelist. An avid reader since childhood, Donna always made up her own stories. She completed her Arts Degree in English Literature in 1994, but it wasn't until 2001 that she penned her first full-length novel and found herself hooked on writing romance. In 2006 she sold her first manuscript and now writes warm, emotional stories for Harlequin Mills & Boon's Romance line.

In her new home office in Nova Scotia, Donna loves being back on the east coast of Canada after nearly twelve years in Alberta, where her career began, writing about cowboys and the west. Donna's debut Romance, *Hired by the Cowboy*, was awarded the Booksellers Best Award in 2008 for Best Traditional Romance.

With the Atlantic Ocean only minutes from her doorstep, Donna has found a fresh take on life and promises even more great romances in the near future!

Donna loves to hear from readers. You can contact her through her website at www.donnaalward.com, visit her myspace page at www.myspace.com/dalward, or through her publisher.

To my girly girls, Ash and Kate.
Love you.

CHAPTER ONE

OF ALL THE MISHAPS that had happened today—stubborn cattle, broken gates, his ATV running out of gas—Wyatt Black definitely hadn't seen this one coming.

His boots scuffed in the dust leading to the sagging porch, his gaze riveted on the oddly shaped lump next to his front door. It was rounded and…pink. Pink? After a pause, he quickened his steps. A sound came from the bundle, a small squeaking sound.

Three steps later his heart pounded as his eyes confirmed his initial assessment. It was, indeed, a baby seat. For a few brief moments he'd nearly convinced himself he was seeing things. But there was no mistaking the pink canopy. He took the veranda steps slowly, confused. What the hell?

Two steps away from the seat he could see a small white chubby hand, the fingers curled in, delicate pink fingernails tipping the tiny digits.

And then there she was. A small mite of a thing, eyes closed and lips sucking gently in and out with her breath as her hands moved restlessly. A hint of dark fuzz peeked out from beneath a stretchy pink hat, and a blanket patterned with white and pink teddy bears covered all of her but her hands. *A baby.* And beside her a navy-and-white cloth bag, as if announcing she was staying for a while.

Wyatt's heart raced as the necessary questions flew through his mind. He put down his toolbox with a quiet thud. Who was this child's mother and, more importantly, where was she? Why had a baby been left on *his* doorstep?

It was inconceivable that this miniature human could be meant for him. There had to be some mistake. The alternative was momentarily staggering. Was it possible that she might be his flesh and blood? He stared at the lashes lying on her china-doll cheeks. She was so little. He counted back several months, then breathed out in relief. No, it was impossible. A year ago he'd been outside Rocky Mountain House working as a roughneck. There'd been no one. He had always kept his relationships on the unserious side and short. There'd been no sense letting a woman get her hopes up when he hadn't been in a position to settle down. He wasn't into playing games.

He exhaled fully. No, this baby wasn't his—he was sure of it. The core of tension in his body eased slightly, but not completely. The baby couldn't be his, but that still left the question—*whose was she?*

And what was he supposed to do with her?

As if hearing his question, she lifted her fringe of black lashes and he caught sight of dark eyes. The hands waved even more as she woke. Then, as if knowing he was the last person she should see, her face scrunched up pitifully and a thin cry pierced the silence.

He breathed a profanity in shock and dismay. He couldn't just leave her there crying, for God's sake! What should he do now? He knew nothing about babies. He glanced around the yard and up the road, knowing it was a futile exercise. Whoever had left her on his doorstep was long gone.

He reached out and grasped the white plastic handle of the car seat, picking it up with his right hand and tugging

FREE BOOKS OFFER

To get you started, we'll send you
2 FREE books and a FREE gift

There's no catch, everything is **FREE**

Accepting your 2 **FREE** books and **FREE** mystery gift
places you under no obligation to buy anything.

Be part of the Mills & Boon® Book Club™ and receive your favourite
Series books up to 2 months before they are in the shops and delivered
straight to your door. Plus, enjoy a wide range of **EXCLUSIVE** benefits!

- Best new women's fiction – delivered right to
  your door with FREE P&P

- Avoid disappointment – get your books up to
  2 months before they are in the shops

- No contract – no obligation to buy

We hope that after receiving your free books you'll
want to remain a member. But the choice is yours.
So why not give us a go? You'll be glad you did!

Visit **millsandboon.co.uk** to stay up to date
with offers and to sign-up for our newsletter

2 **FREE** books
and a
FREE gift

DETACH AND POST CARD TODAY!

S0JIA

Mrs/Miss/Ms/Mr _____ Initials _____

BLOCK CAPITALS PLEASE

Surname _____

Address _____

_____

Postcode _____

Email _____

🌹 **MILLS & BOON**®

MILLS & BOON®
Book Club

FREE BOOK OFFER
FREEPOST NAT 10298
RICHMOND
TW9 1BR

NO STAMP
NECESSARY
IF POSTED IN
THE U.K. OR N.I.

open the front door with his left. He certainly had to get the baby out of the September chill—surely it couldn't be good for her. He didn't even stop to take off his boots, just went straight through to the kitchen at the rear of the house and put the seat on a worn countertop. The thin cry echoed—seeming sharper, stronger in the confined space. Wyatt took off his hat and hooked it over the knob of a kitchen chair before turning back to the unhappy bundle.

He lifted the blanket, momentarily marveling that a creature so tiny and fragile could emit such a shrill, ear-piercing cry. A quick search of the recesses of the seat revealed no clues to her identity, and he ran a hand through his hair as the cries increased, feet wiggling furiously now as well as hands.

"Shhh, baby," he murmured, his stomach sinking beneath the weight of the situation. He couldn't just leave her this way. He reached out to unfasten the buckle strapping her in and pulled back once he caught a glimpse of his hands. He'd been herding stubborn cattle and fixing run-down fences all morning. Pulse still hammering, he rushed to the sink and the bar of soap he kept on the rim in an old chipped dish.

He scrubbed his hands in the water, all the while looking over his shoulder at the baby, his nerves fraying as the cries grew more impatient. Instinct told him that he should pick her up. Babies needed to be soothed, right? After all, he'd be pretty ticked off at being strapped into a seat all day. He threw the hand towel next to the sink and went back to the seat. "Shhh," he repeated, desperate now to stop the crying. "I've got you. Just stop crying."

He released the strap and reached out, took the baby, blanket and all, from the seat and rested her on the crook of his arm.

The red blotchy face signaled more crying, and the wee body stiffened with outrage.

"Hey," Wyatt cajoled, wondering now if he shouldn't call 911. Surely this was an emergency. How many people came home to find a baby on their doorstep, after all?

How had this possibly happened?

Dimly he recalled that a bag had been on the veranda along with the seat. It was his best hope for a clue, he realized, so, baby and all, he opened the sagging screen door with his hip and retrieved the bag. His boots thunked on the scarred hardwood as he went back to the kitchen and the counter, putting the bag on top. Trying to ignore the crying, he wrestled the zipper with one hand while holding the baby tightly with his other arm. Perhaps in here there would be a name, an address. Some way to sort out this horrible mistake and return the baby to where she really belonged.

He pulled out a handful of tiny diapers, then a pair of pajamas with soft feet, and a stuffed animal. One, two, three bottles…and a can of some sort of powder added to the collection on the counter. Then more bottles. He ran his hand along the inside of the bag. More clothes, but nothing else.

Irritation flared, now that the initial shock was fading away. This was craziness, pure and simple. For God's sake, what kind of person left a baby on a stranger's porch and walked away? What kind of mother would do such a thing? What if he hadn't come back for lunch and she'd been left there all day? He let out a frustrated breath. Okay. Without a doubt the smart thing to do would be to call the police.

And then he felt it. Something stiff near the front of the bag. He lifted a Velcro tab and reached into a front pocket. An envelope.

Adjusting the baby's weight on his arm, he opened the flap, went to a kitchen chair and sat down. Heavily.

His eyes scanned the page. As if sensing something important were occurring, the infant quieted and she plunged a fist into her mouth, sucking noisily and whimpering. Wyatt read the brief words, his back sagging into the chair, staring at the plain paper and then at the tiny girl in his hands.

Holy jumpin' Judas.

Her name was Darcy. He said her name, tried it out on his tongue, his throat closing as the sound of his voice faded away in the quiet kitchen. The answer that greeted him was a fresh wail punctuated by a sad hiccup.

The break had helped only to increase the baby's vocal reserves. Her crying rose to a fever pitch and Wyatt closed his eyes, still reeling from the contents of the letter. He had to make her stop so he could think what to do next. His stomach rumbled loudly, reminding him why he'd come back to the house in the first place.

Maybe *she* was hungry, too.

As the inspiration struck he grabbed one of the bottles off the counter where he'd unloaded the diaper bag. At the first touch of plastic nipple to lips, Darcy opened her mouth and frantically started sucking at the milk inside. That was it! A sense of pride and relief raced through him as he went to the living room, sitting on the old couch with its sagging cushions and wiggling arms. He leaned back, rested his feet on a wood box he had pressed into use as a coffee table. Blessed silence filled the room as she drained the small bottle, her tiny body nestled into the crook of his elbow. She felt foreign there, unlike anything he'd ever held before. Not unpleasant. Just…different.

Her eyes drifted closed once more. Had he actually put her to sleep, as well? Thank God. With some peace and quiet, he could take a look at that letter again, try to sort it out. One thing was for sure…Darcy—whoever she was—couldn't stay here.

The little lips slackened and a dribble of milk slid down her chin into the soft skin of her neck. He was struck by how tiny, how helpless she was. As gently as he possibly could, he slid her back into her seat and covered her with the blanket. Then he went to the fridge, got out an apple to substitute for the lunch he'd missed. He took a bite and returned to the letter he'd left open on the table.

He read it again, and again, and once more for good measure. Half his brain told him there was some mistake. The other half, the part that nagged and taunted him each day of his life, nudged him cruelly and said he shouldn't be surprised. The apple tasted dry and mealy in his mouth, and he swallowed with difficulty.

Darcy was his niece.

Born to a sister he'd pretended hadn't existed.

He rubbed a hand over his face. Oh, he'd known for a long time that his father wouldn't win any awards for parent of the year. But he recognized the name at the bottom of the plain sheet. Barbara Paulsen had been two years behind him in high school. All the kids had known that she had no dad. She'd borne her share of ridicule, all right. *Bastard Barb,* they'd called her. He cringed, thinking about the cruelty of it now. He'd never joined in the teasing. It would have been too easy for the tables to be turned. He'd deserved the name as much as she had. There'd been rumors back then, of his father having an affair with Barb's mother. Barbara's dark hair and eyes had been so similar to his—and to Mitch Black's.

He'd always hated that he'd favored his father rather than his mother in looks. He didn't want to be *anything* like his father. Ever.

He'd chosen to turn a deaf ear to the rumors, but inside, a small part of him had always taunted that it was true.

According to the letter, they shared the same father. It wasn't much of a stretch for Wyatt to believe her. It had been no secret in his house that Mitch Black had married Wyatt's mother to do the right thing after getting her in trouble. And it had been a disaster.

Wyatt scowled, staring at the wall behind the table. Hell, even dead, his father still created ripples of destruction. Now Barbara—claiming to be his sister—found herself in the same position, and was asking for his help. Temporarily. But asking for it just the same.

The fact that she had left Darcy on his step meant one of two things. Either she was as great a parent as their father had been, or she was desperate. Reading between the lines of the letter, he was leaning toward desperation.

But it didn't solve a damn thing where he was concerned. He was now in possession of an infant. And he was a single man, trying to run a ranch, who knew nothing about babies. Maybe he should simply call the authorities.

He ran a hand over his face, heaving a sigh. The authorities, though, would call child welfare. He knew that much. And if Barbara were truly his half sister, she'd already suffered enough. He'd made no contact with her since leaving Red Deer. It had been easier to pretend she didn't exist. Easier to ignore yet another symbol of the disrespect Mitch had shown his family.

No, if he called, Family Services would take the baby away. Not just from him, but maybe from her, too, and the thought made his stomach clench.

Once he made the call, there would be no taking it back. What he needed to do was buy some time. He needed to talk to Barbara. Figure out the whole situation and make a better decision.

An ear-splitting scream shattered the air, scattering his thoughts into tiny fragments and making his eyes widen with the sheer panic echoing in his ears. He looked over— Darcy's face was red and the cries had a new, desperate edge to them. What now? He walked the floor, holding Darcy in the crook of his arm, at his wit's end. Until today, he'd never held a baby in his life.

He needed help. Even to make it through this one day so he could figure out what to do next. Maybe he shouldn't, but he felt responsible. Even if it turned out not to be true, he felt an obligation to make the right decision. It wasn't Darcy's fault she'd been left here. If what Barbara Paulsen said was true, she was family.

You shouldn't turn your back on family. He'd always believed it somehow, but had never had the chance to prove it.

His muscles tensed at the persistent wails. He couldn't do this, not alone. Who could he possibly call? His parents had been gone nearly five years. He'd been in the house only for the summer, after drifting around the upper half of Alberta for years now, earning his fortune in the oil patch and never staying in one place for long. He was alone, and for the most part that was how he liked it.

Until now. Right now he could really use a helping hand.

And then he remembered his neighbor. Not technically his neighbor either. He'd met Ellison Marchuk exactly once. She was housesitting for the Camerons, and despite being incredibly attractive, had no more sense than God gave a flea. Whatever possessed a woman to go traipsing through a pasture housing his bull—in search of flowers!—was beyond him. And then she'd had the nerve to call him grouchy, with a toss of her summer-blond hair. Grouchy as a wounded bear, if memory served correctly.

Ellison Marchuk would not have been his first choice, but she was a woman and she was next door, both qualifications that put her head and shoulders above anyone else he knew. Surely she would have some idea what to do with a baby. At this point, looking at the tiny face twisted in agony, *anyone* would know what to do better than he did. His nerves were fraying more by the minute. He just needed help quieting her crying. He'd take it from there.

Amidst the shrieking cries and against his better judgment, he wrapped the blanket around Darcy and headed for the door.

Elli rubbed her eyes and slid a bookmark into the textbook, pushing it to the side. If she read any more today about profit-and-loss statements she'd go cross-eyed by the end of the week. Taking the courses by correspondence had benefits and drawbacks. Still, they'd help her get back on her feet, something she needed to do sooner rather than later. Being laid off from the hospital was just the icing on the cake after the year from hell. It was time to take action. To find a purpose again.

Right now she just wanted a cup of hot chocolate and something to break up her day—make her stop thinking. She'd had way too much time to think lately. About all her failures, mostly.

She jumped as someone pounded on the front door, and she pressed a hand to her heart. She still wasn't used to the way things echoed around the vaulted ceilings of the Camerons' house, including the sound of her footsteps as she went to the foyer. The house was so different from the condo she'd shared with Tim in Calgary. It had been nice, in a good area of town, but this was...

She sighed. This was exactly what Tim had aspired to.

This was the sort of McMansion he'd mapped out for them. Maybe he'd get it yet. Just not with her.

The pounding sounded again. She peered through the judas hole and her mouth dropped open. It was the neighbor, the new rancher who lived next door. Her teeth clenched as she recalled their one and only meeting. Wyatt Black, he'd informed her in a tone that could only be considered brusque at best. He'd yelled at her and called her stupid. The remark had cut her deeply. Normally she would have brushed off the insult—she'd been called so many names as a clerk in the emergency room that she'd developed a thick skin. But in light of recent events, it had made her eyes burn with humiliation. She'd called him something, too, but she couldn't remember what. She vaguely remembered it had been more polite than the words going through her mind at the time. She'd stomped back to the house and hadn't seen him since.

Now here he was, all six brawny feet of him. Elli pressed her eye up to the peephole once more and bit down on her lip. Dark hair and stormy eyes and a mouth pulled tight in a scowl. And in his arms…

Dear Lord. A baby.

As he knocked on the door again, Elli jumped back. Now she could hear the thin cries threading through the solid oak. She reached out and turned the heavy knob, pulling the door inward, and stepped out into the afternoon sun.

"Oh, thank God."

Elli's eardrums received the full blast of the infant's cries mediated only by Wyatt's deep but stressed, voice.

"What on earth?"

Mr. Dark and Scowly stepped forward, enough that his body started to invade her space, and she stepped back in reflex.

"Please, just tell me what to do. She won't stop crying."

Whatever Elli's questions, they fled as she looked from his harried expression down into the scrunched, unhappy face. First things first. Her heart gave a painful twist at the sight of the baby. He clearly expected her to know what to do. She hated how her hands shook as she reached out for the soft bundle. The little girl was clearly in discomfort of some kind. And this rancher—Black—was certainly not calming her in the least.

Elli pushed the door open farther with her hip, inviting him in as she moved aside, trying to ignore her body's response to feeling the small, warm body in her arms. This baby was not William. She could do this. She pasted on an artificial smile. "What's her name?"

He swallowed thickly as he stepped over the threshold, his Adam's apple bobbing. Elli's gaze locked on it for a moment before looking up into his face. He had the most extraordinary lips, the bottom one deliciously full above a chin rough with a hint of stubble. The lips moved as she watched. "Darcy. Her name is Darcy."

Elli felt the warm little bundle in her arms, the weight foreign, painful, yet somehow very right. She pressed a hand to the tiny forehead, feeling for fever. "She's not warm. Do you think she's ill?"

Black came in, shutting the door behind him, and Elli felt nerves swim around in her stomach. He was not a pleasant man. And yet there was something in his eyes. It looked like worry, and it helped ameliorate her misgivings.

"I was hoping you could tell me. One minute she was asleep, the next she was screaming like a banshee." He raised his voice a bit to be heard over the screaming racket.

Her, tell him? She knew next to nothing about babies,

and the very reminder of the fact hurt, cutting deep into her bones. She scoured her mind for the things she'd learned about soothing babies from the books she'd bought and the prenatal classes she'd attended. Food seemed the most obvious. "Did you try feeding her?"

"She seemed to be fine after I gave her the bottle from the bag," he explained, rubbing a hand over his hair. "She drank the whole thing, sucked it right down."

Elli wrinkled her brow, trying to recall if Sarah Cameron had mentioned that their reticent neighbor had a child. She didn't think so. He certainly didn't act like a man who'd come into contact with babies before. He was staring at her and Darcy with his eyes full of concern—and panic.

A detail pierced her memory, a remnant of classes taken what seemed like a lifetime ago. "Did you heat the milk?"

The full lips dropped open slightly and his cheekbones flattened. "I was supposed to heat it?"

Elli's shoulders relaxed and she let out a small chuckle, relieved. Immediately she lifted the baby to her shoulder and began rubbing her back with firm circles. "She's probably got cramps," she said above the pitiful crying. It seemed the easiest solution at the moment. She began patting Darcy's back. Hungry, gas, cramps. Elementary. At least she could fake knowing what she was doing.

"I didn't know," he replied, a light blush infusing his cheeks beneath the stubble. "I don't know *anything* about babies."

"You might as well take off your boots and come in for a minute," Elli replied, not wanting to admit that she knew little more than he did and determined to bluff her way through it. She knew she'd made a mistake going into his bull pasture earlier this summer and she already knew what he thought of her common sense. She'd be damned if she'd let him see a weakness again.

They couldn't stand in the foyer forever. An enormous burp echoed straight up to the rafters and a laugh bubbled up and out of Elli's lips at the violence of the sound coming from such a tiny package. She was pleased at having discovered the cause and solution quite by accident. The expression on Black's face conveyed such abject surprise that she giggled again.

"I'm Ellison Marchuk," she introduced herself, her shoulder growing warm from the soft breath of the baby as she sighed against her sweater. "I don't think we met properly last time."

"I remember," he replied, and Elli felt the heat of a blush creep up her neck straight to her ears. "Wyatt Black, in case you forgot," he continued pointedly. "Thank you. My ears are still ringing. I was at my wit's end."

Elli ignored the subtle dig. Of course she remembered meeting him. It wasn't every day a perfect stranger yelled at her and called her names. She was more polite than that, and had been making an attempt to start fresh. She lifted her chin. "You're welcome, Wyatt Black."

Goodness, Elli thought as the name rolled off her tongue. The name matched him perfectly. She watched with her pulse drumming rapidly as he pushed off his boots with his toes. Even in his stocking feet, he topped her by a good four inches. His shoulders were inordinately broad in a worn flannel shirt. And his jeans were faded in all the right places.

She swallowed. She needed to get out more. Maybe she'd been hiding out in the Camerons' house a little too long, if she was reacting to the irascible next-door neighbor in such a way. Especially a neighbor with rotten manners.

Elli led the way through the foyer into the living room,

determined to be gracious. The room faced the backyard, then south over the wide pasture where Wyatt's herd now grazed—the very pasture where she'd indulged herself in picking late-summer wildflowers in an attempt to cheer herself up. The fields here were huge. She'd had no idea she was in the same pasture as one of his bulls.

"The Camerons have a nice place." His voice came from behind her. "I haven't been inside before."

"My father used to work for Cameron Energy," Elli remarked. "The Camerons are like second parents to me."

Wyatt remained silent behind her and Elli added lack of conversational skills to his repertoire of faults.

She took him straight to the conversation pit with its plush furniture. Windows filled the wall behind them, flooding the room with light, while French doors led out to a large deck. She gestured toward a chair, inviting him to sit. "Would you like her back now? She seems much more contented."

She held out her arms with Darcy now blinking innocently, her dark eyes focused on nothing in particular.

"She looks happy where she is," Wyatt replied, looking away.

Elli took a step back and went to the sofa. She sat down and put Darcy gently beside her. He couldn't know how caring for a child—even in such a minor way—hurt her. She worked hard to push away the bitterness. If things had gone right, she would have been in her own home cradling her own son right now. She blinked a couple of times and forced the thoughts aside. It could not be changed.

"Won't she fall off?" Wyatt's hard voice interrupted.

The rough question diverted her from overthinking. She didn't know. How old were babies when they could start rolling over? She didn't want him to see her indecision, and she adjusted the baby on the sofa so she was lying safely, perpendicular to the edge of the couch.

"How old is she?" Elli guessed at a month, maybe six weeks. She still held that newborn daintiness. A precious little bundle who had been through what appeared to be a rough day if the mottled, puffy cheeks were any indication. Could a day with Wyatt Black be described in any other way? Elli ran a finger down the middle of the sleepers, smiling softly as the little feet kicked with pleasure. At least she'd elicited a positive response rather than more crying.

When Wyatt didn't answer her question, though, she looked back at him again. He was watching her speculatively, his eyes slightly narrowed as if he were trying to read her thoughts. She was glad he couldn't. There were some things she didn't want anyone to know.

"What do you do, Ellison?"

Ah, he hadn't wanted to answer her question, and she didn't want to answer his either. It wasn't a simple question, not to her. Answering required a lengthy explanation, and it would only add fuel to his comment in the pasture that day, when he'd called her stupid. Maybe she was. A fool, certainly.

Maybe it was time he left. There was something not quite right in the way he'd avoided her question, something that didn't add up. He could mind his own business and she could mind hers and they'd both be happy.

"She seems fine now, but perhaps tired. You should take her home and put her to bed."

Wyatt looked away. Elli's misgivings grew. Her heart picked up a quick rhythm again. The only information he'd offered was that her name was Darcy, and it wasn't as if the baby could dispute it. He didn't answer how old she was, he didn't know to heat a bottle... What was this man doing with an infant? Was the child his? And if so, shouldn't he know *something* about caring for her?

She braved a look. As much as she didn't want to get involved, she could still smell the baby-powder scent on her shoulder, feel the warmth of the little body pressed against her like a wish come true. She took a breath. "She's not yours, is she?"

His eyes captured hers, honest but betraying no other emotion. "No."

"Then whose…"

"It's complicated."

She put her hands primly on her knees to keep from fidgeting. She briefly thought of all the news stories about noncustodial kidnappings. Sure, he was a crusty, grouchy thing, but was he capable of *that?* She didn't want to believe it. "I don't feel reassured, Mr. Black."

His steady gaze made her want to squirm, and she fought against the feeling. Should she be frightened? Perhaps. But she hadn't put herself in the middle of the situation. He had. A man with something to hide wouldn't have done that, would he? "You don't know what to do with babies," she remarked, screwing up her courage. "You don't even know how old she is."

"No, I don't. I've never held a baby in my life before today. Does that make you feel better?"

There was a little edge of danger to him that was exciting even as warning bells started clanging. "Not exactly."

She had to be crazy. Despite their first meeting, Wyatt Black was a stranger with a strange baby, in a situation she didn't understand and she was alone in the house in the middle of nowhere. Calling the police had crossed her mind more than once. But then she remembered the look on his face as he'd handed Darcy to her. It wasn't just panic. It was concern. And while he said little, there was something about him that she trusted. She couldn't explain why. It was just a feeling.

She'd learned to trust her gut feelings. Even when it hurt.

She picked Darcy up off the sofa cushion, swaddling her in the blanket. She simply had to know more to be sure. To know that the baby would be safe and cared for. "I need you to explain."

"Darcy is my niece. I think."

The ambiguous response made her wrinkle her nose in confusion. "Mr. Black…"

He stood up from his chair, his long, hard length taking a handful of steps until he paused before her, making her crane her neck to see his face. His jaw was set and his eyes glittered darkly, but there was a hint of something there that elicited her empathy. A glimmer of pain, perhaps, and vulnerability.

He reached behind him into his back pocket and withdrew an envelope.

He held it out to her.

"Read it," he commanded. "Then you'll know just as much as I do."

CHAPTER TWO

ELLI STARED AT THE piece of paper, all the while aware of Wyatt standing before her, the faded denim of his jeans constantly in her line of vision. She read the letter aloud, her soft voice echoing through the empty room. Listening to the words made it more real somehow. Wyatt seemed to look everywhere but at the baby.

"'Dear Wyatt, I know right now you're probably wondering what on earth is going on. And believe me—if I had another choice…'"

Elli risked a glance up. Wyatt was staring at a spot past her shoulder, his jaw tightly clenched, his gaze revealing nothing. She looked back down at the plain piece of paper, torn from a notebook, with the edges rough and careless. Her stomach began an uneasy turning. This wasn't stationery chosen for such an important letter. This was hurried. Impulsive.

"I don't know if you were ever aware, Wyatt, but we share a father. I am your half sister. I tried to hate you for it, but you were never mean to me like the others. Maybe you knew back then. Either way… you're all the family I've got now. You and Darcy. And I'm not good for either one of you. If there were

any other way…but I can't do this. Take good care
of her for me."

The letter was signed simply "Barbara Paulsen."

If the letter were genuine—and she was inclined to think
it was—then he was telling the truth. Darcy was his niece.
More importantly, the words themselves disturbed her.
Twice she had said she had no choice…why?

"Your sister…" she began quietly.

His boots did an about-face and she looked up from
the paper. He was no longer directly in front of her. He
had moved and stopped at the front window, looking out
over the hedge and small garden. There was a stiffness in
his posture that caused Elli a moment of pause. Surely a
mother's care was better than this detachment. Faced with
an infant, Wyatt showed the same cold, stubborn side as he
had the afternoon they'd first met. Babies needed more than
bottles and a place to sleep. They needed love. She wondered if Wyatt Black was even capable of tenderness.

She cleared her throat. "Your sister," she continued, her
voice slightly stronger, "must trust you very much."

"My sister?" The words came out in a harsh laugh. "We
have a biological relationship, if that. I went to school with
her, that's all."

"You don't believe her?"

He turned slowly from the window. His dark eyes were
shuttered, his expression utterly closed, and she couldn't
begin to imagine what he was thinking. Nothing about his
face gave her a clue. She wanted to go over and shake him,
get some sense of what was going through his mind. It was
clear to her that there was a plea in Barbara's note. She
was asking for help. And he was standing here like some
judgmental god doling out doubt and condemnation.

"There were rumors…I ignored them. It certainly makes

sense—most of it anyway. It's not much of a stretch to think that my father…"

There, there it was. The flash of vulnerability, in his eyes and flickering through his voice. Gone just as quickly as it had surfaced, but she'd caught it. What sort of life had he had as a boy? He wasn't shocked at the discovery of his father's betrayal, she realized. But he was bitter. She had to tread carefully. She folded up the letter neatly and handed it back to him.

"What if it's not true?"

His lips became a harsh, thin line. "It probably is," he admitted. "But I need to find out for sure. In the meantime…"

"Yes," she agreed quietly, knowing he had to see that Darcy was his first priority. "In the meantime, you have a more immediate problem. You have Darcy. What are you going to do?"

"I am hopeless with babies. I know nothing about them." His dark eyes met hers, looking as if he expected agreement.

"That goes without saying," she replied, crossing her arms. "But it doesn't change that Darcy has been left in your care."

"I don't know what to do. A few hours and I've already screwed up. I've never been around babies."

Elli offered a small indulgent smile. At least he seemed concerned about getting things right. Maybe she was judging him too harshly. "You were one, you know. A baby. Once."

"My memory is a bit dim," he reminded her, but she could see her light teasing had done its work. His facial muscles relaxed slightly and she thought there might actually be a hint of a smile just tugging at the corner of his lips. Just as soon as it came, it disappeared, so that she wondered if she had imagined it. The moment drew out and Elli's gaze remained riveted on his face. When he wasn't looking so severe, he was really quite…

Quite good-looking.

Darcy kicked on the sofa, a tiny sigh and gurgle breaking the silence. Elli looked away, wondering what on earth the child might be thinking, totally oblivious to the chaos around her. She thought briefly of Darcy's mother, Barbara, and felt a flash of animosity. How could a mother, any mother, simply drive away and leave this beautiful child on a stranger's doorstep? Did she not know how lucky she was? And yet…there was a sense of desperation between the lines of her letter. For some reason Barbara didn't think she could look after her own daughter. She was so afraid that she'd left her on the front porch of a man little more than a stranger.

Wyatt sat down on the sofa on the other side of Darcy, the cushions sinking beneath his weight. "I know," he said, as if replying to the question she hadn't asked. "I don't know how she could do it either. I haven't seen her in years. Maybe it is all made up. But maybe it's not. And I can't take that chance with Darcy."

"What do you mean?" Elli turned to face him, keeping her hands busy by playing with Darcy's feet, tapping them together lightly. She was already feeling the beginnings of resentment toward a woman she had never met. Darcy was so small, so precious. Elli had learned from years working in the emergency room that she shouldn't judge. But it was different when faced with an innocent, beautiful child. She *was* judging. It was impossible not to. She would give anything to be playing with her own child's feet at this moment. She knew in her heart that if William had lived, nothing could have pried her away from him.

Wyatt scowled slightly, resting his elbows on his knees.

"If she is my niece, I can't just call the police, can I? Because we both know what will happen to her then."

Elli nodded, pulled out of her dark thoughts. She had to look away from Wyatt's face. Was that tenderness she'd glimpsed in his eyes? The very emotion she'd doubted he possessed only moments ago? He might be inept, but he was trying to do the right thing.

"I can't just let her go into foster care. If I do, maybe there's a chance that her mother will never get her back. I can't let that happen. At least not until I know for sure. I need to find Barbara, talk to her."

Elli tried hard to fight away the surge of feeling expanding in her chest. She could already feel herself getting involved, getting sucked into a situation not of her making. Coming here, housesitting for the Camerons—that was supposed to be her way of taking a first step toward building a new life. Her chance to try again away from the drama and pitying looks. *Poor Elli. Bad luck comes in threes. Whatever will she do now?* She'd had enough of it.

A bachelor next-door neighbor with a baby wasn't exactly the type of special project she'd been looking for. She drew her attention back to the letter.

"This woman, this Barbara, even if she is your sister, Mr. Black, deliberately left a six-week-old baby on the doorstep of someone she barely knew with no guarantees that you would even be there." Elli fought to keep the anger, the frustration, the passion, for that matter, under control. This wasn't a subject she could be rational about. She knew it. It was the exact reason she should steer clear of the whole mess.

"Doesn't that tell you how desperate she is?"

Without warning, tears stung the backs of her eyes and she bit down on her lip. She got up from the sofa so that he couldn't see her face. So he couldn't see the grief that bubbled up.

She went to the kitchen, going instinctively for the kettle to give her hands something to do. Losing William had nearly destroyed her. It had certainly destroyed her marriage. And now that baby Darcy was quiet and content, the emergency was over. There was no way on God's green earth she was going to tell Wyatt Black—a man she'd just met—the sordid story of her disastrous pregnancy and resulting divorce.

She plugged in the kettle and took out a mug, hesitating with her hand on a second cup, trying to regain control. She should send him on his way. Remind him to warm up the bottles and wish him well.

He appeared in the doorway to the kitchen, filling the frame with his solid figure. She paused, the cup in her hand, looking up into his unsmiling face. He had Darcy on his arm in an awkward position.

Elli sighed, putting the mugs down on the counter. She'd taken the new-baby classes with Tim by her side. Back then it had been with dolls and smiles and laughter as the instructor showed them how to do even the simplest things. She'd blocked out those times from her mind deliberately, because they were so painful. But with Wyatt and Darcy only footsteps away, they came rushing back, bittersweet. She'd been excited to be pregnant, but also overwhelmed by the impending responsibility of caring for a baby. How must Wyatt be feeling, thrust into the situation with no preparation at all?

"Here. Let me show you." She went over to him and was careful to touch him as little as possible. Her fingers brushed the soft flannel of his shirt as she adjusted the pink bundle just the way she'd held the doll in classes. She forced the pain aside and focused on the task at hand.

Darcy looked up, eyes unfocused, seemingly unconcerned. Elli moved Wyatt's hand slightly. "You need to support her neck more," she said quietly, remembering what she'd read and heard. "Babies can't hold their heads up on their own at first. So when you pick her up or hold her, you need to make sure she has that support."

He cradled her close. "Maybe I should call someone. I really don't have a clue. She'd be better off with someone else, right? You said it yourself. I'm hopeless."

His eyes were dark and heavy with indecision, and shame crept through her. How could she have said such a thing, knowing how hurtful it could be? No matter how grumpy or grouchy he'd been, she could do better than throwing insults around. Elli could see that he was trying to do the right thing.

"No one was born knowing how to look after a baby, Mr. Black." She kept up the use of his formal name. The last thing she wanted was familiarity. It would be too easy to get involved. The instinct to protect herself fought with the need to help. "And if it's true, you're family. Doesn't that count for something?"

"More than you know," he replied, but there was no joy in the words. "Well, she's here now. I have a ranch to run. How can I possibly look after a child and do all that too?"

It did look as if he was beginning to think of the issue beyond *Could you get her to stop crying.* The kettle began to whistle and Elli swallowed thickly. "Do you want some tea?"

He shook his head. "No, thank you. I should get going, try to figure this out. First of all, I need to find Barbara."

"You seem to place a lot of importance on family, Mr. Black. That's to your credit."

His jaw tightened again, and Elli flushed slightly, not

knowing how what she'd intended as a compliment had managed to give offense.

"People tend to appreciate what's in short supply, Miss Marchuk."

He'd reverted to using Miss Marchuk now, too. The heat in her cheeks deepened and she turned away to pour the boiling water into her mug. His footsteps echoed away from the kitchen down to the foyer again, and she closed her eyes, breathing a sigh of relief.

She heard the door open and suddenly rushed from her spot, skidding down the hall in her sock feet, wanting to catch him before he left altogether. "Mr. Black!"

He paused at the door, Darcy now up on his shoulder and her blanket around her. A gust of wind came through the opening and ruffled his hair, leaving one piece standing up, giving her the urge to reach up and tuck it back into place.

"Yes?"

His one-word response brought her back to earth. She'd remembered something else, like a page torn from a book. "Heat the bottle in hot water. Then put a few drops of the formula on the underside of your wrist. When it's warm, but not hot, it's the right temperature."

For a few moments their gazes held, and something passed between them that was more than bottle-warming instructions. She didn't want to think about what it might be; even the internal suggestion of it hurt. She took a step back and lowered her gaze to the floor.

"Thank you," he murmured, and she didn't look up again until she heard the click of the door shutting her away from them both.

Elli struggled for the rest of the afternoon, all through her tea and while she made herself a grilled cheese and ham sandwich for supper. It was comfort food, and one she rarely allowed herself anymore. The months of criticism from Tim had caused her to burrow further into her grief. And like a nasty cycle, the further she withdrew, the more she had satisfied herself with food. His cutting remarks about her figure had been only one hurtful part of the disintegration of their marriage.

She put her plate into the dishwasher and cleaned the crumbs off the counter. The problem was, she couldn't get Wyatt and Darcy off her mind. Remembering how William had died made her want to run away from the situation as fast as her legs could carry her. And on the flip side was knowing that on the other side of the line of poplar trees, in a very modest bungalow, there was a rancher who knew even less than she did about babies. One who cared about what happened. At the same time she knew that Darcy would be the one to suffer while he tried to figure things out.

She swallowed, went to the windows overlooking the fields to the south. Wyatt's cattle roamed there, the red and white heads bobbing in the evening dusk, where she lost sight of them over a knoll. How was he managing now? Was Darcy crying, and was Wyatt trying to soothe her?

Elli wiped her fingertips over her cheeks, surprised and yet not surprised to find she was crying. She'd never even had the chance to hear William's cries. The absence of them had broken her heart cleanly in two. She got a tissue and dabbed the moisture away.

What would Wyatt do when he had to work? Had he managed to feed her properly? It wasn't fair to Darcy that Wyatt learned these things in trial by fire. And it was only Elli's stupid fear preventing her from helping. Shouldn't the welfare of the baby come before her own hang-ups?

She wiped her eyes once more, pity for the infant

swamping her. Shouldn't someone put that baby ahead of themselves?

Before she could reconsider, she grabbed her jacket from the coatrack and made the short trek across the grass to his house.

Wyatt paced the floor, Darcy on his shoulder, her damp lips pressed to his neck. His shoulders tensed as he thought about all he should have accomplished around the farm this afternoon. He'd managed to boot up the computer long enough to find Barbara in an Internet search, but when he called the number listed, there was no answer. He'd tried twice since, during moments when he'd thought Darcy was asleep.

She managed exactly seven minutes every time, before waking and crying. Crying that stopped the moment he put her on his shoulder and walked the floor. Which was great in the short term. But at some point he needed to eat. Sleep. Do chores.

More than once he'd felt his control slipping and wondered if he was more like his father than he'd thought. God, he didn't want to think so. From Wyatt's earliest memories, crying hadn't been tolerated. Mitch Black made sure of that. Wyatt wanted to think he had more self-control than his father. More compassion.

But baby Darcy was testing him.

He'd try Barbara's number once more. And then he'd call someone. He tried to ignore the end of the letter. The part where she apologized and said she trusted him. He'd given her no reason to. And yet…something about it made him feel as if he would be failing her if he didn't do this.

He sighed, turning back toward the kitchen, craning his neck at an odd angle to see if Darcy was asleep. It was almost as if he was operating on two levels—the one that needed information and planning, and the one with the immediate, pressing problem of keeping a baby's needs met.

Suddenly he had a new respect for mothers who seemed to juggle it all with aplomb.

A knock on the door broke the silence and Darcy's hands jerked out, startled. A quick check showed her tiny eyes open again. Wyatt pushed back annoyance and headed for the door, with a prayer that it was Barbara saying it had all been a mistake.

Instead he found Ellison Marchuk on his dilapidated porch.

"Oh," he said, and she frowned.

"Disappointed, I see." She pushed her hands into her jacket and he fought against the expansion in his chest at seeing her again.

This afternoon he'd been an idiot. He'd rushed over there thinking only of getting help, but he'd been inside all of thirty seconds when his priorities had shifted. He was supposed to have all his thoughts on his predicament, and instead he'd been noticing her hair, or the way her dark lashes brought out the blue in her eyes, or how her sweater accentuated her curves. He wasn't disappointed at all. Even though he should be.

"Not at all," he mumbled roughly. "I was just hoping it was Barbara, that's all."

"It would solve everything, wouldn't it?" She offered a small smile. His gaze dropped to her full mouth.

"Are you going to invite me in, Mr. Black?"

Of course. He was standing there like a dolt, thinking how pretty she looked in the puffy fleece jacket. Clearly she wasn't thinking along the same lines, as she persisted in calling him Mr. Black. Her body language this afternoon had spoken volumes. She couldn't even meet his gaze at the end, and she'd taken a step back.

And now here she was.

He moved aside and held the door open for her to enter.

Instantly his eyes saw his house the way hers must— in stark comparison to the pristine, high-class Cameron dwelling. They were from two different worlds. It couldn't be more plain from the look on her face.

"I haven't had time to pay much attention to the inside," he explained, then mentally kicked himself for apologizing. He didn't need to apologize, for Pete's sake! It was his house, purchased with his own money. He could do what he damned well pleased with it. He'd be a poor rancher if he put dressing up the inside ahead of his operation.

"I expect you've been busy," she replied softly.

"Something like that." He forced himself to look away, away from the brightness of her eyes that didn't dull even in the dim lamplight.

"I just wanted to see how you were making out with Darcy."

"I can put her down for exactly seven minutes. After that, she starts crying again." He shifted the slight weight on his arm once more. "So I keep picking her up."

Her gaze fell on his arms and desire kicked through his belly, unexpected and strong.

"Babies like to be snuggled," she murmured. "Think about it. If you had spent the first nine months of your life somewhere that was always warm and cozy, you'd want that on the outside, too."

Was it just him, or had her voice hitched a little at the end? He studied her face but saw nothing. He realized she was standing in front of the door with her coat and shoes on. He should invite her in. She'd helped once today. Perhaps she could again.

"I'm sorry, Miss Marchuk…" He paused, hearing how formal that sounded. "Ellison. Please…let me take your coat and come in. I managed to make coffee. I can offer you a cup."

She looked pleased then, and smiled. His heart gave a slight thump at the way it changed her face, erasing the seriousness and making her look almost girlish. She unzipped the fleece and put it in his free hand.

"Coffee sounds great," she replied. "And please…call me Elli. Ellison is what my mother calls me when she's unhappy with something I've done."

She looked so perfectly sweet with her blue eyes and shy smile that he answered without thinking. "You?"

She laughed, the sound light and more beautiful than anything he'd heard in a long time.

"Yes, me. Don't let the angelic looks fool you, Black."

He turned away, leading her to the kitchen while his lips hardened into a thin line. Angelic looks indeed. He'd been captivated by them twice today already. As he considered the bundle on his shoulder, he knew that one complication was enough. No good would come out of flirting with Elli Marchuk. He'd best remember that. His life was here, this house, this ranch. Anything else was transient, capable of moving in and out at a moment's notice. He'd built his life that way on purpose, one planned step at a time. The last thing he wanted was to be foolish and impulsive and end up as unhappy as his parents had been.

Being careful to support Darcy's head, he tried once more to put her into her seat. He'd only just retrieved mugs from the cupboard when she squawked again.

He sighed. There was a reason he'd never aspired to parenthood.

"Have you fed her?"

Elli's voice came from behind him. It sounded like a criticism and he bristled, knowing full well it was a legitimate question but feeling inept just the same.

"Yes, I fed her. She burped, too."

The squawking quieted as Elli picked her up, and Wyatt turned around, trying hard to ignore feelings of inadequacy as Darcy immediately stopped fussing.

"Maybe she's uncomfortable. What do you think, sweetheart?" Elli turned her conversation to the baby.

"What do you think is wrong?" Wyatt asked, putting the coffeepot back on the burner.

A strange look passed over Elli's face, one that looked like guilt and panic. But it was gone quickly. "I couldn't say," she replied.

"But you were so good with her this afternoon." Wyatt put his hands on his hips.

"Lucky, that's all. I just…remembered a few things." The same strange look flitted over her features once more.

Wyatt took the coffee to the table. "You fooled me. You looked like you knew exactly what you were doing." So much that Wyatt had felt completely inept. A feeling he despised. He was used to being the one in control.

Elli and Darcy walked the length of the kitchen and back. After a few moments she admitted, "I haven't really cared for a baby before. The things I thought of were simply things I'd heard about. Not from experience, Mr. Black."

Her chin jutted up, closing the subject but making him want to ask the questions now pulsing through his mind. But then he remembered the old saying, "Don't look a gift horse in the mouth." He'd benefit from whatever insight she had and be glad of it.

"I don't really know what babies need," he admitted. "I

fed her, patted her back like you did, walked her to sleep, but every time I put her down…"

Wyatt almost groaned. Of course. He'd forgotten one important thing. He'd been so focused on getting formula the right temperature that he'd forgotten to check her diaper. Not that he had any clue what to do there either.

Pulling calves and shoveling out stalls was far less intimidating than one tiny newborn.

"She's probably due for a diaper change, isn't she?" He tried to sound nonchalant. This was a perfect opportunity. Elli must know how to change a diaper. He could simply watch her so he'd know better for the next time.

Instead, Elli came around the corner of the counter and placed Darcy back in his arms. "Here you go, Uncle Wyatt," she said lightly. "You get diaper duty. I'll fix the coffee. Cream and sugar?"

Oh, boy, Wyatt thought, looking down into Darcy's pursed face, his smug plan blown to smithereens. He was in for it now.

CHAPTER THREE

WYATT HELD DARCY straight out in front of him. There'd been many firsts for him over the past few months, but this was something completely out of his league. For the first time in his life Wyatt Black was going to change a dirty diaper.

He glanced over at Elli, who was spooning sugar into cups without so much as a concerned glance in his direction. The last thing he wanted to do was look like a fool in front of her twice in one day. He did have a level of pride, after all. And he was generally a competent sort of guy.

But people—babies—were different than cows and horses and machinery. He wasn't nearly as sure of himself when it came to human beings. And not just babies. Each time he met Ellison, his tongue seemed to tie up in knots and nothing seemed to come out the way it should.

He went to the diaper bag, retrieved a diaper and laid the baby on her blanket. He removed her sleepers and some sort of snapped-on undershirt and then the diaper. Good Lord. Wyatt paused, unsure, completely out of his element. Darcy, who'd been sucking on two fingers, took the digits from her mouth and began to squall again, protesting against the cold. He heard Elli go to the fridge and back to the counter. He refused to look up to check if she was watching.

"Hang on, hang on," he muttered, trying to remember

how he'd taken the wet diaper off so he could put the new one on the same way.

"Do babies always cry so much?" he grumbled as he cleaned up Darcy. He reached inside the bag for a new diaper.

Elli came to his side, laying a hand on his arm. "It's the only way they have of saying what's wrong," she said quietly. His arm warmed beneath the touch of her fingers. It felt reassuring and friendly, not the kind of caress he was used to. The touches he was accustomed to were more demanding. Wanting something, rather than giving.

"Do you know how to do this?" he asked, holding up the tiny diaper.

"I haven't done it before…on a baby," she replied, her gaze darting away from his.

"Meaning you've done it *not* on a baby?" he teased, wondering what had put the dark look on her face.

"A doll," she replied, her lips firm. "I've diapered a doll before."

There was something in her voice that reached inside him and grabbed his attention. A defiance, and a defensiveness he hadn't expected. But did he want to know? No, he decided, he didn't want to dig into whatever reasons Ellison did or didn't have for anything. But it didn't mean he was insensitive to her feelings, whatever they were.

"Can we figure it out together?"

Her gaze went back to him now, the irises of her eyes a glowing sapphire. "Wyatt…"

She'd dropped the Mr. Black and used his first name. His gaze dropped to her lips—he couldn't help it. They were pink and finely shaped and very soft looking.

He had to be careful here. Very, very careful.

"Which bit goes at the back?" He shook the white diaper gently.

She pulled back a few inches and looked away. "I think this way," she said, sliding the diaper underneath Darcy's bum, tabs at the back. "And diaper cream. There should be some of that, right?"

Elli watched as Wyatt dug in the bag and pulled out a tube. When he handed it to her, their fingers brushed and she pulled her hand back quickly. The contact seemed to spiral straight to her tummy and she held her breath for a tiny instant.

"It doesn't bite," Wyatt quipped, and Elli forced a smile. Maybe it didn't, but she wasn't so sure about him. Unsure how to respond, she hesitated and looked at the label—it said barrier cream. Logically, it provided a barrier for the baby's tender skin. She smoothed some on with her fingertips, ignoring the odd sensation of knowing Wyatt was watching her.

"You don't want her getting a rash, right? And then…" She pulled the front up and went to fasten the tab. Only, she folded it over so it stuck to itself.

"Heck, I could have done that," he said from behind her, and she heard humor in his tone as her cheeks flamed. Darcy was looking up at her with wide eyes, as if to say, *Come on, people. What's the holdup?*

Elli began to laugh. Lordy, the situation was comical when she stopped to think about it. She heard Wyatt's warm chuckle behind her and then felt his body—*oh, God,* his very hard, warm body—pressed against hers as he reached around her to retrieve another diaper from the bag. "I hope we get it right this time," he murmured, his lips so close to her ear that she could feel the warmth of his breath. She suppressed a delicious shiver.

"We'd better. Or else you're going to run out of diapers in a hurry."

Elli slid the diaper under once more and this time

fastened the tabs securely to the waistband. "Ta da!" She slid away, needing to get away from him and his sexy voice and body. She avoided his gaze, the one she suspected was leveled right at her. Self-conscious, she tugged her thick sweater down over her hips, smoothing it with her palms. "Now you just have to get her dressed again."

She left him there and went to toss away the diaper and wash her hands.

He took out a new undershirt and pajamas and carefully dressed Darcy. Then he placed her in the seat and sighed, moving to tidy up the mess before taking his place at the table. After only a few hours, things that were not usually there were cluttering countertops. Bottles and creams and rattles, where there were normally gloves and keys and perhaps the odd tool. "I haven't had two moments to take a breath. And now I have to say thank you again."

"It was nothing," she replied quietly.

Wyatt's eyes narrowed. She had let down her guard for a moment, but there was something in her voice, something in the way she refused to meet his gaze right now. It had happened several times today. Evasion that told him there was a whole lot to Ellison Marchuk he didn't know. Whatever it was, it was her business. He took a sip of hot coffee.

The immediate issue was solved, but he was beginning to see there would be more. He had no proper baby equipment, a handful of diapers, a few more bottles left. He still had chores around the ranch to look after tonight—and more repairs in the days ahead than he could possibly imagine. Barbara had been a fool to leave her daughter here. Darcy belonged with her mother, not with him.

Elli watched Wyatt over the rim of her cup. She could almost see the wheels turning in his head as he mulled over what to do. She wondered if all that stuff ever erupted. She guessed it did. She suspected it might have been the case the day he'd read her the riot act in his pasture.

She was glad now that she'd followed her instinct and come over. Wyatt was trying to do the right thing, she could see that, but he was totally out of his depth. And he was proud. Watching him try to change the diaper had shown her that. He didn't want to ask for help. Men never did. And who would be the one to suffer? Darcy. Darcy couldn't explain to Wyatt that she was hungry or wet or uncomfortable or tired. Elli wasn't much more qualified. Everything she'd done today had been because of her pre-natal classes. She'd been so afraid of caring for William that she'd signed up for a baby-care course. Until today, she hadn't had a chance to put those classes to use.

Being with Darcy, feeling the tiny body in her arms, smelling the baby-powder scent of her was so bittersweet it cut deeply into her soul, but the alternative had been staying at home and wondering and worrying. What would Wyatt do with her during the day? There would be formula to mix, baths to give, diapers to change. How was he supposed to do that and maintain his ranch? He already looked exhausted.

Her gaze fell on the car seat, and the half-closed lids of the angel within it. Then back to Wyatt, his dark hair curling lightly over his forehead, his eyes dark with fatigue and worry.

"I can't thank you enough, Elli. Twice today I was at the end of my rope."

Elli knew that to get mixed up with the situation was a mistake. He just needed to focus on the good. "You're doing fine," she replied. "Not many men would have the patience to walk the floor with an infant."

"But that's just it." He ran his fingers through his hair.

"I'm not that patient. I…I don't want to lose patience with her."

He wouldn't, Elli was sure of it. Even this afternoon, when Darcy had been screaming incessantly, his expression had been one of utter concern and helplessness. She reached across the table and squeezed his arm. "I think you're just experiencing something every new parent does," she said. "You want to do everything right. I can see how you care for her already, Wyatt. You'll do what's best."

"I wish I had your confidence."

She smiled brightly, wanting to finish her coffee and get out of there. At the moment she didn't know which was more dangerous—Darcy and her baby-powder-scented sweetness or Wyatt's dark sexiness. "You'll be just fine."

She was just finishing the last swallow of coffee in her cup when Wyatt asked plainly, "What if you stayed to help?"

Her mug hit the table with a solid thunk. "What?"

"I know it's a huge imposition, but I need to find Barbara, and do chores, and I can't take her to the barn with me and I can't leave her alone in here. I'd like to hire you to help me."

Heat blossomed in her cheeks. Wyatt didn't strike her as the kind of man who liked admitting weakness. The very fact that he was asking meant he was admitting he was over his head. But she wasn't the solution. "I'm not sure I'm cut out to be a nanny for hire," she replied, hearing the strain behind her voice and knowing the source.

"Look, it'd only be temporary."

"I'm sure there must be services in town, or nearby. Someone more qualified." Caring for a baby full-time? Oh, she could just imagine what her friends and family would have to say about that. They might even be right.

"I can't run the place and watch her at the same time.

I need help. And if it's you…" He coughed. Looked over at the car seat. "The fewer people that know about this— at least for now—the better. I can't be sure someone else wouldn't make that phone call. I just want to keep her safe and do the right thing."

"You trust me, then?"

"Is there some reason I shouldn't?"

She shook her head. "No. I'm just surprised, that's all."

Wyatt took a sip of coffee. "At this point, you're in as much hot water as I am. You're an accessory."

The words came out as serious as a judge, but the tiny upward quirk of his lips was back. Was he teasing? He was, she was sure of it. Warmth seemed to spread through her as she realized it. Moreover, she *liked* it.

Elli didn't know if she should feel relieved or panic. Right now a little of both was running through her veins. This was all she'd ever wanted, in a sense. She'd never been keen on a career the way the other girls in school had been. She'd known all along she wanted to be a mother. To have a house full of children, a home.

She thought once more of her friends and family. They would remind her that this wasn't her home, and this wasn't her family. They would be right. But maybe it was high time she confronted all those hurts. And Wyatt…she could tell he was a proud man, but not too proud to put Darcy's needs ahead of his own. How could she say no to him when his motives were clearly honest?

She looked around her. Lord knew the house needed a feminine touch and it was a sad business, cooking for one. She should know.

"All right," she replied. Considering her unemployed status, she'd be foolish to turn him down. But only for a little while, until he could get things sorted out. She couldn't get attached. And it would be very easy to love the tiny pink slumbering bundle. Elli knew she could love Darcy without even trying. Yes, eyes wide open. That was how she had to look at it.

His breath came out in a rush. "Thank you," he said, his relief clear in each syllable. "You have no idea how grateful I am."

"We have two things to do, then," she said quietly. "First, Darcy needs things. Diapers, formula, clothing. Is this really all her mother left her with?"

Wyatt nodded.

Elli sighed. If she were going to tackle her fears head-on, she might as well tackle them all. Perhaps it was finally time to let go. There was a whole room in Calgary filled with unused baby items. Why was she keeping them? As a shrine to William? It made her sad thinking about it. If she lent them to Wyatt, at least they would be of practical use. She could make a quick trip to Calgary and pick them up, and simply tell him that she'd borrowed them from someone who didn't need them.

"If you're looking at short-term, I know where you could borrow some items. No need for you to buy things you may never use again. It does mean a trip to Calgary tomorrow…"

"I can watch Darcy while you go. I don't want to totally disrupt your life, Elli."

"Thank you, Wyatt." She was glad to be able to go alone. It saved a lot of explaining at both ends. If she didn't have Darcy with her, she could avoid the questions at her parents' house, the probing, motherly kind. And if Wyatt stayed here, she needn't explain why she was in possession of a complete layette.

"Perhaps you can get a lead on Barbara in the meantime."

"I agree," he said, rubbing his lower lip pensively with a finger. "I can't help feeling she's in some sort of trouble."

This wasn't quite as easily solved as baby amenities. Wyatt pushed away from the table and went to the sink, putting his cup within it and bracing his hands on the counter.

"I found her number, but she's not picking up. The address didn't have a street number. It appears to be a Red Deer number, though."

Red Deer. A spark of an idea lit, one that might be able to solve all their problems. Elli got up and retrieved the cordless phone from a dock. "May I? I might be able to find an address."

"By all means."

She dialed in a number, then pressed in more keys for an extension, hoping Joanne was working tonight.

She was, but the query came up empty. Elli hit the end key and thought for a moment.

"She didn't have the baby in Red Deer," Elli said, furrowing her brow. "If she had, there'd be a record of it at the hospital. Let's try Calgary."

"I thought they wouldn't give out patient information," Wyatt said, leaning back against the counter. He ran a hand through his hair, leaving the ends of the nearly black strands slightly mussed, and very, very sexy. Elli swallowed. She was tired, that was all, and the dark outside made the cozy kitchen seem more intimate than it truly was. She could still feel the shape of him pressed against her back earlier and tried to ignore her body's response at the memory.

"They're not supposed to." She hit the talk button on the cordless phone once more. "I used to work in the emergency department. I have friends who will do me a favor, that's all."

A smile creased his face and Elli's breath caught. It was a slow, devilish sort of smile that she hadn't seen up to this point. The kind of smile that could do strange and wonderful things to a woman's intentions.

"Are you breaking the rules, Ellison? Because I had you pegged as Miss Straight and Narrow."

The words stung even as she knew he was teasing. How often had she faced that criticism? His perusal of her sparked her self-conscious streak once more. Why couldn't she have hit the treadmill more often? She crossed an arm around her middle, attempting to hide the flaws he must see. "You wouldn't be far off," she murmured. "But that particular title isn't all it's cracked up to be."

"Your secret is safe with me."

The phone grew slippery in her hand as her nervousness went up a notch. She hadn't been this alone with a man since Tim. In fact, she'd gone to great lengths to avoid it. And now Wyatt was working some sort of spell around her.

She was here for Darcy, that was all. She was being neighborly. There were all sorts of reasons she should have accepted his offer, beyond her cash-flow problem. It was the right thing to do. She might not know exactly what she was doing, but so far she and Wyatt had stumbled their way through the day, hadn't they? Four hands were better than two, right?

"Do you want me to make the call or not?" A note of annoyance crept into her voice. Annoyance at him, and annoyance at herself for worrying so much what Wyatt Black thought. Her mother always said if there was a wounded bird around, Elli wanted to nurse it to health. It had always frustrated her, both the teasing and the criticism inherent in the words. Was it so very wrong? So many times she'd felt her choices were looked down upon simply because they didn't line up with others' expectations. "If you have a better idea…"

Wyatt's smile faded. "Make the call."

She dialed the number she knew by heart.

Five minutes later she hung up, the address jotted down on a notepad. "She had the baby in Calgary. I've got her address in Red Deer. Darcy is five weeks and three days old."

Wyatt's dark eyes met hers. "I think we should go by Barb's place before you go to Calgary, don't you?"

Elli nodded. "It doesn't make much sense to stock up on baby things if she's going to be going back home, right?"

But even as she said it, she got a heavy feeling in her stomach. Barbara wouldn't be there. Looking into Wyatt's face, she could see they both knew it. All tomorrow would be was confirming what they already guessed.

"There's something else," Elli said, putting the paper down on the counter. "She listed you as her next of kin."

Wyatt's mouth fell open and he pushed away from the cupboard. "She did?"

"Either she's telling the truth or she's planned this from the beginning. Somehow…"

"It doesn't make sense, right? If she weren't going to keep the baby, she would have come to me before. Or given it up for adoption."

His thinking was along the same line as hers. "I think so, too."

"Which means Darcy is, likely, truly my niece."

Elli fiddled with the pen. "How can you be so sure?"

Wyatt's brow wrinkled. "Without seeing Barbara, talking to her…I suppose I can't. We both know we're not expecting to find her tomorrow, are we? But Elli, I can't see her making all this up."

Elli couldn't either. Too many things fit together. "What

if she's simply gotten in over her head? She didn't mention the baby's father."

"I get the impression she's doing this alone," he replied, his voice sounding weary.

"Me, too."

"Then the best thing is to find her and talk to her, right?" Wyatt went to the fridge, avoiding her gaze. "Did you have dinner? I haven't eaten. I can make us a sandwich or…"

Wyatt stood, the fridge door open, a packet of roast beef in his hand. The whole conversation felt surreal to Elli. This morning she had been working on an accounting assignment. Tonight she was contemplating sandwiches with Wyatt Black and trying to help him figure out what to do with a baby.

He shut the door of the refrigerator, holding the meat, mustard, and a bag of lettuce. Elli eyed the roast beef, but declined once more as he held up his hand in invitation. She'd eaten already. And the last ten pounds she wanted to lose weren't going to fall off on their own.

"You haven't mentioned any other family."

"That's because there isn't any." He took a plate off a shelf and slapped two slices of bread on it.

"So if Barbara is your sister as she claims…" She let the thought hang.

"Then she's the only family I've got," Wyatt confirmed.

Elli thought about that for a moment. As much as her mother's meddling and worried phone calls drove her crazy, at least she wasn't alone. She knew she could go home and her mom would make her homemade cabbage rolls and perogies and her dad would convince her to stay to watch the hockey game. She couldn't imagine not having them there.

"Can I ask you a question, Elli?" Wyatt went about

building his sandwich, layering lettuce and meat on the bread.

"I guess." As long as it wasn't a question she didn't want to answer. There were lots of those.

"Why did you agree to help me?"

Ugh. She didn't want to answer, simply because there were so many possible responses. Granted, he'd barged into the Camerons' house today and demanded her help, but she'd come back tonight under her own power. It was a chance to feel as if it all hadn't been for nothing. All the hope and loss should have a purpose. Wouldn't this be a chance for something good to come out of all the bad?

And if they were going to care for Darcy, shouldn't she at least make an attempt at being friendly? Surely she could ignore the way her pulse seemed to leap when he was close and how her cheeks flushed when he touched her.

"Look," she said, "I'm going to be honest here. I'm housesitting for the Camerons because I'm at one of those places in my life. I lost my job in some recent streamlining and I…" She felt the words clog up her throat but forged on doggedly. "I got divorced not long ago as well, so I agreed to housesit to help make ends meet. I've been doing some courses online to upgrade my skill set. But for the most part I'm out here in the boonies with only myself for company and feeling fairly useless when all is said and done. When you came barging in today, I wanted to help. Because Darcy is innocent. And because at least I feel somewhat useful again. So you see, you're kind of getting me out of a jam, too."

Wyatt had stopped chewing and put down his sandwich during her speech. Now that it was over, he masked his surprise, finished chewing the bite that was in his mouth, and swallowed.

"I bet that felt good."

And his lips curved. His dark, scary scowls lost all their power when he smiled, replaced with something even more potent.

"It did. Maybe I danced around stuff far too long today. I don't make a habit of going around and spilling my life story." She found herself smiling hesitantly in return. As the seconds drew out she realized they were standing there grinning openly at each other, another notch in familiarity gained. She turned away, embarrassed, shoving her hands into her pockets. Wyatt Black could be darned alluring when he wanted to. And she'd bet he didn't even realize it.

"I'm sorry about your marriage."

His words were sincere, and she sighed. "Me, too. We shouldn't have married in the first place. We were very good at pretending we were what we wanted in each other. He's not a bad man, he just wasn't…the right man." Losing William had been the final blow to a marriage already failing. That was the true grief, the part she wouldn't share with Wyatt. Once William had died, there wasn't any point in keeping up the charade any longer.

"This isn't my usual method of meeting people either," Wyatt acknowledged. "In fact…I tend to keep to myself most of the time."

"I hadn't noticed," she returned, and then felt sorry she'd been sarcastic, even if it had been meant as teasing. It was a reaction to remembering their first meeting and the disapproval on his face as he had spoken so harshly to her. She hurried to cover the barb by turning the tables on him. "So…turnabout is fair play. Now it's your turn to tell me about yourself."

He considered for a moment. "I don't usually talk about myself."

"Me either, but I spilled. Now you owe me." She raised an eyebrow and let a teasing smile touch her lips.

The comfort level in the room rose. Now that Darcy was sleeping peacefully, some of the tension had dissolved and they were suddenly just a man and a woman. There were so many things she didn't know about him, like where he came from and why he'd bought this run-down farm in the first place. He was a big question mark. She'd spent these past weeks all alone. Despite their rocky beginning, he was turning out not to be a bad sort. It was nice to have someone to talk to who didn't know about her past, bringing her baggage to every single conversation. Someone who didn't think of her as *poor Elli*.

"The fact that I'm willing to believe that Barbara is my half sister tells you a bit about my home life, don't you think?"

"I take it your parents weren't divorced, then."

Wyatt shook his head. "Nope. If Barbara's my sister, then it's because my dad had an affair with her mother." As if he suddenly found the sandwich distasteful, he put the remainder on his plate and pushed it away. "I know Barbara's mother had a rough time making ends meet. You can bet that my dad didn't offer any support. If it's true he was her father, he left them high and dry. My dad—"

But then Wyatt broke off, took his plate to the garbage and dumped the sandwich into it.

"I'm sorry."

They were the only words Elli could think of to say. Anything else would sound trite and forced.

"Not your fault," he replied. "And none of it helps us now."

He moved as if to leave the room, but paused beside her, close enough that if he shifted another inch their sleeves would be touching. He smelled like coffee and fresh air and leather—a manly combination that had her senses swimming. Her breath caught simply at the powerful nearness of him.

"Nothing will change who my father was. He wasn't a very good man. Even if he isn't Barbara's father, I know he could have been."

Elli turned her head and looked at Darcy, sleeping so peacefully, and felt her heart give a painful lurch. Her mother and father had somehow found the magic formula. They'd always had a good, strong marriage. It was another reason her own failure cut so deeply. She turned her head back again and found herself staring at Wyatt's shoulder. Now here she was with Wyatt and his own dubious beginnings. Stuck in the middle of them both was Darcy.

"What about you, Wyatt?" She found she wanted to know, for Darcy's sake and for her own. She put her hand on his sleeve. "Are you a good man?"

His head tilted sharply downward as he looked at where her fingers met his arm. Then his eyes, nearly black in the dim kitchen light, rose again and captured hers. Her chest thumped again, but for an entirely different reason. There was something edgy and mysterious about him, all mixed up with a sense of unsuitableness. And the package was wrapped very nicely. Surly or smiling, Wyatt Black was unlike any other man she'd ever known.

"I doubt it," he replied. "I suspected the rumors about my father were true but never asked. I ignored it instead. What does that say about me? I stuck my head in the sand, just like my mother."

Her heart softened at his confession. "You're not like him, though," she said gently. "You're too good for that."

He pulled away from her grasp. "I wish I could be as sure of that as you."

CHAPTER FOUR

DARK CIRCLES SHADOWED Wyatt's eyes when he answered the door the next morning. He looked less than stellar, in faded jeans and a T-shirt that had seen better days. A suspicious spot darkened one shoulder. His hair was mussed on one side, as if he'd crawled out of bed only moments before. The thought made Elli's blood run a little bit warmer.

Elli stepped inside, out of the frosty chill. The mornings this week had been cool enough that she could see her breath in clouds. Wyatt's home, despite the run-down condition, was warm and cozy, and smelled deliciously of fresh coffee.

"Rough night?"

Wyatt raised an eyebrow, let out a small sigh. "Kind of. How did you know?"

She smiled, pointing at his shirt. "Spit up."

He angled his head to stare at the fabric. "I'm just tired enough to not be amused." Even as he said it, he offered a wry grin. "I didn't get more than a few hours. You?"

Elli hadn't slept much either. She'd lain awake a long time, wondering how he was faring with Darcy and if she had settled at all. When Elli had finally drifted into a fitful sleep, it had been to a mixture of dreams of Wyatt and William all jumbled up together. Her head kept drumming out a warning that getting involved was a grave mistake.

But her heart told another story, one of an innocent child caught in an impossible situation.

Personal wounds or not, it just wasn't in her to walk away and forget that someone needed her. Despite what she'd told Wyatt, this had nothing to do with the money. It had been so long since she'd been needed for anything— even if it meant learning as she went along.

"I worried about the two of you a little. How is Darcy now?"

"Napping."

She couldn't help the relief that flooded through her, knowing that things were going smoothly and there was no emergency that needed her attention. As much as she wanted to help, she wasn't very sure of herself. Laughing as she practiced diapering a plastic doll in baby-care class wasn't the same as caring for a live, breathing infant, not knowing how to soothe upsets or interpret crying. Yesterday she'd done a decent job of faking it. But the whole time she'd doubted herself.

They needed to find Darcy's mother and make things right again. She was skeptical they'd find Barbara at her home today. Elli held on to a little strand of hope that her intuition was wrong.

"You look like hell, Wyatt." She followed him into the kitchen, careful to step quietly in her stocking feet. "Did you get any rest at all?"

He shrugged and went for the coffeepot. "A little. Here and there. It was harder than I anticipated."

Elli hadn't expected him to admit such a thing. He seemed so proud and determined. Even yesterday he'd sought her help, but only when it clearly became too much for him to deal with. "Why don't you go sleep now? I'll stay and look after Darcy." The words came out far more confidently than she felt.

He handed her a cup and she heard him sigh once more. The thought had crossed her mind last night that she could stay at his house and give him a hand, as Darcy was sure to wake during the night. That's what babies did, right? Between the two of them surely they would have figured out what to do. But that also would have meant staying there, in his house, *with him*. Her visceral reaction to him last night had been unexpected. It had been attraction: elemental, surprising and strong. Staying overnight would not have been a good idea, and so in the twilight she'd made her way back over the dry grass to her house.

"I'm fine. I've gone on less sleep before, Elli. As soon as I've had something to eat, we can get going to Barbara's. The sooner we talk to her, the better."

"You don't want to go alone?"

"I was thinking that having Darcy with us might be a good idea."

Maybe Barbara would realize she'd made a mistake and Darcy would go back to her mother. Either way, surely Barbara would want to see her daughter and make sure she was okay.

While Elli sipped her coffee, Wyatt fixed himself some toast and spread it liberally with jam. He offered her the plate, almost as an afterthought, but she'd grabbed some yogurt and fruit already and waved him off. The quiet of the morning held a certain amount of intimacy. The past few months she'd spent utterly alone. To share coffee with someone over a breakfast table was a level of familiarity that seemed foreign. But surprisingly, not unwelcome. Perhaps she'd licked her wounds in private long enough.

Darcy was still sleeping when Wyatt came in from his chores, so Elli carefully fastened the safety buckles, getting her ready for the car. "We should put a blanket over her, right?" Wyatt looked up at Elli, waiting for confirmation.

Her heart thumped nervously. How could she explain her own trepidation and lack of experience without delving into a topic she had no wish to discuss? She couldn't, so instead of specific knowledge she relied on simple common sense.

"It is chilly this morning. A blanket is a good idea."

She was thinking about fastening the seat inside the vehicle when she remembered something else, a hang-on from her baby classes. "Babies should be in the backseat, Wyatt. But you just have your pickup, don't you?"

"Do you mean I can't take her in the truck?" He paused, hanging on to the car seat handle. He ran his spare hand through his hair.

"It has something to do with the airbags."

"I am so not cut out for this," Wyatt muttered. "I can't imagine what Barbara was thinking, leaving Darcy here."

Elli said nothing.

"Well? How am I going to put her into the truck?"

Elli's mouth opened and closed. "I don't know." She clenched her teeth, hating to admit she really didn't know.

"I thought women knew about these things."

Feelings of loss bubbled so closely to the surface that Elli grabbed his comment and answered sharply simply to cover. "That's a sexist comment if I ever heard one. And not the first time you've brought it up, by the way. I hate to disillusion you, Wyatt, but just because I was born female doesn't mean I'm hardwired to know a baby's needs."

"All the girls I knew in school babysat."

"You didn't know me in school." Her heart had started tripping over itself. She should have kept her mouth shut. Would he start asking questions now?

Would she answer him if he did? She bit down on her

tongue. No, she would not. She barely knew him. He didn't deserve to know about William. That was a treasure she held locked up, close to her heart.

His face blanked, his eyes and cheeks flattened with surprise. "I'm sorry. I guess I assumed all women want children. I didn't mean to touch a nerve."

And oh, that stung. It had nothing to do with wanting. No baby had ever been wanted more than her own. She blinked rapidly and turned away, opening the front door. "Wait here, and I'll get my car," she replied, knowing her tone was less than cordial but caring little. "We can take it instead." They would go and find Barbara, Darcy would go back to where she belonged and she could go back to ignoring Wyatt just as she had before.

On the walk to the Camerons' house, she felt her temper fizzle out, to be replaced by bleak acceptance. There was no sense questioning why she was helping Wyatt when on a personal level she didn't like him very much. It didn't matter that he seemed to rub her the wrong way or that she felt inept when caring for Darcy. It was quite simply that William was gone and his death had left a vast emptiness within her. But Darcy was not William, and Elli knew it quite well. It didn't stop the need to help. Or to hope that this would ease some of the grief she still felt whenever she thought of her son.

Back at Wyatt's, she helped him fasten the seat in the back, and spread a blanket over Darcy to keep her warm. She looked like a china doll, all pink and white, with delicate lashes lying on her cheeks as she slept. Wyatt paused for a moment, looking at Darcy, and Elli saw the hard angles of his face soften as he gazed down at her. When he caught her watching him, he turned away and got out of the back, shutting the rear door behind him. Elli, on the other side, touched the soft dark hair, wondering at the sheer circumstances that had landed her in the middle of such a situation. Wyatt was trying so hard. He could be irascible, but she also knew that he genuinely cared about Darcy already. He acted as if he was positive Darcy was his niece. And she'd seen the look in his eyes just now when he'd let down his guard. He would do the right thing by her.

The smart thing would be to resolve it as quickly as possible. To make things right and move on.

She motioned toward the driver's side. "Do you want to drive? You know where you're going."

At his brusque nod she handed him the keys. They'd check out Barbara's house first. And if they had no luck, they'd come back here and then she'd be off to Calgary. She could stop at her parents' house while her mom and dad were at work. She hadn't been able to bring herself to get rid of William's things before, but now was a good time. Someone should get some use out of them.

The drive to Red Deer was quiet, and when Wyatt pulled up outside a small bungalow, he got an eerie feeling. There was no car in the yard. The shades at the windows were all closed. No summer flowers bloomed outside like the surrounding yards.

Ellie stayed in the car while Wyatt got out, approached the front door. He knocked, rang the doorbell. No answer. Tried the doorknob; it was locked.

Getting back into the car, he sighed, then his lips formed a grim line. "No one's there. And I don't think anyone has been there for a while."

Ellie's face fell. "What about friends, other family?"

He shook his head. "None that I know of. I haven't been in contact with Barb for years."

What should he do now? The address was the only clue

he'd had. He couldn't even begin to know where to look, and he was still uneasy about bringing any authorities into it. He might not know much about babies, but the more he looked at Darcy the more he believed she was his niece. How could he do that to the only family he had in the world?

He couldn't. So it was up to him to come up with an idea.

"Wyatt, look." Elli pointed to the house next door. An older lady, slightly stooped and with tightly curled gray hair, had come outside. She paused when she saw the car, then picked up a watering can and moved to a tap on the side of the house.

"It's worth a try," he admitted, and got out of the car again.

"Morning," he called out.

The lady looked up, turned off the tap as Wyatt approached. "Good morning." She watched him with curious eyes.

"I'm looking for Barbara Paulsen. She lives here, right?"

"And you'd be?"

Wyatt swallowed. The answer had to be true and it had to put this woman at ease. She was looking at Wyatt quite suspiciously now, and he noticed her fingers tighten on the watering can.

"Family, but I haven't seen her in years. This is the last address I have for her, but nobody's home."

The answer seemed to appease the woman. "She lives here. We don't see much of her, though. She keeps to herself. Hardly ever see that baby she brought home. It's been a beautiful summer and last year she planted a whole bunch of petunias and marigolds. This year, nothing."

A huge lump of unease settled in Wyatt's stomach.

Dropping off a kid to a stranger, changes in behavior…he wasn't getting a good feeling.

"You don't know where she might be, do you?"

"Sorry." The lady put down her watering can. "I saw her leave yesterday morning, but I haven't seen her since. I can let her know you stopped in…"

She left the words hanging in the autumn air.

"Tell her Wyatt was here and I'd like to catch up with her." He aimed a smile in the woman's direction. At this point he felt he could do with any ally he could find.

"I'll do that."

Wyatt thanked her and went back to the car. No further ahead than before, except he now knew that she hadn't been back home since dropping Darcy off at his doorstep yesterday morning.

There was nothing to be done right now except go back to the ranch and try to come up with a plan on the way. Darcy's needs came first. He didn't want to have to go to the police, but if he kept coming up with dead ends, he'd have to.

He got into the car and shut the door, taking a moment to look back at the baby. "Darcy's still sleeping. Let's head home."

Elli nodded. "I'd like to get on the road. There are several things I can bring back that will make caring for her so much easier. A stroller, for one, so I can take her for walks, and something better than a car seat for her to sleep in."

He nodded and backed out of the driveway as Ellie's cell phone rang.

Wyatt kept his eyes on the road as Elli spoke on the phone. Seeing Elli this morning had made the day seem sunnier. For a small moment. Then he'd realized how stupid that was and he'd locked it down.

He passed a car and stared resolutely ahead. She looked so cute and cheerful, so sunny and blonde and…free. Just as she had that afternoon he'd encountered her in his pasture. He'd bet anything she was a real Pollyanna. She'd surprised him with her harsh words this morning, but he supposed he'd deserved it. He'd made a rash assumption, and he hated it when people did the same thing to him.

At least she'd walked away, so he hadn't felt the need to apologize.

Truth be told, he was glad for her help. Any attraction he'd felt last night in the intimacy of his kitchen was easy to tamp down. He wasn't interested. Certainly not in her. She had complication written all over her, and he avoided complications like the plague.

And the bit about his father…there could be no more of that. He'd felt an odd little lift in his heart when she'd expressed such confidence in his temperament. But she didn't know. She had no idea where he came from.

A snuffle sounded from the backseat and he glanced back. Darcy was still sleeping, the tiny lips sucking in and out. She was exhausted from her long night, just as he was. He wished he could catch up on his sleep as easily as she seemed to be able to.

A sigh slid past his lips as Elli chatted on the phone in the background. Like it or not, Darcy was his responsibility for now. If he wanted uncomplicated, he was in the wrong situation.

Elli's voice registered through his thoughts. "He's right here," she said. "Oh. *Oh.* I see. We'll be there soon."

Elli clicked her phone shut. "Wyatt, I have good news and bad news."

He looked over at her, unsettled by the anxiety that darkened the deep blue of her eyes. She bit down on her lip as he scowled back at her. Her teeth caught the soft pink flesh, and he had the momentary urge to kiss away the worry he saw there, to bring back the light, unfettered smile he remembered.

He pulled his attention back to the road. "Hit me."

"I know where Barbara is."

The flash of relief was quickly replaced by the knowledge that this was the good news and the bad news was yet to come; that it was likely about where Barbara was and he wasn't going to like it. "So? Where is she?"

"She was just admitted to the hospital." Elli tucked the phone back into her purse and straightened. "That was my friend—the one I called yesterday. She tried your number first, since you're next of kin. When she couldn't reach you, she took a chance and tried me."

Heaviness settled around his heart. Hospital? Was she sick? Barbara had trusted him because she was ill? How sick exactly? Scenarios ran through his head, none of them good. He kept thinking about her note and how she'd said she couldn't do it. A rock of worry settled at the bottom of his stomach. "Is she okay?"

"She was admitted to the psych ward."

Wyatt swerved and nearly put them off the road. "What?" His hands began to shake on the wheel and he pulled off onto the shoulder, putting the car in Park. Now he knew what had nagged him about Barbara when he'd read the note, the uneasy feeling he hadn't been able to put his finger on. Her mother had passed away when he'd been working in Fort St. John. The next time he was home and out having a beer with a few buddies, he'd heard the gossip about her death.

At the time he'd barely paid attention; small-town rumblings were really not his thing. But now he remembered, and the memory only added to his dread.

"Is. She. Okay." He ground out the words, fearful of the

answer, his mind on the innocent child in the backseat and what a huge dilemma this all was.

"Physically, you mean?"

He nodded, blocking out images that threatened to flood his brain. Awful possibilities. Scary ones.

Her hand came to rest on his forearm, lightly but reassuring. "Wyatt, what is it? You're white as a sheet."

Wyatt's muscles tensed beneath the weight of her fingers. Admitting to a complete stranger that he had a half sister in the world was bad enough. How could he explain to her that he already felt guilty about keeping quiet all these years? When they were kids, it was understandable. It would have caused trouble, trouble he tried to avoid at home. But once he was grown, he could have gone to Barbara and…who knows. He would have been away from his father's censorious anger and his mother's fearful glances. He might have had *family*.

Maybe that hadn't meant anything to his father, but it had meant something to him. When Barbara's mother had died, he'd let shame and embarrassment rule his good sense.

If he hadn't been so weak, maybe she wouldn't have been driven to what he suspected right now.

And he couldn't tell Elli any of it. He clenched his teeth. After all this time, it still ate at him.

"I just…the *psych ward*," he said meaningfully. "That's not good."

"You are listed as next of kin, remember. At least we know where she is now. They'd be contacting you regardless."

"They would?" He turned and studied her profile. Something was troubling her, more than the situation. He'd glimpsed it several times in the past twenty-four hours. As if she was remembering something unpleasant, and it was weighing her down. Much as he was feeling the deeper in he got.

She nodded, but wouldn't look at him. "Oh, yes. A new mom, showing up at the emergency room, needing a psych evaluation?" Finally she turned toward him, and her earnest gaze hit him like a punch in the gut.

"Don't you see? You can't protect her now. The first thing they are going to want to know is where her baby is."

CHAPTER FIVE

ELLI'S WORDS SANK IN, one heavy syllable at a time. Of course. He'd watched the news enough to know that a new mother coming into an emergency room without her baby would set off alarm bells. Added to that he really didn't know what sort of state Barb was in. All he could feel was the heavy weight of knowing that Darcy was relying on him completely.

"Then we have to go there, don't we." The situation had changed now and the weight of responsibility grew heavier on his shoulders. This was no longer a few days of child care—it was now complicated by bureaucracy. Everything would be recorded, noted, in some chart. He felt the walls closing in and hated it.

Elli nodded. "Yes. If we don't, like I said, you're listed as next of kin. You'll be the first place they look for Darcy anyway. And this way, Wyatt…well, it wouldn't hurt to have Darcy looked over, as well."

"Will they take her away?" He looked at Elli, needing her to say no. The very thought of losing Darcy now to complete strangers was incomprehensible. He might not have been prepared, but he was family. Surely that counted for something. He had Elli to help him. It disturbed him to realize how much he needed her.

Elli felt her heart leap at his question, not so much the

words but the way he said them—unsure, and slightly fearful. The man had been up most of the night; he had never
looked after a baby before, by his own admission. But the
concern, the fear she saw on his face now touched her,
deep inside. She wished she could put her arms around
him and tell him it would be fine. But what would he think
of her if she did such a thing? He'd read more into it than
she'd intend. And they had to keep their relationship—the
completely platonic one—separate from Darcy.

There was more to Wyatt than she'd initially thought.
He wanted to do right by this baby. How could she fault
him for that?

She couldn't. She applauded him for it.

He checked his rearview mirror and then pulled a
U-turn, heading back the way they'd just come, back to the
highway. She had to answer him honestly. "I don't know,
Wyatt. I'm not in social services, though I would think they
would want her to stay with her family. Let's just take it a
step at a time, okay?"

Wyatt nodded, but she saw the telltale tick in his jaw
anyway. She reached over and patted his thigh, meaning
to be friendly and supportive. Instead she was struck by
the intimacy of the gesture, the warmth of his denim-clad
leg beneath her fingers, the way the fabric wrinkled just
so at the bend of his knee. The small touch made her feel
a part of something, and that scared her. She pulled her
hand away. "It'll all work out," she reassured him. It had
to. If not for her, for them. She'd do whatever she could to
make sure of it.

She was relieved they had found Barbara, but as they
drove south Elli twisted her fingers. This wasn't how she'd
planned on today playing out. The agenda hadn't included a
visit to the hospital, faced with old coworkers and remind-
ers. And now Wyatt would be with her when she went to

pick up the baby things. How could she possibly explain why she had a roomful of newborn paraphernalia at her mother's? What if she broke down? She didn't want to cry in front of him.

She would get through it somehow, she promised herself as she stared out the window. She had come this far. She would fall apart later. After all, she'd spent months pretending and going through the motions in public. She only had to do it for one more day.

Once they were inside city limits it took just ten minutes to reach the hospital. They parked in the parkade and made their way through to the emergency department.

"I'll stay with Darcy," Elli suggested, taking the baby seat from his hand and adjusting the strap of the diaper bag on her shoulder. She needed space from him, space to think without him always so close by.

She wished that Barbara was anywhere but here, at the Peter Lougheed Hospital. Inside were her old coworkers, many who had been her friends but who had drifted away from her since William's death and her divorce from Tim. There had been so many awkward silences in recent months. But she lifted her chin. What did she have to hide? Nothing. Why shouldn't she face them? Their whispers didn't matter anymore. Steeling her spine, she gave the car seat a reassuring bounce, tightening her grip. It didn't matter, not anymore, and she was tired of running away.

"You go ahead and check with the triage nurse," she suggested to Wyatt. "I'll stay in the waiting room with Darcy. She's waking up and you need to find out what's going on."

Wyatt went to the triage line and spoke to a nurse while Elli sat in one of the padded vinyl seats. She undid the chest strap to Darcy's seat and lifted the baby out, cuddling her in the crook of her arm.

Oh, she felt so good and warm, smelling of powder and the scent that was distinctly *baby*. "Hello, sweetheart," she murmured softly, not wanting to be overheard by the others in the room. She fought away the insecurities that had plagued her on the drive and decided to enjoy whatever time she had with Darcy. Being with her made her feel better, not worse. "You were such a good girl in the car," she whispered, touching the tiny fingertips, looking into the dark blue eyes that stared back at her, slightly unfocused. The little fist moved and clasped her finger tightly.

And just like that, Elli lost her heart to the tiny girl in the pink blanket. She blinked several times and swallowed past the lump that had formed in her throat. "Your uncle Wyatt and I are going to do everything we can for you, little one. I promise."

It felt strange joining their names together that way, but Elli knew she meant it. She already cared about Darcy so much, and Wyatt couldn't do it alone. She just wouldn't deceive herself into thinking it was something more, no matter how much her senses kicked into overdrive when he was around. She wasn't interested in fairy tales. She was interested only in reclaiming her life.

Wyatt returned, his face looking pinched and his gaze dark with worry. "Her doctor wants to speak with us," he explained. "Both of us, and to see Darcy."

She nodded. "Yes, but she's going to be wanting a bottle soon."

Wyatt picked up the empty car seat. "Okay." His shoulders relaxed as he turned away. But then he turned back once more and reached down for her free hand.

His strong fingers gripped hers and her heart thumped in response.

"Thank you, Elli. For everything over the last twenty-four hours. It helps knowing that Darcy is being taken care of, that I…" He paused, and a slight tint of pink stained his cheeks. "That I don't have to do this alone. It means more than you know."

He spun back toward the sliding doors, which opened on his approach. Elli's jaw dropped a little as she followed him; he expressed more confidence in her than she had in herself. Taken care of? Elli was feeling her way through this as much as Wyatt. But she couldn't stop the glow that spread through her at his words. Her confidence had taken such a beating since William's death. There were times she felt she'd failed at everything—wife, mother, even her job. Wyatt Black—ornery, pigheaded cowboy—had offered more encouragement than anyone else had in the past months. Not just with Darcy, though that was part of it. When he looked at her, she almost felt pretty. Desirable. That was as much of a miracle as anything.

She gently touched Darcy's nose as she passed through the doors. "I'd better be careful, huh, little one?" she whispered. "Before long I'll start *liking* him, and then we'll really be in trouble."

They were shown not to a curtained exam room but a different room, one with four walls and a door that the nurse shut behind them. They waited only moments before the doctor came in and shut the door behind her.

"Mr. Black, I'm Dr. McKinnon." The young woman held out her hand and Wyatt shook it. "I'm the one who admitted Ms. Paulsen earlier this morning. We admitted her for postpartum depression, and we'll be meeting and assessing her over the next several days."

"I'm just glad she's all right," Wyatt replied, but Elli noticed his face was inscrutable. The emotion he'd shown her only moments ago was gone, and in its place a wariness she thought she might understand. This hospital had been her home away from home, yet she was no more looking forward to the questions she'd face today than Wyatt was. At least she had the choice not to answer. A month ago standing in this department would have filled her with dread. Today, with Wyatt beside her, it didn't matter quite as much.

Dr. McKinnon looked at Elli now, smiling easily. "And Elli. It's good to see you, but surprising under these circumstances."

"Thank you," she replied carefully.

"Mr. Black, I'm going to talk to you about your sister's condition, but as you can understand there was significant concern about her baby."

"Yes, she left Darcy with me yesterday," Wyatt offered. Elli noticed he didn't elaborate on how Barbara had left her. He was trying to protect his sister. Every time there was a development, Elli could see how Wyatt took on the responsibility himself. It was admirable, but she imagined it must be a very heavy load to carry at times.

"At what time?"

"Late morning," he replied without missing a beat. He met the doctor's eyes steadily. "I'm not used to babies, so Elli has been giving me a hand." He smiled at Elli now, but the smile had an edge to it. He was nervous, she realized, and seeking her support.

She smiled back at him, and then at Dr. McKinnon. "Between the two of us, we've muddled through."

"Darcy does need to be examined, though." Dr. McKinnon was firm. "Elli, I'm going to have Carrie show you to a curtain and we'll have the peds on call come down. In the meantime, I can speak to Mr. Black about his sister."

McKinnon's voice softened as she rose and stopped to touch the downy crown of Darcy's head. "Would that suit, young lady?"

Darcy's answer was to pop two fingers into her mouth and start sucking.

"I'm afraid she's hungry," Elli replied. "Could someone heat a bottle for me?" She no longer had access to the rest of the department, nor did she want it. Her presence had already been noted, she suspected. People here knew her. There would be questions and murmurings when she showed up with a baby in tow. She knew how it looked. Granted, it was awkward considering Tim was still on staff. But her job loss had been cutbacks, pure and simple.

She wondered if she'd stayed married to Tim if it would have made a difference when it came to the chopping block. Then she wondered if she would have wanted it to. She had just enough pride to know the answer right away. Despite the financial hardship, being made redundant was a blessing, freeing her to begin again.

She resolutely clipped Darcy back into her seat and picked up the bag of supplies. Well, let them talk. It wouldn't change anything. She didn't work here anymore, wouldn't have to see these people on a regular basis like before. She was starting over.

"I'm sure that can be arranged. I'll be right back, Mr. Black."

She opened the door and Wyatt stood. "Stay with her," he said to Elli. There was a fierceness in his voice. "I'll come find you."

Her heart thumped at his words, knowing he meant them. Even knowing he meant them for Darcy, the effect was the same. It made her feel warm, protected. Wyatt would do whatever was in his power to protect them both.

She'd never met a man quite like him before.

"I won't leave her side," Elli promised, wishing she could touch him somehow to reassure him. She was too shy to do such a thing beneath the gaze of an old colleague, so she offered a small smile instead and cast her gaze down, following Dr. McKinnon out the door.

At the desk her friend Carrie hung up the phone. "Ellison." She got up and came around the desk, giving her a quick hug. "Gosh, it's good to see you."

"Hello, Carrie." Elli couldn't help but smile at the warm reception. Of all the staff, Carrie had been the one who'd remained the most normal when it came to Elli's ordeal. "Interesting circumstances, huh?"

The clerk's face broke into a wide grin in response. "You know the E.R. Something needs to break up the boredom."

"Can you show Elli to a curtain, Carrie? And page Dr. Singh—we need to do a physical on the baby." Dr. McKinnon smiled at Elli. "It is good to see you again, Ellison."

She went back to continue her meeting with Wyatt while Elli and Carrie looked at each other.

"Let's find you a spot," Carrie suggested, and led the way through the twists and turns of the unit. She entered a curtained cubicle and put the car seat next to the bed.

"Thank you, Carrie. Could I trouble you to heat a bottle?"

"Of course you can. What a shock, though, seeing you here with a baby, when…"

But Carrie's voice drifted off and her cheeks colored. "I'm sorry, Elli. That was insensitive."

"You were going to say 'when it's so soon after William died.'"

"We were all so sad for you and Tim."

Funny, Elli realized—saying William's name had come more easily than she'd expected. And the mention of Tim didn't upset her as it might have. Maybe she had Wyatt to thank for that, too. If he hadn't asked for her help, she'd still be hiding away instead of facing things.

"It gets better," she said, trying a smile for Carrie's benefit. "I'm not sure I'll ever get over losing William completely, but at some point you have to start living again."

Elli stood rooted to the floor, dumbstruck. Had she actually said that? *Start living again?*

"Can't say as I blame you…your Mr. Black is pretty easy on the eyes."

Elli felt her body grow warm all over at the mention of Wyatt. "It's not like that…."

"What a shame."

She looked over and found Carrie watching her with an amused expression. "It's that obvious?"

"He's very good-looking. Tim would be jealous."

Elli shook her head. "I doubt it. It doesn't matter anymore anyway."

She realized she meant it. It didn't matter. How had all this happened since yesterday? Yesterday she'd merely been thinking about what to do next. Afraid of taking a wrong step.

"I'll go heat your bottle." Carrie tapped her arm lightly and scooted out of the cubicle.

Elli sat on the edge of the bed, covering her mouth in surprise. She thought of Wyatt's wild eyes as she'd opened her door and chuckled. "Well, I guess when you're thrown in the deep end, you have to swim," she murmured.

A few minutes later Carrie returned with the warmed bottle. "I wish I could stay and chat," she said, taking a quick moment to sit in the seat next to Elli. Elli picked Darcy up and cradled her in her elbow, then reached for the bottle. As Darcy began to suckle on the nipple, Carrie let out a sigh. "I've missed you. But I can only spare a minute. Forgive me, Elli, but…does it hurt? Just knowing?"

Elli didn't need help interpreting. Of course it hurt, knowing what she'd missed. She smiled wistfully at the young woman who had been her coworker for nearly two years. "A little. She's precious, isn't she?"

"A doll. And this Black, he's her uncle?"

Elli ignored the leap in her pulse at the thought of Wyatt. "Yes, and he lives next door to where I'm staying at the moment. Thank you for calling me today," she added. "We'd gone to Barbara's home to find her but came up with nothing."

"It was just a chance I took, after you called me last night. I'm glad it worked, though. That woman came in here all alone, poor soul. She needs someone in her corner."

And that someone was Wyatt. Elli could think of few better.

Darcy took in too much milk, coughed, spluttered and sent up a wail. At the same moment Carrie's pager went off.

"I've got to go."

"I'll be fine," Elli replied, settling down in the chair and giving Darcy the bottle once more.

Familiar sounds, hospital sounds, filtered through the curtains—the hushed footsteps of nurses and the quiet, confident tones of doctors. The odd moan or catch of breath of those in pain, and the sound of gurney wheels swishing on the polished floors. For a moment the memory of it was a bittersweet stab in her heart, a reminder of a past life that she'd once considered perfect. She was at home here, the sounds and smells so familiar they seemed a part of her. Once she'd waited out a particularly tense bout of Braxton Hicks contractions and Tim had checked on her every ten minutes.

With a free finger Elli stroked Darcy's hair. She had to stop thinking about what might have been. It never *would* be. She was so tired of feeling sorry for herself. It was exhausting. Nothing she could do could bring her own precious baby back. Being with Wyatt and Darcy had made her face it head-on, making her want to get on with simply missing him rather than the futility of wishing for what she could never have.

She looked down into Darcy's face—the closed eyes with the lids that were nearly transparent, the way one tiny hand rested on the side of the bottle as if to keep it from disappearing. "Who knew," she whispered, "how important you'd turn out to be?"

The curtain parted and Wyatt stepped through, with Dr. McKinnon behind him. "How's she doing?"

Wyatt's eyes were troubled, but the fear had subsided slightly. She smiled up at him. "We're right as rain. How about you? What's the news on Barb?"

"I'm going to see her," he replied. He reached out to tuck the blanket more securely around Darcy's feet and Elli noticed his hand was trembling.

"Wyatt?"

He finished fussing with the blanket and looked up. "They're letting me visit her, and then…" He cleared his throat. "And then I have to talk to a social worker."

The tone of his voice made it sound like the seven tortures of hell. Wyatt was a private man—Elli had sensed it from the beginning. He'd been reluctant to give her any sort of details at all, skirting around issues to give her just enough answers. Elli knew that speaking to social workers was going to be intrusive at best.

She tried to smile reassuringly. "All signs point to her trying to get help, Wyatt. This is a good thing. And it fits with the letter she left you, don't you think?"

"I hope so. I just…I don't want her going into foster care, Elli."

"I know that, and they will, too. Once Darcy's had her checkup, I'll meet you. How about—the cafeteria downstairs?"

"Okay."

Elli was aware of Dr. McKinnon waiting for Wyatt and wished for some privacy so they could talk without being overheard. "Unless you'd rather I went with you." Elli doubted Wyatt was prepared for what he'd see in the psychiatric ward. "It's good she's admitted, but it's not an easy place to visit, especially the first time."

"Knowing you're caring for Darcy is all I need," he responded, his gaze sliding away from her. "I'll find you once I've spoken to her."

He looked so uncomfortable her heart went out to him. She stood, Darcy resting along her shoulder, and went to stand in front of him. He was desperately trying to do the right thing, and he hadn't seen his half sister in years. These were hardly optimum circumstances for a reunion.

Damn the doctor and whatever scuttlebutt was filtering through the unit. Elli didn't care anymore. She lifted her free hand and touched his cheek lightly. "It will be fine," she murmured. "Darcy's safe and Barbara is in good hands."

He placed his hand over hers, sandwiching it between his palm and his cheek. It was warm there and soft, with only a slight prickle of stubble from his jaw. "Why are you being so helpful, Ellison? This is not your problem." He closed his eyes for a few moments as he inhaled and exhaled slowly.

"Because I can see you're trying to do the right thing and at great personal sacrifice."

Without saying another word, he turned her palm, pressed a quick kiss into it. His lips were warm and firm in contrast to the stubble on his chin. Emotions rushed through her at the tender gesture, so sweet and so unexpected.

He cleared his throat and squared his shoulders. "The cafeteria," he reminded her, and without another word left the curtained area.

Elli pressed her hand to her lips, shocked at the intimate touch, flustered, and…my word. She was pleased.

This wouldn't do. Wyatt was only reacting to the situation. He had said it himself. He was thanking her for helping, that was all. Everyone's emotions were running high. She couldn't read too much into it.

She struggled to remember that he'd never had any interest in getting to know her before Darcy had come on the scene. They'd been neighbors for two months and had crossed paths only once. And yes, maybe they were getting to know each other better, but she also knew that if they'd met elsewhere—on the street, in a shop—his head wouldn't have been turned. Heck, he'd shouted at her the first day they'd met. She was still carrying around an extra ten pounds she'd put on during her pregnancy, and her looks were what she'd consider strictly average. The caress meant little when she put it in perspective.

She took a moment to change Darcy's diaper, slightly more comfortable with the task than yesterday as she dealt with sticky tabs and squirming, pudgy legs. In less time than she might have imagined, Darcy was dressed and happy. Elli took out a rattle and smiled as the baby shook it in her tiny fist.

The curtain parted once more and Dr. Singh entered. He saw Elli and his face relaxed into a pleased expression. Then his gaze dropped to Darcy, kicking and cooing on the white sheets of the bed.

There was a flash of consternation on his face and Elli felt a sickening thud in the pit of her stomach. She'd conveniently forgotten why she'd avoided coming to the hospital over the past few months. Now she remembered. She hadn't wanted to have to deal with explanations and platitudes. Carrie was one thing; they'd been close friends. But every other person she knew in this hospital saw her as Elli who had married a doctor, carried his child, lost it, lost her marriage and finally her job. *Poor Elli.*

"I understand this is our missing Baby Paulsen." He covered the momentary awkwardness with a smile.

"Yes. Her name is Darcy."

"You brought her in?" He went to the bed and watched Darcy for a moment while Elli looked on anxiously.

"Yes and no. Darcy has been with Barbara Paulsen's brother, and he's a friend of mine. I've been giving him a hand."

"He must be a very good friend."

"A friend in need is a friend indeed," she quoted, trying to make light of it. She knew how it would look if she admitted they'd only truly become "friends" yesterday. But looking at the outside of a situation was rarely like looking at it from the inside, so she kept her mouth shut.

Elli waited while Dr. Singh gave Darcy a thorough check. He turned to her and smiled. "She's perfectly healthy," the doctor stated.

Elli stared into Dr. Singh's chocolate eyes, surprised at the concern she saw there. Was there something wrong with Darcy he hadn't wanted to say?

Dr. Singh sat on the edge of the bed and rested his hands on his white coat. "This isn't about Darcy," he said quietly. "It's about you, Elli. I want to know how you're doing since William's death."

His quiet concern ripped at her insides at the same time as it was comforting. People didn't know what to say to her—she got that. But no one asked how she was, or spoke

William's name. Even today—it was the first time she'd been able to say his name without her voice catching. To everyone else he was always called "the baby," as if he'd never been named. As if keeping him nameless would make it somehow easier. It wasn't.

"I'm doing okay. Better now." She was happy to realize it was true.

"How did you end up caring for Darcy?"

"Wyatt didn't know what to do," she said, trying to lighten things by giving a light laugh. "Of course, neither did I, really, but I was conveniently just next door." She smiled then, genuinely. "Tell me, Dr. Singh, how can a person resist an adorable face like that?" She motioned toward Darcy, who seemed intent on the rattle clenched in her tiny fist. The pieces clacked together as she shook her pudgy hand. Only, Elli knew it wasn't just Darcy's adorable face that counted. Wyatt's was becoming more of a pleasure each time they were together.

Dr. Singh smiled. "You can't. I just want to make sure you're okay with this. I know you must be grieving still."

Elli swallowed, but was surprised that the tears she expected were nowhere to be found. When was the last time before today that she'd thought of William without crying? She was getting stronger. "I am grieving, of course. But it's different now, and I think helping care for Darcy is good for me. I can't always wish for what will never be. I have to look forward rather than backward."

"Good." Dr. Singh put his hands on his knees and boosted himself up. "I am glad to hear it. It is good to see some roses in your cheeks, Ellison."

The roses bloomed pinker than before, because Elli knew it was Wyatt and his caress that had put them there. And she didn't want to start having feelings for him. She was finally just starting to get a handle on her emotions.

The last thing she needed was to get mixed up with someone again. To rebound.

Maybe she should just look upon this time as a lovely gift. For the first time in months she felt alive.

"Thank you, Dr. Singh. Wyatt will be involved with social services because I know he wants to look after Darcy until Barbara can again. Would it be okay if he listed you as her pediatrician?"

"By all means."

Elli gathered her things. "It was good to see you, Doctor."

"And you." He smiled, then left the room with a flap of his white coat.

Now at loose ends, Elli realized she hadn't eaten all day. When there was no sign of Wyatt in the cafeteria, she hefted the car seat and made her way to the coffee chain near the west doors. A steamed milk and a muffin would do the trick, she thought. Carrying the paper bag and car seat while balancing a hot drink took more dexterity than she'd expected, and she went slowly back to the cafeteria, where she could at least sit down and wait.

When she returned to the entrance of the cafeteria, she came face-to-face with Wyatt. It took only two strides of his long legs before he caught up to her. "Where have you been?" He whispered it, but there was a hard edge to the words, so very different than the last time he'd spoken to her.

"I just went to buy a steamed milk," she explained, feeling the color drain from her face at his thunderous expression.

"Your timing stinks." He ground out the words.

"Is there a problem?" A woman's voice came from beyond Wyatt's shoulder and Elli closed her eyes. She'd disappeared with Darcy at the same time Wyatt had come to find her with…

"Ellison Marchuk, this is Gloria Hawkins from Child and Family Services."

Elli handed Wyatt the hot cup, her appetite lost. "Ms. Hawkins," she said quietly, adjusting Darcy's weight and holding out a hand.

CHAPTER SIX

IT WAS PAST DARK BY the time they arrived home again, and on the drive Wyatt had taken the time to cool down. Now he stared around his house with new eyes. In the space of little more than a day his whole life had changed. This run-down bungalow and farm had been enough for him. He'd bought it seeing the potential, and he had lots of time to fix it up the way he wanted. Or so he'd thought.

But this was a bachelor's house, sparsely decorated and functional. He had to make it a home, somewhere welcoming and comfortable rather than a simple place to lay his head. There was more at stake. It needed to be a place for *family*. No matter what happened, he had family now.

Elli was in the kitchen, cooking some sort of chicken dish for dinner. Already he could see small changes in the house, and it put him off balance. His desk was tidy—pens in a can she'd unearthed from somewhere. She'd gone through and straightened what things he had, giving the house a sense of order that seemed foreign. He shouldn't feel as if Elli was taking over—he knew that. She was going above and beyond with helping. But somehow he did. As though the house wasn't his anymore.

Darcy was watching from her spot in the car seat, her dark eyes following Elli's every move from stovetop to counter. Wyatt stood at the doorway, nursing a beer, fighting the false sense of domesticity. It was all temporary, not real. Darcy was not his child, and Elli was not his wife. It was a short-term situation. Before long things would go back to normal.

He couldn't deny he'd had flashes of attraction over the past day and a half, but he wasn't truly interested in Elli. Elli didn't care for him either, he knew. Anything that had happened so far was because of the extraordinary position they were in. When everything settled, they'd each go back to their own lives. He got the feeling that she was too much of a city girl to want the isolated life in the country for long. He couldn't get used to seeing her here. Darcy, on the other hand, was his niece. As things played out, he knew he wanted to have a home where she and Barbara could come to visit as often as they liked.

His mom would have wanted that. She would have wanted him to accept Barbara and make her welcome. Despite her difficult life, he didn't know anyone with as generous a heart as his mother.

But for now, this was reality, until Barbara was well enough to look after her daughter. There was work to do to make this a family home. He'd promised it to the caseworker at the hospital. He'd been so nervous, afraid she would take Darcy away into foster care anyway. And he'd growled at Elli for not being there right away. She had done nothing wrong. Instead Elli had been calm, and she had been the one who had carried the meeting. She'd been composed and articulate and reassuring when Wyatt had been scared to death. He wouldn't let that happen again.

"Do you like squash?"

Elli's voice interrupted his thoughts and he straightened. "Yeah, I guess."

"You guess?" She finished wiping a spoon and put it down on the counter. Her blue eyes questioned him innocently, but he knew there was little of innocence in his thoughts. Lord, but she was beautiful. Not in a flashy way either. At first her looks seemed ordinary. But they grew on a man—the glowing complexion, the blond streaks in her hair. The way her clothes seemed to hug her curves and how those curves caught his eye. Most of all, it was her eyes. Elli wasn't his woman, but those eyes got him every time.

He'd looked into them earlier today and had forgotten himself. That caress in the E.R. had been a mistake, brought on by her understanding and the fact that she was simply there for him. He'd felt it again when he'd tried to explain to the caseworker why keeping Darcy was so important to him, while still protecting himself. He'd fumbled the words, but Elli had put her hand on his arm and smiled at him.

"My mom used to bake squash in the oven," he said, coming forward and putting his empty beer bottle beside the sink.

Elli smiled, her face a sea of peace and contentment. She looked so at home, so…happy. He wondered how it could be so when he'd dragged her into this situation, turning her life upside down as well as his.

"I can do that," she answered. "As soon as I find a baking dish."

He found her a proper pan and put it on the counter. "You like to cook," he stated, starting to relax. His version of cooking consisted of baked potatoes and frying a steak.

"I do," she answered, still smiling. She took a small squash and quartered it, scooped out the middle and slathered the orange surface with a paste of brown sugar and butter. She slid it into the oven beside the chicken in mere seconds. "My mom taught me how to cook when I was just a girl. It was one of the things we did together. I make a wicked cabbage roll. Though I've never quite mastered the technique of her perogies. She makes them from scratch and they're the best thing I've ever eaten."

Wyatt leaned back against the counter and nudged Darcy's hand with his finger. The baby grabbed it and batted her hand up and down while Wyatt smiled. He liked her—when she wasn't crying. A baby's needs were uncomplicated and he liked that. Food, a dry bottom and love, he supposed. A simple love, a warm place to cuddle into and feel safe.

At that moment he missed his mother with an intensity that shocked him. It had been five years, but now and again the grief seemed to come from nowhere. His finger stopped moving with Darcy's and he swallowed.

"Wyatt?"

Elli was watching him curiously. "Are you okay? You look funny all of a sudden."

He shook off the sadness. What had come over him? He never indulged in sentimentality. Maybe it was Elli. She reminded him of his mother, he supposed. His mom had been the one to make their house a home when he was growing up, and he realized Elli was doing the same thing now with him, and Darcy.

"I was just remembering my mom," he replied carefully. "You remind me of her, you know. She was always cooking and smiling. I didn't realize how much I missed it."

Her smile faded and a tiny wrinkle formed between her brows. "I remind you of your *mother?*"

Apparently that wasn't what she had expected to hear. Belatedly he realized that most women wouldn't find that an attractive comparison. He stumbled over trying to find the right words to explain. "Only in the very best ways, Elli. She was the one who made our house a home. You're doing the same thing for Darcy and me without even real-izing it."

Damn it, was that pain on her face? What had he said that was wrong? He was trying to pay her a compliment and it was coming out all wrong. "I'm sorry if I said something to upset you."

"You didn't," she murmured, but she wouldn't look him in the eye anymore.

"Do you want to talk about it?"

He couldn't believe he was asking. But he'd heard snatches of whispered conversations today. There was more to Elli, and he found himself curious. The people at the hospital where she'd worked knew. But she'd said nothing to him about why her marriage had failed. And the bits he'd heard left him with more questions than concrete information.

"There's nothing to talk about," she insisted, moving back to stir something on the stove. But he knew. She was covering. He'd done it a thousand times himself.

"How did Barbara seem to you? You never said." She still had her back turned to him, but there was a slight wobble on the word *said*. He *had* touched a nerve. A part of him wanted to pursue it and another part told him to leave it alone. If she'd wanted to talk, she wouldn't have changed the subject.

But he wasn't sure how to proceed. Talking about Barbara was a loaded topic, too. The moment he'd entered the hospital room Barbara had started crying and apologiz-ing. Her doctor had gone with him, and Wyatt had let her take the lead. Calm but compassionate. Problem was, Wyatt had never seen himself as a very compassionate man.

So Barbara had cried and he'd held her awkwardly. She'd apologized and he'd tried to say what he thought were the right words—that the most important thing right now was for her to get well. He'd insisted that Darcy was well taken care of.

"Seeing her was odd. She was like the Barbara I remembered, and yet she wasn't. There was an energy about her that wasn't quite right."

Elli nodded. "Her perspective is so skewed right now, and she's afraid. When I worked in the E.R.—"

She halted, but Wyatt wanted to know. She'd worked at the very desk where he'd checked in today. How had today affected Elli? It had been so hectic he hadn't asked.

"When you worked in the E.R.," he prodded.

"I was just going to say we saw lots of mentally ill patients. People who for one reason or another couldn't cope. That Barbara could recognize that in herself, that she checked herself in…" Elli met his gaze. "It was a brave thing to do. Certainly nothing to judge her for."

"Did I judge her?" He straightened in surprise. He hadn't, had he? Had he judged or simply been concerned?

"No, but I did. The moment I saw her note and saw Darcy. I'm sorry about that."

She turned back to the stove. Wyatt stared at her back for a few moments before stepping forward and simply putting a hand on her shoulder.

"So did I. I asked myself how a mother could do that to a child. Today I realized how much courage it took for her to do what she did."

"Thank you," Elli whispered.

He took his hand away, already missing the feeling of warmth that had radiated through his palm. He put his hand in his pocket instead. "Three times she asked where Darcy was. Eventually she got so agitated the doctor suggested I come back later. She reassured her that Darcy was getting the best of care. I felt a lot of pressure when he said that."

"You're doing the best you can, and she's got a clean bill of health. Don't be so hard on yourself."

But it was impossible not to be. It highlighted his failure as a brother, if nothing else. Maybe if he'd made an effort years ago, this would never have happened.

"She's going to be okay—that's the main thing. It was easier speaking to her doctor. She seemed very pleased that Barbara was asking about Darcy so much. That she'd taken steps to make sure the baby was looked after."

A memory flashed into his brain, of his mother when he'd graduated from high school. He'd been in a suit she'd bought on discount in Red Deer, and his father was nowhere to be found. *Don't think about your dad,* she'd said, taking his hand. *You remember this. Family is important. Don't let your dad teach you otherwise. Family is everything.*

She'd gotten tears in her eyes then. *You're everything, Wyatt.*

He realized now that she had to have known about Barbara all along. And still she'd stayed with his father. Why? He'd never know now.

"Asking for help is a positive sign," Elli agreed. She fiddled with a set of old pot holders.

"I should have been there," he replied, the confession taking a load off his shoulders. "I knew deep down she was my sister. I knew what had happened to her mother and I pretended she didn't exist. If only…"

"Don't." Elli's voice intruded, definitive and strong. "Do not blame yourself. You were a teenage boy. There is no before. There is only now." She blinked rapidly. "There is only now."

The words seemed to catch her up so completely his thoughts fled. "Are we still talking about Barbara? Or about you?"

His heart pounded as she turned her eyes up at him

once more. He couldn't resist her when she did that. Years of choosing to be alone hadn't made him immune to a beautiful woman. He could rationalize all he wanted, but the truth was he didn't want just any woman—he wanted her. He wanted a connection with another human being, something to anchor him so he didn't feel this was spinning out of control. Elli seemed to get to him without even trying.

He stepped forward, cupped her face in his hands and kissed her. All the self-recriminations vaporized; all the doubts fled in a puff of smoke. Nothing mattered for a few blissful seconds. There was only Elli, her soft skin, the moist taste of her lips, her body close to his. God, he'd needed this, badly. And when she made a soft sound in her throat, he deepened the kiss.

Surprise was Elli's first feeling, quickly chased away by the sensation of his lips on hers and his hands cradling her face like a chalice. Her emotions had been riding close to the surface all day, facing all the things she should have faced long before now. But she'd held herself together, through the hours at the hospital and even facing William's things at her mother's. Tonight, alone with him, the words had sat on her tongue burning to be said. And still she couldn't. But somehow he seemed to know anyway.

Oh, he smelled good. She could still smell the remnants of the aftershave he'd put on this morning, something simple and rugged. His lips were soft, the faint stubble on his chin was rough and the combination was electrifying. She heard a sound—coming from her own throat—and he deepened the contact in response.

She met him equally, nerves and excitement rushing in waves throughout her body as she slid her arms around his waist and put her hands on his back, pulling him closer.

The points where their bodies touched were alive and

she rejoiced, knowing it had been several long, lonely months since she'd felt such an intense connection with anyone. Elemental, raw and feminine.

He gentled the kiss, sliding his hands over her shoulders and down her arms as his lips parted from hers. His mouth hovered mere inches away from hers as their breath came rapidly, the sound echoing in the quiet kitchen.

"Why did you do that?" She whispered it, but the syllables sounded clearly in the silence. His kiss had made her feel like a woman again. But she wanted to hear him say it. She needed him to admit to the chemistry. She had despaired of ever feeling it again, of inspiring it again in a man.

"I don't know what came over me."

For once, Elli refused to let her inner voice speak. She knew what it would say—that he didn't find her attractive. The inner voice would make excuses. But she didn't want excuses. She wanted to believe in the power of the action itself. She wanted to believe in the attraction she'd felt humming between them.

She desperately needed to believe she'd been worth it. As long as he didn't apologize. She couldn't bear that.

"So it was because…" His hands rested on her arms and she kept hers about his waist. She wanted to keep touching him, just a few moments longer. He was so warm and strong.

"You keep looking at me and I—"

He broke off, pushed backward and dropped his hands.

"You?" she prompted. She wanted him to say the words. Her whole body begged him.

"I couldn't seem to help it."

The sweetness of it filled her. This was what she'd been missing. How long had it been since she'd felt desirable?

How long had she been picking apart things she'd done, words she'd spoken, how she looked? Her hair was too flat, her bottom too wide. She still carried weight around her middle from her pregnancy. But handsome Wyatt Black didn't seem to care about any of it.

His gaze probed hers. "But it was probably a mistake. We can't let this complicate things, Elli. We have to put Darcy first."

And just like that the bubble popped, taking the fizz out of the moment. Of course they needed to put Darcy first. He'd told the caseworker that she was a friend helping him care for his niece. He'd stressed how Darcy was the focus for both of them at this moment, and how having two people was vastly better than one. The baby was first priority. And that was as it should be. She was letting her vanity get in the way.

But it hurt. And she didn't know why. It shouldn't matter. Where would it lead? Nowhere. He was absolutely right.

"Of course we do." She gathered her wits and retrieved the pot holders, then went to the oven and took out the chicken. It *did* matter and she *did* know why. She was seeing a new side to Wyatt and she liked it. She was starting to care about him.

"Elli—I don't know how to thank you for all of this." He looked down at Darcy and Elli's heart wrenched at the tenderness in his face. Did he realize he was half in love with his niece already?

She should be thanking *him*. For pulling her out of her half existence and giving her a purpose again. For feeling, for the first time in months, like a woman. But she couldn't say any of that without explaining what came before, so she merely replied, "You're welcome."

Silence was awkward so she made herself busy, filling a

plate for each of them, and with Darcy napping, they took them to the table.

The light was low and so were their voices as they discussed what had happened at the hospital. It wasn't until Wyatt suggested she stay over that she had a moment of pause. A big moment.

"What do you mean, stay over?"

Wyatt put down his fork. "We told the caseworker that you were helping me, right?"

"Well, I know, but…"

"But I have livestock to look after as well, Elli. I know she is my responsibility, but I can't see how I can be up with her all night and work all day." He paused, looked down at his plate and back up again. "We should discuss your wage. I don't expect you to do this for nothing. You've done more than enough the last two days."

Elli's face flamed. That wasn't where she wanted this to go, a discussion of money. "We can talk about it later."

"But Elli…"

"There's no rush, Wyatt. Helping you with Darcy is not taking me away from anything more important, I promise."

"Then you'll stay?"

The idea was so seductive. She wouldn't admit it, but the Camerons' house was big, beautiful and incredibly lonely. Here at Wyatt's, despite the general frayed-around-the-edges look, there was life and conversation and purpose. But what would she be getting into? She had just admitted to herself that she was starting to care for Wyatt. *He'd kissed her.* Being here 24/7 was just setting herself up for hurt down the road.

"I'm right next door if you need me."

His gaze pinned her for several seconds before he picked up his knife and fork and started eating again. He'd taken exactly two bites before he put them down again, the clink of silverware against plate loud in the uncomfortable silence.

"Is this about me kissing you just now, Elli?"

She didn't want to look up, but she couldn't help it. His eyes were completely earnest—not angry, but probing, as if he was trying to understand. But of course, he couldn't.

"No, Wyatt, honestly it's not." It was only a partial lie.

"You can have the bed," he said, his voice low and rough. "I don't mind sleeping on the couch."

"Wyatt…" He was making it so difficult. How could she sleep in the bed, knowing he was just down the hall, folded up on the short sofa? The very thought of it made her heart beat a little faster. "I can help you, but you have to understand…I have assignments due. I'm taking some bookkeeping courses." It was a paltry excuse; she'd just got through telling him she had nothing pressing. She could easily do the assignments on her laptop and log in to the Camerons' wireless connection to send them in.

He was silent for several long moments. Elli looked up in surprise when he straightened his shoulders and squared his jaw. He looked like a man about to face his executioner, like one who was about to say something very unpleasant and the words were souring in his mouth. Butterflies swirled in her stomach.

"Elli, the one thing I cannot do is let that baby go into foster care. I promised. And I cannot do it alone. I barely got a few hours' sleep last night. I need you, Elli. I will not let that baby be taken away by child services. *I need you.*"

She tried to push away the rush of feeling that came upon hearing the words. She hadn't known him long, but she'd thought him too proud, too stubborn to admit such a thing.

He didn't need *her*—she understood that. He needed the help, but not her. She was, however, the one person who was here. And the assignments were an excuse. She'd been waiting for a chance to do something important, so what was holding her back? A crush? Didn't she trust herself enough to be smart?

Surely she could keep that in hand. Wasn't Darcy worth it? If it were William, wouldn't she want someone to do the same?

That was the clincher. Of course she would. She was in a unique position to help a child. To refuse for personal reasons was beyond selfish.

"What makes you think they would take her away?" Elli sipped on her water. Wyatt was more open now than he'd been. It could be a good opportunity to learn more about him. Why did the mere mention of a social worker tie him up in knots? Because even the way he said the words was as if they tasted bitter in his mouth.

"Look at this place." He pushed away his plate. "It is not the picture of a family home. I am not set up for a baby. I am a single man with no experience with infants. All that is working against me. I can't give them more ammunition. I need to make this place into a family home."

"You realize that they aim to keep children with families, right? That you're on the same side?"

But Wyatt shrugged it off. "Maybe so, but there are no guarantees. You don't know what it does to a kid to be taken away."

Her heart ached at the pain in his voice. "Darcy is only a few months old. She wouldn't remember, Wyatt."

"How do you know that? How do you know someone else will be kind? What happens with Barbara? Do you know what the doctor said? She said that Barbara had taken steps to make sure Darcy was safe. She removed herself from the situation. She put Darcy in the care of someone she trusted. Despite being ill she made decisions based on good mothering. I will not betray that faith she placed in me."

"Wyatt." Elli tried to contain her shock at his vehement words. She reached across the table and laid her hand over his wrist. His pulse hammered beneath her fingers as the bits clicked into place.

"When did it happen?" She asked it gently.

Wyatt turned his head to the left and looked out the window at the approaching darkness. "What are you talking about?"

She squeezed his wrist. "How old were you when you were taken away?"

He started to push back from the table, but she kept her hand firmly on his wrist. He paused halfway up, then sat back down. And this time when he met her gaze there was defiance, an I-dare-you edge in the dark eyes.

"I was nine."

"Oh, Wyatt."

"I was gone for a whole week. That's all. It was too long. I ran away twice trying to get back home. They let me go back when he promised."

"Promised what?" Elli felt slightly sick, afraid of what the answer was going to be, sad for the little boy he must have been.

"Promised he wouldn't hit me again."

Her mouth tasted like bile. "Did he?"

"No. Not with his fists, anyway. But he'd done enough. I always knew what he was capable of."

"Weren't you afraid to go home?"

He turned his hand over, studied her fingers, twined his with them. She wondered if he even realized he was doing it, twisting a connection between them as his jaw tightened.

"I couldn't leave my mother back there," he said simply. "I had to be with her. We only had each other, you see. Who does Barbara have if not me? Who does Darcy have?"

Elli's eyes smarted. Over in the baby seat Darcy started to snuffle and squirm, waking from her nap. Wyatt held hurts as deep as her own. So much made sense now, including his burning need to get it right. Did he think he was like his father?

"Wyatt, you could never be like him, you know that, right?"

His gaze was tortured as it plumbed the depths of her face. "How do I know that? When Darcy cries and I don't know how to make her stop..."

"You walk the floor with her. You came to me for help. Don't you see? You're doing a fine job with her. You're patient and loving. You're twice the man he ever was, Wyatt, I just know it."

His gaze brightened before he looked away.

"Okay. I'll move some things over. You won't have to worry about Darcy being taken away from you."

Relief softened the lines of his face. "Good. Because we still have to prove it at the social services home visit."

He rose and took his plate to the sink, then stopped at the seat and picked Darcy up, cradling her protectively against his chest.

How was Elli supposed to come through unscathed now?

CHAPTER SEVEN

WHEN ELLI RETURNED from the Camerons' house with a bag, Wyatt was in the middle of the living-room floor, setting up the playpen they'd brought from her mother's. His dark head was bent in concentration, his wide hands working with the frame. Elli caught her breath and held it, pushing past the flare of attraction. She almost welcomed the stab of grief that came in its wake as she glimpsed the brightly colored pattern on the nylon. Darcy. The playpen had been meant for William, and she couldn't quite squelch the anger and pain, knowing he would never use it.

But why shouldn't Darcy have it now? Wasn't it better that it was going to be put to some use?

Wyatt fiddled with a corner and mumbled under his breath. Elli left her maudlin thoughts behind and smiled at his grumbling. "Having fun?"

Wyatt looked up, a wrinkle between his brows and a curl of hair out of place, lying negligently on his forehead. There it was again—the buzz of excitement. She bit down on her lip.

"There are way too many buttons and levers on baby things," he replied. He stood, gave the side of the playpen a quick jerk and the frame snapped into place. "There. It might not be a crib, but at least for tonight she won't have to sleep in her car seat."

Elli put down her overnight bag and went to his side. A plush pad lined the bottom of the playpen, decorated in farm animals. Darcy lay on the floor next to him on an activity mat, her attention riveted on a black-and-white zebra with tissue paper crinkling beneath the fabric.

"You're trying really hard." Elli knelt beside him and rested her hand on the nylon of the pen. In the short time she'd been gone she could see he'd tried to tidy up the living room. A lamp glowed warmly in the back corner and he'd put a soft blanket over the sofa cushions, covering the worn upholstery. The room was more homey than she'd thought, and the warm light highlighted a framed Robert Bateman print on one wall. It was a fine house, it was just…neglected. It wouldn't take much effort to bring it up to scratch.

"I never really had a reason before," he said quietly, getting to his feet. "I've been on my own a long time." A ghost of a smile tipped his lips. "And in case you haven't noticed, I'm pretty low maintenance."

She laughed lightly, drawn in by the cozy light and the easy way he spoke, but beneath it all warning herself she couldn't get used to it. "And babies aren't."

"Certainly not." He went to another box, one they'd just managed to slide inside the trunk of her car. "I should put this together next." As he opened the top flap, he carried on. "I can't thank you enough for arranging the loan. This stuff is brand-new! Where did you get it?"

She'd neglected to tell him that the house where they'd stopped belonged to her parents, and she'd determined ahead of time that should he ask she would simply answer that they belonged to someone who had lost a baby. The fewer details the better. She'd been spared explanations earlier, as on the drive home Darcy had been fussing.

The last thing she wanted was to tell him what had really

happened with William. But after his own revelation at dinner, she felt compelled to be honest with him. Maybe if she gave him just a bit of the truth, it would be enough to stop his questions. She had to talk about it sometime. Maybe then it would get easier.

"It was for me, for when I had a baby," she said, determined to keep her voice even. She didn't want to see the same pity on his face that she'd seen today at the hospital, facing her old coworkers again. The last thing she wanted from Wyatt was his pity. "I stored it at my mom's, that's all. You know mothers. You mention the word grandchild…"

He slid a flat board out of the box and put it to the side. "Wasn't that jumping the gun a little bit?" He said it easily, even teasing, but Elli was finding it hard to keep up the pretense. The logic of her decision to skim the surface made perfect sense, but she wasn't quite as successful at stifling the emotions that came into play. When she didn't answer, Wyatt looked up. His smile faded and those damnably dark eyes searched hers yet again.

"I've said something wrong."

He got up off the floor and went to her, not touching her, but she could see the wall of his chest and she blinked. She would not cry. Not again. She'd cried enough, and she'd done so well today. At some point she had to talk about it without falling apart. Wyatt didn't come with any preconceived notions about her, or her marriage to Tim. And once she left the Camerons' house, their paths would likely never cross again.

"It's all right," she said quietly. "You couldn't have known."

"What happened?"

"I was pregnant but…" She didn't want to go into too much detail. Concern was one thing, and it was already written all over his face. Full disclosure would bring the pity and sympathy. She'd decided to tell him, so why was it so difficult to say the words? "But I lost the baby," she finished on a whisper, unwilling to elaborate further. "All the things we'd bought we put at my mother's, thinking they'd still be there later."

"But there was no later," he guessed.

She kept staring at the buttons of his shirt, noticing oddly that their color matched the fabric precisely. "No, there wasn't," she answered softly. "Our marriage ended."

And so did the dream, she thought, but the idea wasn't as sad as it might have been. Tim had married her for the wrong reasons. He'd wanted a good wife, a home in a prestigious neighborhood and the picture-perfect family to go with it. In that, they'd been alike. She'd fancied herself in love with him when she'd been in love with her own dreams instead. It wasn't a mistake she planned to make again. She was stronger now. If she ever married again, it would be for nothing less than the real thing.

"I'm sorry," he said, and while Darcy stared intently at a blue elephant on the play mat, Wyatt took Elli into his arms.

It felt so good to be held there, nearly as good as his kiss had felt earlier. His chest was warm and solid, his arms gentle around her. It had been so long since she'd allowed herself to lean on anyone at all that she sighed, feeling a weight lift from her shoulders.

"Don't be sorry. It's not your fault," she murmured, knowing she should pull away but not quite ready to give him up so soon. She hoped that would be the end to the questions. He could go on thinking she'd had a miscarriage and that would be it. He didn't need to know how close to her due date she'd been, so close she could taste the sweetness of motherhood, only to have it ripped cruelly away.

His wide palm stroked her hair and a shiver went down

her spine, a feeling of pure pleasure. A gurgle sounded from the mat as Darcy discovered a new texture.

"The last two days and you didn't say anything. I saw your expression a few times as you tended to Darcy and knew there was something, but…" He pushed her away from him so he could look into her face. Not pity there, then. No, it was pure compassion, and she felt her determination to keep him at arm's length slip another notch. "If I had known…how callous of me," he finished, squeezing her hands.

"I could have said no." She smiled a little, squeezing back. "You and Darcy needed help. You couldn't have known."

Darcy grew tired of being ignored, and squawked. Wyatt let go of Elli's hands and went to the baby, picked her up in his wide hands and rested her in the crook of his arm.

"Yesterday I was terrified to touch her, and already she seems to settle when I hold her."

"You're a natural." Elli smiled, glad to leave the topic behind. She reached up to adjust Darcy's shirt.

"Hardly. But I want to do right by her. And if this is too much for you, I understand. I wouldn't have asked if I'd known how it would hurt you." Darcy's chubby hand grabbed at his lower lip. He removed her fingers gently and kissed them.

Elli was sure he hadn't consciously done it, but there was a tenderness to Wyatt that was utterly unexpected. It was in the way he'd put his arms around her, the way he held Darcy in his arms and vowed to fiercely protect her. She hardly knew him, but in some ways she already understood him better than she'd ever understood Tim. Tim had spoken to her as a doctor would, using technical terms and medical explanations. Wyatt didn't. He simply offered a genuine "sorry" and a hug.

"No, it's good for me. I should have stopped hiding away ages ago. I've put off moving on, and caring for Darcy is helping with that. It hurts, but you're not the only one benefiting from this arrangement."

"As long as you're sure…"

"I'm positive."

The atmosphere in the room seemed to lighten. "Okay, then, can you take her while I put this thing together?" Wyatt smiled, pushing the serious topics to the side and moving back to the present problem, and Elli was grateful. They'd learned something new about each other today and they were still standing. Her initial impression of him, the one where she'd labeled him a complete grump, wasn't bearing out. They were—to her surprise—becoming friends.

"Sure. She's due for a bottle anyway." Elli took Darcy in her arms, realizing she was getting used to her weight there, and liking it. As Wyatt organized hardware and parts, she went to the kitchen and heated a bottle, then came back to the living room, settling in the corner of the sofa. Darcy's warm weight relaxed in the crook of her elbow as she took the bottle, the blue eyes staring up at Elli with what felt like trust.

She sat quietly while Wyatt put together the change table. The silence was pleasant. Wyatt might think his home wasn't good enough, but it held something that many homes with better furniture and fresher paint didn't. It held comfort. A gurgling sound from the milk being pulled through the nipple made Elli smile.

How could it be that she felt more at home here than she had at her own condo with Tim? The thought disturbed her. How could she have been so wrong? How could she have fooled herself so well? Why had she settled when she'd really wanted something so much simpler?

"What do you think?"

Wyatt's voice pulled her out of her musings and she realized that he was standing proudly next to the change table. The maple-colored wood gleamed in the lamplight and a quilted pad fit on the top. No more changing Darcy on a sofa cushion or bed or whatever happened to be near. She had a place to sleep and now a table where they could organize her diapers and supplies. Darcy was settling in. And so was Elli. She wasn't yet sure if it was a good thing or not.

It felt right, which scared the daylights out of her. It would be fine as long as she kept up her guard. Then she'd find a new job, and an apartment somewhere. An apartment that she knew now would be more like Wyatt's home. Set up for comfort, not for style.

Darcy had fallen asleep and Elli put her down on the sofa. "It looks great," she said, going over to the table and running her fingers over the polished wood. "Where should we put it?"

Wyatt shifted his weight, suddenly awkward. "I suppose wherever she sleeps. The second bedroom still needs to be cleaned, and probably painted. I tried to get the rooms I needed livable first."

"And it doesn't feel right putting her in here."

"Well..."

"I still feel funny taking your room, Wyatt. I can sleep on the couch."

"No, I wouldn't feel right. You take the bed. I'm up at six for chores and I'd wake you."

"Then I can keep Darcy in with me."

"You're sure?"

"Yes, I'm sure. Isn't that why you wanted my help? So you can look after your livestock and I can look after Darcy?"

"Yes, but I…"

"Feel guilty."

A small smile played on his lips. "Something like that."

"I can take care of myself, Wyatt."

"Will you let me know if you need anything, then?"

"Do you always try to take care of everyone?"

His gaze slid back to hers and she remembered the way he'd drawn her into his arms, the way his lips had felt against hers. She was determined to make her own way this time, but there was something alluring about the thought of being looked after by Wyatt Black.

"Is that a fault?"

She couldn't help but smile, her heart tripping along a little faster than normal. "That's the standard 'answer a question with a question' technique. But I'll let you off the hook this time. We've got more important things at hand. There's a small matter of needing baby things," she said, taking a step away. Being close to Wyatt was becoming a habit and one she had to break. "We're on our last outfit, and nearly out of diapers. The can of formula I bought isn't going to last, either. If you start a list, I can run into town in the morning and do some shopping."

"That would be very helpful, but I don't want you to feel—"

Elli interrupted, laughing. "Stop it. You asked me to help and what, now you feel guilty about it?"

"You're teasing me." He said it with surprise, and Elli felt a frisson of pleasure skitter along her spine. It did wonders for her confidence to know she could put him off his balance.

"Maybe a little. You're so serious, Wyatt. You need to relax."

Wyatt fiddled with the screwdriver, finally putting it

back in a leather pouch. "I don't mean to be so serious," he confessed.

Elli recognized it not only in him but herself lately, as well. Maybe they both needed to lighten up. These little exchanges with him definitely made her feel better.

"You're concerned about the home visit, right? So let me do this, get the basics covered while you worry about work. A girlie shopping trip is just what Darcy and I need." She rubbed her hands together.

A quiet pause filled the room. She exhaled and continued in a calm, logical tone. "Isn't that why you asked me to stay?"

"I know you're right," he conceded. "About the necessities, anyway. And if it means I don't have to shop…" He strode off to the kitchen and Elli followed, stopping when she heard the tinny sound of a coffee can. Wyatt had relaxed for a few minutes, but now his jaw was set again in what she was beginning to recognize was his stubborn look. He took a wad of bills out of the can and started counting it off.

"How much do you think you'll need?"

Elli gaped. "You keep your money in a *coffee can?*"

"This is my emergency fund. It's easier to give you the cash than it is to sort out banking cards or credit cards." He held out several bills. "Take it and get what you need tomorrow. I don't dare take another day away from the stock, and you're right. It will be a huge help."

She reached out and took the money. "Okay, then."

He put the lid back on the can and returned it to a low cupboard. Elli frowned. Wyatt resorted to a can? It seemed so…old-fashioned. Just when she thought she was starting to puzzle him out, something else cropped up that made him a mystery. Maybe she should just stop trying.

"Come on," he said, turning back to face her, the earlier

stubbornness erased from his features and replaced with a smile. "Let's get the two of you settled."

Elli was following him down the hallway and his heart was beating a mile a minute. He didn't know what to do about Elli anymore. She was such a puzzle. Wounded and emotional one moment, teasing him the next. He couldn't forget the expression on her face when she'd told him about the miscarriage. It all made sense now. The odd looks that shadowed her face at times, the way she had first handled Darcy, as if she was afraid. And then…oh, God. The comment he'd made yesterday about all girls wanting babies. What an ass he was. He wanted her help, wanted her to feel at home and her confession made him feel like a heel.

Inside the bedroom he suffered another bout of embarrassment. The room was, at best, plain. A bed and a dresser, nothing on the walls, nothing inviting or cozy as he'd expect a woman's room to be. He'd never put much thought into decorations or felt the need to clutter things up with objects that held no meaning. He supposed that philosophy made his place look a bit spartan.

"I'm sorry it's not very fancy," he apologized, seeing the room through her eyes.

"It's fine," Elli replied. "I expect you've put your energies into the ranch and not the decor."

As she put down her overnight bag, Wyatt stripped the white sheets off the bed and tossed them into a plastic hamper along the wall. "That about sums it up," he agreed. He wondered what she was thinking. He knew how the house appeared. The petty cash he kept in the kitchen probably didn't help. It wasn't as if he didn't have the money to fix things up. He'd just put his priorities elsewhere.

"I'll get some fresh sheets," he murmured, going to the hall closet. The couch wasn't going to be comfortable, but

Darcy was his niece, not Elli's. She had no reason to stay, but she was doing it anyway. She was his guest. And yet the thought of her sleeping in here, in his bed, Darcy in the playpen beside her, did funny things to his insides.

He hadn't expected an instant family, no matter how temporary. After years of solitude, it was odd to have others sharing his space. In particular Elli, with her shy smiles and soft eyes. She seemed to take everything at face value and didn't judge because of it. And in a few short days she seemed to be everywhere.

It almost made him want to explain things to her. Things he had never explained to anyone.

He returned with the sheets. Elli had put Darcy in the middle of the bed and he heard her coming behind him, carrying the playpen. She brought it into the room and smiled. "If I put it beside the bed, I can get to her easily when she wakes," Elli explained. "A flannel sheet underneath her and the blanket should be enough. The nights aren't too chilly yet."

She put the sheet on the mattress pad and Wyatt picked up Darcy, placing her gently on the soft surface. She blinked up at him.

Then he looked at Elli and felt his heart turn over. She was looking at the baby with such tenderness it hurt him. Now he knew she'd lost her baby and her marriage and her job. And yet she greeted life with a smile. It was more than he'd managed for many years. He'd spent a long time drifting around, working, making enough money to settle somewhere, never getting too close to anyone. He'd lost his entire family and he'd spent his time nursing his wounds. Perhaps he'd nursed them too much. Buying this place—making it into something profitable—was his way of moving on.

But now it was different. He had a family, even if it

wasn't quite the one he'd expected. And Elli was a part of it whether it made sense or not. He was surprised that he wanted her to be.

He smoothed the sheet over the mattress and pulled up the comforter. "Are you sure you'll be warm enough?" Elli's cheeks flushed a little and he was charmed. "There are extra blankets in the hall closet."

"This will be fine," she murmured. "You're going to need the blankets anyway."

"And a pillow. I hope you don't mind if I take one."

"Of course not." She stared at the bed again and the nerves in his stomach started jumping, just as they had in the kitchen before he'd kissed her. The temptation was there. He wondered what it would be like to lie beside her. In his bed. To feel her body close to his, to kiss her in the dark, to hear her whisper his name.

He grabbed the pillow. After everything that had happened today, his libido had to stay out of it. He wanted to ask her what had happened. He wanted to know how her husband could have let her get away, if he'd been there for her or not. By the way she'd melted in his arms, he'd guess not. Not the way she deserved.

"The bathroom is down the hall. I'll bring the change table in and then say good-night."

Elli nodded dumbly and the temptation to kiss her reared up again. But he put it off. She was still a little jumpy from earlier, and it felt wrong to press.

When he delivered the change table, Elli was sitting cross-legged on the bed, a book and a small laptop open in front of her. Darcy was there, too, on top of the covers with a ring of plastic keys clutched in her chubby fist. As Elli turned a page in the book, she absently rubbed Darcy's foot with her free hand.

Wyatt swallowed.

Why did having her here feel so right? Why had he felt like such a miser counting out bills to give her? He wasn't rich, but he had this place and he could certainly afford to put food on the table and buy the necessities. Maybe it was time he put some effort into the inside, bringing the house up to scratch.

Why couldn't he get her off his mind?

He put down the table along the far wall and looked at the two of them, so comfortable and so right. Odd that he'd spent so many years roaming around looking for the right opportunity and here it was, dropped into his lap. Darcy's arrival had thrown a kink into things, but he understood the reason now. It wasn't about the ranch or cattle or making his mark.

It was about family. And it was about Elli.

His mother, even when things were at their worst, had cautioned him not to be bitter. She had begged him not to judge the world based on his parents' marriage. He had anyway, for a long time.

But when he looked at Elli, those jaded thoughts seemed far away. She had obviously been through a lot and she was still smiling. Maybe he could make things better for her in a way he never could for his mom.

She put her hand on Darcy's tummy, rubbing absently, and the bubble burst. How could he be thinking about being with her when Darcy was his first priority? He had to ensure that Darcy stayed with him until she could be reunited with her mother.

"You're staying up for a while, then?"

Elli looked up from her book and smiled. "Darcy's not ready for sleep yet. If I finish this assignment, I can send it tomorrow."

He nodded. "Elli, about the money...you know where

the can is. What I'm saying is, take more if you think you'll need it."

"I don't want to spend you out of house and home," she replied, but she focused on her book instead of on him.

So that was it. Did she think he was so poor a few things were going to strap him? "That's just petty cash, Elli," he explained, putting his hands into his pockets and smiling. "You're not going to break the bank. Besides, I trust you."

That got her attention and she looked up. "You do?"

"Is there any reason I shouldn't?"

Her cheeks blossomed and he thought once more how pretty she looked.

"I did think about picking up a few things to spruce up the house a little, but wasn't sure how to ask."

"Of course. I'm hopeless when it comes to decorating. I think it's a guy thing. I'd be happy for you to pick up some stuff. It might help make things look nicer for when family services does their assessment."

He went to the door and rested his hand on the frame, not wanting to leave but feeling silly staying.

"Wyatt?"

"Hmm?" He turned back around, fighting the strange urge to kiss her good-night. Maybe it would be best if he just got the hell out of there.

"I won't take it all, don't worry."

"Do I look worried?"

She smiled an angelic smile and he clamped down on the desire that rushed through him. "Actually, yes."

"Not about that," he replied, and before he could change his mind, he closed the door behind him and went to make up the lumpy couch.

It didn't matter. He wasn't going to sleep tonight anyway.

CHAPTER EIGHT

ELLI DID A QUICK CHECK of the house to quell the nerves dancing around in her stomach. The phone call had come earlier than they'd expected. The social worker from Didsbury was coming in the afternoon.

She was glad she'd gone shopping early that morning. A cheery new tablecloth dressed up the kitchen and she had also bought matching tea towels and pot holders. Wyatt had finished the chores outside and just after lunch he'd brought in his toolbox and fixed the sagging front door so it opened and closed easily. Now he was taking a shower. Darcy was bathed and sweet smelling and dressed in a new pink two-piece outfit.

Elli now took a moment to brush her hair and twist it up, anchoring it in the back with a clip. The refrigerator was full and the house tidied. Darcy had enough formula for several days, diapers stacked neatly on the change table, and several cute, serviceable outfits. It had been a bitter-sweet pleasure shopping for them, picking them up and choosing the patterns and styles. It was something she'd never had the chance to do for William, and it had been fun. She would have enjoyed the day out, regardless, as she'd finally felt she had a purpose. She hadn't realized how much she'd missed it until she was needed again.

But all in all she was nervous. Both for Wyatt, who

had a lot riding on this meeting, and for herself. She had been with Wyatt at the hospital and now at the house. She knew that she would also have to answer questions. And without knowing what the questions would be, she couldn't anticipate the answers. It wasn't even so much talking to a complete stranger. There seemed to be some safety in that. It was airing everything in front of Wyatt. She shouldn't care what he thought, but she did. His opinion mattered.

She heard the dull thump of Wyatt's stocking feet coming down the hall and she took one last glance in the mirror, forcing the worry lines from her face and pasting on what should look like a pleasant smile. She'd taken extra care with herself, too, dressing in navy slacks rather than her usual jeans, and a soft raspberry-red sweater. When she turned he was standing behind her, and the curve of her lips faltered the slightest bit at his appearance.

He was so handsome. Even in neat jeans and a blue-and-white-striped shirt, he still exuded that little bit of rough danger, of excitement. It was in his deep-set eyes and the just-a-bit-too-long tips of his dark hair. An air of carelessness, when she knew in many ways that *careless* was one of the last words she could use to describe him.

It made for an intriguing package.

"Do I look okay?"

Worry clouded his enigmatic eyes, and she reached out, putting a hand on his arm. "Of course you do."

"Maybe I should have dressed up more."

Elli tried to picture him "dressed up" and it wouldn't quite gel. He belonged in well-fitting jeans and cotton shirts that emphasized his broad shoulders. "I don't think so. This is who you are. And today of all days, you need to be yourself. You can't pretend to be someone you're not."

A furrow appeared between his brows. "Not helping," he replied, and Elli laughed.

"Who would you trust more? Someone who looked great but was clearly uncomfortable? Or someone who looked calm, capable and comfortable in their own skin?"

He moved his arm so that his fingers could twine with hers. A thrill skittered down the length of her arm at the simple touch.

"That's how I appear? Wow. I didn't realize these clothes had special powers." Finally a smile broke through his tense features. "You look nice, too. The red brings out the roses in your cheeks."

When Wyatt smiled Elli felt as if a candle had been lit inside her. Maybe because he didn't bestow his smiles frivolously and they seemed to mean more because of it. "You're teasing me," she accused softly, pleased he'd noticed her extra effort. She resisted the nervous habit of straightening her clothing. She'd had the sweater for ages and had never worn it, thinking it too bold. After last night, and with the social worker coming, she'd wanted Wyatt to see her in something other than her normal exciting-as-a-mushroom colors.

He nodded. "You look as nervous as I feel. You even put your hair up." His gaze roamed over the twist, held with a clip so that a few ends cascaded artfully over the top. "I like it. It makes you look…sophisticated." He let go of her fingers. "Too sophisticated for a run-down ranch in the boondocks."

But Elli had noticed things in the past weeks, too, even if it had just been from a distance, on the deck of the Camerons' house. "This place isn't run-down. You have already made a lot of improvements. It takes time and hard work."

Wyatt's keen gaze caught her once more. "Of anything I expected today," he said quietly, "I didn't expect that. I didn't expect your unqualified support. Thank you, Elli."

The sincerity in his voice made her want to hug him, but she could not. Would not. Sure, she could see the differences and yes, she was attracted to Wyatt. But once this "situation" was resolved he would be back to being a full-time rancher and she would be…not at the Camerons'. This was meant to be a time to forge her own new life, not be sucked into someone else's again as she had been with Tim.

Wyatt's kiss last night was just an indulgence in fantasy. It had been lovely, but she couldn't let it be a life-changing event. She did not want life-changing events. What she wanted was to rebuild and begin again, this time much stronger.

"You're welcome. And try not to worry so much. Darcy should be with you. You're her uncle. It's not like this is forever, either."

She said the words to remind herself as much as him. It would be far too easy to get caught up in the situation and mistake it for reality.

Both of them heard the car turn up the drive, and in concert they turned their heads toward the front door. "This is it," Wyatt murmured, and the wrinkle reappeared in the middle of his brow as Elli straightened her sweater. There was no time to recheck her makeup. She would have to do as she was.

Wyatt opened the door and stepped out onto the veranda. Elli noticed that while the paint was still peeling, there were several pieces of yellowy fresh lumber where Wyatt had shored up the steps and floor. Sometimes it seemed he could do anything with his hands and a few supplies.

A young woman barely older than Elli got out of the car. She was tall and dark haired, the straight tresses pulled back in an elegant sweep. There was nothing about the woman that was ostentatious or over the top, but she was the kind of put-together female who always made Elli feel just a bit dowdy. Now, with only a sheer layer of foundation and some lipstick for makeup, Elli felt the difference keenly. It made her want to fade into the woodwork.

Come to think of it—perhaps that wasn't such a bad idea. The less she was in the spotlight today the better.

She slipped back inside as Wyatt greeted the woman. "Miss Beck, I'm Wyatt Black. I'm glad you could come today."

Oh, he was smooth, Elli thought, envying how he could cover up all that nervousness with charm. She heard the higher sounds of the woman's reply and bit down on her lip.

The door opened and Wyatt held it for Miss Beck to come through. She stepped inside and looked around briefly before moving to unbutton her coat.

"I appreciate you being so accommodating," she said as Wyatt stepped forward to take the coat from her. He hung it on a peg behind the door and rubbed his hands together. Elli watched it all from the living room, where she quietly folded a load of towels she'd taken from the dryer only minutes before. Anything to keep her hands busy and not twisting together as she was tempted to do.

"There was no reason to put it off. Of course you want to make sure Darcy is well looked after. We want the same things, Miss Beck. The best of care for my niece while her mother recovers."

That earned a smile from Miss Beck. "So we do," she agreed. "Please call me Angela. I can't quite get used to Miss Beck. It makes me feel like a schoolteacher."

Wyatt smiled back and Elli held her breath. Perhaps this wasn't anything to be so nervous about. Perhaps the caseworker at the hospital had been unusually stern.

"Like any government agency, there is paperwork that

needs doing, and procedure we need to go over. Might I see Darcy first, though?" Angela suddenly noticed Elli in the living room. "Oh, hello."

Elli swallowed and felt even shorter than her five feet three inches and every ounce of her despised extra pounds. She tried standing taller and held out a hand. "Hello. I'm Ellison Marchuk."

"Elli is helping me out with Darcy," Wyatt explained. Angela nodded, but Elli didn't feel any easier. How would it appear? Like a friend? Like a girlfriend? Which did she prefer? She wasn't sure.

"Darcy's sleeping right now, but I could get her up. Or you could peek at her. I'm sure she'll be up soon."

"That would be fine."

Elli led the caseworker down the hall to the bedroom. She had made the bed and besides the playpen and change table she'd added a few velvety throw pillows to Wyatt's bed and a cute mobile of puppies and kittens in primary colors, attached to the side of the playpen. They both peeked over the side. Darcy was sleeping, covered to her armpits with the pink blanket and with both hands resting on either side of her head in a classic baby pose. Elli's heart twisted as she looked down at the peaceful face. Darcy had no idea of the turmoil going on around her. If Elli could do one thing, it would be to make this as easy on Darcy as possible so she never need suffer any long-lasting effects from being separated from her mother.

They tiptoed out and Angela turned to Elli. "She's a beautiful baby."

Elli nodded. "And good, too. Well, as good as you'd expect a newborn to be." She smiled. This woman felt like an ally. It would be all right. It had to be.

Wyatt was waiting in the kitchen, sitting at the table staring at his hands. When they entered he stood up.

"Shall we get started?" Angela Beck was all business now and she picked up her briefcase, taking out a file folder. "We need to work through your application first, Mr. Black."

The volume of papers she laid out was staggering. Wyatt looked at Elli and she felt his hesitation clear across the room.

"Is this all really necessary? It's such a short-term thing, after all."

"Perhaps, but perhaps not. We don't really know when your sister will be able to resume care for Darcy or how long you will be temporary guardian. Does that present a problem?"

Wyatt's hands unfurled and he looked her dead in the eye. "Absolutely not. Darcy can stay here as long as it takes. I'm the only family they've got and it's only right that Darcy stay with me until Barbara is well."

"Then let's proceed."

Elli went through the motions of putting on coffee while Wyatt and Angela worked through the application. She gave a cup to Angela, then fixed another the way Wyatt liked it and put it by his elbow. His shoulders were so stiff. Despite his easy smiles, she could tell he was wound up tighter than a spring. She put her hand on his shoulder for just a moment and squeezed.

The hands of the clock ticked on as Wyatt went through his orientation. Elli fed Darcy when she woke, changed her diaper and put a load of laundry in the washing machine. Finally Angela Beck tamped the papers together and put them into her briefcase. "That was great coffee. Why don't we take a minute and you can show me around, Mr. Black?"

Elli put Darcy in the new windup swing, and the motion ticked out a rhythm as she tidied up the few dishes in the sink. Wyatt gave Angela a brief tour, outlining how long he'd lived there and what improvements he'd already made to the property as well as what he had planned in the days ahead. "I'd focused more on the livestock and ranch when I first moved in," he explained. "But Darcy changes things."

"How so?"

They paused at the end of the hall and Elli held a cup in her hand, the dishcloth dripping water back into the sink, waiting for his answer.

"Having a child under your care changes your priorities, wouldn't you agree?"

"I would."

Elli carefully placed the cup in the drying rack. Did Wyatt know how rare he was? He wasn't putting on a show for the social worker as some people might. He was answering honestly, sincerely. No one could dispute his dedication to his niece, surprise appearance or not. He was a man who would do what needed to be done, a man who would do the right thing. He'd do anything for someone he loved, she realized. At personal sacrifice to himself. She didn't know many men like that.

"And Miss Marchuk, is it?" Angela Beck's astute gaze pinned her in place. Elli felt awkward and plain next to Beck's efficiency. Lord, the woman was well put together. Not a hair out of place, while Elli could feel a few flyaway pieces fraying around the edges of her face.

"That's right." She curbed the urge to say *Yes, ma'am*. Angela Beck couldn't be any older than Elli was.

"How long have you and Wyatt been living together, then?"

Elli felt her control slipping by the sheer surprise of the question. "Living together," she repeated, somewhat stupidly, then looked to Wyatt for guidance.

Angela raised an eyebrow. "Our eligibility requirements state that if there is cohabitation the relationship must be a stable one for the good of the child. We require a twelve-month minimum."

Wyatt couldn't be disqualified as a temporary guardian simply because she was here. It was wrong. "We're not living together," she replied.

"Oh?" The tone of Beck's voice said she didn't quite believe it.

"Ellison is the nanny," Wyatt supplied. He sent Elli a dark look and gave his head a slight shake just before Angela turned and looked at him.

"Your nanny?"

"Of course. I do have a ranch to run, and I needed help. Elli has agreed to help out temporarily. It's a much better solution than a daycare. I cannot be in the house all the time, and I can't take Darcy with me to the fields and barns."

"Of course."

"This way Darcy isn't being shifted around to different people each day. She is here, with me, and with Elli. Isn't it good to have normalcy? I thought a nanny was a far better option."

Elli stood dumbly through the exchange. She knew why he'd said it and it made the best sense. But it stung. It stung a lot. Was being in a relationship such a bad thing? Not that they were, but the way he'd put it sounded so cold.

"A stable environment is definitely one of the things we look for," Angela replied. She gestured toward the table, inviting Elli to take a seat. "And Mr. Black is paying you, Ms. Marchuk?"

Elli swallowed, but schooled her features. If Wyatt could do this, so could she. "Yes, we've agreed on that arrangement."

"Ms. Marchuk, how do you know Mr. Black?"

Elli couldn't look at him. She knew if she did it would seem as though she were looking to him for answers. She sat at the end of the table, perching on the edge of the chair. "We're neighbors. I've lived next door to Wyatt for the last two months, ever since he moved in."

Angela Beck took the chair opposite, leaving Wyatt standing in the doorway. "And you're not romantically involved?"

Elli thought back to the kiss last night, and it was like being there again, feeling Wyatt's hands on her arms and the softness of his lips against her own. But did a kiss signify romantic involvement? On the surface, she supposed it did. But they had backed off and put Darcy first. And he had just called her the nanny in front of the social worker. The nanny. Not "a friend" or even a neighbor. The nanny. That told her quite clearly where Wyatt's feelings stood.

"No, we're not dating." That at least was truthful. Until Darcy's arrival, the sum total of their interaction had been a brief argument in the middle of a pasture. She still refused to look at him, instead seeing the dark blue denim of his jeans in her peripheral vision.

"And how long have you lived next door?"

Elli lifted her chin. "I'm housesitting for family friends at the moment. I was laid off from my job in Calgary and took the offer to stay at their place while I upgrade some courses and look for work."

She really hoped that didn't sound pathetic. Lord knew she wasn't alone. Lots of people had lost their jobs lately as the economy tanked. Surely she couldn't be judged just because she'd been a victim of budget cuts.

"And you're single?"

"Recently divorced."

She could feel Wyatt's gaze on her and she refused to

meet it. She knew if she did she would blush and that would betray her words. She hadn't lied. They weren't dating. But it didn't mean there wasn't an attraction on her part and she did not want to give that away. There was too much at stake.

"Children?"

She swallowed, held Beck's gaze. "No."

"What do you feel qualifies you for this position, then?"

And finally she couldn't help it. Her gaze rose to Wyatt's. His face was nearly unreadable, but she saw a softening around his eyes. He was thinking—as she was—of the baby she'd lost. And he would not say a word about it. She could tell by the compassion in his eyes. Her secret was safe.

She faced Angela again and offered a smile, bolstered by Wyatt's silent support across the room. "I'm available," she began, "and more than that, I have love to give. A baby's needs are simple—food, sleep, diaper changes. Anyone can provide that. What Darcy needs is love and attention and security. I can help Wyatt provide all of that. Most daycares won't even think of taking a newborn. With me here, Darcy is guaranteed to have the undivided attention of at least one of us at all times. She'll have some sort of consistency."

As she finished, a thin cry came from behind her. "And speaking of," Elli continued, trying very hard to smile while keeping a tight grip on her emotions, "I think someone would like her swing wound again. If you'll excuse me?"

"Of course. It is a perfect time for me to begin the interview with Mr. Black."

Darcy was sucking on her hands again, so Elli quickly warmed a bottle and took it with her to the bedroom. "I'll give you some privacy," she murmured to Wyatt as she passed him. "We'll be in the bedroom if you need me."

The softened look around his eyes was gone, replaced by a hard, distrusting edge. He was so afraid, she realized, and wondered why. Everything she'd seen him do the past three days—everything—had been for Darcy's well-being and at sacrifice to his own. Was he hiding something more that she should be concerned about?

"It'll be fine," she reassured him in a low voice. She wanted to reach out and touch him but held back. It wasn't the time or the place, not when she was simply the nanny. Remembering his choice of words made it slightly easier for her to walk away.

Once in the bedroom she arranged the spare pillows on the bed and got comfortable, Darcy cradled in her arms. "Okay, sweet pea," she said softly, adjusting her position and Darcy's weight until both were comfortable. Darcy eagerly took the bottle and Elli sighed. She could hear Wyatt's deep voice and Angela's feminine one from the kitchen. Her back stiffened against the headboard, and she sighed. The sofa would have been more comfortable, but Wyatt needed privacy. Elli thought briefly of the rocking chair she'd bought but Tim had returned to the store, insisting it didn't match their decor.

The solid wood and Quaker design would have fit in here perfectly.

It would have fit in, but she didn't. Even if she had been pretending she did, she realized. Today had shown her that. She was still on the outside, looking in through a dusty pane of glass. This wasn't about her. It was about Wyatt and Darcy and protecting his family. His explanation today that she was "just" the nanny had shown her that he would do what was necessary to keep Darcy with him. That he was sticking to their original arrangement. And of course he should.

But it was very clear that she was not Wyatt's priority despite their pretty little scenes together. If nothing else, the past few days had shown her that dissolving her marriage to Tim had been the right thing. For even if she didn't belong here, she was coming to understand what it was she wanted. And it had nothing to do with a fancy house and expensive car and having the right things.

She wouldn't settle for anything less than it all. Not ever again.

CHAPTER NINE

WYATT COULDN'T AVOID the house any longer. Not the house in particular, but Elli. Darcy was too little to ask questions, of course, but Elli could. And would. She seemed to notice every little thing about him, reading him better than anyone he ever remembered.

It was incredibly disconcerting.

But dark was coming on and he'd relied on her for too long today. Darcy was his responsibility and Elli was here to help. He couldn't hide out in the barns any longer. Chores were long finished. It was time to regroup and move on.

He made it as far as the veranda, with his hand on the handle of the door, but he couldn't make himself go in. Not yet.

Instead he turned, rested his hands on the old wood railing. The veranda faced north, and he gazed out over the brown, empty field across the road. Next year it would provide hay for his herd, and he could almost see the welcoming green-brown grasses, waving in the prairie wind.

This was all he'd ever wanted. A place to call his own. To leave the past behind him. To find his own way, make his own living. He'd done it, too, relying on himself, putting money away until he'd found this place. His Realtor had looked at him skeptically when he'd said he wanted it. It had been neglected and had fallen into disrepair. His herd for this year was small. But the challenge of rebuilding, of growing it into something vital and important was exciting.

Until today, when he'd had to face his past all over again. All the prying, awful queries that he'd had to answer about his upbringing. He had come away from the meeting angry and resentful and afraid, and those were three emotions he'd worked very hard to overcome. He couldn't explain it all to Elli. He needed her on his side in this and if she knew the ugly truth she'd be gone like a shot. Elli was too good, too pure to get wrapped up in his baggage. He'd do well to remember it.

When he thought of her waiting inside, he tensed all over again. She'd looked so pretty today in her red sweater and makeup. He hadn't missed the little touches around the house either, the pillows and tablecloth and, for heaven's sake, matching dishcloths. He scowled. Before Miss Beck had come he'd recognized them as a good idea. But now… this was his house. Elli's presence was everywhere, in every corner. The past forty-eight hours had moved at warp speed and he was struggling to keep up mentally and physically. Coming in to a bunch of feminine touches was simply too much. Something had to give.

"Wyatt?"

He spun, his breath catching in surprise as she appeared as if she'd materialized from his thoughts. The porch light highlighted her pale hair, making her look soft and alluring. "I didn't hear you come out."

"No, you were in another world."

She was right, and it had been a world with her in it, so he didn't answer.

She stepped up beside him, mimicking his stance with her hands on the railing. Her voice was soft, so that it almost seemed part of the breeze. "Do you want to tell me where you were?"

He deliberately misunderstood her. "In the barns."

She laughed lightly, ending on a sigh. "That's not what I meant."

He expected her to go on, but she didn't. She just waited patiently, as if it didn't matter if he said anything more or not. She simply stood beside him, breathing deeply of the crisp autumn air. Her scent, something light and floral, drifted over to him and he felt his muscles tighten in response. This was why he'd stayed away. Because after Angela had departed, he'd wanted nothing more than to seek Elli out. To have her near, to bury his face in her sweet-smelling hair and feel that everything was right again. And that would have been a mistake.

"Where's Darcy?"

"Sleeping. She had a bath and her bottle. She's such a good baby, Wyatt. When you first showed up at my door, I had no idea what I was doing. But Darcy's shown me, bless her."

"You didn't seem unsure. Angela seemed pleased enough with you being Darcy's nanny." Wyatt turned away from the view and rested his hips against the railing so he could look into her face. It was calm, serene even, while he still felt in such turmoil. Again he fought against the urge to pull her into his arms. No, he was stronger than that. He had to keep the lines drawn.

"Nanny." Elli's voice sounded flat. "That certainly tells me where I stand, doesn't it?"

Was she angry with him? She crossed her arms over her chest, chafing them as if she was cold, but even Wyatt understood the defensive body language. "What was I supposed to say, Elli?"

That caused her to pause, and her gaze flew to his.

"What was I supposed to tell her?" he asked. "That I barely knew you? That we were friends?" He swallowed hard. "That I kissed you last night and it was a mistake?"

"Of course not," she whispered. Her eyes had widened as he'd spoken and he regretted the harsh way he'd said it.

"I had to present everything in a positive way for Darcy's sake. And thank God I did. I might lose her anyway now."

Elli's lips dropped open. He could see she was surprised by his last remark, and part of him wanted to confide in her but another part wanted to lock it all away as he'd done for the past fifteen years.

But Elli's response surprised him. "I'm not just a nanny to you, then?"

"Elli…"

"That was our agreement, but I really hated that part, you know. The part where you cozied up to her with your smiles and saying all the right things and passed me off as only the nanny, like some appendage to the situation that could be replaced at a moment's notice if it wasn't convenient."

She reminded him of a little girl who lifted her chin and accepted a dare while being scared to death on the inside. Defiant and terrified. He wondered why. Was she afraid of him? Of herself?

The air hummed between them while he fought for the right thing to say. "Why do we have to quantify our relationship at all? Elli, are you…" He paused, not believing it was true but wanting to know just the same. "Are you *jealous* of Miss Beck?"

A faint blush blossomed on her cheeks.

"You are." By all rights the knowledge should have made

him retreat, away from messy emotions that had no place in this situation. A solid reason to back away, his head was telling him. She'd managed to insinuate herself into nearly every aspect of his life in the past few days, and without even trying.

He should be backing off. But he found himself slightly flattered. Maybe she hadn't been as immune to his kiss last night as he'd thought.

He stepped forward, mysteriously charmed by the roses in her cheeks. He'd thought calling her the nanny was the clearest and best way of defining the situation, especially to someone who had a say in the matter. Angela Beck, for all her pretty looks and smiles, had more power than he was comfortable with. *He* didn't regret kissing *her,* not really. And it sure didn't stop him from wanting to do it again, despite his better judgment.

He was close enough that now she had to tilt her head to look up at him. It would take only the slightest shift and his lips could be on hers. The idea hovered there for a moment, and the way her breath was coming, in shallow, quiet gasps, he could tell she was thinking about it, too.

"It made me feel…pushed to the side," she finally admitted, lowering her chin and breaking the moment. "Marginalized. Like I was…somehow expendable."

That hurt, because making her feel that way was the last thing Wyatt wanted. Couldn't she see that he cared about her? That he was trying to protect her, too? But how could he do that and still protect himself?

"That certainly wasn't how it was meant," he consoled her. "Do you know what it meant to be able to say that today? To be able to point out that Darcy was cared for so well? And you were here, looking after her, and making coffee, and backing me up, showing her that I was right to trust you." He lifted his fingers to her face, touched the cool, soft skin of her cheek. "No one has ever done that for me before. No one. I never meant to make you feel like less because of it, Elli."

He understood her insecurity and refused to add to it by making her feel unimportant. He leaned forward, just enough that their bodies brushed and he lowered his head, his Stetson shadowing them from the light of the porch. Her lips were warm, pliant and just a little bit hesitant. The sweetness fired his blood more than any passionate embrace might have.

"It was just for show. You are more than a nanny, Elli," he murmured against her lips. "But I couldn't let the social worker see that."

Elli stepped out of his embrace. He could see her fingers tremble as she touched her lips and then dropped her hand.

"You trust me?"

"Of course I do. Why do you continue to doubt it? I would only leave Darcy with someone I trusted."

"But you hardly know me!"

His smile followed her as she went back to the railing, putting several feet between them.

"I know you better after two days than I know most people after two years, Ellison."

She shook her head, her face white now. "Don't. Don't say that."

"Why?"

"B-because it…it…" She kept stammering and his heart beat faster, not sure what her answer would be but knowing what he hoped. Nothing could have surprised him more, but there it was.

"Because it scares you?"

"Yes," she whispered.

The air began to hum again.

Elli blinked, swallowed. He watched each movement with great attention, trying to drink in every nuance of her. She had lost so much over the past months. Wyatt had overcome many of his demons through the years, but Elli's wounds were fresh. Surely, for this once, he could say what he felt if it meant giving her back some of her self-esteem.

"Angela Beck is no more beautiful than you, Elli."

"You're just trying to distract me." Her eyes narrowed. "My hair was a mess and any fool can see I am overweight and…well, she looked so put together and perfect!"

Was that what this was about? Perfection? He'd learned long ago that perfection was overrated and impossible. It was intimidating and unsustainable, as well. "What you are, Ellison Marchuk, is *real*."

He closed the distance between them once more, this time leaving her no escape as his body blocked her from the front and the railing from the back. He put his hands on her waist and drew her closer so that their bodies brushed. His fingers trailed over her ribs and down the curve of her hip. "I don't want you to be perfect. I want you to be just as you are. I like your curves, and the way your hair curls around your forehead, and just about everything about you."

"Oh, Wyatt," she whispered, and he could tell she was tempted to give in.

Elli heard the words and felt his hands slide over the pockets of her pants. She sighed, a sound of bliss and longing and fear. Did he really mean it? When was the last time someone had taken her as she was and it had actually been okay? Everyone always expected more of her.

She should be smarter, more ambitious, neater, prettier, thinner. And yet Wyatt didn't seem to care about any of that. At the same time she wanted to be more *for* him. He was a good man, she could tell. Strong and honorable and gorgeous without even trying.

His hand rested at her waist as his voice touched her, deep and sad. "Whoever told you otherwise isn't here now, Elli. Let it go."

Oh, the kindness was nearly too much to bear. If he kept on, she'd start crying and that would be a horrible mess. The only way to hold it together was to straighten her spine and dismiss his kindness. All of it, and keep only the sweet memory of his words locked inside like a treasure.

"Let it go like I suppose you have, Wyatt?"

She nearly cringed at how harsh her words sounded. Was she so wrapped up in protecting herself that she'd hurt him to do it? Shame burned within her. His hand stopped moving on her hip and she felt him straighten, the intimate moment lost.

"I don't know what you mean." He dismissed her comment, but she knew he was lying. She'd fought back simply to avoid being pulled down into more sadness, but his evasive answer somehow made her mad. She had been rude, but it had also been an honest question. He could see into her so easily—why shouldn't she know more about him? She wanted him to be straight with her. She needed it.

"You know exactly what I mean. You hightailed it out of here after Angela left and hid out in the barns ever since. That had nothing to do with me. What did you mean before, that you might lose her anyway?"

"It doesn't matter now," he replied, backing away. He turned and headed toward the veranda steps.

Elli watched him walk away, and anger warred with remorse for turning the tables on him. She'd thought she wanted to hear him confirm that yes, she was simply there to help Darcy. It would have made it much easier to fight her growing attraction, knowing it wasn't returned. But he hadn't. He'd brought up the kiss, the one she couldn't erase from her mind. And then he'd kissed her again, making her toes curl. Why had he done it? Because he meant it? Every cell in her body wanted to believe that, but a nagging voice in her head told her it was merely a method to distract her from the real issue—the reason he'd disappeared after Miss Beck had departed.

Now he was shutting her out and walking away when she was aching to understand why a mere mention of his interview made his face turn pale and his shoulders stiffen. What had happened to make him seek solitude for hours? Why was he hurting so much?

"Never took you for a runner, Black," she accused, heart in her throat. She deliberately provoked him, knowing that if she went the gentle route he'd simply dismiss her.

Her sharp words had the desired effect. He turned back and his eyes blazed at her. "You don't know what you're talking about."

"No, I don't. But I figure it's something big when it makes you leave the house and hide out in the barns. When you spend hours alone rather than face us in the house. When you miss dinner and bath time with Darcy and choose to spend the evening in an unheated barn. And it's got to be really something if you attempt to distract me by kissing me. I asked a simple question and you ran away."

"It's nothing." He started to turn away again, guilt written all over his face.

"No, it's not. It's a whole lot of something, and I know fear when I see it. If I'm staying here, if Darcy is staying here…" She paused, afraid to speak her mind, but wanting to be stronger than she'd ever been before. "If we're starting something, I think I deserve to know."

He spun on her so quickly she could react only by stepping backward. "I don't owe you anything," he growled.

"And if we want to talk about running, what exactly are you doing, Elli? I'm not blind. What are you doing at the Camerons' if not hiding away from life, huh? Running, hiding…we all have something, don't we?" He scoffed. "What are you doing here anyway? Playing at reality? You and your tablecloths and doilies and God knows what else."

Elli recoiled inside as the harsh words sliced into her, but she held her ground and lifted her chin. He would not intimidate her, even if he was one hundred percent right. She knew what pain looked like; she'd seen it in the mirror for months, and now she saw it in the hard planes of his face. They weren't so different in that way. Wyatt was simply afraid. Of what? What could be so bad that he'd fear Darcy was going to be taken away from him?

"I certainly didn't mean to overstep," she said stiffly. "I thought you wanted me to do those things. If you don't like them, I'll put them away and you can keep things just as you want them. And for the record, Wyatt Black, you don't owe me." She had taken Tim's insults, but those days were gone. She was stronger than that now. "Except not to play games." She slid her hands into her pockets, attempting to keep them warm. The evening suddenly seemed much colder. "If what happened just now between us was a game, it was very cruel of you, Wyatt."

His lips dropped open for a moment before he shut them again, forming a firm line. His hat shadowed his eyes, but she could feel the apology in his gaze.

"Oh God, I'm sorry. I don't play games, Elli. I never should have said that."

She knew in her heart he was being honest. Which meant what he'd said was true, and she tried to keep her pulse from spinning out of control. Lord, everything about him was so intense. What would it be like to be loved by a man like Wyatt Black?

"I know," she acquiesced.

His lips relaxed and his shoulders dropped. "I do owe you for all you've done. But not this. Please don't ask me this," he breathed.

Elli sighed, touched by the anguish in his voice. What was she doing? She could feel herself falling. Any plans and decisions she'd made about her future seemed to fly out of her head when he was around. Wyatt was *dangerous.* And it was *exciting.*

Sympathy and provocation hadn't worked. Maybe he had a right to his own secrets. "I'm going back inside, then. There's dinner in the fridge if you want to heat it up."

What an idiot she was, letting herself have feelings for Wyatt, giving in to the intense attraction that seemed to grow with each minute they spent together. He couldn't give her what she needed. He had too many things pulling at his time. Whatever else was between them was only muddying the waters.

Nothing surprised her more than the sound of the door as it creaked open, then clicked shut behind her.

She turned to see him standing in the doorway, his jaw set and his hair slightly messed as if he'd run his hands through it. His hat drooped negligently from his hand. "I am not a runner," he said firmly. "Not anymore."

"Then why did you take off? I came out from feeding Darcy and you were gone. I didn't know where until it got darker and I saw the lights in the barn."

He stepped forward, his eyes pleading with hers, as if they were begging her to understand. "Do you know the kinds of questions she asked, Elli? We're not talking generalities here. Every single last thing you'd rather not talk about? That's what they ask."

He tossed his hat onto a chair and covered his face with his hands.

The gesture was so sudden, so despairing, Elli was at a loss as to what to do. She felt his pain keenly, as piercing as a cold knife, the hopelessness of it. He exhaled slowly and pulled his hands away from his face. She almost wished he hadn't. His eyes were bleak, his cheekbones etched with agony. He looked the way she'd felt the morning she'd awakened and truly realized that William was not going to be in her arms ever again.

"Don't," she said, shaking her head. "I'm sorry I pushed. Don't say it, Wyatt, if it hurts too much. It doesn't matter."

But now he ignored her, as if he'd opened the door and couldn't help but walk through it. "She poked and prodded and pried for every detail you can imagine about any topic you can come up with. That interview invades every single aspect of your life. Perhaps now you can understand why I had to be alone."

"Did she ask about your relationship to Barbara?"

He snorted, a harsh, hurtful sound. "Top of the list. When did I find out she was my sister. Why did I want to look after her child when we barely knew each other. The fact that Barbara was the product of an affair started the probe into our family life."

Elli blanched. Of course. Digging around in painful events would make anyone want to turtle into themselves. "About being taken away? Your father's abuse?"

"Oh, yes." His hands fidgeted and he shoved them in the back pockets of his jeans. His eyes were wild now, like a cornered animal. "My father, that paragon of parenthood, and whether or not I'm cut from the same cloth. Do I solve things with physical violence. What are my thoughts on discipline."

"I'm so sorry, Wyatt."

He took several breaths before responding. "All the things I never wanted to talk about with another living soul. All the demons I've tried to outrun. That's what it was. So I could somehow prove myself worthy."

Elli felt tears sting the backs of her eyes. She understood that the last thing Wyatt would want was to be compared to his father. He was so gentle and caring with Darcy, so dedicated and determined to do the right thing. To insinuate otherwise would cut him to the bone. What if she'd been faced with the same interrogation? Would she have passed? Would she have been able to talk about all her mistakes?

Now she looked at him and saw him swipe at his eyes. Compassion overruled every bit of self-preservation she possessed and she rushed forward to take his hands. "Oh, Wyatt, I'm so sorry," she repeated, not knowing what else to say. "What can I do?"

He led her by the hand to an old battered wing chair. The light from the kitchen highlighted his sharp features as he sat, then tugged her down onto his lap. "Just let me hold you," he murmured, and she felt her heart quake as his arms came around her.

Mentally she'd been trying to push him away for hours. But it felt so good to be held. When William died Tim had pushed her away, pretending everything was all right, denying her the physical touches that might have given some comfort. She was beginning to see that Wyatt, with all his baggage and secrets and sometimes prickly exterior, was far more giving than Tim had ever been and yet he had more reason to hide. She curled into his embrace and tangled her fingers through the dark strands of his hair, wanting to give back to him just a little bit.

"I can do that," she whispered, and for long minutes they sat that way, absorbing strength from each other.

And somehow without meaning it to happen, Elli felt a corner of her heart start to heal.

"Do you know what the saving grace is in all of this?" Wyatt's soft, deep voice finally broke the silence.

"Hmm?" she asked, her eyes closed as she memorized the shape and feel of him, the scent, the way his chest rumbled when he spoke.

"My mother. When I think of Barbara, I think of my mother. Mom would not have turned Barbara away, even though she would have been a reminder of my father's infidelity," he said. His arms tightened ever so slightly. "My mother was kind and generous, and had every reason to be bitter. But she wasn't. The only way I've gotten through this at all is thinking about her. If I was cursed with one parent, I was blessed with the other. I've always tried to be more like her...even if I do look like him."

Of course, Elli realized. What must it be like for Wyatt to resemble someone who had betrayed the very nature of fatherhood? Of course he would want to emulate his mother. "What was she like?"

She felt his facial muscles move as he smiled. "She could do anything. Cook, sew, sing...not that my father gave her much to sing about. But she did it when he was away. She always tried to make things special for me, and she seemed to apologize when she couldn't."

"Why did she stay? Why didn't she take you and leave, Wyatt?"

His response was typical and sad. "Where would she have gone? She was afraid he would find her. Or that he would try to take me. Not that he really wanted me. It was about possession with my father."

She was starting to understand why all the prying questions had affected him so deeply today. "This all came out this afternoon?"

He nodded. "I will not be like my father, Elli."

"Of course not." She straightened and cupped his chin, tilting his face up so she could look him in the eyes. "And you're not. Looking after Darcy isn't about possession for you. I know that. It's about family, and acceptance, and responsibility."

"You see that. But I'm not sure Angela Beck did. It isn't so pretty when it's in black and white."

"What happened to your parents, Wyatt?"

His gaze was steady on hers. "I was working in Fort McMurray. They'd been traveling together and my father had been drinking. The crash killed them both instantly."

She let the news sink in, knowing there was nothing she could say that would be more than a useless platitude. And after today's interview Wyatt was afraid he was going to lose Darcy, too. Darcy and Barbara were the only family he had left. He was determined to look after them both, she could tell. What would happen to Wyatt if he failed?

He couldn't fail. She was here to help ensure it.

"They need to be sure, that's all. They are putting Darcy first, just like you are. They'll see that you're the right person to care for her until Barbara is well again."

"It doesn't make it easier," he replied, calmer now. "So now maybe you understand why I called you the nanny today. I can't let them all down. They're all the family I have left. That's why I can't jeopardize the situation by keeping on like we have been."

She slid off his lap, took the chair opposite him and put her hands on her knees. "What do you mean?"

Wyatt's gaze was apologetic as he leaned forward, resting his forearms on his knees and linking his hands. "I know I said that you were more than just the nanny, but do you think today's visit is the end of it? What if Beck comes back and finds us like we were tonight?"

"We were hardly doing anything wrong," she replied, feeling a sudden chill on her shoulders now that his arms were not about her anymore.

"Maybe not, but how would it look to her? I insisted you are the nanny. I made it clear we're not in a personal relationship. You heard what she said. People cohabiting need to be in a relationship for at least a year, and we've known each other only days. I told her there was nothing romantic between us. If we continue on this way it means I've *lied*. And I simply can't risk it. Darcy is too important to me."

A part of her ached as he said it. She had enjoyed being held by him so much. But Darcy had to come first, and they both knew it. Tonight, she had only fooled herself into thinking she was important to him. And perhaps she was, but she was way down on the list. The new life she wanted to build wasn't here. She'd left the old dreams behind. Wyatt and Darcy were sidetracking her, and at times most pleasantly. Tonight she'd forgotten all her self-promises the moment he'd put his lips on hers. But she had to keep her eye on the big picture.

"Elli...I'm sorry. Sorry I've dragged you into this."

Her heart tugged, hearing him say her name that way. But her resolve was stronger, especially now that he wasn't touching her. She wouldn't let him see he had the power to hurt her. "No, Wyatt. I'm here of my own choosing. You're right. If she got the wrong impression, you could lose Darcy, and I know how much that would eat away at you. You have to do what's best for Darcy."

He nodded. "She's the most important thing now. And lying about our involvement would be a mistake I don't want on my conscience." His eyes were sober, and she thought perhaps held a glint of resentment. "Lies have a way of coming out sooner or later."

She thought of his father denying his own daughter and leaving Barbara's mother to fend for herself. She thought about all that she hadn't told Wyatt about William and felt a niggle of guilt. She hadn't exactly lied, but she hadn't told him the whole truth either. She wasn't sure she ever could.

"You are not your father, Wyatt. You always do the right thing."

The truth was bittersweet. The right thing was costing her. Just when she was starting to feel alive again, she was cruelly reminded of her own unimportance.

A thin cry sounded from the bedroom; Darcy was awake once more.

"So we keep it simple," she said, pushing on her knees and rising from the chair.

"Simple," he echoed.

Elli left him sitting in the dark and went to get Darcy. As she picked her up, warm and nuzzly from sleep, she realized that nothing about their relationship would ever be simple. Not after tonight.

CHAPTER TEN

THE DAYS THAT FOLLOWED set a pattern, and Wyatt was true to their agreement. He was always pleasant and friendly, but there was no more talk of pasts and fathers or any other hot-button topics. Elli cooked meals, cared for Darcy and finished up accounting assignments, e-mailing them to her supervisor. Wyatt asked her quietly to leave the things she'd bought, but there were no more shopping trips to the home décor shop. The fall air turned colder and the leaves scattered from the trees, leaving a golden carpet on the grass. Wyatt cared for his stock, spent hours outside making repairs and moving the herd to different pastures. When he came in his smiles and touches were for Darcy.

As Darcy watched from her swing, Elli washed up the breakfast dishes and put them away in the cozy kitchen. Elli wasn't jealous. It was impossible to be jealous of Darcy, who was an absolute darling. But she found herself wishing that Wyatt could spare a few soft words and gentle touches for her. She missed him. She'd had a taste and she wanted more. Seeing him work so hard and lavish his affection on his niece only made him more amazing in her eyes. She'd promised herself never to settle again, but as she got to know Wyatt even more, she saw so many qualities she admired, wished for in a partner. Stability. Tenderness. Patience. Love.

She was falling in love with him, sure as spring rain.

But the way he'd put on the brakes and then slipped into their daily and functional existence so easily told her that the feeling wasn't reciprocated. Her hands paused on the handle of a cupboard door. Those first days together had been so intense. Emotions had run high and things had been in flux. Now things had settled into a routine. Whatever her feelings for Wyatt, they weren't returned, she was sure of it.

She should be relieved, she supposed. Soon Barbara would be out of the hospital and the Camerons would be back. Elli had to start thinking about what she was going to do next. She told herself that because her feelings were one-sided, there would be fewer complications when it came time to move on.

As she passed Darcy, she reached out and gave the tiny cotton-covered toes a squeeze. It was going to be difficult to see Darcy leave, too, but she'd always known she would. Wyatt would not be a part of Elli's life after that happened and that wouldn't change even if she wished it to. No, she needed to start looking for a job and a place to live as soon as she finished her course.

She heard Wyatt's boots on the veranda and checked the clock on the microwave. Right on time. The past few days he'd come in at precisely ten o'clock for a cup of coffee and a sweet. He did have a sweet tooth and she was more than happy to oblige. She'd enjoyed the looking after Darcy, and Wyatt's house, and cooking meals for more than herself. As the screen door slapped against the frame, she cautioned herself not to get too accustomed to it. She was going to be hurt enough when this was over; forming habits would not help.

Wyatt stood in the doorway, grinning as if he was holding some sort of secret, looking unexpectedly youthful. The lines that had crinkled the corners of his eyes were gone, and there was an air of hopefulness about him.

She couldn't help the smile that curved her lips in return. He looked so pleased with himself, his dark eyes alight with some mischief and his hair even more windblown than usual. He held his hat in his hands, and she noticed he was crumpling the sides.

"What are you up to? And I know it's not my banana bread making you smile that way."

He made a show of sniffing the air. "You're right, although now that you mention it, it does smell good in here."

"It's just out of the oven and too hot to slice, so stay away from that cooling rack." She struggled to keep her lips stern as she brandished a mixing spoon, but felt the corner of her mouth quiver. What was it about him that made her smile so easily? He looked like a boy with a new toy.

He came across the kitchen and tipped a finger at Darcy's nose. "I have a surprise for you both."

"A surprise?" Elli folded the tea towel in her hands and draped it over the handle of the oven door. Curiosity got the better of her and she couldn't resist asking, "What kind of surprise?"

"Just something I've been working on the last week or so."

Elli's mind whirred. The past week—that would be ever since the night they'd agreed to keep things platonic and he'd started spending more time in the fields and barns. What could he possibly have to surprise them with?

"Stay here, okay? I've got to bring it in."

She wanted to refuse but couldn't, not at the hopeful look he sent her before he spun and disappeared out the door.

She heard an odd clunking as he came back. "Close your

eyes!" he called out from the porch, and she did, anticipation causing a quiver in her tummy. No one had surprised her in a very long time.

"Are they closed?" More clunking and thunking came from the entry.

Elli giggled. "Yes, they're closed. But hurry up!"

Some shuffling and scraping and then Wyatt came back to the kitchen. "Bring Darcy," he said, and Elli could see he was practically bouncing on the balls of his feet. His Stetson was pushed back on his head, making him look even more young and boyish and very, very attractive.

She picked Darcy up out of her swing and said, "Okay. Lead on before you burst."

He led the way into the living room. "What do you think?"

In the corner where the makeshift table had been now sat the most beautiful rocking chair Elli had ever seen. Stunningly simple, with a curved seat and perfect spindles along the back, painstakingly sanded and stained a beautiful rich oak. On the seat was a flowered cushion in blues and pinks.

A lump rose in her throat as she tried to think of the words to say. "It's beautiful, Wyatt," she murmured, holding tight to Darcy.

"I found it in the back shed, of all places," Wyatt explained. He went to the chair and stood behind it, resting his hands on the back. "It was dirty and scratched, but it just needed some love. Some fine grit sanding and a few coats of stain."

He had done this himself? With his hands? Somehow it meant much more knowing he hadn't just gone to a store and picked it out. It almost felt…like a lover's gift. But that was silly, wasn't it? Who gave a lover a rocking chair?

There was also the small matter of things being strictly friendly between them lately.

It felt intimate just the same.

"You did this?" The words came through her lips tight and strained. She tried to smile encouragingly to cover.

"It was a bit of a shock at first, you know," he said, undaunted by her cool response. "When I came in and saw all the...well, the feminine touches around the place. I've been a bachelor a long time, Elli, but you didn't deserve the criticism I doled out. And you know, I've gotten used to it." His eyes danced at her. "Now I even like it. I wanted to make it up to you and didn't know how. Then there it was and I realized you need a proper chair. Come and sit in it with Darcy."

Elli's knees shook now as she walked across the room. She hadn't meant to make Wyatt uncomfortable in his own home, and his apology had made things right. He didn't need to do this. She was touched.

"I didn't mean to overstep," she whispered.

"You didn't. You just had the sense to do what I wouldn't do for myself. Come on," he cajoled, giving the chair a little rock. "I've tried it. It's stable, I promise."

For days she'd lamented a comfortable seating arrangement for feeding the baby or for soothing her as she fussed. She'd remembered the chair she'd bought and returned while expecting William, and wished she had something similar, especially when Darcy seemed particularly difficult to soothe and Elli's back ached from leaning against the headboard of Wyatt's bed. But her reaction now was immediate and frightening. Grief and longing hovered on the edge of her heart as she was faced with the actual object rather than the thought. She inhaled deeply, struggling for control. How could she refuse to sit in it when Wyatt was looking so pleased with himself? And he deserved to be.

She could do this. She could stay in control. She sat tentatively on the seat, the weight of Darcy in her arms awkward in a way it hadn't been since the very first day. Her shoulders tensed as she leaned against the back. "It's wonderful, Wyatt. Thank you."

But he'd gone quiet behind her, as if he'd sensed something wasn't quite right. "You're tense," he observed, and his hands settled on her shoulders. "What's wrong?" His fingers kneaded gently, trying to work out the knots that had formed. And as he moved his hands, the chair began to rock.

Elli looked down into Darcy's contented face, saw the blue eyes looking up at her, unfocused, the tiny, perfectly shaped lips, and in the breath of a moment her control slipped and everything blurred.

Once the tears started, Elli couldn't make them stop. The chair tipped forward and back but each movement pushed the tears closer to the edge of her lashes until the first ones slid down her cheeks. She caught her breath on a little hiccup, trying desperately to get a grip on her emotions.

But the memory was so utterly real that she lost the battle.

"Elli…my God, what is it?" Wyatt came around from behind the chair and knelt before her. He swept the Stetson from his head and put it on the couch beside them. Her heart gave a lurch at the action, gentle and gallant. His face loomed before hers, his eyes shadowed with concern. She did love him. There was no way she could have avoided it. Knowing it was one-sided, on top of the pain already slicing into her, only increased the despair cresting over her.

"It's just…just that…" She gasped for breath and felt another sob building. "The last time I rocked…it was…"

But she couldn't finish. Her mouth worked but no words

came out. Only an oddly high, keening sound as she sat in the chair he'd made for her and finally fully, grieved for the son she'd lost.

It had been William in her arms, her son, unbearably small but perfectly formed, painstakingly bathed by the nurses and swaddled in the white-and-blue flannel of the hospital. No breath passed his lips; his lashes lay in rest on his pale cheeks. But she had held him close and rocked him and said goodbye.

Wyatt reached for Darcy, but Elli held on unreasonably, turning her arm away from Wyatt's prying hands. "No! Don't take him yet. You can't take him yet."

Then her ears registered what she'd said and she broke down completely with shame and grief. Wyatt took Darcy gently from her now unresisting arms and laid her on the play mat on the floor.

When he returned, he simply bent and lifted Elli out of the chair, an arm around her back and the other beneath her knees, lifting her as if she weighed nothing. She clung to his hard, strong body, putting her arms around his neck and pressing her forehead against it. He went to the sofa and sat, holding her in his lap. "Let it out," he whispered against her hair, and she felt him kiss the top of her head. "For God's sake, Elli, let it out."

She did, all the while clinging to his neck as the pain and anger and grief finally let loose. This was what she'd held in for months, trying to keep up appearances, determined to show the world she could function. It had been building all this time, brought to the surface by loving Darcy as she cared for her, and now spilled over by loving Wyatt, by trusting him.

And she did trust him. Even if he never returned her love, she knew she trusted him completely. In all her life she'd never known a better man. Gradually her breaths slowed, grew regular, and exhaustion and relief made her limbs limp and relaxed. He felt good, solid. Tim had scoffed at her tears, turning her away. Perhaps that had been his way of handling the grief—by not showing it at all—and she'd been forced to hold it in, too. With Wyatt there was no pretending. She could be who she had to be.

"I didn't know," Wyatt said softly, once she was in firm control. His hand rubbed over her upper arm, soothing and warm. "How long have you been holding that in?"

Elli sighed, her eyes still closed so she could focus on the feel of him, warm and firm, the way his fingers felt through the fabric of her sweater. "Thirteen months."

Over a year. William had been gone over a year and she suddenly knew she was no closer to being over it than she'd been then. She'd only gone through the motions.

Darcy lay on the floor, looking up at the colors and shapes of the baby gym above her. Watching her caused a bittersweet ache to spread through Elli's chest. She missed the opportunities most. The opportunity to see her son grow, change, to be able to love him and see the light of recognition in his eyes at the sound of her voice or the touch of her hands.

"I had been waiting so long to have my baby," she confessed, finally giving words to the pain. "I never had the chance to learn with him. To feed him or change him or rock him to sleep. I imagined what it would be like for months, but theory is different than practice." She tried to smile, but it wobbled. "And then you showed up with Darcy...." Her voice trailed off, uncertain.

He lifted his head and looked at her face. Oh, she knew she looked dreadful. She rushed to wipe at her cheeks, to smooth her messed hair. But Wyatt didn't seem to care about her appearance. He never had. He raised his left hand and wiped away the moisture beneath her eyes with the pad of his thumb.

He touched her cheek softly, cupping her jaw lightly in his hand and applying gentle pressure so she would turn her face toward him. "It was a boy," he said, and she remembered what she'd blurted out in the chair.

For a moment it had been as if she was back in the hospital with William instead of there in the living room with Darcy.

Wyatt kept a firm hold on his emotions. There was more going on with Elli than he had ever dreamed and somehow the chair had set her off. He'd done the only thing he could—held her until the storm was over. She tried to turn away, but he kept his fingers firm on her face. "Elli?"

"Yes, he was a boy," she whispered, and he caught the glimmer of remnant tears in the corners of her eyes. Her teeth worried her lower lip.

And if she knew it was a boy, it meant she'd carried him long enough to know. How long? Months, certainly. He couldn't comprehend what that must be like, to carry a life and then just…not. He thought she'd told him that she had miscarried. But it didn't add up, not now. When a person thought of miscarriage, they thought of pregnancies ended in the early stages, the first few months. To know her baby was a boy, and the rocking chair today… It didn't take much effort to connect the dots.

"You were further along in your pregnancy than you let me believe, weren't you?" He said it gently, urging her to talk. She clearly needed to. And he wanted to listen. Not because he felt obligated in any way but because there was something about Elli that reached inside him. He couldn't explain it, or quantify what or why. He just wanted to. He wanted to help her the way she'd helped him.

"I was six weeks to term," she murmured, and the tears

that had been sitting in the corners of her eyes slid silently
down her cheeks. "My water broke and I knew it was too
early. It should have been okay. We just thought he'd be
small, and spend some time in the neonatal unit."

It took her a few seconds to collect herself. "There was
an additional problem with his lungs we hadn't known
about, a defect. I…"

She stopped, lowered her head.

"You don't have to say it," he said gently, feeling his
heart quake for her. He'd been hiding out in the barns and
thinking only of himself, first to escape the false domesticity she was providing and then thinking how proud he'd be
to present her with that stupid chair to make up for hurting
her feelings. He'd thought about making it easier for her to
care for Darcy, and a way to say thank-you, since she had
yet to cash the check he had written. It had hurt, brushing
her aside and insisting they keep things platonic. If circumstances were different, he would have pursued her.

She was the first person he'd willingly told about his
past, and it hadn't been easy. But his pain was nothing
compared to hers. His loss was nothing when held up to
the loss of a child.

She carried on, even though he could barely hear the
whispered words. "I never got to hear him cry."

There was a plaintive plea in her words and he tightened
his arms around her. "I'm so sorry."

"I thought I was over it more than this," she whispered.
She wasn't fighting his embrace, and he settled more deeply
into the cushions. Her weight felt good on his lap, holding
her the way he'd wanted to for days. Just being close to her,
connected, felt right.

"Sometimes it takes people years to really grieve." He
sighed, knowing how long it had taken him to accept that
his mother was truly gone. It had been just recently that

he'd made peace with it. And only then that he'd been able to sort out his life and know what he really wanted. This ranch was that resolution put into action. A testament to his mother's faith in him and finally his faith in himself.

"Back in Calgary, everyone kept asking how I was doing. I could never answer them honestly. I had to put on a smile and give them some stock response."

"And your husband?"

"Grief either brings you together or drives you apart. Our relationship didn't have the right foundation, and it didn't weather the stress of it. Tim buried himself in work and I…"

When she paused, Wyatt gave her hand a squeeze. She was being brave, though he doubted she knew it.

"I built myself a shell."

Wyatt smiled. "Oh, I can relate to that, all right."

And finally, a smile in return, with puffy lips and red-rimmed eyes. "I guess you probably can." Then the smile faded.

"Ain't life something?" Wyatt shrugged. "I realized a while back that it's not the disaster that defines a person, Elli. It's what you do afterward that counts."

"And I haven't done anything." Her eyebrows drew together. "I've just put it all off."

"There's always today. Today's a good day to make a new start."

Wyatt knew what he wanted her to say. That this platonic relationship was a waste of time. That she would make a new start with him once Darcy went home. Barbara's doctors reported she was doing well and soon Darcy would be going home. There wouldn't be a social worker standing in their way.

"I'm not sure I'm quite ready for that yet. I just…oh." Her voice caught again. "I miss him," she said simply.

"No one said you had to do it overnight," he replied, disappointed. "But making a start—and getting it all out, if that's what it takes—is good."

"You're a good man, Wyatt Black."

She cupped his face in her hands and he felt her blue gaze penetrate. Even with the evidence of crying marring her face, he could honestly say he wanted her, more than he'd ever wanted a woman. It was deeper than a simple physical need. His gaze dropped to her lips and back up again and he saw acknowledgment in her eyes. "Not as good as you think," he murmured. His resolution was forgotten when faced with her sweet vulnerability.

Her fingers still framed his face and he leaned forward, needing to touch her, taste her, wanting to somehow make things right for her in the only way he knew how.

He put his lips over hers and kissed her softly, wanting to convince her to open up to him that little bit more. For a few seconds she seemed to hold her breath, and the moment paused, like standing on a ledge of indecision.

But then she relaxed, melting into him, curling into his body as her mouth softened, warm and pliable beneath his. As his body responded, he wondered how in hell any man in his right mind could have let her go.

Elli heard the small sound of acquiescence that escaped her throat as Wyatt took control of the kiss. Oh, his body felt so hard, so reassuring. He knew everything now and he wasn't running, he wasn't changing the subject. He was a man in a million, and he was kissing her as if she was the most cherished woman on the planet.

She melted against him, letting him fold her in his arms as he shifted his weight on the sofa. Want, desire such as she hadn't felt in months slid seductively through her veins.

His body pressed her into the cushions and she welcomed

the weight, feeling at once wanted and protected. As his mouth left hers and pressed kisses to her cheeks, down the sweep of her jaw, she suddenly understood that she wasn't cold, or standoffish, or any of the things Tim had accused her of. She had simply been waiting. Waiting for the right person to come along and set her free.

And she was. As Wyatt's mouth returned to hers, she slid her hands over his hips and up beneath his shirt, feeling the warm skin beneath the cotton.

His hips pressed against her and her blood surged.

"Elli…"

"Shhh," she replied, touching her lips to his neck and feeling his pulse pounding there. She licked along the rough skin, tasting, feeling pleasure not only in what he was doing to her but from knowing what she was doing to him. After months of feeling powerless, it was liberating, affirming, and she craved more.

Wyatt pushed against the arm of the sofa with his hands so that he was looking down into her face. Elli noted with satisfaction that his breath came in ragged gasps and his lips were puffed from kissing.

"I definitely need a new couch," he murmured, his voice a soft growl. "Not here. My bed."

Taking it to the bedroom was a logical next step and one Elli thought she was ready for, but a thread of nervousness nagged. "But Darcy…"

"Has fallen asleep on her play mat."

He looked into her eyes, took one hand and slid it over the curve of her breast.

It was almost impossible to think when he was touching her like that, and thinking was starting to sound quite overrated.

She ran her hand over the back pocket of his jeans and offered the challenge with her eyes.

In a quick move Wyatt was off her, and she felt the lack of him immediately. It was quickly replaced by exhilaration as he scooped her off the sofa and carried her down the hall to the bedroom. Once inside, he laid her on the bed, sat beside her and began unbuttoning his shirt.

Elli's heart slammed against her ribs. A slice of well-muscled chest showed as his shirt gaped open, and she wanted to touch it. She wanted him, but modesty fought to be heard. What would he say when he saw her body? She fought against her insecurities, trying to ignore the hurtful comments in her memory. He hadn't turned away yet. She had to believe he wouldn't now.

She swallowed as she knelt on the mattress and pulled her sweater over her head.

Wyatt was there in the breath of a moment, kneeling before her, pulling her forward so her skin was pressed against his. She thrilled to touch it, to feel the heat and strength of it against her. She reached to push his shirt off his shoulders.

And then they both heard it—a knock on the front door.

For a split second they froze, then Wyatt jumped off the bed and went to the window.

"It's Angela Beck."

"Oh, my God!"

The seriousness of the situation hit them both and Elli scrambled for her sweater as the knock sounded again. "You've got to answer the door!" she whispered loudly. "Go, Wyatt!"

He was already buttoning his shirt. "You're already dressed."

"Yes, but look at me!" She tried to keep the panic out of her voice, but didn't succeed very well. What had they been thinking, getting carried away? "My eyes are blotchy and my hair's a disaster!"

"All right. Take a moment to collect yourself." He gave her arm a quick squeeze. "It'll be fine."

But the worried look in his eyes belied his reassurances.

This was her fault. He had been clear about keeping things platonic and why. She should have stopped him at the first kiss. He hadn't put her first, and so she had done it for him. And now what a mess they were in!

Elli scrambled to tuck her hair into a ponytail as she heard Wyatt answer the door. She should have stopped him, but she hadn't wanted to. If they hadn't been interrupted, she would have made love with him.

And now, with the faint sound of Angela Beck's voice coming from the other end of the house, the insanity of it grabbed her. She wasn't sure how she was going to walk out there and pretend everything was normal, not when she could still feel his body against hers and taste him on her lips.

And beneath it all was a nagging fear. Would he blame her if today's visit went wrong?

CHAPTER ELEVEN

WHEN ELLI ENTERED the kitchen, Angela Beck was seated at the table with a cup of coffee and Wyatt was calmly slicing through the banana bread. She exhaled slowly, thankful he'd been able to collect himself so quickly, giving her time to regroup. Fixing her hair, a reviving splash of cold water on her face and a good foundation had done its work, she hoped.

"Ellison!" Angela turned in her chair as Elli stepped forward. "I'm glad you're here. I stopped by to check on Darcy, of course, and give Wyatt an update."

Elli stole a glance at Wyatt, wondering what he'd offered for an explanation and afraid to respond lest she contradict anything he may have said. "Darcy's doing well. She really is a good baby."

"Yes, I saw her sleeping on her mat."

Darcy at least was a safe topic. "We put her down to play, and she just drifted off."

Wyatt broke in to the exchange as he put a plate of banana bread on the table. "Did you get your assignment sent, Elli?"

Elli took her cue and hoped to heaven she wasn't blushing. "Yes, I did, thank you. Only two more to go."

Wyatt smiled easily at Angela. "Elli is taking accounting courses online."

The conversation went well for several minutes as they sat and had coffee and sweets and talked about Darcy. Angela's face turned serious, though, when she began to speak with them about Barbara.

"The good news is, Barbara is making excellent progress. Her doctors are very pleased, as I'm sure you're aware."

Wyatt nodded. Elli knew he'd spoken to his sister's physician a few days earlier and had been encouraged.

"We do want to place Darcy back with her mom as soon as we can. As a mother, she needs to spend time with her baby, to develop that important bond. From our side, we need to ensure that the baby is in a safe, secure and loving environment."

"What does this all mean?" Elli asked, the banana bread suddenly dry in her mouth. Would this go on longer than planned, or shorter? And which did she want? The idea of staying here with Wyatt, especially after this morning, was heady. But scary, too. They'd nearly been caught, and she knew Wyatt would blame himself if Darcy went into foster care even for a short time simply because he'd fudged the truth about their relationship. The other option was that he'd be even more determined to keep their relationship businesslike, an arrangement that didn't suit her at all. Then of course, there was the chance that Barbara would be out of hospital quickly and Elli wouldn't have a reason to stay.

"It means that your situation here is hopefully going to resolve very soon. It also means that Barbara is going to need a lot of support. Because she went to the hospital, she'll get the help she needs. Her doctor will be monitoring her health, as will child and family services. Really, going for help was the best thing Barbara could have done. She'll have access to many resources to help her through this, some mandated and some not, including support groups."

"And family," Wyatt replied, folding his hands on the table before him. "I'm her brother. I'll be there, as well."

Angela smiled. "You haven't known you were a brother for long, though."

His smile was grim. "I certainly haven't acknowledged it. But I am her brother, and I intend to help." His lips relaxed a little. "Besides, I've grown very attached to my niece. I hope to see a lot of Barbara and Darcy."

"That's very good news, Wyatt."

Angela pushed back her chair and stood. "I should be on my way. Thank you for the coffee and cake."

"Anytime," Elli responded, relieved that their guest was leaving. She felt as if she was playing a very bad game of charades, and that at any moment Angela Beck would see clear through both of them.

"Any idea how long Barbara will remain in hospital?" Wyatt retrieved her coat and followed her to the door, while Elli hung back at the doorway to the kitchen.

"My understanding is that the doctors are evaluating her every day. While I don't have a specific time line, I believe it will be soon." She smiled then, buttoning her coat. "Your life will be back to normal before you know it, Wyatt." She looked over his shoulder at Elli. "You, too, Ellison."

Wyatt walked her to her car while Elli went back to the kitchen to tidy the mess. Back to normal? The idea was not as grand as it might have been a week ago. Did she want her life to return to normal? Back to the Camerons', back to looking for a job and a place to live, back to a world without Wyatt in it?

She knew the answer already. A world without Wyatt was gray, rather than filled with dazzling color. Was it so wrong to hope that today meant something more? As much as she would miss Darcy, didn't an end to their foster care mean that they wouldn't have to pretend, too?

Wyatt came back inside, shutting the door quietly behind him. The nerves in Elli's tummy started twisting and turning, both in anticipation and a little afraid of what to say now that they were alone. The first private words since being seminaked with him on his bed.

"That was close."

She put down the sugar bowl and went to the arch dividing the living room and kitchen. "I'm sorry." She felt she needed to offer an apology. She should have thought more and felt less. She had let her need for him cloud her judgment and they'd nearly been caught.

"Don't be sorry. I shouldn't have taken advantage."

Her head whirled. "Advantage?"

Wyatt's jaw tightened. "You were vulnerable this morning. It wasn't fair of me to…" He swallowed, as though there were something big in his throat he was trying to get around. "To kiss you."

She wanted to say *Maybe I wanted you to,* but the words wouldn't come. Because he wasn't looking conflicted about it at all. If he had gazed at her now with some sort of longing, some sort of indication that restraint came at a cost, she might have pushed. But his back was ramrod straight, his expression closed where earlier it had been transparent. The shrinking feeling in her chest was the dwindling of hope. Hope that he'd feel about her the same way she did about him.

"I can take the chair back out," he suggested.

"No!" She straightened, took a step forward. "Please don't. It's a beautiful chair, Wyatt, and you did a lovely job refinishing it. I'll be fine now. Really."

"Are you sure?"

She nodded. "Yes, I'm sure. It was so thoughtful of you

and it will make things so comfortable. I didn't realize I'd react so strongly. But it's over now, right?" Emotional hurt became a physical pain as she lifted her chin. "Don't give this morning another thought."

"Only if you're sure, Elli."

"I'm sure."

"All right, then."

She fought against the shock rippling through her as he ended the topic of conversation. They weren't even going to talk about what had happened? What had almost happened? Did he regret it that much? The thought made her crumple inside.

He moved to the sofa and retrieved the hat he'd dropped there earlier. "I'll be out moving the herd to back pasture," he said, and without another word he left.

Elli woke, an uneasy feeling permeating her consciousness. Moonlight sent faded beams through the window blind of the bedroom, and it was utterly quiet. Too quiet, she realized. Blinking away the grit in her eyes, she slid out of bed and went to the playpen to check on Darcy.

She wasn't there.

But the bedroom door was half-open and Elli padded over to it. She opened it the rest of the way with only a small creak and tiptoed down the hall. The blanket on the sofa was crumpled in a heap and the pillow held the indentation of Wyatt's head. In the slight light of the moon, Elli saw them.

Darcy's hands peeped out from beneath her blanket and her lips were open, completely relaxed with the telltale shine of a dribble of milk trailing from the corner of her mouth to her chin. She lay ensconced in Wyatt's arms, the latter clad in only a T-shirt and navy boxer shorts. His jeans lay neatly folded across the arm of the sofa. Heat flooded her cheeks at the sight of his bare feet and long legs. His eyes were closed, but she knew he was not quite asleep. One foot flexed slightly, rocking the chair gently back and forth.

He would be such a wonderful father, she thought as she watched them. Not once in this whole ordeal had he ever put Darcy somewhere other than first. She couldn't think of one single man who would have stepped up in the same circumstances with equal dedication and without resentment. There had been moments at the beginning that they'd fumbled with knowing what to do, but he had taken it on and he'd done it out of not only obligation but love.

He had so much to give. She wondered if he realized it, or if what he'd told her about his past crippled him the way her grief had crippled her.

The toe stopped pushing against the floor and the chair stopped. Wyatt's eyes opened and met hers across the living room.

Elli struggled to breathe, suddenly feeling as if there wasn't enough air in the room to fill her lungs. She was drawn back in the flash of a moment to yesterday morning, and what it was like to be held and protected in his arms. They'd been stilted and polite since, but now with her feet bare and wearing nothing but a nightgown, she felt the awareness return, sharper and stronger than before.

In the gray light his eyes appeared darker than ever and her nerve endings seemed to stand on end. The soft curves of the rocking chair and the pink-blanketed baby were in contradiction to the ruggedness of Wyatt's body. In that moment, with his gaze locked with hers, she understood what people said about men with babies. Strength and frailty, shadow and light, toughness and tenderness. It was a combination Elli was helpless against.

"She woke up," Wyatt whispered in the dark, setting the chair in slow motion again.

Elli put one foot in front of the other and perched on the edge of the sofa, only inches from where his bare knee moved as the chair came forward. "I didn't hear her," she replied, as quietly as she could. Not only because of Darcy, but because she was afraid to break the tentative shell around them.

"You were sound asleep," Wyatt answered, and she saw the corners of his lips tip up slightly. "You never moved when I went in to get her."

Elli looked away, staring at her fingers as they rested on her knees. Wyatt had been in the bedroom, watching her sleep? It was intensely personal and she wondered what he'd thought as he'd seen her there in his bed.

She'd been exhausted tonight and had to admit that she'd had the deepest, most restful sleep in months. It didn't escape her notice that it followed the purging of her grief earlier.

"What time is it?"

"Nearly five."

Goodness, she'd gone to bed before nine. For the first time in weeks she'd had a solid eight hours of sleep.

"I'm sorry I didn't get up with her." Elli noted the empty bottle on the table. She'd slept through it all, including Wyatt heating a bottle.

"I enjoyed it," he replied, smiling. "It wasn't long ago I would have thought it crazy to say such a thing. But for someone so small, she sure has a way of making us come around, doesn't she?"

The way he said *us* sent another warm curl through Elli's insides. Right now, in the predawn hours, it could almost be easy to believe that they were a perfect little family. It felt that way—adorable child, tired mother, husband who got up instead with the baby so mom could rest.

But that wasn't reality. It was a fantasy, a life she'd wanted more than anything before having to trade in her dreams for new ones. They were only playacting. Darcy was not theirs, and Wyatt was not hers.

"Let me put her back to bed," Elli suggested. "You need your sleep. You can get a couple more hours before breakfast."

She and Wyatt stood at the same time, and Elli put her arms out for Darcy. But switching her from Wyatt's embrace to Elli's was awkward, the more so because they didn't want to wake her. Wyatt's arm brushed hers, firm and warm. As he placed Darcy in the crook of Elli's arm, his fingers brushed over her breast.

Both of them froze.

Elli bit down on her lip, realizing that she was braless and once more aware that she was clad only in a light cotton nightie that ended at her knees. And Wyatt…he was holding himself so stiffly, careful not to touch her in any way. Her teeth worried at the tender flesh of her bottom lip as she tried not to be hurt by that. He was so close she could feel the heat from his body, the soft fabric of his T-shirt. And oh, the scent of him. The faded woodsy notes of his body wash from his earlier shower, mingled with sleep.

What would happen if she moved an inch closer? Two? If she tipped up her head to ask for his kiss? Would he accept the invitation?

Or would he step back, as he had that night on the veranda, and as he had yesterday after Angela Beck's visit? She wanted to tell him how she felt, but needed some sign from him first, something to encourage her that she was not alone. And since the accidental touch, he was not moving any closer.

So she moved back, adjusting Darcy's weight. "Good night," she murmured, too late realizing how silly it sounded, since it was already nearly morning. She turned away and took Darcy to the bedroom, not looking back.

It didn't matter.

The sight of him there, standing in the dark, was already branded painfully on her brain and heart.

Exactly two weeks after Darcy had been deposited on Wyatt's veranda she went home to her mother.

Neither Elli nor Wyatt were prepared for the news; despite Angela Beck's visit they had expected temporary care to last longer as Barbara regained her feet. For Elli it was too soon and yet too long as well; she already loved Darcy and felt a bond between them. There was no question that Darcy belonged with Barbara, but it was equally true that Elli had become attached to the blue-eyed angel who had been dropped into her life unceremoniously and was now leaving it under much different circumstances.

She had her goodbye moment with Darcy as she put her down for her morning nap. She kissed the warm temple, her nostrils filled with the scent of baby lotion and sweetness. She was determined not to cry, but wiped below her eyes anyway at the bit of moisture that was there. She had a lot to thank Darcy for—she could feel in her heart that healing strides had been taken. Sadness for William now wasn't as piercing as before. Somehow between Darcy's innocence and Wyatt's gentleness she'd been able to let go of the grief that had stopped her from living.

But goodbyes of any sort hurt, and she knew she had to do it now and get it over with, so that later she could simply pick up her things and leave.

She was folding the freshly laundered sleeper sets she'd

bought and laying them in the bottom of the diaper bag when Wyatt came in.

He said nothing, just went to the change table, picked up a soft stuffed bunny and turned it over in his hands. Elli kept folding and packing until there was nothing left to fold.

She looked up at Wyatt, who was watching her with worried eyes.

"Are you okay with this?" She voiced the question that he would not.

"You mean her going back to Barbara?"

Elli nodded.

"I don't have a choice," he replied, but Elli knew he was avoiding the real answer.

"I didn't ask that. I asked how you felt about it."

It felt good, being direct with him, especially since they'd danced around any type of personal topic since Angela Beck's visit. Darcy would be leaving today. So would she. There was no more time to leave things for later.

He stopped worrying the bunny and put the toy down on the bed. "We were told it wasn't going to be long," he said. "But of course I'm worried. I'm happy Barbara's done so well and that the doctors think she's ready. But she has a long road ahead of her, especially as a single mom. It is so much for her to handle."

"Family services will still be involved."

"Yes, of course. And her doctor, too. I spoke to her doctor this morning, and there are support systems in place. It all sounds fine."

"Yet you don't sound convinced."

He looked up and met her gaze. "I worry, that's all. One thing I know for sure. Barbara will have me behind her.

I'm going to be there for her. As her brother and as Darcy's uncle. Lucky for her, now I have practice as a babysitter."

"More than a babysitter, Wyatt." Elli zipped up the bag. "A father. You have been a father to Darcy these last two weeks."

His expression was difficult to decipher. Elli saw pleasure, but also pain, and perhaps denial. Knowing what she did about him, she could understand where such emotions might come from. But he wouldn't talk to her, not anymore. Ever since that morning when Angela Beck had shown up, he'd been closed off. And any softening that had happened in the dark at 5:00 a.m. was gone now. Perhaps there had been a mutual attraction, and something more than friendship between them. But there wasn't the trust she thought. Not from Wyatt. He'd backed away and hadn't had any trouble keeping away.

She'd already been in a relationship where they hadn't talked about their true feelings, and it had been their downfall. She wouldn't do it again. So she tried to make this, the end, as amicable as possible. "You made everything right for Barbara and Darcy," she said.

"You were the one who made this work," he replied, refusing to accept her words. "You were with her day and night, caring for her, making this place a home. And you accepted nothing for it. You didn't even deposit the check I wrote you. I checked. Why?"

Because I needed you. She heard the answer inside her head, but it never reached her lips.

With that answer, she began to doubt. Were her feelings for him solely wrapped up in overcoming her own problems? The answer hadn't come to her as *I love you.* It had been about need, and grief, and moving forward. She didn't want to think she'd used him, and she certainly hadn't meant to, but there was no denying the possibility that her feelings had been influenced by her needs. And with that possibility, the seeds of doubt were planted.

"I did it because I wanted to."

Wyatt stepped forward and reached for her arm. "Not good enough."

His hand on her biceps was firm and she shook it off. "I'm sorry if you're not satisfied."

She reached for the bag she'd already packed. She couldn't wait around for Barbara to arrive, to see Darcy put in her car seat and to watch her leave, taking a piece of Elli's heart with her. She had to get out now. Just his hand on her arm created a maelstrom of emotion she didn't want to deal with. Not today. Not with everything else.

"Elli…" His voice had a strain on it she hadn't heard before. "You're leaving. Can't we be honest before you go?"

Her heart pounded, wanting to be. But over the course of the past few years, so many of the things she'd thought were true had been only illusions. Could she say for certain this wasn't the same thing?

The issue of propriety during Darcy's stay was ended as of today. And yet he hadn't once said, *Please don't go.* He'd said, *You're leaving.*

"What do you want me to say, Wyatt?" She turned around to face him, willing her voice not to quiver. "Our deal was that I would stay and help you as long as Darcy was here. But she's not going to be here any longer and I am no longer needed as your nanny. Because that's what I've been, right? Darcy's nanny."

Her fingers gripped the handle of her bag, while every pore of her wanted to hear him contradict her. Not long ago he'd said very clearly that she was more than a nanny. Had that changed? The other morning, in the dark, her invitation couldn't have been more clear, but he hadn't stepped forward and taken what was offered.

"You weren't a nanny that morning here on my bed, were you." He said it as a statement, not a question. And the snap in his voice put Elli's back up.

"You cooled off soon enough." Oh bravo, Elli, she thought, seeing Wyatt's shocked expression. He hadn't been expecting such a quick response, she could tell. He couldn't put this all on her. If she'd given mixed signals, she'd taken the lead from him.

"Angela Beck at the door put things in perspective quite quickly," he replied. His forehead seemed to flatten as if he were displeased. "Getting caught would have been a disaster. Like you said before—our relationship had to be platonic."

"I don't want to argue before I leave, Wyatt. Please, can't we just leave things on good terms? You got what you wanted all along. You got to keep Darcy and fulfill your responsibility to your family. You did the right thing. Let's just leave it at that."

"And did you get what you wanted?"

The words hurt, because he didn't know what she wanted and she was too afraid to tell him. She was too afraid to ask how he felt about her and get pushed away again. Twice had been more than enough. Every single time in her life that she'd tried to be open with her feelings she'd been shut down. And Wyatt wasn't offering her anything in return, any level of safety that if she did open up would make it worth it.

"What do you *want* out of life, Elli?"

As he said the harsh words, the planes of his face changed, more angled and taut. He ran a hand through his hair that even when messy looked as if it was that way deliberately. She wanted to throw off the cloak of all her misgivings and just tell him how she felt. But she couldn't. She could still hear Tim's words in her ears, the ones she'd passed off as coming from bitterness and pain. She understood now that there had been a kernel of truth in them just the same and that they had affected her even if she hadn't wanted them to. Words that had cut her to the quick. *Go ahead. Walk out on our marriage. You failed our baby and I'm just another casualty.*

The words came back with disturbing clarity now because she knew they were true.

She did blame herself for William's death, and she did walk out on their marriage.

CHAPTER TWELVE

WYATT WATCHED THE COLOR drain from Elli's cheeks. Her eyes loomed large within the pale skin of her face. It was a fair question. What did she want, and why wouldn't she just say it? Now that Darcy was leaving, nothing stood in their way. Why wouldn't she come to him?

He had seen her face when she'd come into the kitchen the day Angela Beck had visited. Maybe they'd both been carried away in the moment, but he hadn't expected her cool response. They'd both known what could have happened if they'd been caught together, what else could he have done? And he'd tried to bridge the gap by offering to remove the chair, but she'd stared at him with those huge eyes and he'd felt the gap between them widen.

She was afraid, and he knew it. This morning he'd tried pushing to see if he could make her react with honesty, but if anything she was withdrawing further. And he couldn't do it anymore, not knowing how fragile she was. Maybe she needed more time. He would never push where he wasn't wanted; he'd seen his father muscle his way through relationships enough to know making demands and bullying didn't work. You couldn't force love. And he was pretty sure he was falling in love with Elli.

What would she do if he just came right out and said it? As they stared at each other, her chalk-white and him with tension cording every muscle, he knew exactly what she'd do. She'd run.

"I've got to go."

"Elli." He took a step forward, and in spite of his determination not to push he found himself gripping the tops of her arms, forcing her to look up at him, wanting to grab one last chance. "Don't run."

The color rushed back into her cheeks and her blue gaze snapped up at him. "What are you offering, Wyatt? What do *you* want out of life? Because knowing that would help me out a lot. I can't figure you out, I really can't. And the last week and a half, you've gone out of your way to stay out of *my* way."

His hands felt burned and he dropped them away from her arms. Is that what she thought? That he couldn't stand to be near her? "Me?"

"You were the one that set up boundaries!" she cried.

Their gazes clashed and his dropped to her lips briefly, watching them open as her breaths seemed to accelerate.

"To protect Darcy!" Frustration was suddenly added to the cocktail of feelings rushing through him.

"Only Darcy?"

She'd very effectively turned the tables on him and he felt a slide of guilt run up his spine. All right, so maybe he was being cautious. And maybe he'd used Darcy as a shield to keep from admitting how he really felt. But he kept quiet now because he wasn't sure of her. He'd been there when she'd fallen apart and he'd seen her withdraw into herself afterward. She wasn't ready. He knew she was afraid. What woman wouldn't be after what she'd been through? He couldn't force her to open up.

"Fine. You want to know what I want, Elli? I'll tell you. I want this ranch to prosper, I want this house a home, I want a wife to love and a couple of kids. I want the kind of marriage my mother and father never had and I want to provide my children with the childhood *I* never had. I want the past to stop defining me and I want to prove that a pattern doesn't have to be continued." It all came out in a rush and it felt damn good to say it.

"Now go ahead." He lowered his voice and looked down at her, knowing she hadn't expected such an outburst. "Run. I know that's what you want to do."

She hadn't moved a muscle, but it seemed suddenly as if an invisible wall rose between them. Her complete withdrawal was cool and palpable. This was why he'd resisted. Because he'd known exactly how she'd react.

"I have to go," she whispered.

Her response didn't surprise him, but he felt the dull ache of disappointment. He couldn't beg for someone to love him. He'd left that little boy behind him long ago and he had too much pride. He went to the end of the bed, picked up the bag she had dropped when he'd grabbed her arms. "I'll walk you out."

Silently they went to the front door and Wyatt opened it. The fall air had a bite to it; in the low places of the yard the grass was still silvery with frost. Sunlight glinted off the few golden leaves remaining on the border of aspens. It was a perfect fall day. And yet there was no joy in it for Wyatt. By tonight he would be alone in his house again, only this time he'd feel the solitude much more keenly.

They hesitated on the porch for only a moment. Wyatt held out her bag and Elli took it without meeting his eyes. "Thank you for everything," he said, knowing it sounded formal, but pride kept him from speaking more intimately. "If there's ever anything you need…"

"Don't," she commanded softly. "Please, not this cold politeness. Not after everything."

She walked down the steps and half turned, and he

thought he caught a glimpse of moisture in her eyes before she blinked and it was gone.

"Goodbye, Wyatt."

He waited on the porch, watching her walk away down the dirt drive, feeling his heart go with her. Wishing she'd turn around and come back, hoping she'd be as honest with him as he'd been with her. If she would only do that, they might stand a chance. He needed her to stop. To come back to him. To let him make everything right somehow.

But she didn't. She walked on, her strides never faltering.

And as she reached his mailbox, a car slowed and made the turn into his driveway.

Barbara was here.

Elli felt every pound of her bag as the strap dug into her shoulder. She wouldn't look back. She couldn't. If she did, her resolve would falter. No, she reminded herself, holding the strap for dear life, she had to be strong. This time she had to be strong. This time she had to see the reality, not the dream. And the reality was Wyatt didn't love her, not the way she needed him to. Not the way she loved him.

As she stepped onto the interlocking blocks of the Camerons' front walk, she couldn't help but look over toward the house. A woman—dark hair, tall, like Wyatt—got out of the car, and Elli paused. It was like watching an accident and being unable to turn away even though she knew she should. Wyatt went down the steps with Darcy bundled in her blanket. Across the two lawns she heard Barbara's exclamation and saw her take the baby from Wyatt's arms. The way she held her, close to her body and with her head dropped low, made Elli's eyes sting. Barbara rocked Darcy in her arms even though she was standing, and Elli saw her kiss the perfectly shaped forehead.

She couldn't watch anymore.

Numbly she unlocked the door and stepped inside. She'd once been awed by the foyer's perfection, its opulence. Now it felt cold and empty. The cavernous foyer echoed with the closing of the door. She trudged up the tile steps to the living room, stared out the huge windows at the prairie extended before her, so vast and unforgiving. She took her bag to the guest room, dropped it inside and waited. For a sound. For anything.

But nothing came.

Next door, Wyatt was reconnecting with his sister and reconciling his past. Darcy would be going home, but he would see her often. She imagined them sitting in his kitchen now, perhaps drinking coffee, laughing, talking. He hadn't had to say goodbye to Darcy, as well. But she had lost both of them. She was alone.

And the worst part of it was that she knew she'd brought it on herself.

She'd said yes to his plea for help. She'd gone and fallen for him despite all her self-warnings to stay detached. And in the end she'd been too afraid to tell him how she felt, and so here she was. Alone. Again.

She told herself it didn't matter, because her feelings weren't returned anyway. She told herself it was better this way, because it wouldn't be right to stay so attached to him, or to his niece. She couldn't leave Darcy out of this either; she loved her, too, and felt the loss of her deep inside. And in that moment Elli realized an important truth. She was a mother. Maybe she hadn't had the opportunity to watch William grow, but she had loved him. She had a mother's heart.

Bereft, she buried her face in the pillow and let out the tears she'd held in all morning.

* * *

With a broad smile Wyatt refilled their soup bowls and sat back down at the table. He wasn't much of a cook, not like Elli. He missed her smiles already. He pushed the thoughts aside, to bring out later when he was alone. Tonight marked a milestone, even if his best efforts managed only canned soup and a sandwich. Reuniting with his sister seemed to eclipse his lack of culinary expertise.

"Sorry it's not fancier."

"Don't be silly." Barbara picked up her spoon and smiled. "Thank you. One of the things I promised the doctor I'd do for myself was eat better. This is just what I needed."

"Are you really okay?" Wyatt halted the progress of his spoon and his smile faded a bit. "I mean, you're going to be back to caring for Darcy full-time again. You're sure you're ready?"

Barbara's smile faded as the mood turned sober. "I'd be a liar if I said I wasn't scared. But I'm learning coping skills and I have a number to call anytime, day or night. Don't worry, Wyatt. Everyone is following up on me."

"That day or night thing," he said, putting down his spoon and taking her hand. "That goes for me, too. I suspected about our father all along, but I was a coward and said nothing. But not anymore. I'd like to be your brother, if you want me to."

Tears filled Barbara's eyes and she squeezed his hand. "You always were a good kid, and you turned into a good man. Even when I wasn't thinking clearly, I know I wouldn't have trusted you with Darcy if I hadn't believed you'd do your best by her. You went home with a black eye because of me once, Wyatt. I haven't forgotten."

"It's good to have family again," he said simply.

"Yes, it is. And I know you had help. Where's Ellison?"

Wyatt suddenly became engrossed with his soup bowl,

feeling pain at even the mention of her name and not wanting to show it to Barbara. "She's gone home."

"I want to thank her for all she's done."

Of course she did, Wyatt realized. But not now. "Now is probably not a good time, Barb. I think it was very difficult for her to leave Darcy."

He felt Barb's eyes assessing and stood up, taking his bowl to the sink.

"Only Darcy?"

A heaviness settled in his heart. "I don't know." He braced his hands on the edge of the counter.

"Is there something between you two?"

Wyatt turned around. Maybe he and Barb had a lot of missing gaps, but she had known him a long time, since they were children and in school together.

"Even if there was, there isn't now."

"I'm sorry, Wyatt. Are you in love with her?"

He had known his father's cruelty, but she had known his neglect. Now she was dealing with the results of her own failed relationship and making her way as a single parent. The way she was looking at him now told him she understood a little of what he was fighting against.

"I am."

"So what's stopping you from fighting for her?"

"We're not the only ones damaged here, Barb. Elli's had her own troubles to deal with. I got to a point where I was ready to move past it and take the life I wanted. But she's not there yet. And I can't do it for her."

Darcy made happy-baby noises from her seat and Barbara smiled. "I should get her home."

She rose and went to the seat, buckling Darcy in and picking up a blanket to lay over her.

"You'll be okay?"

"I'll be fine."

"You'll call me tomorrow?"

Barbara smiled. "You getting all big brother on me now?"

Wyatt grinned. "Feels weird, huh? But yeah, I guess I am."

To his surprise, Barbara came to him and hugged him. "Thank you," she murmured, and backed off slightly. "Sometimes the worst part in all of this is feeling alone. I think I'll like having a big brother."

He walked her out, taking the bag of clothes while she carried the seat. As they secured Darcy in the backseat, he added, "I kept the playpen and change table. Any time you need a break, Darcy's welcome to come stay with Uncle Wyatt."

"Thank you."

As Barbara started the engine and backed out of the driveway, Wyatt stood and lifted his hand in farewell.

When she was gone he went back inside, but the house felt instantly different. Empty, and lifeless. For two weeks it had been filled with noise and discord, but also with happy moments and somehow, family. Darcy had gone home with her mother, but he would see her again. He was her uncle. But Elli—soon she'd be leaving and heading off to wherever life was going to take her. And he missed her most of all. The way she looked sitting across from him at the table, or the way she joked with him about his sweet tooth. How she looked cradling Darcy in her arms, giving her a bottle, and how sweet she tasted when he kissed her.

He stared out the kitchen window, looking over the dark fields. They undulated like inky-black curves as cloud covered the rising moon. Droplets of rain began to splash against the pane, suiting his mood. He had tried to tell her what he wanted earlier today and she had been too afraid to reach out and grab it. He knew he couldn't force her to change.

But he also knew he didn't want to give up.

She was still at the Camerons', and he was here. Both of them alone. It didn't make sense, not when he wanted to be with her so much.

Energized, he went to the door and pulled on his boots, followed by his oilskin. All the things he should have said this morning he'd say tonight. It didn't have to be too late. He opened the door and was flipping up his collar when he saw her.

Standing at the bottom of his steps, her hair in strings from the rain, her shoulders huddled in her jacket.

For a split second they both hesitated, stared. Then he took one step outside and held out his hand.

She came up the steps and took it, her fingers ice-cold as his wrapped around them. Without saying a word, he pulled her into the circle of his arms.

They stood that way a long time, with the rhythmic patter of the rain falling on the roof of the veranda and the door wide-open behind him. Finally he kissed the top of her head, the scent of vanilla and citrus filling his nostrils.

"Come inside," he murmured, and he drew her in out of the cold and damp.

Once inside he could see the evidence of hard crying in her pink face and puffy eyes. It gave him hope. She'd been so contained, so cold today he'd had moments wondering if maybe he had imagined their connection. And then there was Darcy to consider. He knew part of the reason she'd left first was so that she wouldn't have to watch Darcy go.

"Darcy's gone home with Barb," he said, watching, gauging her reaction.

"I know."

"The house seems empty without her."

"I know."

She said it so sadly he wondered if that was the cause of her distress, and not him at all.

"Where were you going just now?" She tilted up her face, droplets of rain clinging to her pink cheeks.

"I was coming for you."

The world opened up for Elli as he said it. Her heart, so withered and afraid, expanded, warm and beautiful. She had been coming for him, too. But hearing him say it, seeing the agony etched on his face, gave her a rush of hope.

Her bottom lip quivered with emotion and she reached out for him. Her hands spanned his ribs through the heavy jacket and he threaded his fingers through her hair. Firm hands tilted her face until she was forced to meet his gaze.

"I was coming for you," he repeated, and then he kissed her.

When he finally released her, she admitted, "I was coming for you, too."

Elli had spent hours crying and hurting, but at the end of it there had been no solution. The pain of letting go of Darcy was what she'd dreaded, but in the end it wasn't the loss of Darcy that cut deepest. It was Wyatt. She didn't want to be held prisoner by fear anymore. She'd known that even if it never worked out, she had to make the important step of telling the truth. She would never know unless she asked. His welcome was more than she had dared hope for.

"Wyatt, I...I want to answer what you asked me this morning."

They were still standing next to the front door, water dripping from their coats, but Elli didn't care.

"Okay."

"You asked me what I wanted," she began, tucking the

wet strands of her hair behind her ears. "And my answer is the same as yours. It's all I've ever wanted, my whole life. I was always a puzzle to my mom, and my friends, and then my coworkers. I didn't have lofty aspirations like they did. I didn't want to be a lawyer or a doctor or a model, or even rich. All I wanted was a home, with a husband to love and a couple of kids. I wanted the kind of marriage my mother and father had and I wanted to be a mother more than anything. And for a while I had all that, or very nearly. And it all went up in smoke. And now, finally, I know why."

"Elli, I'm so sorry about that—"

"No." Elli cut him off. "I want the past to stop defining me and I want to prove that a pattern doesn't have to be continued, just like you. I'm done with settling, Wyatt. I convinced myself I could have it all with Tim, and I was wrong. I know I was wrong because..."

The next part was the hardest. It was putting herself out there, being emotionally naked. But what was the alternative? What more did she have to lose? Nothing. This afternoon had shown her that. She had cried and felt a bleakness unlike anything she'd felt before, even in her grief about William. Today she had, for a moment, given up hope, and the emptiness was more than she could bear.

"I know I was wrong because I didn't really love him. I loved the idea of him, I loved the fantasy of the perfect life I could have with him. I thought we would have it all. But it turned out it was nothing. Because I know now what it is to really love someone. The way I've fallen in love with you."

Her voice faltered to a near whisper as she finished, trying desperately not to cry, trying to fight back the fear she felt in admitting such a thing. Wyatt was gaping at her, saying nothing, his face a mask of surprise. And well he should be surprised. After holding things so tightly in her heart, letting them out in such a rush was unexpected.

"I gave up last time without a fight. Maybe because it wasn't worth fighting for. But you are, Wyatt. I don't want to walk away from you. I want those things with you. Is there a chance you might want them with me, too?"

She stood back, chin quivering, waiting for his answer.

He exhaled, the sound an emotional choke as he stepped forward. "Look at you—you're soaked."

She let him unzip her jacket and slide it down her shoulders. It dropped to the floor in a damp puddle. He cupped her jaw in his hands and forced her to look into his eyes.

"I love you, Elli."

He dipped his head and kissed her, the sweetest thing she had ever known. "It took you long enough," he murmured against her lips, and then he wrapped his arms around her ribs and lifted her off her feet. "I told myself I had to wait for you to be ready. But tonight, alone…I just couldn't."

She nuzzled against the collar of his jacket, smelling the unique scent of leather and rain and man mixed together. Joy rushed through her, chasing away the fear. Wyatt wouldn't say it unless he meant it. He loved her. She closed her eyes. She could handle anything if he truly loved her.

A laugh bubbled past her lips. "Long enough? We've only known each other a few weeks."

He only squeezed tighter. "We spent more time together the last two weeks than most people do dating. We shared things, things I hadn't told another person. What does time matter, anyway? I knew the night on the porch when we kissed."

"Then? When you pushed me away and decreed our relationship had to be platonic?"

"Yes, back then."

She laughed again. "You were faster than me. I couldn't admit it to myself until I saw you in the rocking chair with Darcy." Tenderness overcame her. "Loving you meant facing a lot of things I was trying not to face, you know."

He finally eased his hold on her and drew back. "There's so much I want to tell you. I don't know where to start. About Barbara today, and about me, and my plans…"

His dark eyes glittered with excitement and Elli felt uplifted by the possibilities. "One thing at a time," she teased.

"Come here," he said. He shed his jacket, hung it on the hook and took her hand, leading her to the rocking chair. This silly chair, responsible for so many things, shaped and polished by his hands. Hands that were capable of so much. As he sat and pulled her onto his lap, she lifted his hands to her lips and kissed them.

"I was so scared to come here, afraid you didn't really feel the same."

"I'm glad you did," he replied, turning his hands over so he could grip hers and mimic her action. "I wasn't sure how I was going to manage without you."

"Me?" She looked at him, surprised. "Are you kidding? Look at this chair, the porch, the door. All the improvements you've made around here. Is there anything you can't do, Wyatt? That's one of the things I noticed right off. You're so very handy."

"I had to be, growing up. God knows my dad was never around. I looked after my mom."

"Like you're looking after Barbara?"

The easy expression on his face faltered a little. "I suppose. I felt like I let her down."

"Why?"

The hesitation lasted only a moment. "Because my parents only got married because my mom was pregnant with me. And my father never let me forget that he was stuck in that marriage because I'd been born. When things went badly, he made sure I knew it was all my fault."

"Oh, Wyatt, that's a horrible thing to say to a child!" Suddenly pieces began to fit. "So you take on responsibility for everyone?" Her stomach began to twist. "For me?"

He closed his eyes. "Maybe at first. Maybe I did, because I could see you were broken and I wanted to fix things for you. I tried for a long time to make things okay for my mom, even though she kept telling me it wasn't my responsibility. But this morning I knew I couldn't. I couldn't fix you. That's something you have to do for yourself. It killed me watching you walk away. But I kept thinking that if I pushed, if I didn't give you that chance, some day you'd blame me, too. And it would be too hard to truly have you and then watch you walk away."

Elli leaned back against his chest. "It wasn't until this afternoon when you weren't there anymore that I realized. Being without you made it very clear how much I love you. I couldn't picture going on without you. I knew I had to try."

"I was looking out the window thinking what a fool I'd been to let you get away. I was going over to ask you to give us a chance."

"I left because you said you wanted those things but you never said you wanted them with me."

He sighed, putting his chin on the top of her head. "And I didn't say it because I was afraid of scaring you away completely."

"We're idiots," she decreed, and felt him smile against her hair.

"No, we're not. Because we both came to our senses."

For several minutes they rocked in the chair, absorbing each other, forging a new bond, two parts of a bigger whole.

"What now?" Elli finally asked. She wanted him to ask her to come back so they could work on their relationship. What she didn't expect was what he said next.

"How do you feel about ranching, and this house?"

She sat up a bit so she could turn her head and look him square in the face. "It's very cozy here."

"Could you be a rancher's wife? I'm no doctor, and I know we had very different upbringings."

Could she! "What difference does that make? What does it matter what you do?" She touched his cheek. "I just need to be where you are. I love it here. I've felt more at home in this house than any place I can remember. It doesn't pretend to be something it's not."

"And children? I understand that's a touchy subject. Are you okay physically? God, I never even asked that before. And I get you must be scared…"

Having children *was* a scary idea, only because she knew what it was to love so deeply and lose. But the dream had just been traded in—it hadn't died. She still wanted to be a mother, more than anything. "Nothing comes without risk," she said quietly. "And the idea of babies…oh, Wyatt," she whispered, and the back of her nose stung. "Not just babies. Your babies."

She couldn't say any more. Instead, they let the idea flower, fragile and tender.

"Whatever happens, we'll weather it," he said in response.

"I know," she replied. And she did know. This was what the real deal felt like.

"I love you, Elli."

He looked up at her, his brown eyes so incredibly earnest

and that little piece of hair flopping over his forehead. She reached out and smoothed it away.

He grabbed her finger and kissed it. "Marry me?"

"In a heartbeat," she replied, and she knew what it was to be home at last.

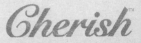

All the magic you'll need this Christmas...

When **Daniel** is left with his brother's kids, only one person can help. But it'll take more than mistletoe before **Stella** helps him...

Patrick hadn't advertised for a housekeeper. But when **Hayley** appears, she's the gift he didn't even realise he needed.

Alfie and his little sister know a lot about the magic of Christmas – and they're about to teach the grown-ups a much-needed lesson!

Available 1st October 2010

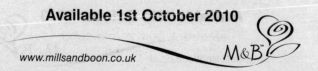

FIVE FABULOUS FESTIVE ROMANCES FROM YOUR FAVOURITE AUTHORS!

A Christmas Marriage Ultimatum by **Helen Bianchin**
Yuletide Reunion by **Sharon Kendrick**
The Sultan's Seduction by **Susan Stephens**
The Millionaire's Christmas Wish by **Lucy Gordon**
A Wild West Christmas by **Linda Turner**

Available 5th November 2010

M&B

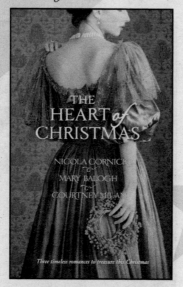

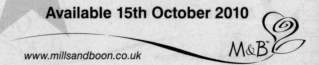

2 FREE BOOKS
AND A SURPRISE GIFT

We would like to take this opportunity to thank you for reading this Mills & Boon® book by offering you the chance to take TWO more specially selected books from the Cherish™ series absolutely FREE! We're also making this offer to introduce you to the benefits of the Mills & Boon® Book Club™—

- **FREE home delivery**
- **FREE gifts and competitions**
- **FREE monthly Newsletter**
- **Exclusive Mills & Boon Book Club offers**
- **Books available before they're in the shops**

Accepting these FREE books and gift places you under no obligation to buy, you may cancel at any time, even after receiving your free books. Simply complete your details below and return the entire page to the address below. You don't even need a stamp!

YES Please send me 2 free Cherish books and a surprise gift. I understand that unless you hear from me, I will receive 5 superb new stories every month, including two 2-in-1 books priced at £5.30 each, and a single book priced at £3.30, postage and packing free. I am under no obligation to purchase any books and may cancel my subscription at any time. The free books and gift will be mine to keep in any case.

Ms/Mrs/Miss/Mr _____ Initials _____

Surname _____

Address _____

_____

_____ Postcode _____

E-mail _____

Send this whole page to: Mills & Boon Book Club, Free Book Offer, FREEPOST NAT 10298, Richmond, TW9 1BR